Murder in Estoril

EDITH TEMPLETON

Murder in Estoril

FOURTH ESTATE · *London*

First published in Great Britain in 1992 by
Fourth Estate Limited
289 Westbourne Grove
London W11 2QA

A catalogue record for this book is available from the British Library.

ISBN 1–85702–056–1

Typset by York House Typographic
Printed in Great Britain by Biddles Ltd, Guildford and King's Lynn

Murder in Estoril

IT WAS YOUNG MCGREGOR AND HIS MOTHER, who together ran the estate agency under the arcades, that took me to Stafford's bar.

'Not another *fado*-singing joint, is it?' I asked. 'I don't want any more of it: the bird has flown away, like my love has flown away, and how can it ever return?'

'It's English owned,' said young McGregor. 'Home from home, don't you know.'

'Dinna fear,' said his mother, who, though she had a Portuguese surname, Fonseca, from her second marriage, never used it, and was eager to show to newcomers that she was entirely Scots.

She added, 'No Portuguese daftness there; it's purely for the English-speaking colony. Nothing rowdy, quiet drinking and quiet talk. And another thing you'll like is this – a young lady like you can go there on her own and no one will think any the worse of you. It's not a pick-up place.'

Behind her back her son made a sarcastic face and raised both hands. But I could not guess what he meant by this mime. Was it a pick-up place, after all? Or was he trying to convey that his mother had a dislike of amorous approaches and that I should not engage in any, in her presence?

They were both short and lean of build, with scanty fair reddish hair, bulging forehead, jutting craggy nose and deep-set blue eyes; and this leanness and this bold, honest face made him a fairly good-looking man and her a plain woman.

The son and I followed her as she made her way to the car parked at the far end of the arcades, near the side entrance to the casino building. She had a pitifully bad limp, which distorted her walk to such an extent that she seemed to be moving forward on a rocking horse.

We drove uphill past mansions glimpsed behind stone pillars or iron railings which were, mostly, surmounted by square-trimmed hedges, and turned into a street lined with trees looking like overgrown and underfed acacias.

'These are jacarandas,' said the mother. 'Native of Brazil.'

The son said, 'They are from Brazil, where the nuts come from,' and I burst into the laughter which was expected of me.

The mother was clearly annoyed. Whether she disliked the frivolity of the well-known quotation from *Charley's Aunt* or whether she was afraid that we were getting on too well together, she cut through our gaiety by saying, 'The flowers come out in June. That's in three months' time. I hope you will be settled by then. The trees look like they're covered with blue butterflies, you've never seen anything like it.'

She was speaking in the reverend tone of voice she used when saying 'three-car garage, five bathrooms and oil-fired central heating.'

The entrance to Stafford's was tucked into a row of modest shops, between a hairdressers and a haberdashers. Coming out of the whitish glare of the late sunny March day, one stepped into a brown velvety gloom which could be depressing or soothing, according to one's mood.

The bar was at the far end of the room, facing the door. A row of two-branched wall-sconces in pleated fawn shades shed their light on the barman behind the counter. His face was hidden from sight. He was stooping down, busying himself among those treasures, invisible to the customers, which bartenders like to range and polish.

By the time he had straightened up, my eyes had got used

to the dimness. Dark brown velvet curtains and dark brown panelled walls and the scrolled outlines of rococo chairs and settees.

Behind a pillared archway there was another, larger room, with more chairs grouped around tables and in front of the window a short grand piano, painted white, with swags of flowers. Two men were leaning against it.

'We're first, they've only just opened,' said young McGregor. 'They open at six. The one over there, the one in the blue blazer, that's Mr Wilkinson, the owner. English. Retired from Darjeeling. Very nice fellow. You'll meet him.'

'Where shall we sit?' asked the mother, pulling down the waist of her beige knitted dress, so that her flat chest and bony shoulder-blades became still more apparent. Like most people I had seen about, she wore no coat, which made me wonder whether I too would get hardened against the never-ceasing chill wind.

Without waiting for my reply she added, 'Let's get nearest to the source,' and she mounted a high stool in front of the bar counter with surprising, dashing speed, despite her infirmity.

She beckoned me to sit on one side of her and her son on the other. Undoubtedly she thought it wiser to keep us apart.

The barman was now in full view, raising a glass above his head against the light, and gazing at it with an air of thoughtful cynicism, as though saying, 'You may think you are clean, but you can't fool me.'

As soon as we were seated, he put down the glass. He stepped forward, laid both hands on the counter and said, 'Ladies and gentlemen, I herewith declare the meeting open. What will you have?' I began to smile and he gave me a grave, reproving look.

My companions wanted brandy. I asked for a white port, not too dry.

Several times I heard the door behind me squeak in its hinges and fall shut with a muffled bang. There was movement and voices, but no one came up to the bar; they all went into the room beyond the archway.

'This is just a wee trickle now,' said the mother, 'life here starts late,' and she went on to tell me how the opera in Lisbon started at ten and went on till two in the morning.

I barely listened. I tried to make out the faces of the people in the other room, in between returning my attention to the barman. His white coat and white neck-cloth gleamed with a frosty brilliance against the sombre mosaic composed by the darkly glossy variegated bottles.

A curly-headed, chubby-faced youth in a red coat and black trousers, and with a smile so steady that it seemed part of his livery, came up asking for drinks.

The mother was now telling me about the bridge club and the English lending library, both housed in a villa near the arcades.

'I don't play bridge,' I said, watching the red-coated youth, who, again, came up with a tray containing empty glasses. Looking beyond his shoulder I saw him once more, curly-headed, red-coated, and with his unvarying smile, bending above a table close to the piano, lowering a chunk of ice held by tongs into a glass.

I caught my breath and held a hand to my throat.

'Yes, madam, you are seeing double. No, madam, you are not drunk,' said the barman in his deep, low voice.

My companions had not noticed my upset.

'They are twins, are they?' I asked.

'Not twins, madam,' said the barman. He left me to attend to an order.

'Then what are they?' I asked. 'Brothers?'

'That I'm not allowed to say, madam,' said the barman. 'That's Mr Wilkinson's department. He loves being asked questions like this, especially by a lady; especially by a lady like you. But you may find it helpful if I tell you that the first one of them looks tremendously like the other one. But that the other one looks less like the first one.' And he moved away from my part of the counter.

It took me a few seconds to realize that he had given me a nonsensical explanation dressed up as sense, and it vexed me that I had been taken in.

He spoke in the same leisurely, beautiful, almost English-sounding way as the American I had been meeting in the coffee house under the arcades, for two days running.

The American was from Boston. He had promised to meet me today again, in the early afternoon. But he had not turned up.

I started listening once more to my companions, and found they were engaged in a mild quarrel about the fees in the lending library. Before I could join in the debate, the talk was shattered by the tempestuous arrival of a tall, buxom young woman who came charging at us in a tiny-stepped run, like a carthorse trying to be dainty.

With her silver-blonde hair, large blue eyes and button-nose, she had the revolting prettiness of an outsize Victorian china doll.

She threw her arms round young McGregor and his mother, exclaiming, 'Katie, just the very person I wanted to see! The lease of the cottage's gone bust again. They flitted last night because today the rent was due, and it wouldn't matter so much because I had this one month's rent in advance – but they've taken the electric iron with them!'

Oppressed by her obnoxiously cloying perfume and the closeness of her plump body, I tried to move my stool but did not succeed. Probably it was nailed to the brass rail which joined the rim of the counter to the floor.

'And they've run up bills with the tradesmen,' she went on, speaking in a breathless husky voice, 'and of course, I was never told. But now, when it's too late, the idiot tradesmen aren't backward in coming forward. Next time you let it for me, Katie darling, do try and get me some low-class people, the scum-of-the-earth and the salt-of-the-sewers sort of thing. They're much more tidy and keep things clean and show some respect.'

She had a hard-looking bust on which her string of pearls

reposed horizontally, as though laid out on a cushion, and I fell to wondering why tall, large-breasted women always had such aggressively domineering ways.

Young McGregor said, turning to me, 'Frightfully sorry and all that, but we've got to leave, we must go off with poor darling Ginny straight away to her cottage. Would you mind frightfully staying on, on your own?'

'Dinna fash yoursel,' said his mother, 'it's impor-rtant we go now to see the state it's been left in, before the gur-rl comes in the mor-rning to clean up,' and she gave a few more explanations of this kind, sprinkling them with a liberal amount of Scottish 'r's.

'You can walk it back easily,' said the son, 'just keep cutting downhill, facing the sea. But if you don't feel like it, there's a cab rank just across the street, next door to the Monte Estoril Hotel.'

I watched them leave, Katie leading the way with her rocking limp.

When I turned on my seat facing the bar counter again, I found the barman watching me with the same doubtful, cynical interest he had given the upheld glass, when I first had seen him.

I tilted my chin up and looked him full in the face for the first time.

He was in his early thirties, black-haired, narrow-headed, with long, heavy lips and a heavy jaw, and with that thick smooth skin which neither blanches nor blushes with emotion. He looked calm, clever and brutal. It was a bad mixture, and a bitterly fascinating one.

Embarrassed by my thoughts, I hastened to think up a suitably conventional remark. I said, 'She's really too good to be true, this estate agent woman, isn't she? That dreadful limp. And yet she's on the go at all hours. The true Scots determination.'

'As you say, madam. But it's not too good to be true, it's too true to be good for her.'

'How do you mean?' I said.

'Her deter-rmination,' he said, imitating her, 'came first. And the limp came afterwards. Because one day her husband came into the room and she said, "If you take one step nearer, I'll jump out of the window"; and he did, and she did. Second floor it was, an old house in Lisbon. High stairs and high ceilings.'

'Oh, God,' I said. 'It must have been her second husband in that case, the Portuguese, Fonseca. Wasn't it? Everybody tells me they make vile husbands.'

The barman said, 'They don't make good husbands. And they don't make bad husbands. They make husbands. And it isn't often that you are right, madam, but this time you are wrong; it was her first husband. With the second one, the Portuguese, she just walked out through the door. I daresay she figured that one jump wasn't sufficient training.' He stopped my smile with a reproving look.

'Was the port to your liking, madam?' he asked.

'It was,' I said.

'Just as I thought,' he said. 'I didn't give you anything decent; I knew straightaway it'd be lost on you.'

I looked at him in silence.

'Your drink's been paid for, madam,' he said, and, turning his back to me, began to range bottles on a high shelf.

I wondered how tall he was. It was not easy to tell because I fancied that the floor inside the bar-enclosure was raised.

Now that his back was half-turned toward me I saw how ill-fitting his white coat was, how it strained over the wide, massive shoulders. The sleeves, cut too short, stopped an inch or more above the wrists.

He obviously did not think I was going to order any more. I slid down from my stool and left.

On the following day I walked up all the way, from the arcades to Stafford's bar, in about twelve minutes.

The weather was deceitful, double-faced, with a gentian blue sky, a glaringly bright light, and a stabbingly cold wind. It made me glad I had on my warmest coat.

10

This time the barman stood motionless behind his counter, watching me, as I came in. He was still watching me as I clutched the brass rail and pulled myself up on to a high stool. He did not answer my smile.

He gravely inclined his head. 'What a pleasant surprise to see you, madam, once more, after so many weeks. Or is it months? How time flies.'

I was the only customer here, but in the adjoining room, beyond the archway, there were two tables occupied, one by a largish group, among whom I recognized Mr Wilkinson, by the cornflower-blue colour of his blazer.

'What is yours, madam?' asked the barman.

'A white port,' I said.

'A white port for a change?'

'A white port.'

'Ladies are so unpredictable,' he said. 'Now, I'd have thought you'd want a white port. But as you insist, I'll give you a white port.'

I started to smile against my will and was cross with myself.

He poured out my drink and said, 'Your girlfriend of yesterday, she's here again.'

'Oh,' I said. 'Katie?'

'No,' he said, 'Ginny darling. Over there by the window. Would you care to walk over and stick a finger in her eye?'

I said, 'How do you know that I don't – but really, of all the blustering ill-mannered – '

'No need to explain, madam. Some like steam-rollers and some don't, it's a matter of taste. You don't. Of course, she made a mistake in your case, when she walked into you and trampled you underfoot. She pretended not to see you, but she'd taken a good look at you from down yonder, before she came cantering along. She thought you were down-at-heel and insignificant, so she turned her back on you. If you'd looked prosperous, she'd have gone out of her way to make herself pleasant to you.'

I took a sip of my drink.

He went on, 'Ginny darling made a mistake with you, but a pardonable mistake. Because, if I may say so, you are deceptive, madam; you are easy on the eye but not easy to make out. For one thing, she only saw your shabby tweed. Handwoven and home-spun, I grant you. But still – you must have been wearing it for ten years, at least. Look how the bloom is rubbed off and the threads are showing. There. On the edge of the sleeves.'

'Nine years,' I said, looking up at him.

He inclined his head as though thanking me for a compliment I had paid him.

He went on, 'But Ginny darling didn't see that the inside is lined with beaver, prime Canadian beaver, and in first-rate condition, I'm happy to say.'

'New last year,' I said.

'To continue,' he went on, 'from Ginny darling's point of view, madam, you are stark naked in the way of jewellery. Sadly, she missed your tiny eight-hundred-dollar watch. She didn't have the advantage of seeing you the way I do.

'What else have we got, apart from the watch? Which one needs for telling the time. And which therefore, is not a luxury. Only a wedding ring, plain gold, nothing fancy. Fair enough, that's all a woman needs.

'But does she need it? Does not that frail band of gold weigh heavily on that little hand of yours? Working up to a divorce?'

I gave him what I intended to be a haughty look.

'Purely professional interest,' he said, pushing forward his heavy lower lip and contemplating me with cynical curiosity, 'I've got a degree in law and one in economics. And divorce has got those two sides to it – wouldn't you agree?'

I kept silent while one of the red-coated twins came forward to collect an order.

As soon as we were alone again, I said, 'In that case, what are you doing here?'

'Earning one hundred and fifty dollars a week with tips,' he said.

He slid aside a panel in the wall behind the counter and took hold of a tray of clean glasses, held by the hands of someone unseen, behind the partition. Then he closed the hatch.

'Darling Ginny,' he said, while stacking the glasses away on a shelf, 'always hangs around the other one, whom she is sitting with now, the one with eyes blue as forget-me-nots. Yet forget-he-did her. Forget-me-not's husband ran away with his wife's maid and Ginny darling's husband ran away with Ginny's best woman friend. So they are very close and never short of talk. You can always discuss what is worse, being left for someone of your own class or for someone below it. An interesting point. An endless source of delight.'

I smiled.

He said, 'Don't be shy, madam. Say it.'

'Say what?' I asked.

'What's just passed through your mind,' he said.

I half turned away from him, and gave him a glance from beneath lowered lashes. I felt embarrassed. I said, 'That I am sorry for you. That you've fallen on hard times. That you've to do this kind of work.'

'Sorry, be damned,' he said. 'That's not what you've been thinking. Shall I do the telling?'

I did not reply.

'You are relieved, tremendously relieved, madam, not sorry. Because all along, ever since yesterday, you wanted to talk to me and you've been feeling guilty about it, awkward, with me a humble barfix. And yet, you couldn't help enjoying it. Which made it so much worse. Correct?'

I did not reply. I twisted the stem of my glass, took a sip and, bending my head, went through the pretence of searching for something in my handbag, while all the time feeling his eyes on me.

I heard the door squeak and bang behind me. Then there was the tired, demanding voice of a man close to my shoulder: 'I say, you, Johnny, or whatever your name is. What d'you have in the way of sandwiches?'

13

Looking round I saw a vigorously built man of about fifty, who was taking a handkerchief from his sleeve and passing it over his bald head.

The barman said, 'We don't do them with ham, sir, and we don't do them with cheese. You can take your choice.'

'Take my – oh, I see. Then, you don't do anything in the way of food, do you?'

'No, sir. We don't eat our customers. We only drink them.'

'And what about some milk, what d'you call that, trying to be a scream, eh?'

'I'd call it a drink, sir. Would you care for a glass of milk?'

'Would I, by Jove,' said the man, stepping up to the counter and giving me a suspicious glance, as though expecting that I too, though harmless-looking, might turn treacherous.

He said, 'But none of that powdered whipped-up stuff, d'you hear?'

'I hear, sir.'

'And not that condensed filth, watered down, either.'

'No, sir. A glass of milk, fresh from the dairy cow, which provides us with milk, butter, eggs and cheese, as we used to learn at school.'

'And I'd like it iced.'

'Iced, sir? But the milk will already be white.'

'How's that again – oh, I see.'

The barman said, 'If you'll take a seat, sir, in the room yonder, I'll have it brought to you. I cannot let you have it here at the counter, sir. Rules and regulations. And, besides, absence makes the heart grow fonder.'

He added, watching the guest make his way toward a window-seat, facing Ginny darling and her friend, 'Though I'd find it hard to get fond of him. Pathetic, isn't it? You spend all your life fighting for Queen and country and now you turn round and there's no one to bark at. He'll start a turkey farm – regimentation of birds being the nearest thing to commanding a brigade, and he won't want to rule over something as vulgar as chickens. That's what the military usually go in for, when they settle in this country.'

'And you'll really get him the milk?' I asked.

'I will. We don't carry it here, but there's a taxi-drivers' joint two doors away from here, I'll send round. It's good for business. You see if he doesn't chase the milk with whisky,' and he slid aside the panel and called something through in Portuguese.

'You speak it well?' I asked, hoping to draw him out. 'Have you been here long?'

'I don't speak their Portuguese,' he said, 'I speak Brazilian. Though you wouldn't know the difference.'

'You have been to Brazil?' I asked. I was disgusted with myself, with this trite questioning. Yet unable to resist the temptation to satisfy my curiosity.

He ignored my question.

Turning his head toward the archway and the room beyond, he said, 'Look. The glass of milk has joined the Wilkinson crowd. He doesn't really fit in, either.'

'How can you tell,' I said, 'you've never seen him before.'

'I've seen him now,' he said. 'And had the privilege of entering into conversation. He's too dumb, too straightforward, too decent. I'll give you a guided tour. I'll explain some of the fauna and flora at Stafford's. Stick with me and I'll set you on the right path.

'The large white thing in the foreground, that's the piano, correct? Now, the large white thing next to it, with the piano legs, that's not the piano, although you might not be able to tell the difference. The customers sometimes pour whisky into the piano to make it play better and she does the same to herself. She's Canadian. A tobacco heiress. Her husband gave her cause for jealousy, so she pitched both their children out of the window. The law being the same for rich and poor alike, she was shoved for one year into a private clinic for the mentally deranged. Now she lives here with thirty-eight dogs and a young native photographer. No servants. He does all the housework too.

'The one next to her, the one in beige, she's English. A few years ago, her son, a boy of nineteen, at a private ball in Cascais, in full sight of the two hundred guests present, was shot dead. By the host. Lovers' quarrel. That man, that murderer, was never caught. He belongs to one of the eleven top families in this country. How could he have been brought to justice when there were no witnesses. The law is alike for the rich and the poor. Sorry to repeat myself.

'Now, the gent facing her, with the cigar. He's a Swiss baron. Yes, they do exist, and when they do they are older than Switzerland itself. During the war he worked for the Germans as a spy while the going was good; and it was very good here in Lisbon, even better than in Zurich. Then when the German regime faded out, he faded out too, and made the German embassy funds fade out along with him. Which was kind of him. Because the Germans had to leave in a hurry and he saved them sleepless nights. After the war he bought up enormous tracts of land in Angola, plantations, and he turned round and married an English Jewess. That's true Swiss neutrality for you.

'That's her, in green, sitting next to him. She's got her back turned to you, you can't see her. Just as well. She makes him happy with that unique thing she's got, beyond the price of pearls and rubies, which she shares with only four hundred million women in the world.

'And next to her, the old goat on the settee, with winter in her hair but summer in her heart, patting her head all the time to feel if the hairpiece is still in place, too mean to go the whole hog and buy a proper wig – she's resting between husbands.

'The last one, it was her third, she caught him in bed with her chauffeur and she threw out the husband and kept the chauffeur.

'It wasn't that she was surprised – she'd always known that he was double-gated – but when you have a large house with a large staff you can't afford to lose the servants when you've taken years training them. And you don't want to set them playing at guessing games about who made those stains on those sheets and with whom.'

A few more people came in.

For a while the barman was kept busy by the red-coated twins who came for their orders.

I saw one of them carry out the milk on a small tray with a fringed napkin, then saw him return and whisper to the barman.

'What did I tell you?' said the barman. 'But I didn't read my crystal ball quite right. It's gin he's on now, gin and water. That means navy, not army. I give him half an hour and he'll come and tell me there's something funny-tasting in the gin. I know the type.'

By now there was so much noise from raised voices and laughter that it drowned the sounds of squeaking hinge and banging door but I could tell, from the barman's glancing above my head, that more guests had come in.

'Ah, look what the cat's brought in now,' he said. 'See him? Crossing over to the piano crowd? He's a Dane and a painter. So what's wrong with being a Dane and a painter? Plenty, if you ask me.

'Because if you go in for painting twelve-year-old boys and the Danish government doesn't like the way you paint them, they put you in prison. Better sit it out here, nine years I think it is, then they close your police files and you can go back safely. Start all over again.'

By then several guests had come to the counter, sitting or standing near the walls, but I was still on my own in the middle.

The barman reached down and brought up six silver shells, three in each hand. I noticed how skilfully he held the dishes, holding them together at only one point in the centre.

He had the large, square, massive hands that one would have expected him to have after seeing his face and shoulders; they were smoothly pale and well kept. They gave nothing away.

As he set out the shells on the counter I saw they were filled with almonds and raisins. It vexed me to think that he had produced them only now, when the place was getting crowded, and not earlier, when I was still the only one seated at the bar.

Seeing me look at the dish nearest to me, he said, 'You leave those raisins alone, madam.'

'Why?' I asked.

'Because I say so, madam,' he said, and went to the right-hand side of the counter to deal with a clamouring group.

Still vexed, I picked up a raisin and put it in my mouth. It tasted dusty and spread a biting fire.

By then, he was back and, after one look at me, he put a glass of water in my hand.

'What on earth – ?' I asked, while dabbing the tears from my face.

'Piri-piri, madam, strong stuff for vodka drinkers.'

'Why didn't you tell me?'

'I warned you.'

I did not speak.

He said, 'Have an almond, madam.'

'No,' I said.

'Have an almond, madam,' he repeated.

I said, 'No, I won't. I've had enough of your surprises.'

He gave me a grave, searching look which disconcerted me.

He said, 'To show that you trust me. To please me.'

'Oh, very well,' I said, trying to sound indifferent. I reached out and took an almond. It was bland, oily, gritty with coarse-grained salt. He watched me with a deep smile of satisfaction. It was the first time I had seen him smile.

'Just like a child,' he said. 'I could make you do anything.' He left me to take a tray from one of the red-coats and I watched him receiving clean glasses from invisible hands behind the hatch; then pouring water on an ashtray in which a guest had set alight a nest of matches and for which he was being applauded by those standing near by.

I felt it was time for me to leave.

As I watched him, still dealing with the clamouring group of those around the fire-setter, I was drowned in a wave of naggingly cloying scent.

I knew, even before looking over my shoulder, that Ginny darling was standing close behind me.

The woman with her, probably the forget-me-not, was as tall as she and twice her age, haggard, dried up and stooping, and with such an air of high breeding that it made her dishevelled hair and dress look like a provocation to those who beheld her.

'Look here, barman,' said Ginny darling, 'I've been with the Baron Vierwald party yonder, and that's taken care of, but I want a gin fizz now, here, on my own, and I'll settle this myself.'

She had been speaking listlessly, as though begrudging every word she had to impart to the barman. Now, turning to her companion, she continued with a burst of conspiratorial animation, 'I didn't want to mention it in front of them, considering. Now, do tell me. I'm going to be a sheep this day week. Gathering round the shepherd. Will you be a sheep too?'

'He hasn't asked me,' said the forget-me-not.

'Well, I suppose it will be a smaller do, this time. The pastures are not as green as they used to be, the dollar's slipping, dipping, but once in a while after so many free meals he feels he must hit back. And very handsomely he does it, too. Used to, anyway.'

'He got rid of his valet,' said forget-me-not. 'He told me he can't afford him any more.'

'Oh, rot,' said Ginny darling, 'that valet's been dismissed and taken back so often it's like a shuttle service.'

'No, he swore to me, this time it's final.'

'Oh, rot,' said Ginny darling, 'you know what they are like. That lot. They always fall out and make up again. Treacherous queers. It's part and parcel of their – '

I said to the barman who was now standing facing me, 'How much do I owe you?'

He said, 'Pay me tomorrow, madam; I've got my hands full now.'

I said, 'You'll have a sleepless night, worrying if I'll pay up.'

He inclined his head. 'As you say, madam. I'll have a sleepless night worrying if you'll pay up.'

Though he had spoken in his deep low voice, indifferently and smoothly, as though uttering a phrase of conventional politeness, I did not like his reply. It made me shiver.

I took hold of my handbag which had lain in my lap, made sure that my gloves were still tucked into the pocket of my coat, and slid off the stool.

When I got outside I was astonished to see that night had fallen. The shops were shuttered. On the opposite side of the street, near the illuminated portals of the Monte Estoril Hotel, there were three taxi cabs lined up, easy to recognize by their green roofs and black bodies.

I moved a few steps away from Stafford's and stopped in front of the haberdashers, under the light of a street lamp, to see if I had any small change in my purse.

Then I heard women's voices. Ginny darling and the forget-me-not were coming out. They were speaking in the loud, arrogantly unconcerned way of women who have been brought up at expensive boarding schools and who know that they are so far beyond reproach they need not care who might overhear them.

They pretended not to see me.

Ginny darling was saying, 'No, I don't think you're bats in the belfry. I think there's a lot of good sense in what you say. I'm really in two minds if I shouldn't back out of it altogether. You see, I'm beginning to – he's had a very bad do in his flat only three weeks ago, a break-in. You didn't know, did you? He didn't own up to anybody. That's understandable, he's ashamed of course. I got it in the usual way, the grapevine up and down the servants' back-stairs. Don't let on I told you.

'That means he's into the really bad lot now, from Lisbon, the bullring crowd and from the Alfama quarter; all petty crime. He's scraping the bottom of the barrel. Till now it was his own valet. Or other people's footmen. All quite harmless. But once he starts on that underworld – not that I care – that is, I do care. Because this kind of thing does spread, you know. I've seen it happen a hundred times over. All around me. Next thing will be I ask him to my house and he'll appear trailing a creature, what he calls a "young friend", along with him, and I can't tell him to clear out – not in front of all the other guests. Next thing I know I'll have my place entered and burgled.

'And it's no use explaining to them; they never understand, these queers. They get mortally offended if you put your foot down and say no to their little curly-headed chums. And they're so frightfully pleased to be the way they are and they are so frightfully touchy, and if you don't like their boys, they hate you for it and they think it's morals. But it's not. It's just that one gets afraid.'

'God, don't I know it,' said the forget-me-not, 'they make me sick. Last week Nicky Lassiter asked me to lunch across the river on the other side. My brother and he, they were in the same house together at school. He waits for me at the ferry-place and I get out and we walk over to his place. Suddenly he stops. Excuse me for a minute. There's a street cleaner in the road. He goes up to him and shakes his hand. And his cousin is Colonel Lassiter, head of protocol at Buckingham Palace.'

'I know,' said Ginny darling, 'and his cousin from the mother's side was ambassador in Madrid.'

'But what you don't know,' said the forget-me-not, 'is that Nicky Lassiter always wanted to be a painter and his people wouldn't let him. But they had a butler. Who was in love with Nicky. He gave him his life's savings so that Nicky could go to Paris and get going. Now, the butler's still alive, old as the hills, and once every year he comes over on a visit and sits about in the drawing-room in his socks. He doesn't even wear bedroom slippers. Don't ask me why, it's all beyond me.'

'I know,' said Ginny darling. 'What I always say is, give me some healthy, wholesome adultery any day.'

'Want a lift?' asked the forget-me-not.

'No, thanks,' said Ginny darling, 'I got here under my own steam.'

Quite soon after beginning to eavesdrop on their intriguing talk I had stopped bending over my opened handbag, feeling that I could not endlessly pretend to count over my change, and I had started, for their benefit, a pantomime of taking and retracing a few steps and of looking up and down the street, as though waiting to be collected by a car. Toward the end I had stopped this show of make-believe, feeling that, as they were so consistently ignoring my presence, it was not worth while. However, just to be on the safe side, I waited till they had disappeared round the corner. Then I crossed the street to where the cabs were parked.

When I had first met the McGregors and told them where I was staying, young McGregor said, 'Your hotel is called Coimbra after the university town up north.'

Katie said, 'It is one of the oldest universities in Europe.'

Young McGregor said, 'Not only that. It is the finest university in the world. And do you know why? Because there they make doctors even of the Portuguese.'

His mother, whose benevolent air at the beginning of his utterance had changed into one of annoyance, accompanied by a nervous tugging at the string of pearls at her throat, now said, 'I don't think this is a very nice way to talk. Anyone overhearing us might get offended. Besides, I'm cer-rtain it's a *passe-partout* joke. Told of Cambridge and the English, too.'

And she raised her chin and directed our glance at the office girl who was sitting in the background over her typewriter, cheek in hand, staring sullenly into space.

She was a coarse-looking young woman with a thick snub nose in a broad face, a blotchy skin, and brown hair that lay in greasy strands on her shoulders. She had a vigorously built, remarkably well-shaped body, and though I found her grubby and repulsive, I realized that she was one of those girls who, wherever they go, attract the attention of every man and the resentment of every woman. I wondered if young McGregor was carrying on an affair with her.

My room in the hotel was separated from the main landing by its own hallway, with sliding doors for the built-in wardrobes on one side and the entrance to the bathroom on the other. The carpet was of a synthetic weave, grey and glinting like pewter, and though it was hard to the touch it swallowed all sounds of footsteps with a sponge-like efficiency to which I could not get accustomed. The chunky easy chair covered with grey corded cloth and the grey telephone belonged to the same usefully dull breed as the carpet. But the bed, with its small table, the desk and the corner cupboard had been provided by a graceful hand. They were in the Portuguese Alentejo style, of a slim, tapering, countrified Louis Seize design, painted yellow and with the panels framed in chains of cornflowers.

The telephone on my bedside table did not ring as it did in London. It came to life with a steady sound which did not cease until I lifted the receiver, a sound which made me think of the purring of a bad-tempered cat. Which, in any case, was an absurd conceit, because angry cats do not purr.

When the telephone rang that morning, it was about half-past nine.

I had finished my breakfast and had not yet taken a bath. I had no wish to get dressed in a hurry because a wall of thick white mist was standing outside my window, low enough to afford a view of pure blue sky, yet high enough to blot out the palm trees and the fake Moorish castle above the beach. The sound of two foghorns came whining from the sea like a naggingly insistent complaint.

I took my time before lifting the receiver.

'This is the hall porter speaking. Good morning, madam. Sorry to disturb you.'

'Oh, yes?' I bet he is. If he is the one I think he is, and he must be, because the others don't speak English so well. He is a morose man of about sixty with a narrow fleshless tight-skinned face, who reminds me of Monsieur Ruelle, my former Latin teacher, and I feel I get a bad mark from him every time I hand in my key. When I tip him, he receives the money with averted eyes and afterwards he is still more disagreeable, so as to show that his favour cannot be bought.

'There is a gentleman here from the police who wants to speak to you.'

'I see. Well. I'm not yet dressed. Tell him I'll come to his office, I know where the place is, in Cascais. Any time that suits him this morning.'

It was Katie who had pointed out the building to me while we were driving through a street leading uphill from Cascais harbour. It was a shabby, wide-fronted house with sentry-boxes flanking the carriage-way.

'That's where you'll have to get your permit of residence,' she had told me, 'once you decide to come and live here. That's the aliens' police department, on the first floor.'

'Ask what time will suit him,' I repeated.

'That's not possible, madam,' said the porter's voice. 'The gentleman is not from here on the coast, he's come down all the way from Lisbon; he's got to see you urgently. I can send him up, madam.'

I said, 'All right. If he doesn't mind, I don't mind.'

'Thank you, madam. He is much obliged.'

The police. The very word seemed like an open-mouthed O of surprise, tapering out into a long eee, like a shriek of fear.

I went through to the hallway to unbolt the outside door, returned to the room, put on my dressing-gown, opened the corner cupboard and looked at myself in the glass lining the inside of its door.

My dressing-gown was of thin white cambric with inset

panels of lace. James had bought it for me in Paris two years ago and Bianca said he had a lecherous taste, that it was not decent, because in places you could see through. When I told him, James had said, 'Look who's talking, that old tart with the paint chipped off.'

Bianca too, had once had some trouble with the police. She had had an affair with the police officer afterwards. He was the best ever, she had told me.

The breakfast tray was still on the desk. In the breadbasket, lined with a napkin, were two slices of Dundee cake and a cellophane-wrapped pile of that Swedish bread which looks and feels like a grating-iron. There were no rolls, no fresh bread of any kind. This was because, I realized only now, today was Sunday. I had quite forgotten.

This was a bad show; this was ominous. He did not come from the coast, locally; he was from Lisbon. And he had come out here on a Sunday. But where was he? *Quousque tandem, Catilina, abutere patientia nostra; combien de temps encore, Catiline, abuseras-tu de notre patience?* I still kept translating Latin into French because I had been brought up in a French Lycée. Monsieur Ruelle, the Latin teacher, who looked like the hall porter downstairs, was a defrocked priest. But he was a good teacher. The stuff still sticks; all the famous shreds come floating out of the rag-bag when life gets patchy and torn at the seams, a kind of sticking-plaster and soothing lint provided by culture.

There was a rap at the door, quite faint, and already he was inside, without waiting for me to call 'Come in.'

He had left the door open. As he was entering the room, I heard the hall door click shut and saw that another, younger man was approaching through the hallway. Why had not the porter told me that there were two of them? This was going to be a very bad show indeed. Bad for whom? I did not know.

Now they were standing side by side, the first one looking down at his feet, as though lost in thought and unaware of my presence. He was in his late thirties, middle-sized, stocky. He looked obstinate, narrow-minded and self-absorbed and the long face with the downward-sloping eyelids and the tightly curled hair gave him a remarkable likeness to the mask of a ram. He was dressed in cheap, ready-made tweeds. He had the air of a small-town man of low origin and seemed ill at ease.

The other one was almost two heads taller, an elegant young go-getter in his mid-twenties, with fluffy ash-blond hair, a sharp nose, a runaway chin and a short upper lip which left his front teeth exposed most of the time. Despite these facial drawbacks his appearance was altogether that of a charmer. He was dressed in the formal way of Portuguese gentlemen, not because they are in mourning but because they like it, in a dead-black suit. The sleeves were cut too short on purpose, so as to show a large strip of brilliantly laundered white shirtcuff, an extravagant style of dress, demanding careful service. He now brought his hands together at the waist, with a sparkle of oval gold cufflinks, saying, 'It was very good of you, madam, to receive us.'

'Not at all,' I said.

Truly, not at all. I had no choice, had I? The way the barman had said it last night at Stafford's, so devastatingly, 'We don't do them with ham, sir, and we don't do them with cheese. You can take your choice.'

'I don't want to say good morning,' he continued, 'it is not exactly a good morning, is it? But it is not a London fog, madam, it is a speciality of Estoril; it will clear up by midday.'

The ramshead was still staring at the carpet but he was getting restless. I imagined his English was so scanty that he did not wish to make himself seem ridiculous by using it, but he had, clearly, understood 'fog' and 'morning' and he felt that there had been enough of this kind of talk.

He now raised his hands like the leader of an orchestra who wants the musicians to come up with a *forte*. His hands were long and cushioned, with gleaming, well-cared-for nails. I imagined him polishing them in his office for hours, while pretending not to listen to the indignant denials of evil-doers.

I was leaning with my back against the window-sill and the young man stepped up to me and showed me a photograph. He had not taken it out of his pocket. He must have been holding it, concealed in his hand, all the time. This made me still more convinced that the matter was serious.

For a moment I could not see anything at all because the glossy surface reflected the white glare which came from the mist outside.

'Do you recognize this person?' he asked.

It was a passport photograph, over-exposed, and in the whitish-grey tints I saw the round face, as though made of dirty snow, and the small round eyes stuck into it, wide apart and not quite at an even level. They had that look of amused malice and cosiness, exactly as I remembered it.

'Of course,' I said. 'It's the American from Boston.'

'And what's his name?' he asked.

'No idea,' I said.

'You were observed talking to him in the coffee house under the arcades,' he said, 'for about an hour each time, on two occasions. On Wednesday and Thursday last week.'

'That's right,' I said.

'You had never met him before?'

'Never,' I said.

'Will you please tell us what you were talking about? Just give us the topics. How did you enter into conversation?'

I said, 'He happened to be sitting at a table next to mine and he saw that I was fascinated by the shoeshiner. Then he said he'd seen me in Lisbon, at the opening of the picture show in the British Institute. Watercolours. Done by Nicky Lassiter. He had seen me; I hadn't seen him, though. But this was what really set us going, who was there and who was who, and then we talked about – that's to say, he talked about – what it's like living in Portugal. Then we got on to Italy. Venice. Italian painters, mainly Caravaggio. We got on like a house on fire.'

During all that time I could see that the ramshead was listening with an air of resigned disgust, with a face that said, 'I told you so.'

I added, 'And then he told me about the rows he had had with his servant.'

The ramshead had raised his head, though he was still not looking at me. He held his hands with the outspread palms downward. He was telling the musicians to go *piano* and *rallentando*. He said a few words in Portuguese.

The young man said, 'Did you think that he was afraid of his manservant?'

'No,' I said, 'just annoyed.'

'Now, altogether,' he continued, 'what was your impression of Mr Shepherd?'

'Is that his name?' I asked.

'Forget it.' He tossed his head, smiling, clearly very proud of his idiomatic English, 'Let us return to our Bostonian. Did he seem depressed? Worried?'

'Depressed, no,' I replied, 'on the contrary; he was very full of himself.'

'Full? Full like an egg, as we say?'

'No, not drunk. Full of the joys of spring. But, at the same time, I think he was worried.'

'Worried? What about? Did he tell you?'

'About robberies and break-ins.'

'Did he tell you he had been burgled?'

'He didn't. Not in so many words. He made out it had been happening to friends of friends, that kind of thing.'

'He didn't tell you outright, then?'

I shook my head.

There was another murmured order from the ramshead, who, with outspread arms, demanded another *rallentando*.

'Was he – did you have the impression he was afraid of being attacked? Did he feel threatened?'

'No,' I said.

They conversed in low voices, the ramshead looking still disgusted and resigned. Then he gave another order. His hands, held in fists in front of his chest, told me that he was going to bring the orchestra to a grand finale.

'Do you know anything about the Bostonian's plans and movements? When he left you on the Thursday, did he tell you what he was going to do?'

I said, 'First he was going for his usual walk on the beach. Then he was going to the cinema. At four o'clock. The matinee performance.'

At the word 'cinema' the ramshead left his spot on the carpet and joined us at the window.

'With a friend?' asked the young man.

'He didn't say so.'

'Which cinema, do you know?'

'The Palace,' I said.

The ramshead murmured, 'Palacio.' It was a reprimand; he resented my anglicizing the name.

'You are sure it was the Palacio? How do you know?'

I said, 'Because we discussed it. The Estoril Casino cinema has the matinee at five and the Palace starts at four, and he said he never went to the Casino because the Palace is more handy and just round the corner where he lives, and then he told me it had to be the matinee because he was invited that night to a reception somewhere near Cascais and the film would be over by half-past six and that would give him plenty of time to change and get ready.'

All the time I had been speaking, the ramshead kept nodding in an encouraging way, while looking out of the window. He still looked disgusted. But the resignation was gone. He spread his arms and brought them together in a rounded gesture. I could almost hear the last chords of the *pianissimo* trembling and fading away.

He turned and walked to the door, with the young man following. There they remained, the young man listening, while the ramshead, speaking in a monotonous voice, in chopped-off sentences, kept slapping a fist into the palm of the other hand.

Now there was silence. The two had come to the end of

their deliberations and were both standing by the door, facing me. The young man said, 'The chief of the brigade wants me to tell you he is sorry he had to disturb you. But it had to be. We were born to suffer and this earth is a vale of tears.'

I looked at him astonished. Then at the ramshead. They were standing upright, arms to their sides, gravely composed, as though posing for an official photograph. Yes, the ramshead meant it. He was not the jokey kind. Not he.

I tried to look serious, and said, 'Never mind, I quite understand. Anyway, what with this freakish weather, it made a change.'

'Change?' repeated the ramshead. His outstretched finger made a semicircle, then pointed downward. 'Is near. Is Banco Toto and Azores. Or Banco Spirito Santo.'

A last bow, and he entered the hallway.

Behind his back, the young go-getter twisted his face into a grimace of exasperation and raised his hands in a show of despair over the misunderstanding. Then he too left, at a running pace, and reached the outer door in time to hold it open, so that the ramshead could pass through first.

The elegant young policeman's forecast turned out to be right. By eleven o'clock, looking out of the window, I could see the tops of the palm trees and the crenellated rooftop with the square tower of the fake castle, as though bathed in milk. By midday the palm trees stood fully revealed, though not clearly, as if swathed by veils of gauze, and I could tell by the stillness of their fronds that there was no wind.

By one o'clock I was sitting in the coffee house at a table close to the wall, the same table I had had when talking to the Bostonian.

From there one commanded the entire view of the Casino gardens, laid out in an immense oval between the Casino building at one end, and the Estoril railway station opposite, with both curving sides bracketed by the equally curving, pillared arcades.

The inside of the coffee house was of modest size and there was only one row of tables ranged against the wall outside, sheltered by the arcades. The largest number of tables was set out beyond, about fifty or so, in the open air, beneath the vast domed crown of a tropical oak which grew out of the mosaic pavement patterned white and blue. It was there that the gathering took place which I called 'the ladies' circle'.

The ladies' circle, a daily event, started at about midday, even when it was raining; no water could trickle through that metallic-looking close-leafed foliage, just as no wind could ever ruffle it. Sometimes there were only a dozen ladies present, sometimes as many as thirty, and, after having watched them for more than a week, I still could not tell them apart. It was all the more difficult because none of them ever appeared in the same dress twice over.

They were all between the ages of forty and fifty. They all had their hair dyed in discreet shades of brown and dressed in the same off-the-forehead and ballooning style which hid the shapes of their heads. I knew from Katie that they went every day to the hairdresser, some of them three times a day.

They were none of them seductive. Their bodies had lost the youthful curves and they had the trim, straight, small-breasted, flat-hipped and flat-bottomed figures of middle-aged women who have starved themselves into fashionable slenderness. From Katie I also knew that none of them were dependent on their husbands. They received revenues from country estates, from villas and apartments, the leasing of which provided them with incomes of their own. They all held crochet work in their laps at which they pecked from time to time, as though wishing to defy onlookers to accuse them of idleness.

As their circle was large and as they were all talking, across each other, as well as to those sitting further away, they shrieked and yelled to make themselves heard. And, as though anxious that they might not be fully understood, they acted out their tales with such a furious passion that I was able to follow the subject of their talk from where I was sitting and without being able to understand the language.

Clothes were the troublesome theme which took up the greatest part of their attention. The quarrel with the dressmaker over the ill-fitting collar, the dipping hem. Servants and shopkeepers were recalled by re-enacting scenes full of indignation: how mildly the lady had protested; with what impertinence she had been met. The family was mentioned with sullen resignation and some grudging patience.

By half-past one they started calling for the waiters and furling their crochet work. By two o'clock they had driven off, each in her own car, sometimes in the company of a chauffeur, who was, however, never allowed to take the seat behind the wheel.

What struck me as remarkable about the ladies of the circle was that they were never in a good mood and that they never seemed to dwell on pleasurable incidents. Smiles were rare, forced, and disdainful. There was never any laughter. Recriminations, grievances, wounding wrongs tinted all their gossip. I wondered whether it was part of Portuguese womanhood to see themselves as victims. On a lower level too, I had observed a steady, resentful, barefaced sullenness: in salesgirls in the shops; in maids standing at the gates of the villas, talking to the gardener or to the delivery boy; in the McGregors' office girl.

I had mentioned it to the Bostonian.

'Yes, there's something in that,' he said. 'Take the bullfight, for instance. The Spanish have it and the Portuguese have it. But the difference between them is that, during the bullfight, the Spaniard identifies with the conquering matador and the Portuguese feels as one with the slaughtered bull.'

It had been on the Wednesday, at about one o'clock, with the ladies' circle in full shriek and fury. I had noticed the tall, stout, long-legged man walking toward the arcades across the Casino gardens. He had a peculiar walk, paunch forward, as though pushing himself on a wheelbarrow, and he looked eccentric because of his little blue linen hat, stitched around the seams, of the kind worn by small children on the beach.

I knew at once that he intended getting into conversation with me, choosing the table next to mine, though most of the other tables along the wall were empty.

He was in his late fifties. With his cheeks and nose empurpled and incarnadined, he looked like a heavy drinker. He was dressed with slovenly expensiveness in stained, pale linen yachting trousers, a frayed, beautifully cut hacking coat of a greenish small-checked cloth and a dark blue jersey which might not have been laundered for days.

After he had taken off his coat, the short-sleeved jersey revealed plump arms. Despite his tall figure he had the small padded hands of a woman.

The shoeshining was going on at a nearby table and I had not been aware of it at all. It was only when I heard a cracking bang, as from a gunshot, that I began to look around me and after two further sharp bangs I realized where they came from.

'You can relax,' said the Bostonian, 'The revolution hasn't broken out yet; it's only the shoeshine. You are obviously new to this country.'

'Why do they do it?' I asked.

'It must be something to do with the suspicious character of the Portuguese,' he said. 'If he didn't crack down from time to time with his cloth, the customer wouldn't believe he was getting a good shoeshine. Now there'll be an interval of silence. Look how he's putting on the cream with his fingers. Then the brush. Then, with the cloth, bang bang again. Every shoeshiner has his beat, like a prostitute. This one does the arcades. And most of them are police informers; they listen when people shoot off their mouths. Some even understand English.'

I looked at him without speaking. I could not make out whether he wanted me to be amused or indignant.

He said, 'And do you see the lottery tickets he's laid on top of his box? Shoeshiners always sell lottery tickets. An American journalist got hoofed out of this country a year ago, because he wrote that the Portuguese economy consists of one half of the nation selling lottery tickets to the other half. He was from *Time* magazine. For six months afterwards *Time* was not allowed on sale.'

I did not speak.

'And I'll give you another tip. When you go to a night club and the photographer comes round to take a picture of cheerful you, having the time of your life, never let him have his way with you. Because he's got to hand in a copy of every snap to the police. Nothing in it, and yet, one never knows. The police are the only efficient body in this place. They are the golden nail that holds this country together.'

He gave me a look of cosy malice. I still could not make out what he wanted me to say.

'By the way, didn't I see you the other day, in town, at the opening of Nicky Lassiter's pictures?'

'That's right,' I said. 'I didn't see you, though.'

'You couldn't have,' he said, leaning his plump arm on the table and dropping his hand from the wrist, with the gesture of a woman settling down to a prolonged gossip, 'You were in the second room and I was passing you on my way out. I was quite piqued, actually. I said to myself, here's a new face in the old crowd and she hasn't wasted her time in getting the right foot inside the right door. You were talking to the Visconde de Moreira. How come you know him?'

I replied, 'That's business, not social climbing. I'm looking for a house and he's got three in Cascais, all to let and he came down from Lisbon the other day to meet me there; the McGregors took me. But I wasn't in love with any of them. All grand but down-at-heel. All right for summer. But not for living in all the year round.'

'What did you think of the show?'

'For my money,' I said, 'the best thing was the ambassador's aide, the blonde one in the kilt. I asked him what it was. It's Hunting Sinclair.'

'How very naughty of you,' he said. 'Did you tell him, Jock, it isn't the glint in your eye I'm afraid of, but the tilt in your kilt?' And, after another wrist-dropping gesture, he went on, 'But, seriously now, what did you think of the pictures? I'm very fond of Nicky's work.'

I had hardly looked at the watercolours. All I could recall was that they were mostly townscapes, smudgy, washed in pink.

I answered, pretending to be thoughtful, 'I'd say he is more of a colourist and less of a draughtsman.'

'So very true,' he said, leaning back in his chair and wriggling his body with an air of contentment. 'That's what makes his work so delicate. I bought one of his pieces yesterday. I already have three. That will make it four. I hope it will break the curse. Bad luck always comes in threes.'

I glanced at him questioningly.

'The first was when the servant I had at the time knocked one of Nicky's pictures off the wall and broke the glass. He said it wasn't him, that there'd been an earthquake. It must have been the 1755 Lisbon earthquake – delayed reaction.

'Number two was when I had a cabinet-maker in, to reframe the pictures. There was glue spilled on the Afghan rug. He said he couldn't understand it, he'd never come near the drawing-room, he'd been doing all his work in the kitchen. If you ask me, he hadn't done it, either. He was a nice boy and I suppose I made a bit of a fuss over him, gave him drinks to keep him happy in his work, and my servant must have got jealous. They are like that. I can have as many people as I like in for cocktails, but if it's one of their own kind, they won't stand for it. I couldn't pin the glue incident on my servant. But I kept it in mind.

'Number three was when I moved house and the packer drove a nail through my favourite Nicky picture. He was impertinent, too; said it was a mere hole in the paper, and wasn't I lucky he hadn't split the frame. When it comes to servants, one must learn from the Portuguese. They never show they are annoyed. They never turn a hair.'

He had a likeable way, when coming to the end of a story, of turning his face to me and blinking several times over, imparting a feeling of shared secrets.

He said, 'The Portuguese are a rum lot. They live in what Beckford called the dirty fag-end of Europe. He said it two hundred years ago but it's still true. They've got the ocean all down one side, not the piddling Mediterranean, the way the other Latin nations have, and they turn their faces to the sea and their backs to the land. They don't want to know what's going on in the rest of the world, not even next door in Spain; they walk about in a trance, they don't want to be bothered. Their favourite word is *saudades*, which means "longing" – longing for what? Never mind, as long as it's longing, and when they have a night out they sing the *fado*, a caterwauling of constant misery. That's their way of enjoying themselves.

'The poor are impertinent because impertinence is the poor man's luxury, but otherwise they are exceedingly polite – even the criminals are polite and considerate. When a pickpocket steals your wallet here, he keeps the cash, but posts you back your documents.' He made the gossipy, wrist-dropping gesture.

'When a Portuguese burglar takes your money, he'll leave you, say, fifty escudos neatly laid out on your pillow so that you aren't helpless the next day and can get out and about your business.

'So far so good. But what is one to do in special cases? It keeps happening to a friend of mine, his place gets broken in, but nothing ransacked, only two bottles of whisky gone. The next time it's a stack of new shirts. The next time it's his new topcoat. Nothing disturbed, nothing damaged. Now, he knows exactly who's been doing it but he can't raise the alarm. Because he can't afford to say, yes, I've been entertaining this fisherman from Cascais. And the fisherman can't read nor write but he knows what he knows and next time he feels like it, he'll walk in again and help himself.'

This time he did not blink. He stared at me with his small round eyes which had lost their look of cosy malice and they seemed more vulnerable than other people's because they were set at a slightly uneven level.

When he left he told me he was now going to take his daily walk on the beach, that he couldn't stand curving and tortuous paths, that he only liked straight-out walks, 'and I manage it even in Venice'.

When I refused to believe this, he said, 'I'll let you into my secret tomorrow, here at the same time, to make sure you turn up,' and he wiggled his plump shoulders and gave me a conspiratorial smile.

It was sadly charming, this way of his of pretending that he intended carrying on a flirtation with me.

He turned at the far curve of the arcades and waved a smiling, lady-like farewell, before adjusting his little-boy's hat.

On the following day, when we met for the second time, the Bostonian was fussy when ordering his lunch. A young waiter was in attendance, younger than the one that had served him the day before. The Bostonian gave long-winded instructions as to how runny the omelette should be, uttering the word '*baveuse*', explaining that it meant 'moist' in French, making the waiter repeat it, correcting his pronunciation. All this in order to have the young man dwell by the side of his chair a few minutes longer.

He told me, 'Now that I've dismissed my valet I get my lunch here. Lunch is the only meal I ever have on my own. I am always asked out to dinner; I am in great demand. I am single and unattached, I play bridge and, if required, I'll dance for hours. There's a German princess in Cascais, for instance, an old bag, she is so keen on dancing, she gets a ballet master from the opera in Lisbon to organize her soirées.

'The only crowd where I'm not popular is the American colony here. I'm not their kind. I'm a Bostonian. I do not deal in ball-bearings, I do not represent car-tyres, I do not teach the Portuguese how to tin their tomatoes.'

'What do you do for breakfast?' I asked. 'Do you have it brought from a place nearby?'

'Oh, no. My breakfast is very simple. Just three gins every morning. After the gins I recite to myself a sad poem. To make myself weep. That's good for me. It clears the eyes. I get through a bottle a day and I feel very well and fit on it.'

Sitting as we were, at adjoining tables, and turned toward each other, I could not see the persons who came walking along the arcades toward the railway station, but I could see those who were coming the opposite way. And yet, every time, by looking at the Bostonian's face, I could tell whether someone was approaching behind my back who might be exciting his interest, or if the passer-by left him cold.

By the time he had finished his omelette and was starting on a steak, he was no longer content to appraise the passers-by in silence. In a rather skilful way, he made me share his erotic preoccupation.

He would say, 'Now, look, this boy who's just passing. He's got good hips, don't you think? You're drawn. Admit it.'

From time to time he would furnish some particulars, taking for granted that I would find them of interest.

'This one, now, he's doorkeeper at the Casino. This here, he's liftboy. Used to be at the Atlantico but now he's changed to the Montemar.'

By the time the ladies' circle had vanished, I had formed a clear idea regarding the Bostonian's taste.

His eyes lit up only for proletarian youths of slight, short build, rarely handsome, often grubby. The well-groomed young clerks from the nearby bank who came strolling by during their lunch break, and the neatly dressed young men from the Casino offices, did not excite his attention.

At times he would find a pretext by means of another

device, remarking, 'Now, look at this one. Hasn't he got a head like out of a Caravaggio painting? The young David, say, holding up the head of Goliath, in the Borghese gallery in Rome? You know, the one where the chopped-off head is Caravaggio's self-portrait?'

I said, 'Yes, rather; I see what you mean.'

He went on, 'You should go and see the gipsies in the Alfama district, if you want to find something really marvellous. Or the barrow-boys on the Cais de Sodré who sell stolen goods.'

'Not interested.'

'But you are wrong,' he said, 'so wrong.' And he added with sparklingly lecherous animation, 'It's just the seamy side of life that's interesting.'

'Not to me it isn't,' I said. 'To me it's just low cunning, rude, smelly and spitting on the floor.' Then I added, 'And besides, it's frightfully risky. You told me yourself, yesterday, remember? Your friend entertaining the wrong kind of people.'

'Ah, but that's just it,' he said, moving cheeks and lips as though he were sniffing and tasting, 'it's just when they are a shade underworld, on the criminal side, that you get that thrilling sense of danger. Besides, in one way they're safer. There's no rifling through your letters, your bank accounts, no capers with your cheque books, because they are all illiterate. There's eighty per cent illiteracy in this country. That's the beauty of it – though mind you, people like us get the backlash too.

'When you go to a notary for a document, he's bound by law to take your thumb-print because the law assumes that you can't sign your name.

'You can't get a driving licence unless you can read and write. You tell them you've got a PhD in English in Harvard and they say they believe you, but can you read and write? If you can't show them your school certificates for the first four years of primary school, how can the Ministry of Transport know that you can read and write?'

He looked at me, blinking rapidly, and went on, 'The upshot of it is, that the American Consul, whom I've never set eyes on, writes a letter saying that he's known me personally for years and that he can vouch for it that I've been through four years' primary school.'

'Devastating.'

'This country is like it's run by the Marx Brothers, I tell you. I've been around; I was in Tokyo for years, teaching at the university; I've lived in Italy, Turin, in Spain, Cadiz, but I've never seen anything like it. And, mind you, I haven't got my PhD in the easy way, like you, for instance.'

Another cosily malicious glance, as I met his eyes.

'What do you mean?' I asked.

He said, 'With you, PhD means your petticoat is hanging down.'

When he was ready to leave for his walk on the beach, I said, 'You still haven't told me how you can walk straight in Venice,' thinking of the map of Venice, which always reminds me of the twisting grooves in the kernel of a peach. He said, 'So be it. I'll tell you. But only if you promise you'll be here, tomorrow, again, at the same hour. It's on the Zattere, along the dogana, with the golden Fortuna figure on top.'

'Of course,' I said, 'how clever of you.'

He had not turned up on the day after.

On the Monday morning there was a thin, steady rain. Sky and sea were like a backdrop of grey velvet and could not be told apart. The palm trees and the fake Moorish castle showed through the rain as if through a curtain of grey glass beads.

Had the telephone been ringing for a long time, or had it only just now broken into the snarling purr? There was no telling, because I had just come out of the bathroom and the bath water was still gurgling down the drain.

I said to myself, if it is them again, the police, this time I'll set them on to Ginny darling and the forget-me-not. Shared pleasure is two-fold pleasure. And even if I don't know the ladies' names, the police are sure to find them.

I lifted the receiver.

'This is the hall porter speaking. Good morning, madam. Sorry to disturb you. There's a telegram arrived for you. I'm sending it up straightaway.'

A click and silence.

This man is a pest. Firm but unkind, that's his motto. If he'd given me the chance I'd have told him to leave it downstairs for me, I'll pick it up later. It's no use ringing back now, the pageboy will already be on his way. One of those dressed-up sad little monkeys; some of them can't be more than ten years old. I hate to see them. It shouldn't be allowed.

The same as those ten- or twelve-year-old child-maids I've noticed, crisply starched and frilled and aproned, on the beach, chasing the toddlers in their charge. And even at the ladies' circle, where, God knows, there are no children to take care of, standing behind the ladies' chairs or fetching carrier bags or fashion journals from the ladies' parked cars. Still, it's nothing to do with me. The McGregors say it's a blessing for those child-servants; they get better fed and better kept than in their own villages. And the ladies even send them to school.

Curse the porter. Now I'll have to find some silver for the page. I must give him something. What if I haven't got a two-fifty escudo piece? I'd hate to have to give him five escudos for the pleasure of being informed James delayed New York return date unspecified. Or, James proceeding Zurichward period of stay uncertain.

And here I am, looking for a house. It's a pity; I don't want to leave London, but James has got to stay out of England.

I don't know what he's been up to – too complicated for me to understand, anyway. That time when I brought in the coffee the lawyer told me it was a perfectly legal swindle, and as long as James kept out of the country the Bank of England couldn't do anything about it. The house in

Campden Hill has already been put up for sale. Then there is the house in Ascona. It sounds grand – a place on the Lago Maggiore – but it's vile, a poky damp cottage, and not even a view of the lake. And if you want a hot bath you have to carry a shovel with glowing coal all down the length of the passage, from the kitchen to the bathroom, to light the boiler. Turn-of-the-century and never been changed since.

It doesn't worry James, he hasn't got to do it; but what if the old girl he's got living there folds up? You don't find domestics in a hurry, not in Switzerland, not with James being as mean as he is with salaries, and I'm not going to walk down the passage with a shovel-full of glowing coal.

It was the right idea to try it here; seaside and never any snow and the Atlantic climate. Never really hot, like in Italy or in Spain, and plenty of cheap servants.

I went through to the hallway and drew back the bolt.

Once I've found a house here I've got to stick it out. Bianca says if I stay with him much longer it won't *be* much longer, because I'll end up in the loony bin.

Bianca says it's quite simple, you pack a suitcase and you clear out, you are not his wife. Bianca doesn't like him – and he doesn't like her either. The first time she came out to Campden Hill and he showed her the stolen Egyptian wall paintings he bought in Zurich, that he's still got cold feet about, he said, afterwards, how he loathed that type of person, because she likes all the right things for the wrong reasons.

It's all very well for Bianca to talk. She's got the right kind of divorce, not like me. In bed he was a zero, she says, but out of bed he was senior partner at Selwyn Reeds, the merchant bankers in the City. And she gets her money year in year out, not like me. And last year they even raised her allowance because of the increase in the cost of living.

James would marry me now. But I can't. I can only stick it out as long as I know I'm not tied to him. That's why I don't want him to give me any jewellery either. I couldn't take it and then clear out; that would be shabby. I'd despise myself for it, even if Bianca says I'm a hopeless fool.

My handbag was on the desk by the window. I took out my purse. I was in luck. There were three two-fifty escudo coins in it.

He'll see me in my bath towel, but never mind, I'm covered right up to my armpits. He has come in just now. I heard the click as he shut the outside door. Didn't even knock. They are hopeless, poor little devils. Maddening, how one can't hear any footsteps on this carpet.

I put the purse into my handbag, picked up the coin and turned round, facing the door.

'What a pleasant surprise to find you here, madam,' said the barman.

I backed away from the desk till I felt the edge of the window-sill cutting into my waist.

'How did –' I began, but my throat was so tight and so dry that I had to stop.

I started once more. 'How did you,' I said, in a shaky, hoarse voice, 'manage to get here? Where is the telegram? I've been waiting for a telegram. I'd never have unlatched the door if I'd known – '

It was only then that I could see him clearly, because my eyes had dimmed with the first leaping heartbeat.

He was dressed in dark green corduroys. The tweed jacket in small brown and green checks was open and showed a yellow shirt, with a yellow Turkish-patterned silk scarf tucked into the open neck.

I still couldn't believe it was really him.

I had only known him in his white barman's jacket and now, as I looked at the smoothly pale face, brutally clever, and heavy-lipped, I felt I was beholding an illusion, one of those pictorial jokes, as when people get themselves photographed at fun fairs, putting their heads through a cardboard cut-out of a fireman or a mountaineer.

He looked sleek, grave and trustworthy, a young executive, dressed for a day in the country.

'But you are not wet,' I said. 'Isn't it still raining?'

'I came here by car.'

'Mr Wilkinson's?'

'Let's forget Mr Wilkinson, madam. Let's talk about you. I'm glad to see you've got your colour back. You went livid when I came in just now.'

'Nonsense,' I said. 'I'm always pale.'

He said, 'I have noticed your lovely ivory complexion. But just then you were whiter than you should be.'

I took a deep breath, trying to steady the insistently heavy beating of my heart and, nerving myself to appear calm and reasonable, I said, 'But I still don't understand. The porter rang through about a telegram. He said he'd send it up. I'm still waiting for it.'

'I am the telegram,' said the barman.

'I'm speechless.'

'Then don't spoil it by telling me at great length how speechless you are,' he said, 'and please, don't make fun of my name. I can't help it, I was christened that way. At home they used to call me Telly for short. In Italy they'd say, Telino. In Spain, Telito. And here, of course, Telinho.'

'And that vile porter downstairs. How much did that cost you? To let you come up?'

'Nothing, madam, I'm happy to say. I'm in the hospitality trade myself, remember. Besides, I used to be a hall porter once too. Country hotel, in England. Idyllic. At night, when they needed it, I sat down with the guests and made a fourth at bridge. Do you play bridge too? It's a useful game.'

While talking he had been undoing the knot of his scarf, and now he took it off and threw it over a chair.

'But how did you find me?' I asked. 'You didn't even know my name. Through Katie McGregor? No, you couldn't have. She'd have sent you off with a flea in your ear.'

He said, 'I'd be pissing on granite with Katie. Loyal Scots granite. But don't be too sure. I could have got it from there just the same. The staff. These golden lasses.'

I said, 'Yes, she's got an office girl. I wouldn't call her golden, though.'

I watched him take off his jacket.

'Are you hot?' I asked.

He ignored my question, and said, 'Did you know that the Portuguese government shut down the brothels, as from the beginning of this year? Silly of them. Because it's well known that Satan will find mischief still for idle hands to do. So I started cruising round the hotels. When I got here, I said to the porter, "Can you do me a girl, hefty size, big, blonde, blue-eyed?" And when he said, "no, but I can deliver one small with black hair and eyes that change into green and gold," I said, "Done and done."'

I said, 'You forget one thing, though. "And she must be seventeen."'

'I did not forget,' he said. 'You are eternally seventeen. You have that little-girl look; you still don't know what it's all about; you break my heart. I can't tell you any more just now because I left in a hurry; my speechwriter had no time to produce any more.'

'I still don't understand how you managed to find me.'

'And at such short notice too,' he said. 'Because I'd been hoping to see you in church last night and you weren't there. A fine, God-fearing crowd we had, too, with the Reverend Wilkinson going from pew to pew and dispensing the Christian spirit.'

I watched him as he moved over to the corner cupboard, opened it, closed it and then entered the hallway.

I watched him slide open a door in the built-in wardrobe, take out a hanger, put his jacket on it, put it inside and slide the door closed.

He returned to the room.

He sat down on the grey easy chair and began to unbutton his shirt.

'And what shall we do now?' he asked, taking off his yellow shirt. 'Will you have the first guess? Or shall I?'

He bent down and slipped out of his shoes.

Then he stood up and undid the buckle of his trouser belt. It was of brown crocodile. I wondered, who, where, what woman had given it him as a present.

As I watched him lay the belt over the back of the chair, casually, unconcerned, I clutched at the towel round my body and tightened my grip on it.

I said, 'Get dressed and clear out.'

'Ladies are so unpredictable,' he said calmly. 'Now, I'd have thought you'd say, get dressed and clear out. But as you insist, I'll stay.'

He pulled off his vest. It was yellow, matching the shirt. I left the window-sill, went over to the bedside table and laid my hand on the telephone.

He said, 'Do not put your trust in the telephone. Because you may find it will not be answered. It says so, in the Bible.'

I took my hand away and went back to the window-sill.

'You've thought of everything.'

'I always do my homework.'

'You think you'll win?' I asked.

'Of course, I'll win,' he said, taking off his trousers. 'Shall I carry you to the bed or will you walk?'

'You are mad. You are a sex maniac.'

'Sex, yes; maniac, no. I'll be careful.'

He bent down and pulled off his socks.

'I'll scream the house down.'

'Some women do and some women don't,' he said, indifferently. 'I don't mind as long as it isn't faked.'

He was on his feet again, clad only in briefs, of the same yellow as his shirt.

Trying to avoid looking at that region, I looked straight ahead, at the wide chest, massively fleshed and with no ribs showing, the torso of a man who has been athletic in his youth. There was a thick sprinkling of dark freckles on his shoulders and upper arms, like the chocolate powder that is dusted on the frothy white coffee in Italy.

'So what else is there?' he asked. 'You could run and lock yourself in the bathroom if you could get past me. And that goes for dashing out into the passage too, yelling for help. And a pretty story it would make.

'First you make a date with the barman at Stafford's and when he gets here, on time, as agreed, you tell the porter to send him up. Then you change your mind and pretend it's all been a mistake. Because you didn't like the look of him, once you'd seen him in the altogether. Because you only like them with hair on their chest. Correct?'

I turned my back to him, pretending to look out of the window and seized the ashtray on the sill, hexagonal, of heavy glass, with the name of a tonic water running round the rim in red letters. Behind me there was a silence which unnerved me. I put my hand over the ashtray and found that I could not grasp it properly. Gripping it at one side only, on the rim, I said in a voice which I tried to make sound harmless, 'I believe it's still raining.'

'Is it?'

I was about to turn round, with the ashtray lifted in my hand, ready to hit him. I suddenly sensed him close behind me, the smell of talcum powder rising from the warmth of his body and a bitter-fresh scent like wet tree bark coming from his hair.

His fingers were pressing into the inside of my elbow with a dull, enervating pain. The ashtray slid with a thud on to the sill.

'There is one nearer to the bed, my angel,' he said, with a voice which sounded as though he were smiling.

His body, so close behind mine, still did not touch me, only his heavy hands moved to my shoulders, rounded them and came to rest under my armpits.

I said, 'Don't you dare to touch me.'

I twisted to get out of his grasp and, to my amazement, he let go of me.

I stumbled, and before I could steady myself I felt one arm coming round my waist and the other sliding between my thighs.

He lifted me up.

I heard his voice, low, still as though smiling, 'It's no use, my sweet.'

I closed my eyes.

'Must you go?' I said. 'Don't go yet.'

He was buttoning his shirt.

He said, 'I wanted to stay. But, as you insist, I'll leave.'

I did not speak.

'Do you know what time it is?' he asked.

I shook my head. My wristwatch was still in the drawer of the bedside table where I had put it before my bath.

'It's two o'clock,' he said, 'and I got here around ten. They told me you never went out before eleven.'

'You enquired?' I asked, 'Beforehand? You are so efficient, you make me feel faint the way you think of everything.'

'Only of one thing at a time, my sweet. And now that I've got this off my mind I must go and have lunch. The birds and the bees eat lunch too; it's one of the facts of life. I've just had half a roll from your breakfast tray, but without butter because you didn't leave me any, and that's not the way to keep a man happy.'

'Two o'clock,' I said. 'I could ask them to – '

'You couldn't,' he said. 'The telephone doesn't work, thanks to the hall porter, and even if it did, coffee and sandwiches'd be all you could get at this hour. But what about yourself? I can't take you out to eat, you know that. You can't afford to be seen with me. You're the princess and I'm the swineherd.'

'I'm too dead to think of anything properly just now,' I said. 'I don't even know if I could stand up.'

'Next time I come I'll bring a lobster and a pot of mayonnaise.'

'I don't like lobster.'

He came over to the bed.

'Do you know, my sweet,' he said, raising my chin and tilting my face upward, 'that I could even make you like lobster. I could get you to the point where you'd beg for it.'

I lowered my eyes.

'Don't be so conceited.'

He let go of me. 'Don't be so conceited,' he mimicked. 'Do you know, my love, you wanted me so much that when I touched you and put my hands under your arms, you went quite limp in the knees; you'd have sagged to the floor, if I hadn't held you up. It's always the knees that give first.'

'I didn't know,' I said.

'You needn't know. As long as you do it.'

I did not speak.

'You know, my sweet,' he said, 'you are like one of those regional dishes they write up in the Sunday papers. Requires lengthy preparation and a great deal of care, but is well worth the effort.'

'Oh, stop it.'

'You should be very grateful to me for having so much patience. Because you can be very trying. You can't help being seductive, but you are the kind of woman who says no when she means no, and who says no when she means yes. Correct?' He was standing in front of the corner cupboard of which he had opened the door. The inside of the door was lined with a mirror, so that, sitting up in bed, I could see, as well as his back, one side of his face in the glass.

As I followed the movement of his hand over the well-shaped narrow head, smoothing the straight black hair, I recalled that at Stafford's his hair had been greased down with brilliantine, with the neatness one expects to see on waiters. Now it had an easy crispness. What was he? A barman posing as gentleman, or a gentleman posing as barman?

He moved away from the mirror and I closed my eyes. I could not hear his footsteps but I imagined he had gone to the hallway to take his coat.

I opened my eyes at the sound of his voice.

'You know, my sweet, I have found a two-fifty escudo piece on the floor. Was that what you were holding in your hand when I came in?'

'Yes,' I said, 'I had it ready for the pageboy.'

'And you dropped it when you saw me; you went all to pieces, correct?'

'You know it all,' I said.

'And yet you went through the whole show of what cheek and how dare you and clear out and wanting to brain me with the ashtray. You did not spare me a single act of the comedy. Did you?'

I felt I was blushing.

He kept his eyes on me, the heavy lower lip pushed forward, with the same cynical air he had displayed when looking at the glass raised in his hand. You may think you are clean, but you can't fool me.

He said, 'It wasn't all comedy, though. And it wasn't because you were afraid I'd think you a push-over either. It's very deep inside you. What you really want is to be violated. Do you know, my sweet, when you were quite beyond and lost to yourself, you kept saying, no, no, no?'

'Did I really?' I asked, forcing a smile. I met his glance for an instant, then turned away.

He said, 'You can't remember? No, of course you can't. Just as you can't remember – you never knew you dropped the coin. May I keep it?'

'You may,' I said.

'I'd better go now,' he said, 'before I get sentimental. It must be the hunger. I'm afraid I'll get to a restaurant and when I tell them, I'm so hungry I could eat a horse, they'll say, what a lucky coincidence.'

Like husband and wife united in marriage and sharing the same bed, yet each possessing a personality and function diverging from that of his partner, the hall porter and the receptionist in the Hotel Coimbra, though sharing the same desk and working in close proximity, were each an entity in their own right.

The hall porter, in his gold-braided livery, was always on view and always on his own while commanding a team of pageboys who were partly stationed at lifts and doors and partly roaming about, often out of sight. Up till midday it usually was the lean, morose, cadaverous-looking man who reminded me of my former Latin teacher, Monsieur Ruelle.

In reception there were always two men, one elderly, bald and of military bearing, and a dreamy-eyed youth of about twenty, his cheeks pitted from acne scars. They were both dressed in the black jacket and grey striped trousers proper to their calling, and were mostly half-hidden from view, enfolded as they were by the activities of several girls who took their turn in filing, typing, and serving at the telephone switchboard.

The hall porter's backdrop was of an unproblematical and geometrical simplicity, made up of the shiny mahogany squares of the pigeon-holes with their hooks and keys. His reference library of guidebooks, leaflets and timetables was stacked out of sight under the counter.

The reception part of the desk, by contrast, was untidy and open-hearted, always littered with ledgers, receipts and bills, and behind it there lay a hinterland of unfathomable depth, affording glimpses of standing, moving, sitting figures behind half-open doors of frosted glass, felt-covered and brass-nailed screens and shoulder-high walls formed by filing cabinets.

It was only at midnight that hall porter and receptionist fused and became one, in the person of a short, portly, middle-aged man clad in a black suit with crossed keys embroidered in silver on the lapels, white shirt and black tie, suggesting both livery and gentlemanly wear.

Smiling steadily, as though listening to jokes he was telling himself, uniting all functions and deferring to no one, he might be considered as ruling like an absolute monarch. Or serving as a maid-of-all-work.

The only person behind the desk whose role I could not account for, was a lavishly elegant, short, plump, blonde woman in her late thirties, who could have been a member of the ladies' circle. I used to see her in the afternoons only, never before three and never after six. She was always standing, leaning, lounging about in the reception area. She never seemed to have an occupation. She utterly ignored the two black-jacketed clerks, though she would sometimes exchange a remark with one of the switchboard girls.

As I stepped out of the lift I saw her beckoning to me. It was after three. The barman had left half an hour before.

Whenever I entered the entrance hall of the Coimbra I felt as though I was stepping into one of Veronese's enormously large banqueting pictures. This was partly due to the concealed lighting behind the cornice of the ceiling which, no doubt chosen for the sake of economy, filled the space with the same dull, shadowless bluish glow encountered in those paintings, which unites the melancholy of dusk with the serene clarity of moonlight, and endows Veronese's work with a secretive, trance-like atmosphere. Another reason for this feeling was the crimson-flamed mahogany desk running the entire length of one wall, which took the place of what would have been the banqueting board in the pictures, with people in various attitudes grouped behind it and in front of it. The third reason was that the blonde woman herself was so exactly like the lush blonde women always to be found in Veronese's pictures: gold-blonde, round-faced, with thickened features, of an ignoble prettiness.

She was beckoning to me from the far end of the counter close to the window, leaning with her bosom resting on the mahogany.

She had on a clinging dress of fine cashmere I had not seen her wear before, beige, printed with white flowers, and she was hung with her usual array of multiple gold chains. Her arms, bare to the elbows, were ringed with gold bracelets.

She had spoken to me on a few occasions before, conversing in fluent, faulty French, mostly commenting upon the weather.

I hesitated, giving her a forced smile.

Knowing her habits, she would have only just arrived and could not have seen the barman on his way out.

The morose, cadaverous-faced porter was not on duty any more. He had been replaced now by the young curly-haired one with the nice smile, who, though he must have seen the barman leave, could not possibly have known from which room he had come, and why.

And yet I was afraid.

What if the morose porter had left a message with reception, a warning about my immoral conduct? I thought that this was very likely; she would have been the most suitable person for this task – more suitable than the military-looking gentleman or his young assistant of the scar-pitted face.

I waved to her on my way out and handed in my key.

'Venez, madame,' she called. *'Je désire vous parler pour une petite minute seulement.'*

I joined her at the desk.

'How are you, madame? You are well?' she said.

This was her customary opening, after which she would pause. Because I, then, had to ask her the same question, in my turn.

After I had said, 'Thank you, madame, and how are you?' she would go on to the second part of her customary formula, 'And you have good news from your husband?'

This question I never reciprocated as I knew nothing about her and had never seen anyone who looked like they might be her husband.

Formerly, I had rather liked this second part of her greeting. It seemed to prove that she was ignorant of my circumstances, had not taken the trouble to look up my entry-slip where my status was given as 'divorced', and took for granted that the letters and telegrams I received from James were those from my husband.

She tilted her face up to me with an archly scandalized smile. I knew that smile. I had liked her for it from the beginning of our acquaintance; it gave a spiciness to her countenance lacking in the ladies of the circle, and turned their show of being victims into an amused pretence.

She said, 'As you are from London, madame, will you be

an angel for a little while,' and, opening her handbag, 'just wait till I find it. This bag is so large, not flat and handy like yours. There is nothing like crocodile, is there? I have eleven crocodile bags, three of them black, like yours, but none as sensible.'

I said, 'Have you really? What heaven,' returning her smile heartily for the first time.

She handed me a leaflet which she begged me to translate. It was printed in English and dealt with the mode of use and the merits of a facial mask.

While I was reading it out to her in French, she kept tilting her head up and casting doubting glances at the ceiling, touching her hair, and wriggling her large, beautifully rounded bust.

I could not understand why I had felt so frightened a few minutes before.

As I turned to her on my way out, raising my hand in a farewell gesture, I was pleased and reassured at the sight of her pink-skinned doughy prettiness framed in the glitter of her gold ornaments.

Later in the afternoon I went to the McGregors' office. It had stopped raining. The sky had become a whitish grey and it had turned sultry.

Walking across the Casino gardens with the rain-soaked gravel soft and silent underfoot, on the same track along which I had seen the Bostonian approaching, tall and stout-bellied and crowned with his ridiculous little-boy's hat, I wondered how soon it would be before I saw him approaching again, carrying off a disreputable escapade, a bout of drunkenness, the pursuit of some youthful delinquent with slim hips, facing me with his conspiratorial blinking of the eyelids, with that look of cosy malice, while hiding his vice behind his devotion to Caravaggio's paintings.

There were no clients in the office. Mother and son were both present and the office girl, seated at the closed typewriter in the background, stared at me with her usual air of incurious sullenness.

On a former occasion I had remarked about her to Katie, who had said, 'These gir-rls are all alike. They consider themselves underpaid,' to which the son had added, 'No, it's nothing to do with their having a grievance. It's part of the Arab strain in the Portuguese. Arab women always have these ugly snouts.'

After she had shown me a sheaf of papers with blueprints of houses and a stack of photographs, Katie said, 'I must tell you, as a client you are out of the ordinary. With most people when it comes to houses, they all know what they do *not* want but they don't know what they do want.'

Young McGregor added, 'In our profession, the most loathsome phrase is "it depends". What kind of house have you got in mind? It depends. How many rooms? It depends. Do you care for an all-in living-room? It depends. Depends on what? It depends.'

I said, 'By the way, I wanted to ask you. About this business with the American from Boston; I think his name is Shepherd. I don't read the papers here, but I've heard something about him. I'm interested because I've met him; we got talking by chance, here, over our coffee, under the arcades.'

Mother and son both looked at me without speaking, wide-eyed and close-lipped, as though undecided how to counter an embarrassing remark I had made.

Still more surprisingly, the sullen office girl at the back had raised the chin she had been resting on her fist, broodingly, and was now looking at me too.

I said, hastily, trying to cover up whatever offence my words had given, 'He's great fun to be with, most amusing; frightfully cultured too.'

'Don't rub it in,' said Katie, tugging at the string of pearls on her flat chest.

I wondered why she always wore clinging knitwear instead of something softly draped, concealing. I imagined this was due to her Scottish, uncompromising dislike of deceit.

She added now, 'He's been mur-rdered.' She twisted her face as though feeling with her tongue round a painful tooth.

'Murdered? How?' I asked.

'He wasn't murdered in a nice way,' she said.

Behind her shoulder young McGregor winked at me, as though inviting me to think up nice ways of being assassinated.

'He was hit over the head,' she continued. 'In his flat. He had one floor in an old house behind the Palace hotel, opposite the fire station and the English church. He was found on the Friday morning. In his dressing-gown. He opened the door himself, that's certain, to let the killer in.'

'Have they found him yet?' I asked.

'Not yet,' she replied, 'but they will, dinna fear, dinna fash yoursel.'

The son said, 'It was in the papers on Friday night but we missed seeing it.'

'And do you know how we came to hear about it?' said his mother. 'Ginny Sutcliff rang me up – you met her at Stafford's the other night, only she didn't know then, either. But she rang me up on the Saturday morning. She said, "Something awful's happened," and my first thought was that her boiler had gone bust again. Then she told me.'

'Ginny darling,' I cried.

Then, trying to cover up, I added quickly, 'I mean, she's really a darling, so handsome, and with that white-blonde hair, so striking, and not dyed either, all natural.'

'Oh, she is a darling all right,' said Katie, 'but she can get very deter-rmined when she thinks she's been done wrong.'

'Determined,' said the son, 'you should have seen her at Stafford's last night. You weren't there, were you? We kept looking out for you. She raised the roof. All because of a gin fizz.'

'Why?' I asked.

He said, 'She kept screaming he'd given her rum instead

of gin in it. It was a bloody lie if you ask me, she was just in that mood. She felt like screaming, so she screamed.'

'She just couldn't see what she was doing to poor Mr Wilkinson,' said Katie.

Young McGregor went on, 'He's got trouble with his staff. His barman is away with flu; he'd got in that new man at a minute's notice – and it's not so easy getting someone with English and Portuguese. But he couldn't make her stop bitching and belly-aching, even after she'd been given one on the house.'

I said, 'Was the barman put out?'

'Not he,' said the son. 'That barman is as brazen as a bedbug. It's Mr Wilkinson one's sorry for; he's between the devil and the deep blue sea.'

I took out my cigarette case and offered it all round.

Young McGregor said, 'You've gone rather white. As though you could do with a gin fizz yourself,' and he started to laugh. He was one of those people who laugh at their own jokes, and I thought of the barman, who never laughed and who, seeing one's own amusement, gave one reproving glances.

Young McGregor's laughter was distasteful to me now, though it had never irritated me before. It was abrupt and monotonous, without rising and falling, and it went on too long. Then I thought again about the barman, of his ill-fitting white jacket, for which I now had been given the explanation, and how odd it was that his way of speaking was so close to that of the Bostonian, and whether he was from Boston, too.

I said, somewhat breathlessly, 'But who found Mr Shepherd?'

'His charwoman did,' said young McGregor.

Katie said, 'The charwoman should have come as usual, at two in the afternoon, but she'd left her umbrella at Mr Shepherd's a full week before and each time she went to do for him, she forgot to take it with her.

'So, on that Friday morning, she happened to be nearby

and she made up her mind she'd dash over specially to pick it up, before going to work there in the afternoon, to make sure she wouldn't leave it behind again. She's got her own key.'

I said, with the flippancy I'd learned from Bianca when discussing disasters, 'Well, at least she got her umbrella back.'

'Funny you should say that,' said young McGregor, 'because, you know, she didn't.'

'How very annoying,' I said, still in my flippant vein.

'Very,' he said, 'but she did find it in the end. That's to say, she didn't find it herself; it wasn't anywhere in the flat. But it *was* found by the police and she got it back.'

I said, 'All's well that ends well. And where was it?'

'At Stafford's.'

'At Stafford's?'

'At Stafford's,' he said, 'in the service part of the place. In one of the staff lockers. Where the barman hangs out.'

I stared at him.

There was a sty coming into bud on the upper lid of his eye which I had not noticed before.

I said, 'The barman? The cheeky barman with the shoulders?'

'Has he got shoulders?' he asked.

'Yes, tremendous.'

'I haven't noticed them. But, cheeky, yes.'

'I don't believe it,' I said. 'It's ridiculous; it's too ridiculous for – '

'Ridiculous or not,' he said, 'it was found in the barman's locker – to be exact, where he keeps his rig, Mr Wilkinson told us. Tearing his hair out. Not that he's got that much hair, really. But you get the idea.'

I said, 'Then it wasn't him that took it and put it there; it must have been the other barman who was there before him – or one of the twins, they're such pretty boys, if you know what I mean. It's as clear as day.'

'Clear as day at midnight,' he said.

I gave him a haughty look and twisted my lips.

He said, 'Is it your umbrella?'

'No.'

'Then what do you care?'

Katie said, 'I don't think this is a very nice conversation to have. Anyone overhearing us would think we were quarrelling. And we aren't,' and she gave a sidelong glance at the office girl, who was sitting, cheek in hand, brooding.

I too glanced at her, at the greyish, unclean-looking skin, the hair separated in greasy strands, the provocatively well-shaped body, and wondered again whether she and young McGregor were sleeping together.

They were always indifferent and off-hand with each other when I saw them together, and whenever he mentioned her it was slightingly. Which meant that he had something to hide. Which made me certain that he *had* slept with her; perhaps only once though. Her very sullenness would be an advantage; it would make her too proudly indifferent to pursue him and to make further trouble. She was not a woman to clamour for the attentions of any man.

Katie said, 'Mr Wilkinson told us the umbrella had got tired of soaking up water. It had come to Stafford's to get a proper drink, instead. So brave of Mr Wilkinson. His sense of humour never fails him.'

I said, 'And because the umbrella was found in the barman's locker, Mr Wilkinson thinks it's he who took it? From the Bostonian's house?'

'Mr Wilkinson doesn't think anything,' said young McGregor. 'Mr Wilkinson wants to be left in peace. But other people do some thinking, don't you know.'

I said, 'No, I don't know. Valets, yes. Footmen, yes. The twins, yes – two for the price of one, I can quite see that. But not the barman. You must be mad. I've – I've seen him myself. You took me there. You are not going to tell me that he's queer.'

'Have you asked him if he is queer?' said the son.

'No,' I said.

'Then how d'you know?'

I went on, 'And I still think you must be batty. The barman goes there, to the flat, kills him, takes the umbrella along, goes back to Stafford's and puts it in his locker. To make sure that he gets found out. Whatever that barman is or isn't – and he is impertinent with the customers, I grant you – he wasn't born yesterday. Not he.'

'That's exactly it,' said young McGregor, 'and that's where you fall down. He takes the umbrella and puts it in his locker. So that if anybody saw him going in to Shepherd's, he can always say yes, he did go there, he took the umbrella, he'd been there before, Shepherd American, he American – can't you see it? And the killing? Not he. Someone else. Search him.'

'Clever, aren't you?'

'Yes, I am.'

I crushed out my cigarette in a hexagonal glass ashtray, identical to the one on the window-sill in my bedroom, the one the barman had forced me to relinquish, without touching my hand, by painfully twisting my elbow.

Katie said, 'We are all surrounded by mysteries. No, not that, that's not what I mean, that'll be cleared up, never you fear. I mean, people. The kind of life they lead, drinks and parties, one never knows where the money comes from. But when it comes to paying the rent they suddenly haven't got two pennies to rub together.'

On the following morning the crenellated roof of the fake castle stood outlined against a pleasant-looking, blue, white-streaked sky but the sea was sullen, of a deeper blue, suffused with ashy grey tints and breaking into a harsh diamantine glitter where it was struck by the fitful sun.

I had been wishing intensely, unceasingly, for the telephone to ring. Yet when, shortly before ten, it gave forth its steady bad-tempered buzzing sound, I was, at first, startled, and then I feared that it was not really ringing – that I was dreaming it.

'This is the hall porter speaking. Good morning, madam. Sorry to disturb you. There's a telegram arrived for you. I'm having it sent up straightaway.'

When he came in he was dressed in two whites, bleached-bone white trousers and a thick chalk-white pullover, a young executive dressed for the seaside.

'No tip ready for me today?' he asked.

'No tip,' I said, 'but I've saved the butter for you.'

'You shouldn't have, my sweet,' he said. 'I had a steak for breakfast, so there is no need to worry any more about the facts of life. Correct?'

Later on, as he was getting dressed, he said, 'I've just had a look at that handbag of yours, on the chair; it got mixed up with my clothes.'

'That's not true. Your stuff was on the grey chair. And my bag was on the desk.'

'It's on the chair now. And I had a look at it, anyway.'

I said, 'It's quite old-fashioned, that flat shape. But it's crocodile and it lasts for ever.'

'I wouldn't know, my sweet,' he said, 'but what I do know is it's got Cartier stamped inside it and it has a slide and tongue clasp of metal and four metal corners, with one two three four five six hallmarks, which means it's mounted in solid gold.'

I looked at him, aghast.

'Why are you so upset?' he asked.

'Because you notice too much. No one ever has before. And anyway, if you must know, I never bought this bag. I couldn't afford it. It was Bianca who gave it to me because she's well off and she was fed up with the shape. She was a friend of my mother's and she's my friend now. She was one of the very few who – always – anyway. She's been a wonderful friend to me.'

He said, 'That's nice, isn't it? And your terribly expensive little gold watch, Schaffhausen, yes, I had another look at that too, in the drawer by the bed. And the beaver lining in your coat. Did Bianca give you those, too?'

I did not reply.

'And while we are on the subject,' he said, opening the mirror-lined corner cupboard and putting on a white silk square, tucking it beneath the neck of his pullover, 'is Bianca going to pay for the large gentleman's residence in or near Estoril, you are looking round for?'

'How do you know?'

'Because Katie doesn't racket round buying drinks for twopenny-halfpenny customers. She's Scots. And, quite apart from paying for your drink, she wouldn't drag you to Stafford's after office hours. Waste time on you. It says so in the Bible, about casting your bread upon the waters. Which isn't so far out with Stafford's, when you come to think of it. Whisky means water of life in Gaelic, and vodka means water in Russian, and aquavit means water of life too. Interesting, isn't it?'

'You are overdoing your part as barman.'

'Leave me out of it, my sweet. We were talking about you.'

He came over and sat on the edge of the bed.

'Who is the man you live with? I knew you weren't married the first time I saw you. You don't have that married look.'

'That's true,' I said. 'You mentioned divorce. You were trying to draw me out. And now, you've got it in any case, black on white from your friend the hall porter; status, single, married, widowed, divorced.'

'Who is the man you live with?' he repeated, unmoved.

I did not speak.

'And he is rich,' he said.

I said, 'Not rich rich, like Rockefeller.'

'Very well,' he said, 'he is not rich, he's just got a lot of money. Correct?'

'Yes,' I said, 'as you are so good at guessing. He always says life's been against him, he never had a chance, because he's never had to earn his own living. I suppose he believes it.'

'What's wrong with him?' he asked.

'He is the way some rich men are, nagging, and demanding and eternally fault-finding, because everybody they meet behaves like a doormat. Here I am, please wipe your feet on me.'

He looked at me with his doubting, cynical expression.

I went on, 'And he's afraid of being exploited, and suspicious of being cheated, and he wants to be sure he's squeezed the last drop out of every lemon.'

'That's normal. But I asked you what's wrong with him?'

He was watching me now with the same air of resignation and disgust I had seen on the ramshead policeman.

I could not bear it.

I sat up in bed and threw my legs over the edge, to get up, to get away from him.

He caught me, lifted me on to his knees and forced my head down to his chest.

'I imagine, my angel,' he said, 'that he thinks he is a man, because he looks like one. Correct?'

I tried to lift my head but his hand went under my hair on the nape of my neck and held me tight.

'You have not been with a man for a long time. More than a year; two, three years. Correct?'

I was grateful now that my face was hidden from his eyes. He felt me relax and began to caress me with a steady movement of his heavy hand.

'I could tell straightaway, yesterday. In the beginning. I could feel it and I knew that I was hurting you.'

'I didn't think you'd noticed.'

'What do you take me for?'

'But later on, you hurt me too.'

'That was different,' he said. 'That was all in the day's work; there I knew what I was doing. But not this at the start. This I hadn't bargained for. Now, what kind of a pervert is he?'

'He's not one of those,' I said. 'He likes women. And he's not – a dried-out riverbed. Only he can't – it's all outside.'

'How?'

'With his hand. I couldn't stand it otherwise. Bianca says it's because he's afraid. If he went inside, he'd be trapped and injured and like this he feels safe.'

'Good for Bianca,' he said. 'And in the meantime, he's very pleased with himself and aren't you lucky he's so considerate, you never need worry about getting pregnant. Correct?'

'You are – it's as though you'd been listening behind the door.'

'I'll put you back to bed now and then I'll go. I take it you won't come to Stafford's tonight?'

'I couldn't bear to see you behind the – '

'Yes, I know,' he said. 'We always come back to the good old fairy tales, the princess and the swineherd, don't we? But take care you don't slip out of it.'

'How do you mean?' I asked.

'I can't tell you now,' he said. 'Later.'

I watched him smooth his hair in front of the glass.

'You came to Stafford's twice. When you didn't turn up the third time I knew I had to make a move. Because if you'd been feeling just a sort of harmless friendship for me, you'd have come. Correct?'

'It's true,' I said. 'And you are as clever as Bianca. Once, abroad, she met a man who had been in love with me, and when she got back to London she told me, "He still hasn't got over you." I said, "How can you tell? Did he say so; did he ask about me?" and she said, "No, he never mentioned you; that's just it."'

He said, 'Good for Bianca. And not so good for Mr Wilkinson. He's lost a customer. I'll come tomorrow at the same time. Goodbye, my love.'

Shortly after one o'clock I was sitting at my usual table under the arcades. It was too cold for me to sit out in the open. The blue, white-streaked sky of the morning had turned into white marbled with grey and the wind was chilly.

But the ladies' circle was hardier and they were shrieking and gesticulating with undiminished resentment beneath the domed shelter of the tropical tree. I was observing the arrival of a new lady, admiring the silver heels on her black shoes and the double row of silver buttons running down the length of her black coat, and wondering how she would be able to sit down in comfort, when I was startled by a man's voice, light, pleasant, and vaguely familiar, behind me.

'Good morning, madam. I'm so glad I've found you.' Standing behind my chair was the elegant young go-getter policeman. His attitude of respectful expectancy was so delightful that it lent charm even to the runaway chin and the bared upper front teeth. He said, 'I enquired at the hotel and they told me you were always here at this time.'

'Won't you sit down?'

'If I may.'

He had on a beautifully made grey flannel suit and a pale blue shirt. As he beckoned the waiter, there was a flash of azure from the blue stone in the gold-rimmed cuff links.

'Isn't it strange, meeting like this?' he remarked. 'You look quite changed as you are now, with your hair twisted into a chignon. I admired you so much, the other morning, with your long hair.

'So many young girls wear it long, but it's not the same; yours is much longer of course, down to your waist. And then, they wear it loose all the time. Whereas you – you are a different woman, now. The young girls are silly. They don't realize – '

'Yes, I suppose so,' I said. 'I can see your point. What you meant, was, the story of the famous actress. When she was cut dead by her former lover at a party, she yelled at him, "Johnny, don't you recognize me, with my clothes on?"'

He laughed longer and louder than was necessary.

I, too, was getting tense.

I said, 'You look different today too, more casual, more relaxed. Because of what you're wearing. It was a lovely suit, though.'

'Yes, it is a decent piece. If black is not perfect it is nothing at all. Though it was wrong for a Sunday morning in Estoril, but I couldn't help it; I had to go to church with my people afterwards. You see, one goes to church. It is *chic*.'

'Did they really tell you at the hotel I'd be here? How could they possibly know?' I asked.

'A good hotel porter must always know where a guest is likely to be found,' he replied. 'Especially now that it's off-season. What will you have? You must have something with me, and I won't take no for an answer.'

'That's a very dangerous thing to say,' I said, 'because, what if I wanted champagne? But I'm not really keen on champagne. I'll have another coffee.'

For a while we remained silent.

I said, 'By the way – I didn't understand at the time, when you called – I just thought you were looking for the Bostonian because he was missing – I only heard yesterday – did you get what you were looking for?'

Putting his hands together as though in prayer, he answered, 'I won't say yes and I won't say no. Actually, that's what I came to see you about. I want you to look at a man, just look at him, and tell me if you've ever seen him before. With Mr Shepherd. Or passing by. Or standing about in the Casino gardens.'

'How very disappointing,' I said, 'I'd thought you'd come here to see what I looked like with my clothes on.'

The waiter brought the coffees.

It was the young one, who had been taught the meaning of an omelette *baveuse*. I wondered whether he still recalled it.

I asked, 'Where do you want me to go?'

'Nowhere,' he said. 'I've got him over there, in a car.'

'Here?'

'Of course. I'll have him brought to our table. *On ne se dérange pas pour une bagatelle comme ça*.

'But – that's awful.'

'Not in the least,' he said. 'There'll be no uniforms, no handcuffs; we don't go in much for handcuffs, in this country. Where would he run away to, anyway? Nobody will notice. Excuse me for one moment.'

He leaned forward and called two words to a man I had barely noticed before, who was seated at a table in front of ours, reading a paper. He was dressed in a grey chauffeur's livery. Now he picked up a peaked cap from the chair next to his, set it on his head, and walked away.

'Actually,' I said, 'it's no use showing me anybody because I haven't met anybody, really, since I've been here. Except owners of villas and houses and I haven't kept their names. The only one I really remember is the Visconde de Moreira, and that's because he latched on to me in Lisbon, the other day, at the Nicky Lassiter show; and Lassiter was a friend of the Bostonian – he told me about him right here where we are sitting now. It gives me the creeps.'

He said, 'I promise you I shan't show you the Visconde de Moreira. One of my mother's cousins married a niece of his.'

Now I could see them approaching from the Casino direction, at the far end of the curve of the arcades. There were three of them, walking side by side, and my eyes fastened at once on the tallest, wide-shouldered one, in a desperate attempt to take in the outlines of his figure. Like that of a familiar shorthand scrawl of which one can decipher the meaning at a glance.

But it was not him.

He had the heavy square-built body of a man approaching middle-age.

Still struggling for breath and with my heartbeats pulsing in my throat and ears I looked away, briefly, watching the ladies' circle.

They were coming past the bank now, past the shop with souvenirs, past the McGregors' office, loyal, dependable bloodhounds in cheaply made dark blue suits, with a miserable, mangy fox-terrier of a man between them.

As they stopped by our table, I saw the couple of gendarmes who were usually standing in front of the bank or on the edge of the Casino gardens. Now, they came strolling behind the group, apparently engaged in talk, apparently without aim.

The two plain-clothes men were both smiling, with the patiently indulgent smile of grown-ups who watch children at play. The man in the middle between them was in his twenties, of frail build. He had, as the Bostonian would have said, 'good hips'. He looked grubby because he was unshaven. He had dark, wavy, matted hair and the thin-boned face of a man who has not had enough to eat in his childhood. His narrow blue eyes were beautiful, deeply set and intensely blue, owing to their being shaded by thick black lashes. He was standing hunched forward, his hands in his trouser pockets, whereas the other two were standing up straight, like soldiers 'at ease'. He did not look unhappy. And he did not look scared. He looked truculent. As our eyes met, his lips moved as though biting on something he had been chewing for a long time. He was dressed in a dark red thick pullover and filthy grey linen trousers. He could have been one of the lorry drivers who came to deliver crates of beer and mineral water for the coffee house.

'No,' I said, while feeling the elegant young man's eyes on me.

'Didn't he pass by while you were here, talking to the Bostonian, and didn't the Bostonian say hello to him?'

'No,' I said.

He threw one beautifully clad leg over the other and waved them away.

As the three were going back to where they had come from, the two gendarmes moved from the column against which they had been leaning, and followed them, once more, at a distance.

'I'll have a brandy now,' I said.

'Whatever you wish. I'm sorry about it; I didn't want to upset you.'

I said, 'It had to be; we were born to suffer; this earth is a vale of tears.'

We both burst out laughing.

It was only now that I realized how senseless my panic had been. It must have been due, I told myself, to having listened to young McGregor's flights of fancy. No, this was not true. Young McGregor had only stirred up in me an unease for which I could give no reason and to which I did not wish to put a name.

The elegant policeman said, 'This case is extraordinary. Not in itself, but in relation to you. You gave us the start and now perhaps, you've given us the finish. It's like a circle. The chief of the brigade, he said it too; he said, "Little did she know when she came here from London – "'

'Did he really say that?' I asked.

'He really did. He gets it from the papers. They write this way all the time. When someone gets run over, they write, "Little did he know when he left his house on that lovely day – "'

We both continued to laugh.

'I was the last person, wasn't I, who saw the Bostonian alive?' I said.

'Not at all,' he replied, 'whatever made you think so? He went to a party on the Thursday night; he was killed on the Friday morning. At about nine.'

I said, 'Where do I come into it? We did have two long talking sessions, he and I, that's true. But that doesn't make me important.'

'Yes, you are,' he said. 'You are our trump card. Because in the wallet we managed to get hold of, there was – not your name – but the name of your hotel and your room number, typed, on the McGregors' office paper with one of their typewriters. It was a piece of incredible luck.'

'I don't understand,' I said, turning my face away from his smiling glance and gazing at the ladies' circle. Some of them were already on their feet, furling their crochet work, while never ceasing to shriek their indignation at each other.

'It must be a mistake.'

He recrossed his legs and leaned back in his chair, a picture of charming well-bred ease.

'No mistake,' he said. 'I can't say anything till we get the case closed – but that's the least of it, that's childsplay; we'll do it lying on our back with our left hand.' He stroked his wavy ash-blond hair, and a glint of azure came from his cufflinks.

'Why was the Bostonian killed?' I asked. 'It all sounds crazy.'

He said, 'These homosexual killings are so dull; they are all the same, like a cracked gramophone record. Either the boy wants more money. Or he's disgusted at what's been asked of him.'

He gave me a sidelong glance, and said, 'That's the theory of homosexual murders; nothing to it. But in my profession one doesn't take anything for granted.'

'How do you mean?'

'It may not be homosexual, after all. One's got to keep an open mind. There is a saying, if it's obvious, it's wrong.'

I did not speak.

'One way or the other, that's our worry, isn't it? Not yours.'

'No, of course not,' I said.

'You got into it in all innocence; like walking down the street and being hit by a falling brick, this business with the slip of paper and your room number. You see, Mr Shepherd was going to give a party.'

'I heard about that,' I said.

'And he wanted to invite you and he didn't know who you were. The waiters here told him about your always going to the McGregors, so he went to their office to find out. When we questioned them the McGregors said they couldn't understand it. They have a strict rule about never giving a client's name to outsiders. So they were out of it, we never doubted their word. And we knew who it must have been. Their office girl. She knows the rule, though. She must have been alone in the office when Mr Shepherd called there, and she obliged him, she got round the rule: she was afraid to give your name, so she just put down Hotel Coimbra and the room number.

'She swore black and blue, of course, she hadn't done it. She's that kind of a liar who keeps calm and looks you straight in the eye. But I got around her. I said, "So you are from the Alentejo? I didn't know they were breeding liars there. I'm from the Alentejo too." That got her. Alentejo, my foot. I'm from the north, from the Minho; look at my hair.'

'God,' I said, and I put my hands over my eyes for an instant.

'And this piece of paper was still in Mr Shepherd's wallet when we traced it on a certain person,' he continued. 'You've seen him just now, you've seen what he's like; didn't even bother to get rid of the paper. Sometimes you don't know whether you should laugh or cry, these people are so dim.'

'Devastating.'

'Money is a washout in my profession. Money is dumb and won't speak; but that chit with your room number on it, that was worth its weight in gold. It was just as the chief said, you were sent to us from heaven.'

'Ghastly, the way he talks,' I said.

'Ghastly but true. In more ways than one,' he said, and he gave me another sidelong glance.

He recrossed his legs. 'Now there is another thing I must ask you. It's so pleasant sitting here, I could talk to you for ever, but you must tell me, quite truthfully. Didn't you think, when you saw me last Sunday in that black suit, that the lapels were just a shade too narrow? You are from London, you must have noticed we wear them in this narrow style, not like Savile Row, but even so.

'I was furious with my tailor; I shan't go to him again. The trouble is, he's getting old; he's run away with a young girl of eighteen; he's lost his head.

'I have not paid him; I'm not going to. He'll see me on Saint Nunca's day, as we say here; *nunca* means never.'

I said, 'I didn't think they were too narrow; they were slim, they were elegant.'

'Oh, you are so charming, so kind. I knew you would be, the first time I met you. Now I'll see you get your brandy and then I must leave you. I must go over there and greet two ladies; they're cousins of my mother's.'

He rose, lifted my hand to his lips and released it.

He called to a waiter. Then he went over to the ladies' circle. There he stood behind chairs, bent down and kissed cheeks. He did it thoroughly. Each of the two ladies got both her cheeks kissed, while the others went on re-enacting their stories without taking any notice of him.

By the time the ladies's circle broke up, I had been able to follow a particularly distressing incident, during which one of the ladies had seen her maid, on the other side of the street, wearing her mistress's gloves. I knew the exact length of the gloves. I knew it must have happened on that last Sunday, after the police had left me; when it had turned sunny and hot, after the mist had cleared. Because I had watched the lady re-enacting the shading of her eyes against the sun, while looking across the street in pained surprise.

Now that I came to think about it, it surely must have been happening as the lady had come out of church. Because she would have been to church. It was *chic*. I knew this from a reliable source.

When I returned to the hotel and entered the hall, I saw the blonde woman leaning over the desk, with her bosom resting on her crossed arms, as though leaning across one of Veronese's banqueting boards.

'*Déjà de retours, madame*?' she called.

As I went over to her, I wondered why her presence, scented, glittering, jingling, was so agreeable while Ginny darling's bodily closeness had so oppressed and revolted me.

She said, 'Did the *senhor policieiro* find you? He is *chic*; he is presentable?'

I nodded.

'He is in love with you, madame? Because he was searching for you.' And as I smiled and shook my head, she added, coaxingly and forming a ring with two fingers of her upraised hand, 'Not a little in love, not a little bit, like this?'

'Certainly not.'

'How can you know, madame? she said. 'One cannot always tell. Men are deceitful; they are like water; you can see through it, but you cannot tell how deep it is.'

'Oh, I think one can always tell. One feels it.'

'That is so. Yet, not always so, madame. When you are in love with one and only one you do not notice the other who may be there, biding his time.'

'You are right,' I said.

'And this *senhor policieiro*,' she continued, 'he is nice, he is *très soigné*, and has good manners. Like the army. They are always presentable too.'

I nodded.

'And besides,' she added, 'with a man like him you know where you are. You know who he is exactly and what he is. Not like a *senhor Brasileiro* who may be a good man and who may be a bad man, who is to tell?'

'I don't know any one Brazilian,' I said.

'Perhaps not, madame. It was just a *façon de parler*; we say it because Brazil is rich and far away. In a hotel like this one does get the police from time to time, but we've never had a policeman like him before; they've given you a special one; it's a pleasure to see him. He comes because of the American murder case, doesn't he?'

'He does.'

'The next time he comes, why don't you say to him, "I have heard nothing but good spoken of the roof garden at the Tivoli. And the Avis restaurant is highly esteemed too. Is this really so, do you believe?" That's how you ask him. He will understand. He will take you there.'

'I don't think he'll come again,' I said.

She raised her arm and pushed the bracelets further up to

her elbow and gave me a quick look while pursing her lips. Then she put on her archly scandalized smile.

'Do you find me changed, today?' she asked me, drawing a hand over her hair, which she wore dressed in the same domed style as the ladies of the circle.

'I had it done more *cendré* today – you don't think it's too *cendré*? I didn't want it any lighter, only not such bright gold. I had to change my cream and powder too, to go with it.'

I replied, 'Yes, it's softer now, wonderfully becoming. It makes you look like a pastel drawing; it brings out the pink in your complexion.'

'Oh, you are always so kind, madame; you say such nice things to me.'

And resuming her pose, resting her bosom on her crossed arms, she continued, 'I wanted a touch of *cendré* only, but not that much,' and she threw a glance toward the ceiling as though suspecting the ceiling of having scandalous intentions.

'I was quite upset when I saw it in the end,' she continued, 'but I didn't want to tell her off; she's seven months gone; she shouldn't be on her feet and working at all.'

I said, 'Is this at the place you sent me to? Antoine's? There's a young man there who is marvellous but I think he got fed up with me. I've got this long hair and I didn't let him do what he wanted with it. He said he had no patience with me, twisted and pinned up, I was like any Portuguese maid straight out from her village.'

'Ah, yes,' she said, 'that's because he is a real artist. He is temperamental; he likes to show what he can do, and he gets cross with customers. He is the owner's nephew. So there is no stopping him.

'But I don't have him, I always have Angela, I'm used to her; she comes every day to my house and combs out my hair, and I'm sorry for her now, the state she is in.

'She was weeping the other day. Just imagine it – I wouldn't tell you this in the ordinary way but you are always so understanding, so kind.

'Her brother, he is servant in the Vasconcelos house, that is the big house in Monte Estoril with the black roof and the towers, most noticeable. The police have taken him in because of the American murder.'

'Have they?'

'Yes, madame. Before midday they came. He'd served breakfast like any other day; he didn't behave any different, the *senhora* Vasconcelos said so, everybody said so. But they took him away. Last Friday. And he is not the only one.

'There is one who works at the Casino, he is the fiancé of my maid's sister, they took him too; but my maid doesn't care, she is *canaille*, she says they are welcome to him.

'They have been round at Stafford's too, they've made trouble there. Not that they've taken anyone away; it's an English-owned place; the foreigners all stick together, they haven't let on, but I've got to know about it through their two Portuguese boys.'

'Stafford's?' I repeated.

'Do you know Stafford's, madame? I haven't been there,' she said. 'It's only for foreigners. They say it's a nice place,' and she gave another of her scandalized looks to the ceiling and made a rippling movement which started with her shoulders and set the gold on her arms jingling and glittering.

I said, 'But what could they want at Stafford's? I don't really care; I'm only interested because I went there once or twice. When one's been to a place – '

'Who knows,' she said, touching her hair. 'It's all English and American there, and this Monsieur Shesherd – '

'Shepherd,' I corrected.

'Ah, yes, Shepersh. He was an American. When you think someone is living for years outside of his own country as he has done – it may be for his health and for economy, and it may be he has another reason for living abroad; how can you tell? Perhaps he was killed by one of his own people; there is wickedness everywhere, and some of the foreigners are very nasty types, not *sympathique*, like you, madame. You are kind, madame, and because you are kind, you think other people must be kind too. But they are not.'

'Will you excuse me now,' I said. 'I want to go upstairs, I want to change.'

'I'll go soon myself, too,' she said, touching her hair with her fingertips and turning her eyes to the window, fitfully darkened by the flitting shadows of tree branches.

She added, 'It is still so windy, outside. I must put some more lacquer on. Do you spray lacquer on your hair, too, madame?'

'I never use it,' I said. 'My hair is so heavy it stays put on its own.'

On the following day the weather was double-faced once more, with the palm fronds tossing wildly under a serene, intensely blue sky. I went through the dull pain of waiting for the telephone to ring; when it did, the pain changed into heart-stopping excitement.

He was dressed in the same corduroys and tweed jacket as on the first morning, but his shirt was pale blue and so was the Turkish-patterned silk scarf tucked into his open collar, and while I watched him starting to get undressed, I thought that the only thing about him I could be certain of was that his vest and briefs would be pale blue too.

I said, 'That beast of a hall porter is really devoted to you, I must say. I went to the McGregors yesterday in the afternoon and Katie told me she'd rung me up here, in the morning, and the porter had told her I was out. It's wonderful how you've got round him. Up here the phone is out of order, as long as you are here, and down below I'm out.'

'It's nothing to do with me how their hotel is run,' he said. 'But I must admit it's very well run. I should know, because I was born in an hotel and raised in an hotel and there's nothing in the hospitality business I can't turn my hand to.'

I said, 'And the hotel was in Boston.'

He came over to me and put his watch on the bedside table. He unbuttoned his shirt cuffs without looking at me.

'No, my sweet, I'm not from Boston. I am from Baltimore. And now, children's question time is over.'

A few hours later, while reaching over to the bedside table for a towel, he said, 'These *Vogue* numbers you've got here. That's not like you. A woman who hides a new fur in an old tweed doesn't buy *Vogue*. Who gave them to you?'

'I wish you wouldn't notice so much. Sometimes you give me the shivers.'

'You can't complain,' he countered. 'Come back to me now and lie still,' and he drew me to his chest and began to caress me.

I said, 'It's the blonde woman from reception downstairs. She sent them up to me. She's awfully friendly, I don't know why. I'm not really a desirable guest to have, you'd think, what with having had the police round, but she doesn't seem to mind. You do know about it, don't you? Your friend the hall porter.'

'Yes, I did gather something to that effect,' he said. 'They got at you about that fag murder. These fag murders are so deadly dull, always the same; who cares?'

'That's exactly what the young policeman said to me; I mean, he does *care*, he's got to, but he said it's monotonous. He is very elegant and he doesn't pay his tailor's bills. He says he's annoyed with his tailor, but I don't really believe it. I think he pretends to be, so that he needn't pay him.'

'By the sound of it, my sweet, you must have been a great help to the police.'

'It's getting on my nerves. The first time I didn't mind. But yesterday, with the young elegant one on his own – it's cat and mouse, wash me but don't make me wet; one moment he's got the killer and the next he's got to keep an open mind – I'm getting sick of it.'

'There's two things to be said for the police. One, you don't have to pretend you're glad to see them; and two, you needn't rack your brains thinking what you're going to talk about. Correct?'

'The blonde pudding-face from downstairs,' I continued,

'she'd like me to get off with the young policeman. Because he's so presentable. And because he's Portuguese. When it comes to men, she's got a down on foreigners. She doesn't approve of Stafford's either. She's never been there, but it's all English and American, and she's annoyed because the police have pulled in some Portuguese servants because of the Bostonian murder, and they went to Stafford's too, but there they left well alone.'

'I wouldn't know, my sweet. I've left there. I'm at the Montemar now.'

'I'm not surprised,' I said. 'I'd have sacked you too, in Mr Wilkinson's place. Only the other day young McGregor mentioned how impertinent you are.'

'He didn't sack me,' he said. 'We had a meaningful relationship, Mr Wilkinson and I. What a second-rater. But in India's sunny clime, you can't live on gin and lime, you're a better man than I am, Gunga Din.'

I laughed.

'How did you get on to me, at the McGregors'?' he asked.

I turned cold with fear. The scene at the McGregors' office.

I said, 'I defended you.'

'Defended me from what?' he asked. 'And keep still, don't run away from me,' and he held me tight and continued to caress me.

I calmed down under the steady fondling of his heavy hand.

'I told them you were clever. And that you weren't born yesterday. That was because young McGregor said you were as brazen as a bedbug.'

'You still haven't answered me, my sweet,' he said. 'Why did the McGregors discuss me, in the first place?'

'Oh, now I know,' I cried, raising my head and glancing up at him, trying to look sincere. 'It was because of Ginny darling. She'd kicked up a row with you over a gin fizz.'

He kept looking at me in silence.

I said, 'Is that why you split, you and Mr Wilkinson?'

He said, 'You still haven't answered my question.'

'I can't,' I said. 'I can't, I can't.'

He forced my head down against his chest and went on caressing me till I felt as though I were melting under the weight of his heavy hand. When he spoke again, it was in the smiling-sounding voice.

'I can guess it all, my sweet. When you meet the McGregors next time you can tell them from me that they ought to join the police, the criminal detection department. And the police should come and sell their houses for them.'

I said, my voice muffled against his chest, 'I can't understand you. You know it. And yet, you are not angry.'

'No, I'm not angry, my love,' he said. 'They don't pay me for being angry.'

It was shortly after three o'clock and I was dressed and ready to go out. When the telephone rang, I knew it could not be anyone from the McGregors' office because there they kept a prolonged luncheon-break according to Portuguese custom.

'Yes, hallo,' I said.

A woman's voice was speaking, *'Bonjour, madame, vous allez bien?'*

'Thank you, madame, and how are you?' I said.

'And you have good news from your husband, madame?' she went on.

'Thank you,' I said, wondering what would follow, feeling that even if she wanted to tell me that the hotel was on fire, she would not have omitted her formula of politeness.

'There is a visitor for you, madame, the *senhor policieiro.* But he says it is only because you are friends; if you would care to have a coffee with him.'

I told her I'd be down in a minute.

I wondered why it was she herself who had rung me up. The morose, tight-faced porter with his fluent English was not on duty at this hour. It was he who was in league with the barman. Whereas she, obviously, was in league with the elegant young policeman.

The more I thought about it the less I liked it.

The Shepherd murder had happened and I had nothing to do with it. Yet this was the third time that the police had sought me out. Which meant that they had still not solved the case. There was a tug-of-war going on behind the scenes, in which they made use of me, while leaving me in the dark.

As I crossed the brown-and-yellow-lozenged marble floor of the hall I saw the elegant young go-getter rising hastily from a chair in a corner, shaded by a potted palm tree. And although I knew that it was only his protruding teeth that gave his countenance the hopefully expectant air, as though he was yearning to meet me, I was pleased to see him.

When I extended my hand and he kissed it, I was still better pleased because I knew she was watching us. She was leaning over the counter with her bosom resting on her crossed arms. She was dressed in a close-fitting dress I had not seen on her before, of beige silk jersey scattered with a tiny paisley print in brown and scarlet. A brown and scarlet patterned band formed the rim of the elbow-length sleeves. I noticed with admiration how the obvious, the expected touch, which would have been the banding of the neckline, had been omitted.

As I watched her archly scandalized smile, so different from the everlasting indignation affected by the members of the ladies' circle, and her plump, short, voluptuous figure, so different from the straight, upright noodles of the ladies' bodies, I fell to wondering again who she was and what she was doing there.

'I shan't keep you long, madam,' said the young policeman.

'Let's go under the arcades, shall we?' I suggested.

'That would be perfect. Allow me.' And he took the key from my hand and laid it on the hall porter's desk.

He was dressed in the same grey flannel suit as on the last occasion but this time he looked more flamboyant, owing to his shirt of blue printed foulard, with a butterfly bow and a breast handkerchief of the same material.

As I turned at the door, which he was holding open for me,

and waved to her, she was still resting with arms and bosom on the mahogany and smiling at me fondly, as though seeing me off with a suitor of whom she approved.

'She thinks I'm having an affair with you,' I said, as we rounded the corner and walked past the bank toward the Casino gardens.

'I'm sorry to say she doesn't,' he said. 'She is too well informed about the goings-on.' And he gave me a sidelong glance. I wondered whether he knew of the barman's visits or whether his remark had been of a general, harmless nature.

'She reminds me of the women in Veronese's paintings,' I said. 'Particularly of one who's exactly like her, in the *Marriage at Cana*, at the Louvre. She's at a side-wing of the table, but very noticeable because she's leaning forward and is picking her teeth with a fork.

'Veronese got into trouble about her; he was accused and taken to court, for lack of respect, because one doesn't pick one's teeth in the presence of Jesus Christ. Then there were the two dogs in the foreground, on the steps. The magistrate wanted these painted out too, and in their place a repenting Magdalen.

'He defended himself rather cleverly; playing it humble, that he was only concerned about shapes and colours. But he wasn't going to get off. Things were looking pretty grim for him. What saved him was the pressure put on by some of his influential friends.'

He nodded, and said, 'One hand washes the other. There is nothing – absolutely nothing – like having the right connections.'

We were entering the gardens.

'She is always so kind to me,' I said, 'though I'm sure she too wouldn't mind picking her teeth in Jesus' presence. It was she who gave me the invitation card for the show at the British Institute in Lisbon. Not because of the watercolours, of course. She said it would be nice for me to meet the Ambassador and the Duke of Palmella, who would be opening the show, and then that woman, I've forgotten her name, who's related to all the royal houses in Europe, the one who's the greatest patroness of the arts in Portugal. She told me that when I meet her, I must not be surprised. That she really is a woman. And not a lieutenant of the Guards in disguise.'

'Oh, yes,' he said. 'That's Isabella del Radeina.'

'And she's sent me to an excellent hairdresser too,' I continued. 'Who is she, by the way? Is she the owner's widow?'

'Oh, no,' he said. 'She's never been married. She is a woman of fate, as we say. She was the mistress of the man who was the major shareholder of the Casino society; they own some restaurants and other places too. He left this hotel to her. But she doesn't have all the holdings; three-eighths of the property belong to the family, that's the law of this country. The two men you see in reception, the old one and the boy, they are family; they are a thorn in her flesh and they won't be bought out.

'She thinks if she comes to the hotel every day and wiggles her behind in the office, it will stop them cheating her over the accounts.

'And the hall porter – not the one who was on duty just now, but the other one, on the morning shift, the older one – he's her boyfriend.'

'The one who looks like a death's-head? Who speaks such good English?' I asked. 'I loathe him.'

He laughed, and said, 'I don't know if they are still together, in that way, you know what I mean, but I wouldn't be surprised by the looks of him. There's many a good tune played on an old fiddle. This porter was that man's valet; he travelled with him all over the place, New York, London, Paris, and he picked up French and English.

'He comes from the village where the man and his family had their country seat. That's how he was taken on. That's the usual way with servants in this country; we always feel responsible for our villagers. My mother once took seven little girls, all sisters, into our house, when their parents died, and even sent them to school.

'That hall porter now, he's really the *éminence grise* in the hotel; he's her insurance against being swindled and, of course, he's daggers drawn with reception.'

'God,' I said. 'You make me feel – quite uncomfortable.'

I recalled her, 'And you have good news from your husband,' and twisted my lips at the thought that I had taken this remark at face value.

We had by then passed some flower-beds with ragged fire-lilies and tiger-lilies and half-withered grape-hyacinths, and other beds freshly planted with some unfathomable greenery.

The gravel, dried out from the sun and constant wind, crunched under our feet.

I recalled the Monday afternoon when I had walked along the same path, after the first of the barman's visits, in the mild, grey, moisture-filled air, with the ground soggy underfoot, and silent. How I had barely recovered by then from my scare of the encounter with her, and how I had been reassured by her harmless interest in the cream for the face mask.

I said, in order to break our silence, 'For my money, there's nothing like the casino gardens in Monte Carlo. For one thing, they're not itsy-bitsy like these ones here; they're not trying to be clever; they're laid out in two long strips, that's all, with strips of lawn in between.

'And the flowers are in perfect bloom, all the year round. One day it's, say, tulips all over, and the next day it's cyclamens. I found out their trick, by chance. I happened to be passing through the gardens once, at one o'clock at night. A whole army of men were there, on their knees, in utter silence, digging out one lot of plants and putting in new ones. This way you never see anything growing and anything wilting. It would be wrong anywhere else. But it's right for Monte Carlo.'

We had reached the wall of the arcades where I liked to sit, sheltered from the wind.

The mosaic pavement under the vast tropical tree was deserted except for a group of water-skiers, long-limbed blond youths, in rubber suits.

The inside of the coffee house was empty, and of the tables ranged against the wall outside only two were occupied, both by customers whom I knew to be habitués at this time of day: the teacher of mathematics from the nearby Salesian convent school, who was giving a private lesson to a couple of teenage boys; and the revoltingly fat woman with the protruding lower lip and the duck-bill nose, who was always chewing nuts and biscuits and who looked like a medieval drawing of the Sin of Gluttony.

He pulled out a chair for me in his charmingly deferential way. He ordered coffee. We both refused the pastries the waiter wanted to bring.

'Do you take dinner in your hotel?' he asked.

'I usually do,' I replied. 'What with being on my own, it's the easiest way out. They never change the dishes, only the names on the menu. I get a fish striped black and white from the grill, that looks like it's been cut out from a scarf by Dior. And a slice off the roast which makes me always think of Julius Caesar, who was said to be all things to all people – man to woman and woman to man. The meat is always the same, and I haven't made up my mind yet whether it's beef, pork, veal or mutton.'

He said, 'You should try the Montemar for dinner. They've got a new chef now, French trained.

'The old chef killed himself – hanged himself, horizontally, not vertically, if you follow my meaning. Quite a rare achievement.

'We had a bit of peculiar bother over this. It didn't look like suicide; he had laid himself down on the bed, with cords round his neck, fastened round the bedposts, then down to his feet, the ankles tied together, then up to his wrists, then round the posts again. So that, when he was found he looked as though he'd been tied up and strangled.

'His wife works as a cook at a house here in Estoril; they were on bad terms. She's a great big woman; if she slapped my face I'd fly from here to Lisbon. She could have trussed him up and done him in, easily. We only let her go after we'd found out that he'd tried to kill himself once before, by eating a chunk of weed killer.'

I said, 'I've never been to the Montemar. I don't much like the look of it; it's a factory for tourists. I think it's off-putting.'

'Yes, it's a bit of an eyesore, it spoils the whole coastline; but it's a five-star hotel, the finest in the area. I think you should give it a try. Ah, here is the coffee. Are you sure you don't want anything with it?'

I shook my head.

I knew from the way he was crossing and recrossing his legs that he was getting ready to ask the question which was on his mind.

He said, 'Now, I've been wondering. When you had these talks here with Mr Shepherd. Did you leave before he did?'

'No,' I said. 'Each time I remained sitting here on my own, after he'd gone.'

'Then you saw him pay? Did you notice his wallet? We've found three in his flat apart from the one we've found – elsewhere. But there might have been yet another one, that was taken. When he was killed he was in his dressing-gown.'

I said, 'The wallet he had, here, was dark brown shiny leather, worn. And no initials. No metal corners. About as long as your hand. That's not much help, is it?'

'Could you see what was inside? Apart from the bank-notes? Any papers?'

'He had an air ticket,' I said. 'He took it out, after he had paid; he waited for the change, and then he put it in another fold, so as to have more room for the banknotes.'

'Please, go on.'

'He showed it to me too. He was going to Italy, in a

month's time, for six weeks. He was going to fly to Milan – does this really interest you?'

'Do go on,' he said. 'You are doing wonderfully well; you are a policeman's dream. This policeman's dream, in any case. And, besides, one must always get as many details as one can. In my profession one never knows what makes one fat, when eating. So, he was going to Milan? On what flight?'

'He was going with TAP – that's to say, he had booked it through TAP, the flight was Alitalia. I asked him why he'd booked it so far in advance. He said because to Milan there was only one flight a week; with Rome it wouldn't have mattered, there are flights to Rome every day.

'And then, there was some other reason too, but I didn't quite get it. He'd paid for the ticket with a dollar cheque and not with a cheque out of his bank account here. I'm a bit hazy – I'm hopeless with these things. It was something about him not liking to have a great deal of money here, in a Portuguese bank, as a foreigner.'

'Very interesting,' he said. 'Anything else?'

'He told me how he always went to the same hotel in Milan, with roses on the balcony and a view of half the *duomo,* and fairly cheap, but he wouldn't let on about the name of the hotel. You know, the way people do, when they tell you they've got the best dentist in town and when you want to know his name they say, it's no use their giving it because he wouldn't take you on, he is so booked up, and they get a kick out of putting you down.'

'Anything else?'

'Then I got him on to the *Basket of Fruit* by Caravaggio in the Ambrosiana in Milan, and that, of course, was grist to his mill, because Caravaggio was a raving pansy too. He started to tell me how Caravaggio got murdered in Naples. And then he told me a very interesting thing I didn't know, about the other Caravaggio, Polydoro, also a painter, but one hundred years before the famous one. He's a Mannerist. I know his work, but I didn't know he was a pansy too, and that he was murdered too. Now that I come to think of it, it gives me the creeps.'

'Ah, yes,' he said, 'and now I'll tell you something which you don't know, but Mr Shepherd knew, because he spoke excellent Portuguese. You have just been saying "pansy". That's a flower. And the name of this flower, in Portuguese, is *amor perfeito*, perfect love. Strange, isn't it?'

'Most,' I said.

'Now, on which day did he show you the air ticket? On Wednesday or Thursday?'

'Thursday,' I answered.

'You see,' he said, 'we've traced the air ticket. But the trouble is, it wasn't in the wallet we got hold of. It did not turn up where it should have turned up.'

'You mean, it wasn't in the wallet the killer had on him?'

'No.'

'But that grubby man with the beautiful eyes, he is your man, isn't he? You told me yourself he was so daft he'd kept the wallet with everything in it, even that chit of paper with my room number on it.'

He said, putting his hands together as though in prayer, 'Let me put it like this. It's like being married. I am not unhappy but I am not as happy as I would like to be. This air ticket was returned to the TAP desk at the airport and cashed in. By whom?'

'Not by the fellow with the beautiful eyes.'

'Are they beautiful?' he asked.

'Yes, striking,' I said. 'Put in with a smutty finger – which means thick black lashes.'

'I've got blue eyes too,' he said, tilting his face toward me and passing a hand over his hair.

I laughed.

'How do you know it could not have been him?' he enquired.

I said, 'Oh, do stop pulling my leg; it's so obvious, isn't it? You haven't been waiting for me. This fellow, this poor devil, even if he's had four years of primary school, he wouldn't be able to read an air ticket. Let alone know how to cash it in. You don't need me to tell you.'

'Too true,' he said. 'And he's no problem. Never has been. Doesn't try to be clever. My real problem now is – don't laugh – it's girls. Sales girls. Office girls. That kind. I can't stand them – never could. It isn't that I'm against young girls, altogether, mind you, don't get me wrong. Give me a maid-servant any day, who's strangled her new-born baby and flushed it down the lavatory and then says it was the plumber who put it there. Let's have more coffee, shall we?'

I said, 'I'm sure you've got a description of the person who cashed it in.'

'An exact description. He was not Chinese and he did not wear a lilac suit with green stripes; but don't let's talk about it any more. The police in Venice in Veronese's time had it easier, from what you've told me. At least the woman picking her teeth couldn't run away.'

The coffee was brought and we both drank it in silence.

The coffee grinder, which had been buzzing for the last few minutes, had now ceased. There was such a silence that one could hear the faint, dry cracking sound of the acorns torn off by the wind, as they hit the mosaic pavement.

I said to myself, this is a war of nerves. Why is he telling me all this? And I bent over my cup, stirring it with a spoon, though I had not put any sugar in, and it was by now almost empty.

He said, 'You look worried. But don't let it worry you; we take things slowly in this country.

'Some time ago, the army wanted to put up a statue for a general who had died. They wanted him on a horse because an equestrian monument looks better. More dignified. But the cavalry said they had no right to do so, because he was infantry. This quarrel started eleven years ago and it's still not settled.'

'Devastating.'

'Rather. But, talking of the army, there's an even better story. You know Saint Anthony of Padua, do you? He was born in Cascais. He was a lieutenant in the army. They pay him a salary every year, but last year they promoted him to major, so now he gets an even bigger salary.'

We fell silent once more.

He said, 'By the way, how long are you going to stay?'

'You are not going to hold me here, are you?' I asked him.

'Whatever made you think so?' he said, uncrossing his legs and shifting his whole body on the chair, so as to face me. 'I don't think we'll need you at all. But if we do, as a witness, you can always go to the Portuguese Embassy in London – if you happen to be in London just then – and make a statement there.'

'I see. That's to say, I don't see. I mean, I see that I don't see.'

He looked at me, smiling. 'I shouldn't give it another thought, if I were you.'

'When people say that kind of thing, about never giving something another thought, what it amounts to is that one keeps thinking about it all the time.'

He said, 'I'm afraid you are right.'

He pulled out his shirt-cuffs and straightened up in his chair. He had clearly come to the end of what he wanted to say.

Later on in the afternoon, at about six o'clock, when I left the hotel, there was only the youth with the scar-pitted face at the reception desk.

The blonde woman was gone.

I was glad she was gone because I knew that listening to her ambiguous talk, with hints thrown out between hair-dressers and face masks, would have unnerved me even more.

Further, dressed as I was, in a black dress and a white velour coat, banded with black satin – the same outfit I had worn when I had gone to see the Nicky Lassiter show in Lisbon – she would not have been able to resist asking me where I was off to.

I had been deliberating about what to wear and had decided to make myself look, as much as possible, like a member of the ladies' circle; like a woman who finds herself between a tea party and an evening party, and who drops in at the bar of a luxury hotel in order to kill time.

The Montemar Hotel, with its twenty storeys, was the highest building on the stretch of coast between Lisbon and Cascais. Standing near the highway which followed the curve of the bay, it could be seen from a distance of many miles. Unlike the Coimbra, built on a rise and approached through a small magnificently wooded park, the Montemar stood on flat ground, skirted by the road. The cars and coaches parked in front of it looked like fish laid out untidily on the fishmonger's marble slab.

Two red-liveried, white-gloved pageboys, stationed inside the entrance, opened both doors for me simultaneously, needlessly wide, with an air of deferential urgency. I crossed the vast foyer, with its many doors, counters, shops and show-cases, all with illuminated signs above them, past travel booking, theatre tickets, newspapers, dolls in national costumes. I told the lift boy that I wanted the bar. I was certain that there were several bars in the building. Yet, without asking me which one I wanted, he took me to the central glass-walled floor on which the restaurant, the grill-room and the banqueting rooms were situated.

I turned left, as he had directed me to do, and entered a glassed-in gallery.

It was so long that, though walking, I did not feel that I was moving forward. On my right I kept passing and repassing the same low, square, glass-topped table, with the same vase of red and white gladioli on it.

On my left, beyond the never-ending window, was the slate-blue sea, not moving in waves, nor in ripples, but roughened up like a giant grating-iron, and rimmed in scarlet by the setting sun.

After perhaps the tenth flower vase, I reached the bar, which opened out in front of me, a large square room, panelled in blond wood and hung with English sporting prints.

About a dozen people, with name labels fastened to the lapels of their coats, were gathered round a table at the back, near the door.

Another similar, smaller group were sitting near the window, close to the bar. From the little I could hear I guessed they were Americans and they were discussing the rate of exchange of the dollar.

Four young barmen were standing behind the counter in a faraway corner. They were all medium-sized, fresh-faced, handsome, dark-haired, and with carefully tended sideburns. One of them was reading a newspaper, while the other three, standing behind him and looking over his shoulder, followed the line his finger was pointing in the print.

They kept reading and murmuring to each other, without taking any notice of me, as I heaved myself on to a high stool. With their grouping, their half-open lips and their air of solemnity, they were the grown-up descendants of those lute-playing and singing children carved in marble by Donatello, encountered on choir friezes in Florentine churches.

A door opened out of the panelling behind this group of barmen-choristers and another barman came out, conspicuously different in age, dress and countenance.

Making his way toward where I was seated, he gave, on passing, a slap at their newspaper, but without glancing at them, as though unaware of what his hand was doing. Now he stood facing me.

'*Womit kann ich dienen, gnädige Frau, vous désirez, madame,* what can I do for you, madam?' he said, while placing his hands on the counter in front of him and looking at his nails.

'A white port,' I said, 'not too dry.'

'With lemon, natural, chilled, or on the rocks?' he asked in a low, tired-sounding voice, and continued to gaze at his nails. He was neither short nor tall, about sixty, with scant sandy hair, thin-lipped and square-faced, with a deeply pink skin.

Vexed by his refusal to look at me, I said, with an arrogance I could not control, 'On the rocks. That's priceless. What do you take me for?'

He dropped his hands and raised his head.

He looked highly efficient and businesslike, with a hardness hidden beneath an air of false joviality. He could have been the senior partner in a firm of chartered accountants.

'No offence meant, madam,' he apologized. 'I beg your pardon. I wouldn't have known you were English, just by looking at you. But now, hearing you speak, madam, it's just like old times again. Fifteen years in the Savoy, madam. Long time ago, though. When you were still in your pram.'

I said, 'Oh, the Savoy. What bliss. Do you know, I've never, ever, looked at their menu card, in the grill-room? It must be the only place in London where you can order just anything that comes into your mind and there's no need to ask if they've got it.'

'Ah, the grill-room,' he said. 'Do you know the one about the debutante and the maître d'hotel? Here's your port, madam, just as it should be. Now, this really happened, it's not invented.'

'I'm dying to hear it.'

'Now, she was a deb and she was a regular customer. Then she gets married and still regular. Then off – for ages. Then breezes in again, and it's gush gush gush to the maître d'hotel. "Oh, George, have you been wondering about me?" "I was indeed, madam." "Oh, George, didn't you see it in *The Times*? I've been out of circulation because I've been breeding. I've got a little girl, the sweetest little girl you've ever seen. And, George, she looks exactly like my husband." And George says, "That's always nice, madam."'

'Devastating.'

'And do you know the one where the gent settles down at a table in the grill-room and when George comes over, he says, "George, it's good to see you again. The other day I floated in and you weren't here." "I'm sorry I missed you sir." "I was sorry too, George, because the chap in charge was putrid; he didn't know me from Adam, so he gave me a stinking table. I had to raise a row. I jolly well told him who I was and then he gave me a decent pew." So, George says, "And who were you, sir?"'

'Devastating.'

'Do you find the port to your liking, madam? I hope that little misunderstanding at the beginning, you won't hold it against me. It's nothing but Americans, these days, and not the right sort either. Just now we've got the union of dentists from Colorado. Every year the clientèle gets worse. And this year we've already got next year's clientèle. And they are never satisfied. I do the worst for them I can, and they still are not satisfied.'

'Any English?' I asked.

'Not many,' he said. 'They are about, but they mostly do their drinking in private. And when they sail forth and cross this threshold they don't make me happy either. Last time I got three of them here, all out of the top drawer, first they tried to get at one of my boys, then they were so gone, so tight, they even requested me to show them the family jewels; but I got them out nicely, on the quiet. I said I had to do my accounts; it was too near closing time.'

'How very tactful of you, the way you coped with them,' I said, 'and the port is just right, of course. But – that's not what I came for.'

'I thought not, madam.'

'I've come here to see if you could help me,' I said.

'Quite so, madam. Did anyone send you? There's nothing that cannot be arranged. I can put you on to a first-rate man, touch of the tarbrush because he's Goanese but he's got his medical degree in Edinburgh and is established here, and the English all flock to him. A doctor you can't talk to isn't much use, is he? Might just as well go to a vet. I know it's a big worry when your worry is a little one.'

'No, it's nothing like that,' I said, 'thank God, touch wood.'

'I thought not, madam. It's like the young lady who goes to the chemist and says, "Give me a packet of S.T.s, thank God."'

I said, 'What I came actually looking for, is a barman.'

'Quite so, madam. But only one? I always advise ladies to take two, at least. Ladies do not realise that two men do not cost the double of one. I supply one junior as support, a lad who's waiting for his military call-up, and he gets a third of what the other gets, and a kick in the behind, to keep him happy. If you tell me exactly what you have in mind, the number of guests and so on, I'll fix you up to your satisfaction, I'll guarantee. Chairs too, and all the glasses.'

I said, 'It's nothing like that; I haven't got a house here, not yet. I'm only *de passage*; I'm casting round, looking for a place.'

'I thought so, madam, and very nice too. Look at all the exiles we've got around, they know when they are on to a good thing; this place is unique in the whole of Europe. Kings, dowager queens, regents, presidents, archdukes, royal highnesses, cabinet ministers – you name it, we've got it. Even a Princess Auersberg. They're older than the Habsburgs.'

I said, 'Yes, I know. But what I really came for is, I'm looking for a barman. A certain barman.'

In order to cover my embarrassment I opened my bag and took out my cigarette case. It was made of gold, narrow, with a ruby clasp, with room for five cigarettes only, a lady's piece. It was a present from James.

I took out a cigarette and put it to my mouth with trembling fingers. My lips were trembling too.

I bent my head to search for my box of matches.

'Allow me, madam,' and he clicked a lighter open. He had been watching me all the time.

It was only after he had given me a light that I regained my calm.

I said, 'I'd like to speak to him, if possible.'

'Certainly, madam, this is a free country; say the word and

I'll arrange it. But you didn't meet him in this bar, did you? Because I don't recall having seen you before and I never forget a face. We've got three bars in this place: the one here, one downstairs behind the foyer, and one in the night club. Now what's his name?'

'I didn't meet him here at all,' I said. 'I met him at another place, but he told me he had changed over to the Montemar. I don't know his name. But it should be very easy for you to guess who I mean, because he's not Portuguese, he's American.'

He fell into a silence which I did not dare to break.

Then he said, looking into space, 'You've been had, madam. There is no American employed here, that I can promise you. I've been in this place six years, ever since it opened; it's only got Portuguese staff. It's strictly against the rules to employ foreigners.'

'But he was working – he was employed at this other place – as a barman. I know. Because that's how I met him.'

'Have you been back there, madam, to the other place? And was it they who told you he's here?'

'No, I haven't been there. I couldn't. I couldn't afford to ask and to draw attention to myself.'

'Does he speak Portuguese, madam?'

'I've heard him speak it, just two words or so, but, apparently he speaks Brazilian. And he speaks like the best kind of American, almost English English. And he's highly educated. That I do know. Because we've had – long talks together. You can't fake education. It isn't like a mink coat which you can slip on.'

'I'll try and help you, madam. Now, what does he look like? Tall, dark and handsome or short, strong and wiry?'

I laughed, and said, 'Tall, dark and not handsome. Striking looking, though. In a heavy way. Gorilla shoulders.'

'Which bar was he at, madam?' he asked.

'Stafford's,' I replied.

He said, 'Oh, Stafford's; they are quite small; they've only got one barkeeper there, Senhor Ernesto, been with them for two years, twenty-eight years of age, married, three children. Bob's your uncle. No, wait. Bob's not your uncle. Because – Ernesto's been off duty recently. Got ill or went to his village or went to his village because he was ill – they all like being ill in their own homes.'

I said, 'That must be right. Because I happen to know that the barman – the one I mean – was taken on quite a short while ago.'

'And why did he leave? Did he tell you?'

'I suppose he was sacked,' I said, 'though he told me it was nothing like that, and he left on his own.'

'I thought so, madam. Mr Wilkinson probably told him, he couldn't imagine how he'd carry on without him, but he was going to try and find out. Awkward customer, this man; very awkward, I can see that. And, take your cigarette case off the table, madam, while we are on the subject; real jeweller's piece, don't want to leave that lying about. And have a sip at your port, madam, you've hardly touched it.'

I said, 'Why do you say that? About my cigarette case? I can't see – '

He said, with all the joviality gone from his efficient accountant's face, 'You'll forgive me if I speak frankly, madam. If you've lost your heart to him, that's one thing. The heart is a useful piece of machinery; it mends on its own. But, if you've lost something else – jewellery is always a problem. If you keep it in the bank you've nothing to show and if you wear it, it's the very devil.

'And yet, it's more hopeful than money. Because, when it's a question of money, madam, you can write it off. I hope you haven't been helping him with money, madam. Don't want to call the police in on it. Not in a case like this. Heaven forbid.'

I said, 'You are barking up the wrong tree. Really. It's nothing like this. It's just – that I must speak to him – urgently.'

I was not feeling ashamed any more. He had by now run through almost all the colours of which the rainbow of a woman's humiliation is composed. But I was so exasperated I was afraid I might start to weep.

He said, 'You sit tight, madam; don't bestir yourself, don't panic and leave it to me. I'll find him for you. I won't ask your name or where you're staying; I know better than that. I shan't get in touch with you; you get in touch with me. You may decide to change your mind, after all, in the meantime.'

I nodded.

He said, 'I'll give you my card, with the line that gets through to me, and you ring me tonight between ten and midnight. I'll give you my – ' He paused, beating his flat hand against the breast-pocket of his white coat, then repeated the gesture on both sides of his black trousers below his waist, murmuring, 'I could have sworn – ' Then, addressing me in his normal voice, 'Shan't keep you a minute, madam. You finish your port, in the meantime.'

He left me, disappearing through the panel door in the back, from where I had first seen him emerge.

I thought it strange that a man of his sharpness and efficiency should have been mistaken about having his cards on him.

I looked around me, at the customers seated and standing, at the four red-liveried barmen, none of them idle, all on the move. I said to myself, 'He's certainly got them all hand-picked, all the same age, all the same size, all with the same trim. He wouldn't have taken on my barman, even if he'd been Portuguese, even if he'd descended straight from Vasco da Gama.'

He returned. 'Sorry, madam, to have kept you waiting. A little matter cropped up behind the scenes, that needed seeing to. This is my card and I've written it all down for you. That's my extension. When you phone, don't say my full name, just ask for Senhor Alvaro; that's me.'

'What a lovely name,' I said. 'Is it typically Portuguese?'

'Not entirely,' he said. 'It's Spanish too.'

I paid with a hundred escudo note. It was the largest note I had on me. As I laid it on the counter I said, 'That will be all right.'

He feigned not to have understood me and gave me change. The last sight I had of him, as I got down from the high stool, was in a pose of Napoleonic brooding, with one hand hidden behind his waist and the other slid beneath the edge of his white coat.

Downstairs, getting out of the lift and crossing the foyer on my way out, I found my way barred by a young man, who, after falling into step by my side, preceded me, turned round and faced me.

'Excuse me, madam. You've just been upstairs, in the bar?'

I nodded, looking with displeasure at his cheerless smile, which bared the yellowish teeth and the gums above them.

He was dressed in the black coat and dark striped trousers of a reception clerk and, looking at his frizzy hair and blotchy skin, I thought he would never have the chance to be accepted into Alvaro's handsome brigade of side-burns. He was the shy, nervous type whose palms are always clammy with sweat.

He said, 'Will you please come with me. You've left something behind. They've just phoned through to me from upstairs.'

I opened my handbag. I could see my purse and, through my handkerchief, feel the shape of my cigarette case and little silver matchbox.

'Your lighter, I think,' he said.

'I haven't got a lighter.'

'Please, follow me, madam,' he said, ignoring my words.

My heart gave a leap. I had been slow in understanding. This was Alvaro's way of asking me to return, of telling me that he had found out something, that he had news for me.

'Very well,' I said. 'I'll go up. I know the way. You needn't bother.'

Again he ignored my words. He walked me to the lifts and, though I dismissed him with a nod, followed me inside.

While we were riding up he entered into a bantering, teasing debate with the lift boy and, as we got out on a landing I did not recognize, I fancied that, in his animated conversation with the attendant, he had told him the wrong floor.

He led the way down the length of an enclosed passage.

I said, 'This is not the way to the bar.'

'I am not taking you to the bar, madam.'

'What on earth – ?'

'I'm taking you to Dr – ' and he pronounced a name I could not grasp, like brrsh, trrsh, mrrsh, sounding like the imitation of the noise of a rushing train. 'The doctor wants to see you.'

He halted by a door and held it open.

We entered a small hall and he opened another door for me, which was flanked by a couple of inlaid chests, each surmounted by a narrow gilt-framed mirror.

I entered a small drawing-room.

The daylight was shut off by the grey and green striped silk curtains drawn across the window. The room was brightly, festively, lit by a small crystal chandelier.

A tall, slim, white-haired man with gold-rimmed glasses came forward, smiling, from the corner near the window, where he had been standing behind a chair.

He said, 'I am Barros Torres de Mascarenhas. How do you do.'

I looked over my shoulder and saw that we were alone. The door had closed behind me.

'This must be a mistake,' I said.

He remained as he was, bowing slightly, his arms at his side, too well-bred to offer his hand unless I decided to offer mine.

I said, 'I'm supposed to have left my lighter in the bar, but I haven't got a lighter. I've never owned one. I hate them, anyway, people always fiddle about with them and they never work. And I wouldn't have come up here. Only I thought – I thought – it was something to do with the barman who served me. He's called Alvaro.'

He said, 'He telephoned through to me while you were there and asked me to see you. But won't you sit down?' And, smiling all the time, he led me to a small hard-looking settee in the Directoire style, covered in the same striped silk as the curtains.

After I had sat down he brought a chair from the corner where he had been standing, to my side, took my bag out of my hand, and laid it on the chair. Then, without taking his eyes off me, he moved to the fireplace facing me and stood leaning against the grey marble mantelpiece.

The panelled walls, painted pale green, enclosed the room in a heavy silence. There was a faint smell of stale cigarette smoke and scented wax polish.

He stood there, watching me, still smiling.

I felt my heart beating slowly and steadily, but with an insistence on each beat, as though warning me that I was about to face a menace.

He was one of those young-looking men of fifty, whose youthful appearance is not diminished, but enhanced, by their prematurely white hair. He was very pleasing to look at, slim and supple, with a short, oval face, and the frost-white, slightly waved hair growing out of the low forehead in a perfectly centred widow's peak seemed to underscore his air of mild benevolence.

Though I had never seen him before, this man with the difficult name, who was so agreeable to look at and who smiled with such reassuring constancy, was no stranger to me.

He was the man who says, 'But though we deny all negligence and do not hold ourselves responsible in any way, we would, nevertheless, as a proof of our sympathy, ask you to accept – '

He was the man who says, 'With all the authority of my many years' experience, I can assure you this was the best way out – '

He was the man who says, 'Let me assure you, this is by no means unique, it happens in the best of families, mostly only in the best of families; it is the penalty one pays for high breeding – '

He rested his elbow on the mantel behind him and crossed the ankle of his left leg over the other. It was a well-balanced pose of graceful virility.

He said, 'I think I can explain the mistake over the lighter. The clerk, when I asked him to get hold of you, said the first thing that came into his mind – and a lighter is always on one's mind.

'Because here, in this country, people who carry lighters are nervous about them. The State has the monopoly on matches. If you don't use matches, you are robbing the State of revenue. Therefore you must get a permit to carry a lighter and pay a tax renewable every year. Any policeman, anywhere, if he sees you using a lighter, can ask you to show him your permit, and if you can't produce it, you pay a fine.'

'Devastating,' I said. 'But you speak like an O.E.'

'I am not an Old Etonian, though. I used to work in England. For nine years. I was with the Anglo-Portuguese bank.'

'Oh, yes, where was it?'

'It was in Lower Regent Street and it still is in Lower Regent Street, and I used to be there and now I'm here.'

He carried a small table to where I was sitting, brought cigarettes in a box of green malachite, with a matching ashtray, lit my cigarette with a match and then returned to the chimney-piece, where, with a deepening smile, he lit his own cigarette with a lighter.

He said, 'I was told you had a talk with Alvaro from the Savoy. Did he unload his Savoy folklore on you?'

'Rather,' I said, returning his smile for the first time. I was beginning to feel more at ease with this professional soother in this discreetly opulent room of reproduction Directoire furniture, of grey marble, green-striped silk and green malachite.

I felt convinced that nothing very nasty could be in store for me. Otherwise I would have been dealt with in an office, by a man behind a desk – and a very different kind of man too.

I gave a slight start as a door to one side in the panelling near the fireplace was opened.

A bleary-eyed old waiter, in a long apron of the old-fashioned kind, which nearly swept the floor, came in, carrying a tray.

'You will take a glass with me, now that you are here,' said my host.

The waiter silently opened a half-bottle of Cordon Vert and poured out two glasses.

After he had left, my host went over to a side table. I looked on as, still smiling, he squeezed a halved lemon over tiny rounds of bread heaped with caviar, with an easy swiftness which made one convinced that he was performing an everyday task.

He said, 'I asked for champagne because you've had port. I wouldn't have if you'd had whisky.'

'I can see that Alvaro has really spilled the beans,' I said. 'He's gone to town on it. And people say it's only women who gossip.'

He said, leaning once more against the chimney-piece, glass in hand, 'Well I suppose Alvaro is a bit of an old woman. Anyway, I have no jurisdiction over him. I couldn't tell him off, even if I wanted to. I've nothing to do with the running of this hotel, nor with the other hotels in Lisbon and in the Algarve. I'm only the legal adviser to the company that runs it.'

'I see,' I said.

From the way he changed his easy, leaning posture and straightened up, I knew he was getting nearer to what he had wanted to say all along.

'I gather you were searching for a certain person; a young man, an American.' He smiled into his glass.

I kept silent.

'And Alvaro had the impression you were desperate to find him; that it was not just a whim of yours.'

I still did not speak.

'Now, let's get our facts straight. Alvaro is quite certain from what you said – no, from the way you said it – that you are very attached to this – what shall we call him? Bartender. What I'm driving at is this.

'If you were on good terms with him and if you have not come to any harm through him, in any possible way – and this was Alvaro's conviction – and there's nothing you can teach him about young ladies – now, wouldn't you agree this is true?'

'It is,' I said.

'Fine. We've established that you hold no grudge against him. What I'm driving at is this. If you have no reason to complain about this barman's conduct, I see no reason why you should wish to get hold of him.

'He did not tell you his name. So be it. And he lied to you about his place of work. Because he doesn't work here, of course. So be it, again. Obviously, because he did not want you to find him. Have I made myself quite clear?'

'Quite clear,' I said.

'Now, in these circumstances, in your case, would it not be proper and reasonable to leave it at that?'

He brought over the plate.

'Please help yourself and finish these canapés. As you know, caviar isn't like a brioche; it doesn't taste so good the day after, when you dip it into your morning coffee.'

I forced myself to laugh.

I said, 'Of course, what you say is quite true. And I'm sick of playing hide and seek. With him. And with the police. I know I shouldn't have said that, but the champagne's gone to my head and if he gets hung, drawn and quartered he'll only have himself to blame.'

'This sounds most intriguing,' he said. 'Won't you tell me more about it? You can be quite open with me. As you know,

I am a lawyer. I'll think of you as one of my clients. Being a lawyer, as you know, I am bound to silence.'

He came over and sat down beside me on the small, narrow settee, which was so hard that it did not give under the weight of his body.

He eased the napkin out of my clenched fingers and laid his hand on mine.

His warm, dry touch made me realize how cold my own fingers were, and I liked the lemon-verbena scent which came from his hair.

He said, 'I think I can reassure you.' He did not stroke my hand but he deepened his pressure on it. 'But you must promise to be good and not to make any further trouble.'

I sat quite still.

He said, 'We get a Shepherd murder every year, year in year out, and up till now we've managed these murders quite well on our own; we don't need an American to come over and do it for us. You have let your imagination run away with you. You have put together two and two, but the wrong two and two.'

'I haven't got any two and twos to put together.' I said. 'I only have this feeling – and the police tell me things there's no need for me to know – I don't know what they are driving at – today, this afternoon, I've had this policeman round again.'

He said, 'Yes, I know, the police are dragging their feet over this. Because it's not quite straightforward. It's much more complex than what we usually get; it's got a different background. But that need not concern you. I understand perfectly. You wanted to come here and see him and warn him, but surely you must realize that, if they'd wanted to, they'd have laid their hands on him by now. They'd be better at finding him than you are, don't you think?' And he enfolded my hands in his.

I said, 'You are so right. And it was idiotic of me.'

'What more can I do for you? Do you wish to weep on my shoulder? Here is my shoulder. Do you wish to break a plate over my head? Here is my head. And there is still one caviar sandwich, looking at you reproachfully. You aren't going to let it get away, are you?'

'You didn't have any at all,' I said.

'They are all for you.'

He tightened his hand on mine. Then he released it and got up from the settee.

He walked me down the length of the corridor to the lift. I could see he was still smiling as the lift doors closed behind me.

On the following morning, while I waited for the telephone to ring, I looked out at the crenellated roof of the fake Moorish castle, at the wind-tossed palm fronds and at the serene, glowing blue sky, and I thought that if I were staying at the Montemar, with its barren tree-less frontage, I would never be able to tell whether the double-faced weather was still continuing.

He was dressed in the same dull white and stark white as on the day before. At the sight of his calmly brutal, unmoved face I fell to wondering whether my own thoughts were showing.

It was again while reaching to the bedside table for a towel that he said, 'Yet another *Vogue,* I see. You are well in with this woman from downstairs.'

I said, 'I hardly saw her yesterday. It was brought up this morning with the coffee. She's really most awfully kind. I think if I stay long enough she'll become another Bianca. She's already started to tell me what kind of man is worthwhile and who isn't.'

'Meaning me.'

'How could she? She doesn't know anything about you; she has never seen you; you are always gone by the time she gets here. And she's priceless, really. The other day she told me, when she dresses to go out at night, she puts scent between each one of her toes. She babbles like a brook. I don't know what she'd be like in Portuguese. Probably like the Niagara.'

'How do you talk together?' he asked. 'In Chinese?'

I said, 'She hasn't got any English. We speak French. Hers is slap-dash but modern and mine is perfect but not up-to-date. Because I was brought up in the French Lycée in Menton and I know what *flamme* means in the language of Racine, but Racine never wrote about safety-pins and moisturising face masks, and there I'm floored.'

'So with Bianca it's easier?'

'It's not only that, there's no comparison. For one thing, Bianca's always been like a second mother to me; my mother and she went to school together. Bianca was always part of my life. And then, Bianca has a wonderful sense of humour too. She says there are two things in a woman's life which should be large. The second being diamonds.'

'A great educator,' he said. He slid his hand beneath my hair and began to stroke the nape of my neck.

I said, 'And she's got a favourite spoonerism: women should be bitching and earning and not itching and burning. And she tells me I should never go for anything but diamonds; even if emeralds or rubies are higher, I shouldn't listen, she says, because rubies were low before and they'll drop again. And she gets cross with me. Because I don't look out for myself. I wish I had her strength of character.'

He said, caressing me in his heavy-handed, steady, reassuring way, 'Why did you go to that French Lycée?'

'To learn French, of course.'

'But why in Menton?'

'Because Menton's got a superb climate.'

'But you weren't ailing, were you?'

'Of course not.'

'And how old were you when you were sent to Menton?'

'Fourteen.'

'I see,' he said. 'Then, you were fourteen when it happened?'

There was such a silence in the room that I could hear a tap dripping in the bathroom where the door had been left ajar. It was a reluctant, half-hearted drip, as though the water were hesitating and could not make up its mind, each time, before the drop fell.

I wrenched myself out of his grasp and sat up.

'How did you – ? Leave me alone,' I said.

'Come back to me.' He slid his hands down my shoulders and pressed them into the soft inside in the bend of my elbows.

I gasped with pain. 'Stop it, you are hurting me.'

'I am not hurting you,' he said. 'You are hurting yourself. Lie down and keep still.'

He drew me to his chest and forced my face close to his shoulder.

'You were there when it happened?' he asked.

'No, of course not. It didn't happen at home; it was at a party in Chelsea, in Bianca's place. She had a house then, in Cheyne Walk. A small party only. Five people.'

He started to caress me. 'And when the party was over there were only four people left alive. Correct?'

He went on caressing me.

'How long have you known this?' I asked.

'Since yesterday.'

'How did you find out?'

'I didn't find out. It was handed to me on a silver platter. One of those chances. Like the zero turning up on all the tables in the Casino at the same time. I got it from Alvaro. He recognized you. And then Mascarenhas filled me in on it. He's a lawyer. As you know. He's got that kind of recall.'

'You are such a liar,' I said. 'Alvaro and Mascarenhas. You are not working at the Montemar. You are staying at the Montemar, aren't you?'

'I've got to stay somewhere, my sweet.'

'Why didn't you tell me? Why can't you ever be straight with me?'

'I'm always straight with you. Put your little hand there and feel how straight I am.'

'Why must you keep on lying? Alvaro couldn't have recognized me; he'd never seen me before in his life. Can't you even try to make up a better story?'

'He did recognize you, he never forgets a face. Your face was familiar to him, at once, but he couldn't place it. Then you have a trick, when you are on a high stool, of sitting sideways – I've noticed that myself too – and turning your head to the bar. It's very fetching; it emphasizes that lovely long neck of yours and your beautiful bosom. And then, you say "devastating" – no one says that any more; it's society girls' gush of twenty years ago – just as your mother used to say it, when Alvaro was serving her at the Savoy. Correct? Alvaro knew you must be your mother's daughter.'

I said, 'But my mother was much prettier than I am.'

'Alvaro said, yes and no, it was a matter of taste, your mother was much brighter and full of fun – too full of fun. As you know.'

'And Mascarenhas?' I asked.

'Of course, he got it all from the papers. He was in London too, at that time, as you know. It was the kind of scandal which makes everybody happy; there's something in it for everyone: love, jealousy, cocaine, a Harley Street doctor, and the Hon. Roderick Delavere who was sent off to India, teaplanting. Maybe Mr Wilkinson met him there. Shall we go and ask him?'

'Mascarenhas is a double-faced smiling beast.'

'No, my sweet, he was very touched that you wanted to save me from the gallows. He is convinced you got so rattled with the police questioning you because you were harking back to your mama. It isn't everybody's mother who shoots a man dead.'

I did not speak.

'And gets off.'

'That's entirely due to Bianca,' I said. 'She saved my mother's life. That's what nobody knows.'

'How?' he said.

'James always calls her an old tart with the paint chipped

off, but it isn't true; it's only that she had affairs with useful people. She had a family doctor, he was all tied up in knots, and she slept with him too, just once, and he was grateful to her for ever after, and he'd even come at three in the morning when she called him for a migraine.

'So when my mother shot the doctor who'd kept her on cocaine, and she wasn't jealous of him – it was the other way round, she was getting fed up with him and he wouldn't let go of her – after she shot him, Bianca called her own doctor. He wasn't at home, he was at a party, but she got on to him and he came straightaway.

'And he told my mother how it had happened, how the Harley Street had wanted to shoot her and how they had struggled and how it was self-defence. And only then did Bianca call in the police.'

He said, 'Now I get it. And Bianca's played fairy godmother to you ever since. And your mother had to go abroad and you had to go to school abroad because you couldn't have gone to any school in England. Your mother died young, didn't she?'

'Heart attack,' I said.

'Drink and drugs,' he said.

'Anyway, she kept off men. In Menton, she lived with two women friends, one American and one French. They shared a house.'

He said, 'Shall I tell you why? Because when women are on cocaine for a long time they invariably turn lesbian. One doesn't know why. But it's one of the facts of life. Like the birds and the bees. But I think we've discussed the birds and the bees before.'

'I didn't know,' I said.

'No, of course, you didn't.'

I said, 'It isn't fair. You know everything about me. Even things I didn't know. And I know nothing about you. You have all the advantage.'

He said, 'Just keep your hand on my advantage, my sweet.'

Later on that day, in the early afternoon, upon entering the hall bathed in the bluish trance-enducing light, I saw the blonde woman behind the far end of the reception desk, with both elbows planted in front of her, holding up her hands with outspread fingers and giving me a conspiratorial smile.

'I have been waiting for you, madame,' she called.

I went up to her.

'And you are well, madame? And you have good news from your husband?'

After this she crossed her arms and leaned over the desk.

'How do you find me, madame?' she asked. 'I have put this on today specially for you.'

I considered her for a long time, while she kept silent, though keeping her meaningful smile.

She had on a dress of fine clinging cashmere and it was the same and yet not the same one that I had seen on her before.

'I've got it,'I said. 'The other day you were in beige with the pattern in red and brown and the banding on the sleeves. And this is a replica, but it's light blue and the pattern is dark blue and violet.'

'That is so, madame. And in which do you like me better?' she asked.

'I can't say,' I said. 'Both are lovely – each in its own way.'

'I was hoping you'd say this, madame,' she said. 'And now that you've seen it you must learn how it is done. You are on your own; you are waiting for your husband; you have the time.

'You must go to Lisbon and look round the shops. I'll tell you where. Then, when he comes, he'll want to buy you a dress, and you take him there, and there'll be two dresses, or perhaps three, all your style.

'Then he says, "Which would you like?" And you say, "How can I decide? They are both so *chic*. If I get one, I shan't have the other. I cannot make up my mind. I cannot bear it. Please, have them both taken away, I do not wish to see them any more; please, do not make me weep." So, he buys both dresses for you.

'You do not mind me telling you this, madame? You are always so charming, but charming is not enough. One must have a man one can be charming to. And to have a man one is charming to is not enough, madame, if he is not the right kind of man. And he is not the right kind of man if he does not understand that charm must be rewarded. And if he does not understand it, he is either stupid or mean and not worth wasting one's time on. And all time is wasted, madame, when there is nothing to show for it.' She ran her fingers over the row of gold bracelets on her left arm and, so as to make her meaning still more explicit, she reversed the gesture to her right arm.

Our eyes met.

She was, in her way, as virtuous as the ladies of the circle, if virtue means abstinence, self-control and dedication to an aim to be achieved.

She was a moralist who was reprimanding me for my disorderly conduct and who was demanding that I put an end to it. And though she was, in regard to the ladies of the circle, on the other side of the fence, she was telling me the same as they would have told me, even if they would have used different arguments in order to persuade me.

She said, 'The new *Vogue* isn't yet out, madame, but there is the *Jardin des Modes*. I don't know how you feel about it; it isn't so élite as the *Vogue*; it's more down-to-earth and in its way more useful. Would you care for it?'

'I'd be most grateful,' I said.

When I got to the arcades the foliage of the tropical tree stood rigid, as though cut out of metal, against the luminously blue sky, although the wind came in such violent gusts that it drove whirls of sand over the blue and white mosaic pavement.

The revoltingly fat, gluttonous woman was looking at a magazine picturing lace mats, while picking up the biscuit crumbs scattered on her table and chewing them, smacking her protruding lips.

The mathematics teacher had just dismissed a teenage boy and was beckoning to a downcast-looking girl of thirteen who was waiting at an adjoining table, her copy-books squeezed to her side in the crook of her arm.

There were people in the McGregors' office, getting ready to leave, and I waited till they had gone out. They were two couples in their forties, all looking of the same breed, tall and well-nourished and fair and conspicuous by their dress; one man and one woman both in pale pink slacks and pink cashmeres, the other two in pale blue.

As I came in, young McGregor rose from the floor where he had been kneeling in front of a filing cabinet, shook himself and kicked a drawer shut with his foot.

'Did you hear my knees creak?' he asked.

I said, 'It must be terrible getting old.'

'Haven't seen you for some days,' he said, while looking through the glass door at his mother outside, who was making final farewells to the two pastel-coloured couples.

The sty on his eyelid was still in bud, exactly as it had been the last time.

I turned away from him and glanced at the rear of the office, bracing myself to meet the sullen stare of the girl. She was sitting behind the closed typewriter, blonde, thin, sharp-featured, anaemic. She was sucking the medallion attached to a gold chain round her neck.

I said, 'There have been changes in this office since I came here last, I see.'

He said, 'Yes, one hundred per cent,' he raised his chin in the new office girl's direction and shrugged his shoulders.

Katie returned.

'Americans,' she said. 'Come in their own private plane and find every house around here too expensive. Now they'll try the Algarve. In the Algarve they'll have no water, no milk, no meat, no butter. Let them go to the Algarve.'

'But they'll have three golf courses there,' said the son. 'Let them bleeding well go to the Algarve.'

'Let them jolly well go to the Algarve,' corrected Katie, putting the emphasis on 'jolly' and casting a look at the girl at the back of the room, who had now relinquished the amulet and was chewing on a pair of dark sun-glasses.

'We've got a lot to tell you,' said Katie, and, raising her voice, she added, 'about that house in Monte Estoril you are so keen on. Let's talk it over next door, shall we? Have you had a coffee yet?'

I said, 'When it comes to coffee I'm like an inverted camel; I can drink it for eight days non-stop without doing a stroke of work.'

'Then let's be off,' said Katie. 'She can call us if there's anything,' and, tugging down her pullover in a determined manner, she called a few words in Portuguese to the girl.

'Yes, let's bugger off,' said the son.

Katie said, 'Yes, let us trot off, by any means,' giving her son a reproving look and her sweater a violent tug.

The dust storm had ceased and it had turned milder. Katie led the way with her rocking-horse walk to the table nearest to the office.

We ordered *galao*, the white coffee served in tall glasses with long-stemmed spoons.

The Bostonian had explained the odd origin of this name to me. In Portuguese *galao* means 'gallant', a dashing man-about-town who, formerly, used to wear a top-hat; which in its shape the tall glass was supposed to resemble.

I asked, 'What's with the office girl? Why this change?'

The son said, 'We pay this one less because she's learning English, being with us. She's dead keen on English.'

'No use talking in front of her,' said the mother. 'She only understands a wee bit but it's the same as deaf people. They never hear what you want them to hear and what you don't want them to hear, they do.'

'And the other one?' I asked.

'We had to get rid of her,' said young McGregor.

Katie said, 'She wasn't very nice.'

'I could have told you that the first time I saw her,' I said. 'I've always hated her. I don't know why. It's unreasonable; it's like a girl we had in school who fainted when she saw a dead fly. It's idiotic. But telling yourself it's idiotic doesn't help.'

Young McGregor said, 'It'd take more than a dead fly to make *her* faint. She's opened more flies on men's trousers than she's got hairs on her head, and when I say "head" I'm being – '

'That is not a very nice way to talk,' said Katie.

For a while we were silent. They were stirring the sugar in their glasses and I, though I did not take sugar, was stirring my coffee too, as though trying to show my solidarity with them.

'You are entitled to know,' said Katie, 'because it's to do with poor Mr Shepherd.'

'You're going to tell me,' I said, 'that she gave him my room number in the hotel and it was in the wallet the police found on the killer. But why didn't you tell me this yourselves, before? It wasn't so pleasant learning it from the police.'

Katie said, 'We didn't know ourselves, to start with. And by the time we did know, it was too late in any case, and we were downright sorry you got mixed up in it.'

She was stroking her scanty, reddish hair, which was thinning above her bony, domed forehead, and I fell to wondering again why she did not at least comb her hair down so as to conceal this unsightliness.

The son said, 'So she gave him your room number at the hotel. For crying out loud, that's not a heinous crime, is it? That was a *brincadeiro*, as they say here.'

'A playful joke,' said Katie, 'but that wasn't the end of it. Poor Mr Shepherd, when she gave him that slip of paper, he took out his air ticket to tidy his wallet, and he left it on the table, when he walked out.'

I said, 'The air ticket. I saw it. He showed it to me.'

Young McGregor said, 'Being what she is, she didn't run after him. She kept it. She shoved it out of sight, she didn't tell us, or we'd have asked her why he had been in the office. She was going to sit tight and give it back to him the next day while he was having lunch under the arcades, and squeeze him for a little reward, sort of thing.

'But the next day, that was Friday, he didn't turn up; naturally, he was dead by then. And on the Monday she knew for certain that he was dead. So then she got going.'

Katie said, 'There's a tailor here, behind the market; he works for TAP, he makes their uniforms, and he's got a son who's one of her followers.'

'Followers,' said the son, 'there's another word for it. And it begins with an "f" too.'

Katie said, 'He is one of her followers and he works in the Star travel office opposite the post office; you pass it every day, when you walk out of your hotel.

'So she gave it to him because he works in that travel agency and knows his way about, and he knew it could be refunded, because it hadn't been paid through a bank account here but with a dollar cheque. And he went straight with it to the airport, not to the TAP office in town, and they paid out the money, seven thousand escudos. And he, the follower, split it with her.'

'How did the police get on to her?' I asked.

'Through you,' said the son.

'I never said a word about her,' I said.

'You didn't,' said the son, 'but you told the police how Shepherd took out his ticket and put it in another place inside his wallet, and that got them thinking he might have done the same in our office, when she gave him the paper. Simple, once you know, isn't it?'

I said, 'And I thought, this policeman, he so enjoyed listening to me about the two Caravaggios, Michelangelo and Polydoro, and how they both got murdered. He listened like a lamb.'

For a while we were silent.

Then I said, 'Anyway, I don't loathe her one little bit more now than I did before. It makes no difference. If you like a person, they could be criminal, you still like them. It's something you can't help, I mean; I don't know, I'm only imagining it, because with your office girl – even if she'd been a saint – I'd have loathed her.'

Young McGregor gave me a venomous look, made as though to say something, then thought better of it.

I now had come to the conclusion, from the way he had spoken about her, that he had not had an affair with her, after all. I felt sure that he had tried and had been repulsed.

Katie said, 'It's no use going off the deep end over that wench. Let's come back down to earth; after all, it's all finished and done with.'

'Is it? Since when? How?' I asked.

'You've gone quite pale,' said young McGregor. 'Are you disappointed? That the young policeman won't be coming round any more? Quite a lad, wasn't he?'

Katie said, 'Didn't you read it in the papers today? No, of course, you don't read them.'

The son said, 'They got the killer and everything is honkey dorey. They left out that little intermezzo with our girl, praise be.'

I said, 'If it was in the papers today, that means, doesn't it, they caught him – when – yesterday?'

'Oh, no,' said Katie, 'they must have had him for quite some time, dinna fear.'

'Thank God for that,' I said.

The son said, 'It wasn't a favourite who won the race, it was an outsider. We'd all been banking on the ex-valet. And, failing this, the twins at Stafford's; well not really – they're not really that way inclined, but these lads all like to make a bit of money on the side, and they oblige. The Vasconcelos footman, he was in the running too. But no, it had to be a complete unknown.'

I said, 'I could have sworn it was the ex-valet too. From the very little I knew.'

'Good job you didn't have any money on him,' said the son.

Katie said, 'That is not a very nice way to talk,' trying to sound grieved, but even she could not hide the cheerfulness that came from talking of other people's misfortunes.

Young McGregor said, 'He's from Manique, that's one of the villages between here and Sintra; it's one of these hinterland places where all the charwomen come from, and the gardeners. There was a young man from Manique, who wanted to join the right clique – let's do a limerick about it, shall we?'

I tried to hide my lack of interest while they told me what had been in the papers.

In Manique, the police became suspicious of a young man, employed in a manufactory of furniture, who did not show up at his place of work, though he was not ill, and spent money wildly.

On Thursday, about midday, he had been sent to Estoril to deliver an order.

In the afternoon he had been seen hanging about the Palace cinema and had been seen leaving there, with the Bostonian, who had taken him to his house.

In the evening, the Bostonian had gone to a party.

On Friday morning the young man came back and called on the Bostonian. He had thought it over. He demanded more money.

'How did he kill him?' I asked. I recalled the narrow, blue, deep-lashed eyes, the hunched figure, the truculent bite of the teeth behind closed lips.

Katie said, 'He bashed his head in with the andirons from the hearth; isn't it ghastly? It's really Mr Shepherd's fault, he would insist on having an open fireplace in the drawing-room; that's why he took the flat in this old house, when he moved from his former place.

'I told him he'd have trouble there, it needed retiling on part of the roof to start with and once you start with that you never see the end of it. Imagine being killed for the sake of four thousand escudos. That's what he had in his wallet.'

It sounded as though she might have been more lenient if the murder had been committed for the sake of four hundred thousand escudos; as though getting murdered were only for the rich, like oil-fired central heating and a three-car garage.

I asked, 'Will he hang for it?'

'Oh, no,' said Katie. 'There's no death penalty in this country. They are very humane.'

The son said, 'I'll say they are. Do you know this is the only country in Europe, where incest isn't a criminal offence? There's so much about, they'd never cope with it.'

Katie said, 'I don't think he'll get more than four years.'

'If that,' said the son. 'Wicked exploitation of poor but honest native labour by rich parasitic no-good foreigner, you know, that kind of stuff. Besides, they'll love him for that andiron caper. Proves he didn't go there with murder in his heart, no malice aforethought, don't you see; just a piece of brilliant improvisation, on the spur of the moment.'

Katie said, tugging at the string of pearls at her throat, 'We'd better get back now, see what's cooking. There's no telling with these gir-rls, what they're up to.'

Young McGregor winked at me and laughed. But his laughter, too long, and monotonous, did not irritate me any more now.

I wondered how soon it would be before he tried it on with the new girl.

On the following morning the palm trees stood motionless under two skies, one above the other, the lower a velvety white, and weighed down by a bank of blackish grey like tarnished silver, behind which the sun was hidden, spreading a glare that was dazzlingly oppressive.

I kept silent while he began to get undressed. He unbuttoned his shirt and put his watch on the bedside table.

'Today, I see, it's the *Jardin des Modes*. It's getting to be quite a friendship, isn't it, with the woman from downstairs?'

'It is, and she's getting more like Bianca every day. Trying to talk sense into me. I think she's disappointed too, that the Shepherd case is solved and over. She wanted me to get off with the elegant young policeman. You do know that it's over, don't you? Yes, of course you do.'

'Who told you?' he asked. 'Did you read it in the *Jardin des Modes*?'

He sat down on the grey chair and unlaced his shoes.

'The McGregors told me,' I said. 'Yesterday. Everybody is glad, it's solved and over.'

He said, 'Who cares if it's solved. The main thing is he's dead. And for that we must be grateful. Better a dead Shepherd in the hand than two live ones in the bush, as the proverb has it.'

He stretched out a leg and kicked off his shoe with the toes of his other foot.

'Grateful? You are – you must be joking. Do you mean, because he was queer and you don't like queers? You didn't even know him. But I did. He was something special.'

He pulled off his socks.

'I know, my sweet, that to you he was something special, because you are a bit heavy on culture too. And to me, he was special too, but in a different way. I'll say.'

He got up and undid the crocodile belt at his waist.

He looked at me with one of his rare smiles and threw the belt on the chair, saying, 'This Shapiro case was really like a dream. Like a beautiful dream. Better than a dream, because once you wake up it's still true.'

'The what case?'

'Shepherd, Shapiro – Shapiro, Shepherd. It's really wicked of me, he'd turn in his grave if he heard me, but to me he was always Shapiro. That's to say, he was born Shapiro and died Shepherd.'

'Then you did know him?' I said.

'What do you think?'

He slipped out of his trousers, threw them over the arm of the chair and sat down once more.

'Look, count it out on the fingers of your little hand, and even you will understand it. To start with, he was a fag. That's never good. That's always a risk. Then he got into drink. Then he got into debt. It couldn't go on, could it? And then – to crown it all – he has this break-in, a month ago. That was too much. He had to go.'

He pulled off his yellow vest.

'Correct?'

I gazed at the clever, brutal face. The long, heavy lips were slightly opened, which gave him an indulgently expectant air.

I said, 'I don't understand what you are talking about. And the way you talk – '

'How am I to talk, my love? Of course I was going to kill him. Mind you, I was still in two minds before I got here. But this break-in – no. That's where I said no.'

'But you didn't kill him?' I said.

He laid his vest on his knees and smoothed it out.

'No, by a lucky chance. Do you think I'd have messed him up with a fire-iron? And in his own place? And recognizable? And his car in the garage? What do you take me for? I'm a professional.'

I said, 'I still don't understand. What risk? And why do you keep harping on that break-in? There's nothing to it; all those queers get it. Ginny darling knows all about it. She knows exactly who did it. I mean, not that she could put a name to the boy, but she'd know where to find him; it's either gipsies in the Alfama or barrow-boys in the Cais de Sodré, and it's all commonplace and nothing to get het-up about, and if you'd asked her, she'd have told you. Instead of which you rubbed her up the wrong way.'

He said, 'It isn't often that you are right but this time you are wrong. The day I ask Ginny darling to help me with my job, I'll quit.'

He put the vest on the back of the chair and remained

seated, looking at me with that cynically doubting air which brought back to me my first sight of him on my first time at Stafford's.

He said, 'Can't you really guess who did that break-in? No, of course, you can't. It was the police.

'When they do a break-in, they always behave in the same way: they take as little as they can, just enough to make it convincing. Some bottles and some shirts and stuff. When they find money they always keep it. That's a fringe-benefit.

'But they went to town with Shapiro. Do you realize, they not only took all his documentation, all that he'd written and worked on – they took every piece of paper, clean, unused, stacks of it, blocks, sheets, the lot.

'Very sophisticated.'

I said, 'You mean, clean paper because they thought it was written on with invisible ink.'

'No my sweet, to hell with invisible ink. There is a new machine now, it photographs letters which don't exist – that's to say, letters which have been written and posted and are gone. But this camera shows up the grooves on the writing pad on which you've been writing. You tear the letter off the pad and put it in an envelope, and you don't know that your letter's still there, underneath. Correct?'

'You mean he was a spy?'

'Sort of; gathering information, doing what he could, first Tokyo, then Cadiz, then Turin, then finally Estoril, which means Lisbon, and settling down to being a full-time retired queer and going to pieces.'

'And he was an impostor too? He wasn't a Bostonian?'

'He was no more a Bostonian than Mr Wilkinson. He was born in Boston, that's all; first generation, Polish Jews from Lemberg, rich, in the rag trade, good schools, then Harvard.'

'Did you go to Harvard too?'

'No, my sweet, I went to the other place. And once Shapiro gets to Harvard, he sees he'll never be one of them, and is a fag and doesn't want to stick around at home and is ashamed of the rag trade. And thusly, we find Mr Shepherd,

PhD Harvard, teaching English at Tokyo university. Now, have I made myself clear?'

'You are such a liar. What about the umbrella?'

He got up.

'You know about that? Who told you?' he asked.

'The McGregors.'

'That was wicked of me, I'll admit. I just couldn't resist it. I thought it'd make them happy, at Stafford's, give them a bit of a run-around, give Mr Wilkinson a change from talking about Bombay wallahs and Calcutta wallahs. Made the police happy too. They're still chewing on it.'

'Then you went to the flat, after all?'

'What do you think?'

'But how could you? It was guarded, wasn't it? Don't they always put constables there, in such cases?'

He came over to the bed and sat down on the edge.

'So what? I should worry,' he said, and he tore the bedclothes away.

A few hours later he said, 'I see, my sweet, you haven't eaten anything for breakfast this morning. Again. That's been going on for a few days now, hasn't it?'

'Yes,' I said, 'I only had coffee. I couldn't manage anything else; I got all knotted up inside.'

'I know,' he said, 'because every morning when you were waiting for me you thought I might not come because they had pulled me in. Correct?'

'Yes,' I said.

'But it's finished now. You're off the hook.'

'Yes,' I said, 'but I still think you are a beast.'

'That's what they pay me for,' he said. 'But that's not what we are talking about. In the beginning I wasn't a beast to you, was I, at Stafford's?'

'No.'

'I'll tell you about it. But first come back to me. At once. Before I hurt you. You know me by now.'

I had been sitting on my heels, facing him. He was

propped up by one pillow against his head and resting an arm on another pillow by his side.

It had grown darker outside and in the livid light which filled the room the constellation of freckles on his shoulders stood out more sharply than I had ever seen it before.

'If I am a beast it will make it easier for you to see the last of me,' he said.

'But it doesn't.'

'No, of course it doesn't.' And only then did he reach out and make me lie against him with my head on his chest.

I clung to him, weeping, and he deepened the pressure of his arms on me, each time I was shaken by my sobbing.

He only started to caress me when I had calmed down, with that steady reassuring heaviness which made me feel that I could never get away from him.

He said, 'You remember the other day, when you said you couldn't go to Stafford's, you couldn't bear to see me behind the bar. It was the princess and the swineherd you had in mind; that was the fairytale you had started on, with me, and I told you not to slip out of it. But it was already too late.

'Because you got into the wrong fairy tale. You are not the princess any more. You are little Red Riding Hood.

'You have heard of little Red Riding Hood, haven't you? It's a story invented by Bianca and by the woman from reception downstairs and it means that one should never go with a man who hasn't been introduced by friends in the proper way, whom nobody knows about, what he is, where he comes from and what he is up to. Because one gets hurt.'

He put a hand under my chin, forcing me to raise my face to his, and looked at me with a smile; then he released me and pressed my head down on his chest and went on caressing me.

'But Bianca didn't think of the wolf. For the wolf it was the other way round.

'The wolf was in the forest where he belonged, being in that line of business, and he couldn't know little Red Riding Hood would be coming along with that clap-trap story she wanted to pick a bunch of wild flowers, correct? And even, for all he knew, she might be getting in his way.

'So he swallowed her up and she belonged to him and it was his fringe benefit that he'd got her.

'But they couldn't live happily ever after; they weren't the princess and the swineherd.

'The wolf and little Red Riding Hood belong together, but in the wrong way, in the deathly way, and they can never make a couple. And little Red Riding Hood is so innocent and never gets the hang of things and never knows what it's all about, and then she gets so that she can't even eat breakfast any more while the wolf eats his steak every morning.

'You see, my love, you got squeezed between me and the police; they were biding their time, they thought they'd try to get at me through you, just in case. And I sat it out and let them get on with it, blameless as I am, and butter wouldn't melt in my mouth. And now my time is up and I've got to go, and the fairytale is over and it wasn't your fault that it was the wrong one.' He tightened his arms around me and went on caressing me.

On the following day it was windy still, and there was a drizzle which was so fine that the palm trees and the fake Moorish castle above the beach looked as though they were shrouded in vaporous mist.

In the early afternoon, when I entered the hall, I saw the blonde woman at the far end of the reception desk greeting me with her archly scandalized smile.

She had placed one arm on the mahogany with the hand supporting the elbow of the other arm, the hand of which, in turn, supported her chin.

It was the same pose as those of the child-angels floating on small clouds above the head of the Sistine Madonna and, like them, she was fully conscious of being pleasant to behold.

'I have been so hoping to see you, madame,' she called.

'And you are well? And you have good news from your husband?'

I forced myself to smile. I did not speak.

She said, turning to the window and touching her hair with the tips of her fingers with a reverend carefulness, 'I do hate this kind of weather, madame. The wind is bad too, but when you get this kind of rain your hair gets all soft and soggy and as soon as you comb it up it falls down again.'

She crossed her arms on the counter and leaned forward. She said, 'This weather, it does make one sad. It is making you sad, madame, I can see; I've got eyes in my head. And what if it goes on for days? You are out here all alone and waiting for your husband; but maybe the weather is nice where he is, how can you tell? And even if it is not nice, how can you tell? I'm not speaking now only to make conversation; I'll be sincere with you, madame.

'I've had Dr de Mascarenhas just now on the phone; he's come down from Lisbon to the Montemar for a day or two and he asked me how you were.

'Of course, it was like a bolt from the blue hearing that he knew you; but then again, it wasn't, the world is so small. Now, I need not tell you who he is and what he is, and if he asks you out to dinner there is nothing wrong with it; and there's no question he'd take you to a restaurant, he knows better than that. If he asks you to have dinner with him you cannot turn him down, madame; one does not refuse a man like Dr Mascarenhas. He is married, of course. He lives in the same house as his wife – that is to say, the town house in Lisbon and one in the Douro valley and one in the Alentejo, so that's really three – and when he meets his wife on the stairs, as sometimes does happen, he says good day to her.

'He said he'll send the car round for you at nine this evening. There's nothing to it, madame; it is so easy to be a woman and it is so difficult to be a man.

'And if you wish, I'll send Angela up to your room tonight, at half-past eight, and she shall comb your hair, and if you like her she shall come every night when you go out.

'But please, please, madame, do not tip her; let me take care myself over this matter. It isn't that I am heartless but I don't want her to get spoiled.'

I said, 'You are so right, madame. And thank you very much.'

After the Murder in Estoril

THE BLONDE WOMAN FROM RECEPTION, WHOSE name, I now knew, was Maria Teresinha, had said that he would be sending the car round for me at nine o'clock in the evening. I was confident that the car would come on time.

But at a quarter to the hour the telephone in my bedroom broke into the steady snarling sound, low and yet penetrating, which would persist until one had lifted the receiver. 'I am getting sick of that hall porter,' I said to myself. 'Each time, it is, "This is the hall porter speaking. Sorry to disturb you, madam," and whether the message has a sweet, sour, bitter or salty flavour, each time he gives me the same servile courtesy.'

I went to answer it. 'This is the hall porter speaking, madam. Your car is waiting for you.' Bianca, had she been present, would now have said, 'Just shows you how keen he is,' and I, giving her a wide-eyed stare, would have replied, 'You are telling me.' It pleased me to think that she would have approved of the dinner dress I had put on, which was my favourite dinner dress and which she had given me from her cast-offs and had altered for me, ripping out the sedate black net round the neck and replacing it with a wreath of large-petalled daisies fashioned from the same dull, grained black silk of which the dress was made. 'It was never me, in the first place,' she had said, 'but you are perfect in it. You are one of those rare black-haired girls who can wear black. It's that white pallor you've got.'

When I stepped out of the lift I was astonished to see that the porter who came forth from behind his desk to meet me was the short, squat one, who usually took over at midnight and who had that air of permanent amusement and secretiveness, as though listening to jokes he was telling himself.

I thought, 'Just as well they've changed routines; I can stay out all night and no one will be any the wiser,' and then I thought, 'Not that it matters, I seem to have attracted plenty of attention without going out at night at all.'

The porter stopped the pageboy with a gesture, and insisted on seeing me out himself; and he remained watching, as the driver, cap in hand, hastened to open and close the door of the car for me, and then, gaining his seat at a run, put his cap on, and started the motor.

It depressed me to think that this show of eager respect had, in reality, nothing to do with my person, but served as a token of the devotion he pretended to have for his master.

We went out of Estoril on the highway leading to Cascais, with no buildings hiding the view of the sea on our left and no houses worth looking at on our right, after we had passed the small fake-baroque church of the Salesians and their school. I thought of Mascarenhas and his lovely, soothing, reassuring smile, and of how, once back with Bianca, sitting in her gloomy drawing-room in Curzon Street, I would describe him to her, and how I would say, 'He came to meet me with a lovely smile on his face.' Then Bianca would say, in a deep grating voice, and speaking through closed teeth, 'What kind of idiot talk is this? Where else should his smile be?' And then we would lean back in our seats and scream with laughter, because Bianca would have been imitating one of John H.'s favourite sayings, trying to speak in his voice, and it was one of those remarks which, no matter how often repeated, never failed to make us laugh.

John H., the H. standing for the clumsily pompous Heribert, was John H. Vincent. He was married to Bianca's sister Claire, and he was always referred to among us, even by his own family, as John H. Bianca said that this was because he was not lovable; he was a grouch and a spoil-pudding, and one could not feel intimate about him. There was the oft-repeated remark he had made when standing in Chamonix, contemplating Mont Blanc in what was thought to be awed wonder: 'I'm glad we got up to this height; I've had a blob of phlegm in my throat all morning, and now, at last, I've got rid of it.' Another of his sayings was: 'It's a modern art to understand modern art.' His utterance about the literature of fiction was notorious, too: 'I never read any novels. What's the point of reading novels? I can get the same effect by looking at my secretary's bandy-legs. First, they are together, like the lovers in the book; then they are apart; then they come together again.' Moreover he could be relied upon, if not to actually denigrate, to find every performance and performer in the arts, 'highly overvalued'.

There were no stars, only an almost full moon, and its light poured a strip of white, not shiny, but blunt like melted lard, over the faintly rippled water, and this strip kept moving along with us, till I stopped looking, as we were approaching the twenty-storey façade of the Montemar Hotel.

To my surprise we did not stop there but continued past it, and past the row of adjoining low buildings containing shops with luxury goods and luxury services, such as a perfumery, a beauty-parlour and even a cosmetic-service establishment for a doggy clientèle. By the time we had skirted these, left the highway and turned into a vast yard rimmed by outbuildings which I guessed to be garages, laundries and store-rooms, my good mood had left me and I was beginning to feel tense. The car stopped at the farthest side of what was the rear of the hotel and once more the driver displayed the eager tripping, the show of deference, the preceding me to open doors, the falling back to close them behind me. The lift did not take us on a long ride. I followed the driver out into the corridor and to about the tenth door, where he pressed a bell.

The door was answered by a tall, gaunt, elderly maid with the carefully expressionless face of the well-trained servant.

She was not black-frocked and white-aproned but had on a white and blue striped smock, and I imagined she belonged to the room service of the hotel. She had the straight, flat figure which Bianca would have described as 'a six-o'clock girl, straight up and straight down', and I thought how clever it was of Mascarenhas to have picked her to be in attendance, instead of a young, pretty and pleasant-mannered girl. I thought, 'At least he won't make me feel second-best, whatever else might happen,' and as I handed her my handbag and gloves and watched her laying these with slow care on the shiny half-moon of the console table near the door, it occurred to me that she was of the same gaunt, tall, flat-chested build as Bianca's servant. I thought how odd it was, how bewildering, that all women have this sense of rivalry toward each other, and how even Bianca, with all her acclaimed and acknowledged beauty, was not exempt from it and would never have employed a maid who was younger than she was and charming to look at.

I had seen at a glance that the hall I had entered was not that of the apartment where I had met Mascarenhas before; it was wider, and there were, apart from the entrance door, four other doors leading out of it. The maid stepped behind me to receive my coat. I watched her as she went to the console table, picked up my gloves, and, with my coat over her arm, went out by the door furthest from the entrance. I remained standing, gazing at where she had disappeared, wondering what kind of a room it was and hoping she had not locked it from the inside, in case I wanted to get my coat quickly, and leave, fast.

I was startled out of my day-dream by his voice behind me, saying, 'No, you are not going to leave now, you are not going to run away from our dinner. I've been waiting for you long enough.'

I turned on my heels. He was standing on the threshold of a brightly lit room. He wore the evening dress of a man at home, a deep-red velvet jacket over black evening trousers, a get-up similar to that which John H. liked to put on when there were guests for dinner. I wondered whether he too, like John H., had another jacket, of emerald green velvet. He was smiling, not in the heartening, soothing manner I had expected, but with a tight-lipped amusement I did not like.

I felt myself blushing with resentment that he had guessed my thoughts.

I said, 'You are being ridiculous. How long does it take to the Coimbra in the car? It can't be more than ten minutes either way, there and back.'

'For all you know I have been waiting for you for years, as a dream. And as soon as I saw you, I recognized you as my dream come to life.'

'Did you think this up all by yourself, or did someone else help you?'

'You look like the proverbial wounded deer – not that I've ever seen one. You are upset. Why are you upset?'

I clutched my handbag more tightly. It was made from the left-over border of an antique Kashmir shawl, yellow, with raised embroidery, and it had a clasp made of a cabochon-cut cornelian streaked blood-red and rust-red. Bianca had given it to me, a few years ago. I could still see her, kneeling on the landing in front of the armoire, saying, 'No, don't protest, don't be so modest; I prefer giving with warm hands rather than with cold hands. Would you rather it went to Claire, the old cow, after I'm dead?' And I said, 'Oh, Bianca, don't talk like this, I can't bear it. I can't bear it in a selfish way, because, what'd I do without you?'

She had said, 'Odd, you should say that. You know, that time, when I wound up my place in Cheyne Walk and moved in here, chasing and scuttling from Chelsea to Curzon Street and back, like a bloody weaver's shuttle – I once suddenly stopped in my tracks, and from my inmost bosom heaved a sigh, crying "What would I do without me?"' And then, growing solemn, 'You must wear it only with your black dinner dress, do you hear? And no other touch of colour; and no jewellery, either. That will be the height of sophistication. A cow like Claire'd wear a black bag with a black dress.' I said, 'Oh, Bianca, you are marvellous. Who else but you would have thought of it?' And she had said, 'To you, I am, because you are such a grateful audience to perform to.'

I only wore the Kashmir bag in the evening, and then rarely, because I treasured it, and now, feeling the rough rim of the arabesques of raised embroidery, the thought of Bianca made me feel more secure. I said, 'It's – just – bewildering, coming here through the backyard, like arriving at your seat in a theatre via the stage door and through the wings.'

He said, 'Really?' with a smile and an expression that implied, 'Go on, invent some more.'

My resentment returned. I said, 'And you. Just making an appearance, and not even saying, good evening, and how nice of you to have come, and that kind of drivel one expects to hear.'

He said, 'Let's stop fencing, shall we? Or, if we must, let us at least do so sitting down.'

I followed him into the drawing-room and sat down in the corner of the sofa while he moved to the fireplace and stood leaning there, against the grey marble mantelpiece, in that pose of graceful virility I had seen at our last meeting. We were both silent and, now that he was not smiling, I felt I was seeing him for the first time, as though I had not met him before; and, as he gazed into space, above my head, I looked at him. At the well-rounded chin; the long, straight lips; the narrow, deep-set grey-blue eyes; the low, wide forehead, from which the white hair sprang in a great handsome wave; and the glitter struck by the light from the gold-rimmed glasses.

The room was much more spacious, but furnished in the same way as the one where I had met him before, with the grey and green striped silk, the rigid Directoire elegance. The only discordant piece was the large Chesterfield sofa on which I was sitting, though it too was covered with the striped silk, and I imagined it could be transformed into a divan, in emergencies, as is often the case in hotel suites. I wondered how many bedrooms the suite had.

'Comfortable?' he said, returning his glance to me.

'Comfortable, yes, thank you. And, no thank you, I shan't have a drink just now, though you asked me so very kindly.'

'You are right to reprove me for not having offered you a drink. And yet, you wrong me. I did not think you'd want one. In the house of a hanged man one doesn't speak of the rope. Who should be serving that drink? Alvaro, from the Savoy, from the bar upstairs, fondly reminiscing?'

'Stop it.'

He uncrossed his ankles and straightened up. 'Or would you prefer your drink to be served by that young man who used to be behind the bar at Stafford's, who was probably American and probably not a barman and probably a professional killer?'

'Stop it.'

'Though it might be awkward chasing him up. I was led to believe he took a plane to Angola, with TAP; if you wish I could find out the flight number for you.'

'Stop rubbing it in. You are revolting.'

'In one way, I am like Talleyrand: you can say anything you like to me, and I don't take offence. As to what you call rubbing it in, I've only just started. Would you care for me to try and chase him up in Angola? Might be a bit sticky. Typical policeman. A devious criminal on the right side of the fence. Smooth talker, though, I grant you.'

'Let me go now, before I scratch your eyes out.'

'But why? Have I said anything wrong?'

'Call the maid and let me get my coat.'

'If I call the maid, it will be to tell her to help you to undress. Would you like her to?'

And when I did not reply, he went on, 'How did you manage in the Coimbra Hotel? Do they have room service there?'

I turned round in my corner of the sofa, put my face on my crossed arms and burst into tears, shaking with sobs. I felt him beside me, the warm dry touch of his hands, as I remembered it; the fragrance of his hair, like lemon verbena, as I remembered it; and again, as on that previous occasion, on the hard, narrow, grey and green striped settee, he did not stroke my hands but enfolded them in his, and suddenly deepened their pressure. His words were the same too. 'If you want to weep on my shoulder, here is my shoulder,' and he edged behind me and put my head on his chest. Then I felt him ease open my fist and put a handkerchief in my hand.

He said, 'Do you know the difference between men and women? Men always have handkerchiefs but they never weep. With women it's the other way round. And yet, there must be more to it. There must be another difference. Shall we try and find out?'

He put an arm round my waist and the other under my knees and lifted me on to his lap.

I said, 'You are – you are – an unspeakable beast.'

'Everybody tells me so. I know I am vile.'

'You are vile.'

'And you hate me.'

'And I hate you.'

'And you wish you'd never set eyes on me.'

'I wish I'd never set eyes on you.'

'So far so good. Don't let's waste any more time, shall we?'

His fingers were a small, sleek, narrow animal sliding up between my thighs, gliding inside me, unhesitatingly, and fastening there deeply, twisting me in a vicious grip. I gave a shriek which was at once muffled as he pressed my face closer to his chest.

Gasping between my sobs, I said, 'Let me go; let go of me.'

His voice up until now had sounded as though he were amused, smiling indulgently. Now there was another voice, speaking very low and slowly. He said, 'No. I shall not let you go, and you will stop resisting. Keep still and open up more.'

I had never before been spoken to by this voice, but I

recognized it; it was the voice of authority, of the power to enforce obedience, of unquestioning mastery, of unassailable right.

I gave way under the merciless insistence of his fingers deep inside me and slid lower down from his chest and on to the sofa and was entrapped by his body. For a few heartbeats I tried to struggle against the slippery, vicious, clutching fingers until the slow, calm and effortlessly moving ease of his power made me realize that the fight was over. When, as though to prove that he was in full possession now, he clasped both my hands on either side of my hips, as though putting me in fetters, I must have made a violent movement and I heard a dull thud; I was too dazed to realize, until afterwards, that it was one of my evening slippers falling to the floor.

I kept my eyes closed after he had withdrawn from me. Seizing my ankles, he brought my legs together, slowly and carefully, and said, 'How do you feel about dinner? Are you getting desperate?'

I looked up at him. He was standing at the end of the sofa, with his claret-coloured velvet jacket draped over one arm.

I said, 'I'm not. I don't feel like it at all. I think I'd only like coffee now, with cream. In the mornings, I don't take cream; I take milk with my coffee. I don't have much of an appetite these days; I've had too much on my plate, in a manner of speaking.'

'This I can well believe,' he said. 'But about this breakfast coffee. What makes you think I'll keep you with me, all night through? Aren't you being a bit hasty, jumping to conclusions like that?'

'Yes,' I agreed, 'and you have put it in such a charming way, tactful as you are. But two can play at the same game, and, if it be farewell for ever, 'tis for ever, fare thee well. Those aren't my words; they're Lord Byron's, and what's good enough for Byron is good enough for me.'

'I see I get paid back for what I said before, but I shan't quarrel over it. I don't believe in quarrelling. However, I'll give you a piece of advice – for future reference. Do not be afraid of those who quarrel, but beware of those who retreat.'

He reached under my dress, unhooked my suspender belt and drew it off, the stockings trailing after it. I felt naked beneath my dress and I realized he must have taken off my panties, during some part of the struggle, without my knowing it.

He said, 'Now I'll really call her, you'll get undressed and I'll get you into bed, at last. I've hardly started, and if I don't get through with it, I'll have to repeat and I shan't pass my exams.'

'Why must you be so vile?' I said.

'Keep still.'

He left the room, and when he returned he was followed by the maid, who was carrying some towels and who had some billowing white garments draped over the crook of one arm. He gave me one towel and said, 'Step out of your dress and put this on. I want her to tidy up here and put you to bed. Lie down and wait for me; I want to get undressed too.'

The maid, facing me, raised and unfurled a nightgown, while leaving what appeared to be a similar but long-sleeved garment still draped over her elbow.

It was made of lily-white cambric and so fine as to be slightly translucent, and I knew that, once I had put it on, the flesh tints of my body would come floating through. The hem and the square neckline were edged with a double row of drawn-threadwork, of the costly kind, which can only be done by hand, and now I could see that the other piece was a negligée gown to go over it.

I put my feet on the floor and sat up straight while stuffing the towel between my thighs. I said, 'How dare you. I'll see you in hell first before I put this on.'

And when he did not speak, watching me, smiling indulgently, I said, 'And I shan't go to bed with you, either.'

He said, still smiling, 'This is so sudden.'

'Please, don't try to be funny,' I said. 'I'm not going to put on the cast-off nightwear of your other women. I can't help it if you go in for one-night performances but I want to be left out of it.'

'My dearest child, is that it? You are so touchingly innocent. They are called one-night stands – at least that's what they were called in my London days. I promise you there is no other woman.' And, when I kept looking at him in silence, he went on, 'This lingerie, or whatever you call it, was bought today, this very afternoon, in a shop, with honestly earned cash laid down on the counter. I swear it by all the saints and I'll even invent a new saint for you, into the bargain.' And he enfolded my hands in his and deepened his pressure on them, before releasing me.

He said, 'Be good, now. Don't let her hang about,' and left the room.

When he joined me in the bedroom he was wearing what looked like a camel-hair dressing-gown over pale grey pyjamas; however, it was so thin and soft that I knew it could not be the reliably sturdy, robustly warm camel-hair, but the easily-frayed, nobly fragile cashmere. As with his dinner jacket, the dressing-gown too was almost a replica of the one I had seen on John H., except for the scroll of embroidered initials standing out in glossy relief on the breast-pocket.

On that occasion I had come out to Screes for the day and I had been with Claire in the drawing-room, where she was discussing the new curtains with the draper's woman from the nearby town of Crosswell. John H. had excused his state of undress – he was indisposed; not ill, just indisposed – and while there was no sense in overrating the indisposition, there was no sense in underrating it, either. He had only come down to greet me. The draper's woman had remarked solicitously, 'I only hope it's nothing trivial,' and Bianca, when told, had said she would be dining out on this for weeks.

This short meeting had further been enlivened by his remarking that, spread out on the settee, those curtains seemed inoffensive. But that, once they were put up, and exposed to a stronger and harsher light, they would look vomit-coloured. And that was putting it mildly. Claire, turning to me, had said, 'But you like the colour, don't you? You said so,' and John H. said, 'What kind of idiot talk is this. What d'you expect her to say? What's it cost her more to say, yes or no?'

I felt embarrassed. His statement came near the truth and I had, as usual, preferred to agree than to differ. I now said, so as to gain, at least, a crumb of his approval, 'The colour is pleasant, I think, but once they're up they will be a bit on the dull side, what with being so vast.' John H. said, 'Glad to hear you say that, that'll suit me to a T, because I'm dull myself.'

He now laid the gold-rimmed glasses he had been holding in his hand, on the bedside table, took off his gown and threw it on the nearby chair, and began to unbutton his pyjama jacket with what I felt to be such relentless, matter-of-fact, undoubting masterfulness, that it set me trembling.

He said, 'Have you been to the bathroom?'

'I have.'

'It's all yours. I've got another one, on the other side of the hall, adjoining the other bedroom, so although you can't lock the door, you needn't be nervous when you use it. I shan't come in unless you want me to.'

'Yes, I noticed that,' I said. 'It's got no bolt, only a lock but there is no key.'

He said, 'I took the key away. I don't like the idea of you locking yourself in there.'

I saw myself in the bedroom in the Coimbra Hotel, edged against the window-sill, facing the American who had already taken off his shirt and trousers, and was standing by the chair in his yellow briefs and vest, and I heard him say, 'So, what else is there? You could dash into the bathroom and lock yourself in, that is, if you could get past me.'

I put a hand over my eyes, then against my throat, trying to steady my breathing.

He sat down on the edge of the bed, looking at me for a

long time, and I was convinced that, though he could not pierce my thoughts, he had guessed the nature of my distress. I turned my head away as though fearing that he would find in my eyes the mirror-image of my thoughts.

He said, 'My sweet child, now you are afraid again and want to run away. I know I have tortured you. But I had to break you down. You'd never have given way, otherwise. Are you going to be good now, or do we have to have tears again?'

He took my arms and closed them round his neck and then he enfolded my face in his hands and held it up to his.

'I don't want you to speak of him again. Never any more,' I said.

'I promise, I'll never speak of him again.'

'And you'll never be beastly again?'

'I promise I'll never torture you any more. Not till the next time. When I think you need it,' and I saw his smile. I hid my face against his chest.

He said, 'Turn round and lie on your side. I'll take it slow and easy to start with. And don't get on edge. I can go on forever.'

Later on, he said, 'You are a dream; there's something unreal about you, like the statue of a nymph come to life. You make me feel I'll never quite get hold of you. I know I've taken advantage of you; I got you on the rebound, come and weep on my shoulder, the oldest trick in the world, and you are still under stress and feel guilty and ashamed with me because I know too much about you and you'd like to run away from me and hide, and you know I hold you and that you've got to stay.'

Later on, he said, 'My sweet child, I know I've been much too much for you, yet you still try to fight me, even when you belong to me, but it's no use; I'm not a hurdle jumper, I'm a long-distance runner, and you'll submit to me as we go along, with that frail waist which looks as though it'd break under my hands. And that marvellous long, thick hair; I could strangle you with it ten times over.'

He got out of bed, and reached for his dressing-gown.

I said, 'I wish you wouldn't make that kind of horrid joke. And if I were a nymph, you couldn't strangle me; I'd melt away into the trees, or into the water. Depending on what kind of a nymph I was.'

By now he had put on his dressing-gown and was tying the cord round his waist. He said, 'I'm not joking. And I might just as well tell you so that we understand each other. I'll never let you go. I'll keep you with me always. And if there is ever another man I'll kill you.' He bent down and put on his slippers. And, if the Portuguese maid had been eavesdropping, listening behind the door, she could have never guessed from the evenly pleasant tone of his voice the fateful finality and the menace encoded in his words; the contrast between what he said and how he said it made me feel as though a stream of icy water was pouring down my limbs, and set me shivering.

I watched him stop at the dressing-table, bow down his head in front of the looking-glass and touch his hair briefly with a brush, then return to the bedside and seize his watch and the gold-rimmed glasses from the pink marble top of the little table, which was supported by a gilt-wood pedestal carved in the shape of a bunch of foliage and flowers.

He said, 'Do you know what time it is?'

'I got here at nine, didn't I? What with one thing and another, and more of one thing than the other – about eleven, I should say.'

He said, with his delightfully soothing smile, 'Nearly one o'clock. So you see, my sweet child, you had a dinner date with me yesterday and you never got your dinner. You must get up now, and while we're eating I want her to make the bed and put on fresh sheets. And afterwards, we'll go to bed again, and if you are good, I'll allow you to go to sleep.' He put an arm round my shoulders and raised me up in the bed and held me close to him, while reaching with his other arm to the foot of the bed for the negligée, saying, 'But, where is the nightgown to go under it? It is as elusive as you are yourself.' And then, 'It doesn't vex me, though. Of course, I cannot allow myself to be jealous of your past, and now that I have you, I'll make sure that there's no need for jealousy in the future. I'll take good care of that, I promise you.' Again I was seized by fear, and with it a sense of relief and gratitude, as though I had returned to a home from which I had been absent for a long time, perhaps ever since I was grown-up; and maybe this sense of *déjà-vu* was induced by the familiarity of his dressing-gown, and the caned head and foot of the bed in its carved, scrolled baroque frame, which recalled Claire's bedroom at Screes, and his watch on the massive, chunky-linked gold bracelet, which was so exactly like the one belonging to John H. Still flooded by this mixture of fear and gratitude, I linked my arms around his neck.

He said, 'This is the first time you've come to me of your own accord, my sweet child.'

He found the nightgown on the floor, buried under the folds of a blanket, and put on my feet the white satin slippers finished with roses made out of twisted silk, which the maid had brought me after having taken away my dress and underwear in the drawing-room.

When I was dressed I said, 'This *ensemble* is lovely. It's so discreet, so restrained. So frightfully, what a maid would call "ladylike", you know.'

He said, 'You look enchanting in it. But the ritual answer to this is, it's not the nightgown, but what's inside it. Am I right? I must have read it somewhere, of course. I have no experience with women. That's why, when the question arises as to what the difference is between men and women – I am left wondering.'

I said, 'Stop that, please. Your secretary's taste is better than mine. I'd have chosen something with sprigs of rose-buds and forget-me-nots; what Bianca always calls my provincial bad taste. She is always on at me about it.'

'Who is Bianca?' he said. 'Friend or family?'

'Friend,' I said, 'and almost family; she was really my mother's friend, they went to school together. But there's more to it than that. Her mother and my grandmother – that's the vintage which belongs together, really, what with Bianca being my mother's generation – the two old girls were close friends too – even when they weren't old girls, as young married women. There was always a toing and froing between them and us, and what Bianca doesn't know about me isn't worth knowing.'

'Ah, yes. I see. Bianca. Was it she who had the house in Cheyne Walk?' When I did not reply he repeated, 'Ah, yes. I see.'

Then, as though wiping from his face the calculating look, the look of lying-in-wait with which he had been listening, he said, with his heartening, soothing smile, 'You are wrong though, about my secretary. It wasn't bought by my secretary; it was bought by a woman who knows you.'

I said, 'I don't know any women here. Don't tell me it was Katie McGregor, I'd never live that down. Or her dreadful new anaemic office girl; no, she wouldn't even know the meaning of *à jour*-work, what it involves. Then, there's Ginny darling; I only know her by sight, but I do know she'd tear this negligée off me and trample on it if she had the chance. Because it wouldn't fit her. It'd take three of these to make one for her.'

'It was got by Maria Teresinha from your hotel.'

'Oh, the blonde woman from reception downstairs; she is always so kind and helpful – and she tries to give me sound advice – you've no idea.'

He said, 'She may be as truly kind and helpful as she is blonde. Maybe she is genuinely blonde. Believe me, I have no intention of trying to find out. But even if she was not born a blonde she was born with the knowledge on which side her bread was buttered. There are women like that. On the other hand, she can't quote Lord Byron.'

In the drawing-room, the two half-moon-topped tables flanking the fireplace had been put together, joined by the drop-leaves, formerly hidden and now raised, and they now formed a short oval dining table. The low sofa table in front of the Chesterfield had been covered with a clean cloth too, and, with warming tray and stacked china, had been enrolled to do duty as a sideboard.

He said, 'I'm afraid the dinner won't be up to much. You know the saying – it's really one of Alvaro's gems – some people are never pleased; you do your worst for them, and they're still not pleased. That's how the kitchen operates here. I've given them *carte blanche* and I'm fully confident they'll live up to it and do their worst. Not that I can blame them, with the clientèle they keep getting these days. Mostly American charter plane groups and excursions organized for the union of dental surgeons from Colorado. Who have to take what they can find. And what with this being the only hotel on the coast with a swimming pool on top of the roof, which these dentists seem to go for, and a tunnel under the highway leading to a private beach, the kitchen think they can get away with anything. At the Palace they give you an excellent meal, they've stuck there to their old grandeur, but my hands are tied, so to speak. However, I find it convenient here; whenever I want to stay for a day or two, I get a suite at a moment's notice.'

'Please don't apologize, I quite understand.'

'You are priceless; sometimes, like just now, you talk like a grown-up person – almost. Quite the woman of the world.'

'But what I can't understand,' I continued, 'is people living in hotel suites all the year round; it must be deadly. Like Bianca's former husband, for instance; he's been living for years at the Ritz, ever since they broke up, and frightfully austere, not even a place in the country. When you think of how they lived before, in Hampstead, eleven indoor staff and three gardeners, it's such a come down. I suppose he must have been devastatingly cut-up when she left him and got the divorce, and he hasn't got over it since.'

'What does he do apart from being cut-up and living austerely in the Ritz?'

'He is senior partner at Selwyn Reeds, the biggest merchant bankers in the City.'

'Ah, yes. What's his name? Maybe I know of him, from my City days.'

'He's got a most peculiar name,' I said. 'I've never come across it, before or since. It's Brainylow. Bianca always has trouble when she rings up somewhere for the first time, and the butler on the phone can't get it, and when she says it again he still doesn't get it, and he can't ask more than twice because it isn't good form and it can't be done.'

'Ah, yes. Albert Brainylow.'

'Yes, Albert on top of it, isn't it ridiculous? It makes you think of Queen Victoria and if you knew Bianca you'd –. Oh, God. You said Albert. And I didn't say Albert, in the first place, did I? You know him.'

'I don't know him, I know of him. From my City days. And he wasn't with Selwyn Reed then, he was with the brothers.'

'Lazard Frères, you mean?'

'Who else?'

'That, I didn't know.'

'So, he's still about. Interesting. How old would he be now? Sixty something, I daresay.'

'Yes, and devastatingly good-looking still.'

'You've met him, have you?'

'Two or three times, at Bianca's. And Bianca always tells me, senior partner at Selwyn Reeds, as handsome as Apollo, and in bed an utter zero.'

He said, 'Ah, yes,' and again he gave me a look as though lying-in-wait, and it made me feel uneasy. I said, 'But there's something I can't understand; about Bianca, I mean. He didn't want her to leave him; he begged her not to get a divorce. It was rotten for him in his business at the time, and he gave her complete *laisser aller*, with men, you know what I mean, as long as she was decorously quiet about it. So why did she do it? She says, whenever I ask her, she wanted her freedom. But John H. – that's her brother-in-law, married to Claire, Bianca's sister – he says it's the biggest mistake she ever made in her life, getting that divorce. You can't eat freedom and you can't drink it. And he's right. And where has it got her, I ask you? The house in Shepherd Market, on the corner of Curzon Street, is crummy, even if it is Queen Anne, and if you didn't know you were in Curzon Street you'd think you were in a slum.'

He said, 'Ah, yes, my sweet child, tell me more. I could listen to you for ever; and even if I didn't listen, I'd look at you, you look so enchanting in this dressing-gown.'

I said, 'You are so ignorant. It isn't a dressing-gown, it's a negligée *ensemble*, and I've never had one before in my life. If only Bianca could see me now.'

I was about to go on about Bianca and her sense of humour, when the old bleary-eyed waiter entered, with his shuffling, dragging step and his apron almost skirting the floor, carrying a gleaming, silvery tureen.

Speechless, I looked from him to Mascarenhas.

We remained silent while the waiter ladled out the soup and placed the plates in front of us, filled with a green velouté, and then returned with a bowl with croutons, which he scattered round the rim of the plates.

I said, 'As noiseless and perfect as with the champagne,' and picked up a crouton quickly, and then several more, and crunched them before they got soggy. Then I said, 'But really, this is cruelty to animals. It must be now – getting near two o'clock, for all I know, what with my drivelling on about Bianca and John H. You should have made me shut up, because once I get wound up I get wild like a runaway Rolls Royce, and there's no stopping me – and there he's been waiting all this time, ready to serve us. It's cruel.'

'Do you really care?'

'No, of course not.'

'Besides, I daresay with him it's a case of, the lovely bride she looks divine, the bridegroom he is doing fine, I'd rather have his job than mine, when I'm cleaning windows. Do you know it? George Formby? No, of course not, you are too young. You must ask Bianca, she should know. How old is she, by the way?'

'She's exactly twenty years older than I am, and I am

twenty-seven, so that makes her forty-seven; but once or twice when she took me to the Curzon Club across the street to watch her playing bridge, people spoke about me as "your little sister", and she loved that.'

'Ah, yes,' he said.

I did not finish my soup. It was ambiguous; it could have been lettuce or green pea. I was bored with it. All the more so as its velvety smoothness was due to flour and not to cream. But he emptied his plate. The waiter poured white wine and mineral water, each time holding the bottle wrapped in a napkin, and, instead of going through the usual ritual of offering a few drops of the wine, for approval, he went through the task of tasting it himself, in a glass he had set aside on the table.

He then set out the fish knives and forks in an accomplished manner I had never seen before: he brought the cutlery to the table, laid on a platter, and slid each piece on to the cloth on either side of the plate, exactly straight, with a flip of the wrist.

I said, 'Do you know that people like the Queen don't own fish knives?'

'I didn't.'

'That's because fish knives came into being in early Victorian times, and old English families have old family silver and it's a matter of pride with them not to own any fish knives. I didn't always know that, either. So you needn't be depressed.'

'I shan't be depressed, my sweet child.'

Again the waiter did the dishing out on the side table and set before us the fish course. I said, 'I've never seen anything like this before, have you?'

He looked down at his plate and then at me. On the plate was a wreath, composed of three fillets of a steamed white fish, braided into a plait and twisted to form a ring. It was accompanied by a pink sauce.

Mascarenhas speared a morsel on his fork and held it out to the waiter who was standing at his shoulder. After receiving it, and swallowing it, the waiter stepped round and removed our plates, placing the first on the crook of his arm and the second on the flat palm of his hand, careful not to disarrange the braids. During all this time not a word had been spoken.

The red wine was poured and we both began to break the rolls, laid on the cloth in the French fashion, without plates.

He said, 'By the way, this débâcle might have been avoided if I could have ordered lobster. I was led to believe that you do not care for lobster. Is this true?'

He looked at me with a smile, for a long time, till I turned my eyes away. He said, 'I've been wanting to ask you about that.'

I saw myself sitting up in bed in my room in the Coimbra. He was already fully dressed. He was saying, 'Next time I'll bring a lobster and a pot of mayonnaise.' And then, 'I could even make you like lobster. I could get you to the point where you'd beg for lobster.'

We watched in silence as the waiter came round to my side with an oval deep brown earthenware dish on which the mashed potatoes, piped into rosettes, had been baked into a hard and brittle-looking crust, and, with fork and spoon clamped together in one hand, he served us each first with a triangle of the crust, then with a slice of the veal concealed beneath it, then with the gravy, button mushrooms and asparagus tips.

I said, 'Shall we brave it?' We started to eat.

He said, 'Not too bad. Though it's got what I'd call a tired flavour to it; *feuille morte*.'

'What a marvellous way to put it,' I said. 'I must tell John H. He always carries on about the meat but he never gets beyond grey flannel, blotting paper and boiled string.'

He said, 'Still, the asparagus is all right, they couldn't spoil that; they get it from Spain, in tall glass jars, I happen to know. Come here. On my knee.' I did so, and, one by one, he fed me all the asparagus tips on his plate. Then he said,

'Come on, my dearest child, and eat up the meat, so that if we die, we'll die together.'

For a while he watched me eating, then he said, 'That will do now, I'm satisfied. If you wish you may leave the rest,' and he continued to eat while I crumbled the bread and ate small chunks of it and thought how odd it was that when ordering me to eat the meat, he had used the same voice that he had used before penetrating me and against which there was no recourse, and then I thought, why am I afraid of him? What could he do to me, and why can't I disobey?

He said, 'Is the lobster a delicate subject with you? It is with me. When I was a boy, I had a flat of my own in the square tower of our place in the country and I had a man too, to look after me, all to myself. One day I get home from sailing and I bring a lobster, still alive, and I say to him, "Can you arrange it?" We say this in Portuguese; we say, *arranjar* when we mean getting something prepared or cooked. He gives a horrible laugh. He says, "Yes, I can arrange it. And I can arrange you too." I had him sacked, of course. Odd isn't it, so many men-servants are that way inclined.'

I glanced at him briefly.

He laid down his knife and fork and signalled to the waiter to pour out more wine, putting a finger against his glass to show him where to stop. 'To get back to our lobster. It was rather amusing, I must say, the interview that I had with your professional killer. It could go down as famous last words. He did have a sense of humour, I grant you.'

He broke off, so as to hold a discourse with the waiter, during which the waiter let his glance sweep from one corner of the ceiling to the other as though reading off a text inscribed thereon.

Then, turning to me, 'There's a caramel pudding. It's like death, it's always lying in wait for us. What do you say? Or fruit salad. The cheese I wouldn't recommend, from past experience; they bring it up from the basement every morning on a trolley, cheese *in situ*, dust it off, and return it to the basement at night.'

I said, 'The caramel is so undecided; it can never make up its mind whether it's a cream or a pudding, and when you stick your fork into it, it starts to shake and shiver till you feel you must have pity on it, and leave it to itself.'

He said, 'Fruit salad then?' and when I nodded, he asked, 'Liqueurs?'

'No thank you, I'll just finish my red wine.'

'The lobster, as I was saying. While we had our talk – which I couldn't very well refuse as Alvaro had already spilled most of the beans – during this talk, though nothing was said on either side, he knew exactly what it was all about, and he knew where he stood and he knew where I stood. And that he was leaving and that I was going to take over. And that if he didn't go fast, I'd speed him on his way; he travels fastest who travels alone, sort of thing. I don't think there is any need, is there, to dot the 'i's and cross the 't's?'

I did not speak.

'And thus, when he is already at the door, with superb timing he turns round and says, "By the way, just in case. If you should ever, by the very remotest chance, ask the young lady to dinner, don't give her lobster. I just happen to know she doesn't care for it." '

He paused.

I clasped my hands on the cloth and bent my head over them.

He said, 'Very remotest chance, you see. He could not resist taking that swipe at me. I knew there was a hidden meaning to it, it was his Parthian arrow; but I shall not act out his intention and I shall not ask you to explain. An ugly customer. A good loser, though. But I came to bury Caesar not to praise him. Am I right, about the hidden meaning?'

'You are. But it is of no consequence. I mean, the lobster. I mean, we didn't have it. We just talked about it, the way one talks.'

'One day you'll tell me of your own free will. When you have stopped resisting me.'

'Talking about the cheese you can't recommend, and what you said about Talleyrand and how you are like him – do you know the story about Talleyrand and the Brie?'

'My dearest child, I don't know it, and even if I knew it, I'd pretend I didn't so as to make it possible for you to change the subject. Yes, I know, I'm a beast. I, too, couldn't resist getting my own back. Go on, my sweet child.'

'At a dinner party, Talleyrand said that, surely Brie was the king of cheeses. One of the others replied, "And surely it is the only king you've ever been loyal to." I think it's a case of, *se non e vero e ben trovato,* and for all I know it might have been thought up by the Brie cheese makers, themselves. I think all the best anecdotes are done with hindsight.'

The fruit salad was brought in a cut-glass bowl placed in the centre of a boat-shaped silver dish and surrounded by crushed ice. It was ladled out for us by the waiter into cut-glass chalices.

'Devastating,' I said. 'John H. would now say that this salad is an orphan all alone in the big cruel world. Where is the Chantilly cream and where is the vanilla-and-white-wine custard, and the sponge fingers and the meringue shells and the pigs' tail biscuits? You know the ones I mean, that curl round themselves.'

We were both looking into the depths of our chalices without touching our forks and spoons. Instead of being neatly and minutely diced, the apples, pears and bananas had been cut into slovenly slivers of pale moons and half-moons, floating in an amber-coloured syrup which might have been the left-overs of the ever-present caramel pudding.

I said, 'John H.'d say that we've got to imagine the pine-apple, the apricots, the nectarines and the peeled grapes. Spartan isn't the word for it. Next thing he'll tell us not to come home without our shields, but to be brought home, carried on our shields, heroes to the last.'

'My dearest child,' he said, 'I did see some cherries, though. Would you care for them?'

'Yes, I would.'

'Come here to me.' And while he took me on his lap, he made a sign to the waiter to bring the bowl on its bed of crushed ice and he fed me the cherries, as he had done the asparagus tips.

I said, 'You are devastatingly selfless; you let me have all the caviar too, the other day.'

'I got paid for it, though, in *naturalia*,' and he slid a hand under my gown, adding, 'No, no, don't get me wrong; I only want to make sure everything is still there the way I left it.' He kept me thus, on his knees, while the waiter began to clear the table.

I said, 'As far as I am concerned, the best thing about the dinner was the waiter. Talk about accomplished. If only he could speak.'

'How do you mean?'

'Like a fly on the wall. Or a house; if only those walls could speak, sort of thing.'

'I've told you before, I have no experience of women. What I know I got out of a book. I don't want you to get the wrong impression of me.'

I hid my face against his shoulder.

The waiter went out and returned almost at once, followed by the maid, who was now dressed in black wool but still without an apron. She was looking at us with a mixture of reproach and satisfaction, as though saying, 'I told you so.'

I said, 'God, she's still up.'

He said, 'Naturally. She won't go to bed until we do,' and, turning to her, listened to what she was saying, while the waiter was shuffling about as though unaware of our existence.

After the maid had left the room, he straightened his legs and made me slide down from his lap. He said, 'Let's go to bed, shall we?'

Once back in the bedroom, he said, 'Maria do Carmo tells me your dress is spoiled beyond repair. Split and torn, but that could be set right; however the stains won't come out, not from this kind of silk.'

I said, 'It's crêpe de Chine, and Bianca gave it to me. Not new, it was hers; she had it done over for me and she even had a row with the dressmaker till she got it exactly right; Bianca is so self-sacrificing, you've no idea. And that dress, that silk, it's a quality you can't get any more. Bianca'll kill me. I'll never dare tell her the truth. She wouldn't understand. She'd never let a man – like this – the way you – oh, God – . She just wouldn't allow it to happen.'

'My dearest child,' he said, 'we'll throw Bianca into the dustbin, and tomorrow morning I'll send round to the Coimbra and have some clothes fetched, for you to get back decently.'

'Yes,' I said.

'And before you lie down, here are the creams and lotions you use, for night and day, because I'll keep you here with me tomorrow too.'

'Thank you, you are really wonderfully kind and considerate.'

'In between being beastly, is that it?'

'Yes, that's exactly it. Did Maria Teresinha get them too? From looking at what I keep in my bedroom in the hotel?'

'Yes, of course. But she wanted me to tell you, what's here is not quite everything; there was one thing she couldn't get. Your mascara was an English brand she couldn't find; she got something French instead.'

I said, 'I didn't see any of it in the bathroom.'

He said, 'It's hidden in the left-hand cupboard of the dressing-table. I didn't want you to see it earlier or you might have tried to run away. I thought I'd better break you down a bit first, till you were exhausted and more obedient.'

I turned away from his amused gaze and, kneeling in front of the opened cupboard, saw the familiar jars and bottles set out in a row behind a glass bowl which was filled with a harlequin array of rounded puffs of cotton wool in tints of violet, sky-blue, rose, peach and amber. 'And she's given me cotton wool too,' I said. 'Much prettier than what I get myself, frightfully extravagant; such a waste, really, for throw-away stuff. You can see what pains she took. She is really amazingly kind and helpful.'

He said, 'My sweet child, you are so innocent. What you call kindness she spells as calculation and, as I've told you before, she knows on which side her bread is buttered. And when the bread isn't buttered, she keeps turning it over and over, hoping the buttered side may eventually turn up.'

'You mean, she wants to be of service to you – through me – because she wants to keep in with you. Yes, I can quite see that. With you being legal consultant to the hotel chain here, and she being in the hotel business too, you could be frightfully useful to her, isn't that it?'

He said, 'Yes, that could be it,' and he looked at me with an indulgent smile.

I said, 'In *The Prince*, Machiavelli says there are three kinds of intelligence. The first kind understands without being told. The second kind understands after being told. The third kind doesn't understand even after being told. And when you say that I'm innocent – that's being polite, isn't it? What you mean is I belong to the third kind and I'll never understand.'

'How sweet you are.'

'You know, talking about the mascara reminds me of such a devastating story of Bianca's, when she was still married and living in Hampstead. She had an eyelash cream from Paris, probably rubbish but very special rubbish, and she noticed that every day there was less of it than there should have been and that someone else was dipping into it. Now the only really loyal servant she had was her cook. Bianca had been very good to her, sending her to the kitchens of the Ritz to learn how to prepare a dish Bianca had liked when dining there – the maître d'hotel always liked to do Bianca that kind of favour. So, Bianca knew the cook wouldn't play her false and would tell her which of the maids had been helping herself. When she asked her, the cook said, unhesitatingly, "But madam, it's the second footman."'

And, as he did not speak and only looked at me, smiling, I said, 'It's just as you said, footmen and valets; they're all the same the world over.' Then I fell silent, too.

He said, 'My dearest child, don't get distressed again. I know, I can follow your thoughts. Shepherd is dead and buried and we are here and alive, and we have even survived our dinner. Go and do your face.'

I said, 'Thank God, I shan't have to wash it with soap and water; I'd have hated that.'

He said, 'Yes, I know. Women wash their faces and ladies clean them. There is another saying about ladies, you know. A lady is a woman who behaves well in any situation and can help herself in none. And you can tell Bianca that when she chides you for having let me spoil your dress.'

On that first night I spent with him, after dinner, he had said, 'We'll throw Bianca into the dustbin,' and then, a short while later, when telling me about the nature of a lady, he had said, 'And you can tell Bianca that,' and on both these occasions these remarks referred to my black dinner dress with the garland of black daisies and to the sorry fact that it was irretrievably spoilt and could never be worn again.

I did not realize then, the full extent of these remarks. I only grasped the obvious meaning; I took them at their face value, just as Maria do Carmo, the maid, might have done, had she been present, and had she been able to understand English.

If Bianca had been present, she might have been amused. She had a sense of humour which I lacked, and I admired her for it, just as I admired in her all those qualities which I did not myself possess.

Once, while on a holiday in Switzerland, she had sent me a picture-postcard. It showed a late Victorian landscape, meadows fringed by a wood and with a group of cows grazing in the foreground. Beneath, Bianca had written,

'You will recognize me easily. I am the third one from the left.'

It was during this stay in Switzerland that Bianca had had what she called an 'adventure' and she told me about it. Sketchily, though, and with a malicious, conspiratorial smile.

'He was very good looking,' she told me, and this annoyed me straightaway because I should have liked her to describe his good looks. She could, at least, have said that he was the type of, naming an actor or a royal personage, which would not have demanded much effort, but this secretiveness was part of her nature. I found it bewildering, considering how lavishly generous she was with me, with gifts, advice and letting me stay at her house in emergencies, for weeks sometimes, that she was so parsimonious, so outright mean, when it came to disclosing details about the men in her life. To whom, by the way, she referred as 'admirers' and never as 'lovers', smudging thus the nature of the bond and leaving me in the dark as to its extent.

'Only one night,' she said, 'I wanted to go to Thun and he headed the other way. I, myself, had all I wanted. But he didn't. He was too keen on me, too excited. Not young, either; my own age. I suppose that's something to do with it. If you ask me, once a man is forty, he's had it.'

I understood her utterly and I listened sympathetically, as though in full agreement. But I was distressed.

You could have 'all you wanted', as she put it, and yet not have 'all you wanted' because the essential part, being taken possession of, was missing. It occurred to me for the first time that Bianca was really indifferent to men; that she was really only interested in them as dinner partners or as escorts.

As to a woman's situation in married life, she liked to express it in her never-failing humorous way, such as when discoursing on her nine-year span in Hampstead with Albert.

'There was this young widow in Hampstead who went to

see her doctor for a check-up. She says, "I'm a bit rundown, a bit tired, but as you know, I'm a widow and I have no love-life." The doctor says, "That's nothing to worry about. You are in the same boat as all the married women in Hampstead."'

It was on the same occasion, while talking about Switzerland, that she told me a charming story which had taken place in Zurich and where her sense of humour had turned traitor, against herself.

In the Baur-au-Lac she had been sitting in the lobby one morning, waiting for her husband to come down from their room. A couple were sitting near by, about the same age as she and Albert. English, by the sound and look of them; not County, but, she was convinced, connected with the City.

She went up to them, and said, 'I'm waiting for my husband to join me. He's very bad on people and names and where he's met them and why. Why don't you, sir, go up to him when you see him getting out of the lift and say, "Hello, Mr Brainylow, how d'you do, fancy meeting you here, and how's life been treating you," that sort of thing. And he'll be in a fearful dither and squirming all over the place and not know how to get out of it and we two girls here will be sitting tight and looking on and it'll be as good as going to the circus.'

The couple were delighted with Bianca's idea and she moved to their table. When the lift gets down and the doors open, the stranger gets up and says, 'Hello, Albert' and Albert says, 'Hello, George'. They had been to school together.

There was one kind of situation though, in which I did not like Bianca's sense of fun. It was when, at one of her parties, she would introduce me as, 'This is Eve Badham; you know, spelt like rotten bacon', and then would move away, leaving me either pretending to be amused or wondering whether to enter into conversation by tediously explaining that the 'ham' part of the name was not pertaining to Bianca's utterance, but derived from the Anglo-Saxon word meaning dwelling place, house, home.

There were other occasions when Bianca did not choose to be arch and presented me, plainly, as Mrs Badham and then there arose the not merely irritating but plainly embarrassing chance, faint, yet to be reckoned with, of being asked, 'Ah, so you are Mrs Badham. And where is Mr Badham?'

The easiest, the shortest, the wisest, the most truthful reply was to say, 'He is not here.' If I was lucky my questioner might strike the flirtatious attitude of the man-of-the-world and close the subject with a throw-away remark like, 'Jolly good show, knows his place, what?' or he might get heavily insistent, with, 'Where is he then?' The truthful answer to this would have been, 'Search me', because the last concrete information on this topic had been given me some years ago, by my father-in-law, in a solicitor's office, before the divorce had been concluded. 'He's gone to Canada,' he had told me. 'Hopes to get from there into the US. A great mistake, in my opinion, forsaking the substance and chasing the shadow.'

I had always liked my husband's father, finding him not only more likeable but more attractive than his son. He was a grey-haired man. Whereas my husband would, as Bianca put it, 'grow into a grey-haired little boy, and the world is full of them.'

At the end of this interview the solicitor had seen me out with the words, 'Then, Mrs Badham, I take it you do not love your husband, Mr William Stockwell Badham, any more? Not one bit? Not one teeny-weeny itsy-bitsy little bit any more? Splendid, splendid, I just wanted to make sure.'

And when I had told Bianca about this and we had finished screeching with laughter, she said, 'You should have told the lawyer, you never did love him, from the word go, not one teeny-weeny itsy-bitsy little bit. Still, he's served his purpose. I always said the best thing about him was his name, and you can go anywhere now and look anyone straight in the eye; your name is Badham and not Thurlow and let them all go to hell. There's nothing wrong with being a divorcee nowadays, and even if there were, it'd still be better than having the name of Thurlow hanging round your neck.'

There had been only one awkward occasion after this. It had happened when I had applied for the job of a translator in Kew Gardens, at the offices of the botanical institute. It had been Bianca's idea for me to make use of my French and Latin.

I had been received by a short, bald, thickset man. He said, 'Mrs Badham, I've got all your qualifications in front of me. And I see that your status on the form is given as divorced. Is that correct?'

I said, 'It is.'

He said, in a voice lowered as though with repressed fury, 'In that case, I must ask you, who was the guilty party?' and he looked at me, then away from me, then at his desk, with a flush that had not only invaded his face but could be seen to have spread all over his head, owing to his baldness.

I said, 'I was the guilty party in so far as I deserted my husband. There was no adultery, though, if that is what you mean.'

He had grown urbane after this and had walked me to the door, and two days later I received the offer of the position. I declined, saying to Bianca, 'I couldn't have stood it, working with that creature.'

She said, 'You shouldn't have told him there was no adultery in the case. You should have told him, "There was no adultery my husband knew of."'

I received this remark in silence.

Then I said, 'You know, Bianca, about this adultery business. When I had that last meeting with him, before he left the country and he wanted me to go back to him and how there'd never be anyone like me and all that rot, and how he loved me and how he knew he'd made mistakes. And then, he agreed he'd divorce me for desertion. Because it was clean. And now, listen, it's ghastly; he said that if I'd betrayed him with another man, he'd never have divorced me. And do you know why? Because he couldn't have borne to see his good name dragged into the filth. Can you beat it. Respectability at all costs. Beneath contempt.'

Bianca said, 'You are well rid of him; the only pity is, this way you can't squeeze any money out of him. I was luckier when I wanted out; Albert did the gentlemanly thing and let me divorce him, and here I am, look at me, sitting like a pig in clover. And if it isn't clover, it's the next best thing; it's the corner of Curzon Street and Shepherd's Market, so that makes me a sheep, I daresay; and the pastures are very green, they get greener every month, all the year round, if you see what I mean. I was luckier than you were.'

I said, 'Oh, Bianca, it isn't that you were lucky, it is just that you are clever and know your way about and I am a fool.'

She gave me her malicious conspiratorial smile, and said, 'Maybe. What you don't realize is that with a man you've got to find the point where you can put the pressure on – not that you'd necessarily want to put it on, but you've got to keep it up your sleeve.'

'But Bianca, how do you mean?' I asked.

She said, 'Never mind. At least you realize that you are a fool, and I'm glad of it.'

'Oh, Bianca, what on earth – ?'

'Because the next time, you'll let me pick a man for you. I shan't let you down, remember that. I don't want you to make a move without me.'

'Oh, Bianca,' I said, 'you are wonderful. That no one can deny, unless they tell a lie, as the song goes.'

'They don't sing it at Screes, though, do they?'

'What do you expect?' I said. 'Family is always bloody.'

'You're telling me.'

When I had first returned from Menton, after my mother's death there, I had looked up 'screes' in the dictionary.

It meant a mountain slope covered with small stones and

the word was of Norse origin, and when I told this to John H. and Claire, Claire said, 'What a funny girl you are; quite a blue-stocking, aren't you? Your mother'd turn in her grave if she heard you. You'll never get a man that way.'

John H. said, 'Goody, goody and thank you, Eve, that'll come in useful. I'll put it down on my next income tax return, that I'm living destitute on a mountain slope covered with small stones. Come to think of it, those last toasted buns we had for tea the other day – talking of small stones.'

I said, 'You could use it as a conversation piece – like a queer picture or a curio in the drawing-room – something to talk about when you have guests and run out of things to say,' and Claire had said, once more, 'What a funny girl you are. Who wants to be lectured about Norse? A young girl like you, you should be full of fun and the joys of spring; and when it isn't spring, make a young man take you out, to Odenino's or the Bag of Nails, and you'll feel like spring soon enough.'

Screes was not situated on a mountain slope but in flat countryside, as far as the eye could see, and it was not in a county formerly invaded by Norsemen either, but in Suffolk, and thus there was no accounting for the perversity of the name.

John H. had bought the property while I had been abroad, since he had retired from banking, and nowadays when people enquired what he was doing, they were told by Bianca, 'Nothing', and by Claire, 'He is administering his fortune.'

Whenever I was at Screes, John H. only made an appearance at mealtimes. He spent most of his time either walking about in the garden or sitting in the small study at the rear of the second drawing-room. He telephoned his broker in London every day, singing, as Bianca put it, like the dragon in Wagner's *Rheingold,* 'Here I sit, here I lie, let me sleep,' and never moving from his hoard.

I had never seen him perturbed, either pleasantly or distressingly. Whatever fierceness he might have possessed he managed to discharge most days, at dusk, when he took a gun and went into the wood at the far end of the garden, and shot some of the rooks which used to congregate there at nightfall.

He was of medium height, thin, with a square head, small neat features, and crinkly, unevenly greyed dark hair, and he never laughed and hardly ever smiled and he looked reliable and trustworthy.

He was widely believed to be 'sincere' because he was disdainful of politeness and often rude – a widespread, erroneous belief, as though only liars were given to making themselves pleasant.

Claire, who was Bianca's elder sister, was a visual example of the saying, 'when two people do the same thing it isn't the same'. She was barely handsome as compared to Bianca's beauty, and yet she was very like her, feature by feature. The same wide, domed forehead; the Grecian nose coming in a straight line out of it; the small mouth with the full lower lip which, on Bianca, looked provocatively impertinent but on Claire pettish and sullen; and the well-rounded chin, which gave Bianca's countenance a regal firmness whereas in Claire's case it seemed to reveal the obstinacy which was part of her nature.

Claire was also at a disadvantage as to colouring; she was insipidly fair and grey-eyed, whereas Bianca was black-haired and had those thick-lashed green eyes which one of her 'admirers' had described as mountain lakes in the depth of a firwood.

Their two children, Violet, who was ten years younger than I was, and Peter, a few years her junior, I hardly ever met, except in the summer when they were home from school.

The Vincents had also what they called a *pied-à-terre* in London, in Redesdale Road, one of those residential streets known as 'millionaires' row'. It was a spacious four-room flat in a villa and they kept it for spending the night in when going to the theatre or a concert. John H. liked concerts, a predilection that no one knowing him would have expected. They had three cars, the largest of which was a Daimler, which I had never seen, as I had no call ever to enter their garage. When they went to London, they went by train.

As I have said before, John H. was known to be a spoilsport and a denigrator. Even his own possessions and achievements were not exempt from his habit of running everything down. When talking to an acquaintance about living in the country, for example, he would describe Screes as a 'rural cottage', adding, maybe, when tendering an invitation, 'I've got a couple living in and two chars come to give a hand, from the village. Whatever the place is – I'll say – it's clean.'

It had to be admitted that calling Screes a cottage was not entirely fanciful, because in the sixteenth century it had been a row of labourers' cottages, which, at a later date had been hollowed out and joined together. To this shell had been added two unequal wings, in the beginning of our century, with brickwork, stone, and half-timbering that tried to follow the character of the old structure. It was a twelve-bedroom house now, with a reed-thatched roof which was costlier to maintain in repair than the most extravagant tiles might have been, and it still had an air of humble, crouching modesty and looked deceptively smaller than its size when approached from the drive, owing to the fact that both wings were out of sight, when the house was approached from that angle.

And yet, with all his mania for denigration, John H. had once said the kindest, the most consoling words to me.

It had been toward the end of one of Bianca's parties, in the late afternoon, with about twenty people standing about in the drawing-room and drinking the concoction of brandy, champagne, and lump sugar which Bianca liked to serve instead of cocktails.

I was standing in the doorway leading to the landing, watching the first of the guests leave, looking particularly, with wistful admiration, at an unusually tall, thin, glamorously elegant young woman, who, fully conscious that all eyes were on her, allowed herself, langorously, to be helped into her coat by her escort.

Then I heard John H.'s voice. He had suddenly moved to my side. He said, 'Yes, yes, Eve; you are looking at her with longing, wishing you were as tall and lovely as she is, with everybody looking at her, wherever she goes. But, believe me, she's all skin and bones. And when it comes to undressing it's girls like you who win every time.'

I had never told anyone about this; it seemed pointless; but it was comforting for me to know that at least John H. had guessed that, small and frail as I was, I was very smoothly covered, and had no bones showing, no 'salt-cellars' beneath the throat, no 'sticking-out wings' of the shoulder blades and none of those 'knobs' where the arms join the shoulders, which are the enemies of a woman in evening dress.

I used to go to Screes about three times a month, usually alone, and was always praised for coming by Claire, who said that I was the only faithful one, their other friends preferring to come out only in the summer. But then, I was not really a friend, as I was neither the Vincents' equal in riches, nor did I belong to their generation; I was just a left-over of my mother's, and I was accepted as such, irrespective of my own merits. Which meant that I was regarded by them as part of the family, and I, too, felt the same.

The Vincents and Bianca were the only ones with whom I could ever feel entirely at my ease. With them I did not have to explain who I was and from what kind of background I came and who my parents had been and what had happened to them and why they had both died so young, or why I had gone to school in Menton and what my name had been before I became Mrs Badham.

Upon arrival, Claire liked to greet me with, 'Dear Eve, here you are; just think, I've asked you to come and I've no work for you.'

This was an evergreen joke, an allusion to the fact that

Bianca often made me do an odd job for her, of the kind the maid could not be asked to do on top of her regular duties and which was obnoxious and delicate and nerve-racking, such as washing and polishing the chandeliers in her house in Curzon Street. These were composed of a multitude of cut-glass drops, each suspended from a frail brass hook from the crown of the branches and liable to slide from one's soapy fingers and roll all over the floor, and dealing with them forced me, standing on a chair, and working with raised arms, into attitudes that were painful and perilous.

Both Claire and John H. did not like my being so close to Bianca and they never lost an opportunity of talking about her nastily; and even then I had the feeling that they knew more than they were saying. As it was, they liked to recall little incidents from the past.

John H. would say, 'What is it with you and Bianca? Don't you know that Bianca is the most dreadful liar?' and when I said this was not true, he would say, 'That's just it, you always fall for her lies; you swallow everything she tells you.'

Claire said, 'And she's so greedy, you've no idea; always fishing for presents.'

John H. said, 'But Heaven forbid that Bianca should be a gold digger. She isn't. She only wants shares and diamonds.'

Claire said, 'She can't bear the idea that others have got something she hasn't got herself. Take me, for instance. I was always in the background from the word go; she was always the pretty one, the admired one, with ten men on each finger of each hand. Yet, do you know what she wrote in her diary when I got engaged to John H.? "John H., on your knees, in the dust, you shall grovel before me."'

John H. added, 'It never came off, though; not on my knees nor on any other part of my body.'

Claire said, 'And look what she did to Pat Pershwing, the elder brother of Pershwing cars in Coventry. She was so livid when he had had enough of their liaison, she calls him up three weeks later, "Darling, it's happened; what we were always afraid might happen,'' and he says, ''How much do you need?'' and before dinner, that same day, he sends the cash round, by hand. Not that she ever was – not her, you bet. And she thinks she's clever.'

John H. said, 'And what about that Brooks person, he of the Odeon chain? She did go out with him, that's true, one, two, three times, not much more. Then he's found dead by his man, at the breakfast table, with half a grapefruit beside him. He's always had a heart condition, so there was no mystery about it; and then Bianca turns round and says they were engaged to get married and tries to squeeze the family. She did get something out of them, too, keepsake kind of thing; she even asked me should she buy Gussies with it or St Helena mines.'

Claire said, 'And what about that time we all went and had drinks at that new riverside pub near Hornsey? Never mind Gussies or gold mines, that wasn't bad either, was it? We sit down, and when we get up, Bianca's got a yellow streak down one side of her shoulder, on her new tailor-made coat and skirt, from the chair – wet paint, the pub being newly open, as I said. And the manager begs her to send the suit to the cleaners at his cost, and if the paint doesn't come out, he'll pay for a new suit. The suit goes to the cleaners and comes back, perfect; and Bianca takes a yellow pastel stick from Violet's colouring box and draws a yellow streak down the shoulder where the paint was, and shows it to the man in the pub. He gives her the money for a new suit, and then she rubs off the pastel yellow with the greatest of ease, and there's no trace of a mark.'

John H. said, 'And even when it's not blackmail, she wants to get attention; she can't rest till she's got it. What about that time she met that film star at a reception at the American Embassy? She says, he went up to her and said, ''Cutie, where d'you live? I want to shack up with you,'' and she slapped his face. Now, that's an absolute lie and invention; it never happened; I was there too, with Claire, and we'd have heard about it.'

I said, 'Yes, I know that story, but why shouldn't it be true? I never doubted it; it's like me saying John H. hasn't got a Daimler, because I've never seen it. And, why shouldn't it be true, what with Bianca being as beautiful as she is?'

John H. said, 'Eve, you are hopeless when it comes to Bianca and her beauty. You're like one of those people who fall over backwards when they're given a banker's reference. A banker's reference doesn't mean a thing. It only means that the man in question has got money in the bank. But it doesn't mean he'd be willing to part with it.'

According to the Vincents, Bianca was a cheat, a liar, greedy and mercenary, and I could not contradict them. Whereas to me she was generous, helpful, self-sacrificing and loyal, and they, in their turn, could not deny this, either. Their Bianca was not my Bianca, and to John H.'s query, 'What is it with you and Bianca?' I could not give an adequate reply.

Shortly after having come back to London I had been invited to dinner by the Graleys, a couple who had known my mother, and who had heard about me from the Vincents.

At dinner, after we had all helped ourselves, Mrs Graley said to her husband, 'I see you haven't got any potatoes.' He did not reply.

She said, 'Do have some,' and he did not reply. She said, 'Really, why don't you try them, they are specially good today.'

He said, 'Leave me alone.' He then turned to me. 'Eve, let me explain. One, I have been married for thirty years. Two, I don't eat potatoes. And yet this has been going on, day after day, for thirty years.'

Recalling this scene I felt that the rows, muffled like distant thunder, which I always witnessed at Screes, were not as extraordinary as one might have thought but were just one of the available gutters in which the resentment gathered in a marriage of long duration found an easy way of trickling off, thus preventing what might have turned into a disastrous flood.

It always started at table, usually with the meat.

John H. said, 'Next time you go there, you might tell him from me that the silverside he gave us last week was tough. And next time you see him, you might tell him from me that when I went out into the wood yesterday, in the afternoon, there was his wheelbarrow left at the gate. It had been raining all day; his lordship hadn't even bothered so much as to shove it under the trees for shelter. And next time you meet her, you might tell her from me that I'm going to engage another maid, to follow in her footsteps, and put the light out after her, each time she leaves a room.'

John H. never specified whether he was referring to the butcher, the gardener or one of the maids, as though to imply that these persons were so distasteful to him they did not merit being called by name.

Claire never came to the aid of the maid or the gardener, but when it came to the meat, she always got on the defensive. She said, 'The silverside was not tough at all; it was beautifully tender. It was well hung.'

John H. said, 'You're confusing it with the butcher. The butcher'd be beautifully tender when hung,' and he paused, waiting with a benevolent air for me to finish laughing. Then he went on, 'It was not hard; understand me, I never said it was hard; it was soft, I grant you, but it was tough, it was stringy, it was like chewing a bundle of boiled string; you can boil this kind of meat till kingdom come and you'll still be chewing it in heaven above when you come face to face with your maker. Now, will you tell him?'

And, when she did not reply, 'What about that joint of roast beef on Sunday? Did you tell him about it?'

Claire said, 'But it was perfect, you said so yourself – '

He said, 'I said so myself – what kind of idiot way is that of talking? Of course I said so myself; when I speak no one else is doing the speaking for me. What I said was, that what there was of it, was perfect. And how much was that? Two-thirds of the joint were gristle, yes or no? If he thinks he's going to get paid for that kind of performance he's mistaken.

What's the matter with you? Why are you so afraid of him? What does he think he is? Charity? Dishing it out to beggars? And he's not so far out, there, too, because you behave like a beggar; you accept anything he throws at you on bended knees.'

There was a pause. I lowered my eyes so as to avoid Claire's, who was trying to catch my glance.

John H. went on, 'And while we're at it, and Eve here is my witness, next time she sends in the cheese scones for tea you might tell her to go easy with the sawdust. And also, that I'm no good in the way of imagination; fancy's never been my strong point; and when I'm given cheese scones I expect to taste the cheese, which may be stupid of me but that's the way I'm made; I don't want to eat the scones and have to imagine the cheese.'

Later, when he had retired to the study, Claire said to me, 'You see, Eve, how it is; it's always me who has to be the nasty one, the one who tells them off. He doesn't realize I have to do a balancing act, all the time, between ticking them off and their giving notice. When I was young I thought tight-rope walkers belonged in the circus.'

I said, 'Claire, he does know; he isn't stupid even if he's stupid enough to want cheese in his cheese scones.'

She said, 'Oh, Eve, you always take his part. And he knows it; when you are here he plays to the gallery because he knows you laugh at his jokes; and it's all very well for you, you aren't married to him; you ought to try it.'

I did like his jokes, that was true. He had, for instance, while talking about amateur dramatic societies whose efforts were always 'overrated', remarked, 'I once took part in such a performance. The play was called "The secret behind the hearth". I played the behind,' and I had laughed so long that Claire had got quite cross with me and John H. had said, 'That's one of the many things I like about Eve; she's such a grateful public.'

I always left Screes wistfully. I should have liked to take Claire at her word and been married to John H. myself. It had nothing to do with knowing that he found me attractive. I did not find him so. But he did give me a wonderful feeling of security, of being firmly in a safe place, of knowing who I was, of never having to worry about my future, of always being taken care of; and those discussions about the tenderness or toughness of the meat were not tedious to me but reassuring.

While I thus found John H.'s critical attitudes soothing and even reassuring, I found James's critical attitudes increasingly trying and hard to bear, with his nagging and fault-finding and carping, sometimes whining and sometimes choleric.

There is an erroneous belief that one can get used to anything, given time. The opposite is in fact the case. Take, for instance, the tropical climate. The first two years you usually take it in your stride and do not feel affected by it; but the longer you stay the less you can bear it, as your strength and resistance gradually weaken.

It was the day following the cheese scones debate at Screes. I was sitting with Bianca in her long, dank, gloomy drawing-room, filled with a permanent twilight of its own, owing to the fact that the length of the room giving on to Curzon Street was solid wall, whereas the two tall windows looked out at the narrow alleyway under the arch leading into Shepherd Market and were never gladdened by sunlight. The room was sparsely furnished with a short desk, a love-seat, a folding card table and a few chairs, all in walnut reproduction Queen Anne, though Bianca liked to believe that the card table, with its four wells in the corners for the placing of candle sticks, was genuine.

The only striking feature of the room, vastly grand and overpoweringly splendid, was a wall hanging which covered the entire wall facing the door as you came in from the landing. It was embroidered in a variety of stitches, with raised thread-work and appliqué on a ground of greenish-blue satin of melancholy hue. Two figures were depicted: a heroic-sized, doubled-over giant stood in the foreground, and there was a smaller enthroned madonna to one side. There had never yet been a newcomer to Bianca's house who had not, almost upon entering the room, enquired about the hanging.

'It's seventeenth century,' she would reply on these occasions. 'That's about the only thing that's for certain. It's something of a mystery. It's either Spanish or Portuguese, and the man is Atlas, bearing the weight of the world; the madonna doesn't really belong with it. The Greek Atlas and the Christian Virgin, they go together like chalk and cheese. It must have been patched up and put together at one time in the past, but there's no rhyme or reason to it, and your guess is as good as mine.'

And, if the guest were familiar with her past, Bianca might add that she had never been in love with the hanging, it was Albert who had doted on it; she had only taken it because the Ritz, accommodating though it was, had no suite with a wall big enough to hang the piece.

It was strange for me to realize, only a few weeks later, that it was this wall hanging which was to determine my fate; Bianca's not being in love with the wall hanging gave this an added irony.

She was now seated on a chair she had turned away from the desk, facing me across the room. She had on a *mille-fleurs* silk robe with long trailing sleeves, one of her peignoirs which she used to put on before sitting down at her dressing-table. She had a dinner engagement for that night.

I sat huddled on the love-seat, crouched on my heels. I had thrown my shoes on the floor.

She said, contemplating me with that malicious conspiratorial smile which always delighted me so much, 'So, he was bitching and belly-aching about the cheese scones, was he?'

I answered, 'No, Bianca, before you get on your high horse, he was right. What their cook turns out, it's never actually wrong, but it's deadly dull stodge.'

'You've said it,' said Bianca, adding with a deepening smile, 'you've said it without knowing it; nothing wrong with them but deadly dull stodge; that's what they both are, Claire and John H.'

I said, 'Yes, I grant you; but you must be fair, and when he does carp, he's always right.'

For a while we continued silent.

Then she said, 'Right or wrong, I think he does it to take it out on her because of Violet.' And when I gave her a questioning look, 'Don't you know? Don't you get it? I thought you knew. I thought you've always known.'

I asked, 'What's wrong with Violet?'

'Nothing wrong with her,' she said. 'She's just an eighteen-year-old piece of deadly dull stodge too. And she's not his.'

I half rose from the love-seat and then sank down again, hugging my knees.

'Have you looked at her?' said Bianca.

'Of course I have,' I replied, 'but she looks so like Claire there's no room left for her to look like John H., if you know what I mean. But now that I come to think of it, Peter does look like John H., down to the crinkly hair; he's his son, all right.' Then I said, 'Whose is Violet?'

'Usual thing; no one you knew; John H.'s best friend; in banking too. It's always the best friend, never the second-best friend, is it? Unless it's the chauffeur. Always rising to heights or sinking to depths.'

'So that's why John H. is always so nasty to Violet.'

For a while we were silent. Then I said, 'But you know, Bianca, that's not quite true. I mean, he's not nice to Violet, but then he isn't nice to Peter either, from what I've seen – not that I've seen much. It's fair shares for all.'

'Exactly. It's fair shares for all; he just doesn't believe in making himself pleasant.'

'But in that case,' I said, 'if he's bloody-minded all round, there's really no telling, is there, whether he does know? About Violet. Does he know?'

'It's not the sort of thing you can ask, least of all your own sister. I should think – officially he doesn't know, she's probably done her damnedest to pull the wool over his eyes; but that really he does know, perfectly well. There are things one does know, even when one doesn't know them.'

'I'm sure you are right, Bianca,' I said, 'and that being so, it makes him feel good; I mean he doesn't have to feel guilty about being as unpleasant as the day is long. And you can't blame him, can you? Besides, when you are as rich as he is, you can afford to be a pain in the neck. If I were as rich, I'd be bloodier still.'

'No, you wouldn't, Eve,' said Bianca. 'What it boils down to is that he is a man. Take James, for instance. Isn't he a joy for ever?'

I said, 'That's not fair, because James is so frightfully rich too; and in his case it's much worse, and I'll tell you why. When John H. does carry on he is right and justified every time, but James isn't. When there's nothing to complain about, he invents something, and that's because John H. has always worked and it's made him reasonable and self-controlled, whereas James has never done a stroke of work in his life, he never had to consider anyone, and people as good as say to him, here I am, please treat me as your doormat and wipe your feet on me.'

She said, 'You've got a point there. That was wrong of me. Let's be fair then, if that is what you crave. Take your own William Stockwell Badham, shall we? He was poor all right, not even public school. Airforce engineer trained by the Force, and disciplined to his eyebrows. And was he any less bloody-minded, in his own way?'

I stretched out my legs and sat upright.

'Take any one of them,' she went on. 'You only have to look around you. Men are just ghastly. And they don't need an extreme case, like Violet, as an excuse to be ghastly, do they?'

'I'll buy it,' I said.

Then she said, 'Men can't be altered but skirts can. Your skirt is dipping at the hem, on the left-hand side, did you know?'

'I plead not guilty.'

'I noticed it straightaway as soon as you came through the door.'

I said, 'You are a marvel, Bianca. I've never known anyone with an eye like yours.'

She said, 'This morning I went to Liberty's to get some gold braid to match the one I'd run out of. And the salesgirl says to me, "E'm efreyd, medem, we don't stock it." I say to her, "And what's this you got on the shelf behind you, you bloody fool."'

I said, 'You are wonderful; you are so perfect in everything you touch. I always think of you and pancakes, the way you notice things no one else would.'

'At least you appreciate me, you are a grateful public,' she said.

Pancakes were, indeed, a telling example of Bianca's discernment and craving for perfection. When batter for pancakes is poured into a pan it does not fry smoothly and evenly, but gets mottled and marbled as it browns. When the pancake is turned, this other side takes on a different marbling, which is less handsome than the first. I had never been aware of it, but Bianca was, and when pancakes were made she insisted they should be rolled or folded in such a way as to have the first, the prettier, side uppermost.

I now said, 'Shouldn't I be going soon? You've got to dress. Where are you off to, tonight?'

'Ann Tooth, in Stanhope Gardens round the corner; good address but the woman is really frightful. I was actually in two minds whether I shouldn't call it off, but then – you never know whom you might meet – even in the wrong places.'

'What's so frightful about her?' I asked.

'I drop in the other day and the maid comes in with a telegram – in her hand, mind you – and gives it to Ann. When the wench is gone, I say, "Ann dear, is there in your house such a thing as a silver platter or do you keep all the silver locked away?" Great indignation. I say, "Ann dear, even if you have a dozen silver platters knocking about the place, you still haven't understood my question." In the end I said to her, "You bloody fool, it's not your silver platters I'm going on about, even a cracked kitchen plate would do the trick, anything on God's green earth, as long as the wire is presented to you for you to pick it up. It's like when you give a servant money or a letter, you never give it straight to them. You put it on a table and you let them pick it up." It dawned on her then. She should have paid me for the lesson.'

I said, 'That reminds me, the other day I went to the pictures; there was this family, a Count, living in his castle, and at one point the footman comes in and hands the Count a telegram. I was shattered. But then I realized it was an American picture; what can you expect from the Yanks?'

Bianca said, 'It's a marvel they had any servants in that castle, anyway. Have you noticed, in Yank pictures, there are never any domestics?'

I said, 'You are quite right, Bianca, now that I come to think of it. By the way, while you were at it, you should have told Ann Tooth about the butler and the bathroom.'

'I actually thought of it,' she said, 'but then I thought she'd never believe me and think that I was pulling her leg.'

What I was alluding to was that Bianca, when first married and living in their Hampstead house, had to get used to the custom that a butler never knocks at a door, but always enters, whether rung for or not. Once, when Bianca was in her bathroom and about to rise from the tub, the butler opened the door, said, 'Sorry, sir,' and retreated. This was part of his training. He had to say, 'Sorry, sir,' so as to pretend that although being aware of a presence in the bathroom, he had not been aware that it was his mistress.

Bianca said, 'Well, anyway, she was really quite grateful I dropped in on her. She's still cut-up about that husband of hers and I tried to talk sense.'

'What's he done?' I asked.

'Three guesses,' she answered. 'And got found out.'

'More fool he. Serves him right.'

She said, 'No, Eve, he did have rotten luck. He and she – they had a smash-up in the car. It's most extraordinary, you know; that's the third time I've come across this sort of thing happening. There is such a thing as fate, you know; look at your own father.'

'I didn't get much chance to look at him, did I?'

For a while we were silent. I watched her smile. I said, 'How did you talk sense into Ann Tooth; I'd have thought it'd be a case of Humpty Dumpty.'

She said, 'Oh, no. For one thing, I pointed out to her that he'd only taken a knock on the head, so no harm done, no nobler part of the body damaged. And then I said to her, "Ann dear, don't carry on so; your husband isn't made of soap; it doesn't get smaller every time he uses it." Still. As you know, I'd never touch a married man myself. Not because of morals. It's just distasteful.'

I said, 'God, yes. At least that's one thing I've always kept out of. I want to be the one and only one. That time, you know, I told you about it, when Reggie Burns made a pass at me in the taxi, taking me home, I said the immortal words "But you are married," and he replied with the equally immortal words, "What's that got to do with it?" But he left off.'

'But you should get James to marry you, though. I keep telling you.'

'Oh, Bianca,' I said, 'don't start on that again. I can only bear living with him as long as I know I can up and away – any moment.'

She said, 'That's not the right way to look at it. Once you've got the ring on your finger, you go out and play bridge and are never at home more than you can help and he can whistle for you. And in the meantime – look at yourself; what's he giving you? Where are the furs and the jewels?'

'If I stick it much longer,' I said, 'by the time I get the diamonds and the sables, I'll be wearing them in the loony bin.'

She said, 'I only know one thing, as soon as there's another man in the offing, James won't see you for dust. But he doesn't know it. He thinks he's so desirable it doesn't even occur to him that he could be jealous.'

I said, 'And he's right, in a way. Not because he's so desirable, as you put it, and he thinks he's a man because he looks like one. But show me a man that attracts me. Where is he? I haven't seen one for years and when it comes to men, London is a desert. So you see, Bianca, I'm betwixt the devil and the deep blue sea; there is no man for me to run away with, and I'm afraid to cut and make the jump on my own, with nowhere to go.'

She said, 'You know you can always come and stay with me; any time, day or night, you can knock at my door and I'll be here for you.'

'Yes, I know, Bianca,' I said. 'You are so never-endingly good to me; and it's really only knowing that you are here and that I've got you, which keeps me going.'

'It's just such a pity that you are poor.'

I said, 'But Bianca, I'm not poor; it's only that I haven't got any money, and that's what keeps me going too. Because when I am at Screes or here with you, I'm the same as John H. and Claire and you; we all belong, and I know it and they know it, and money doesn't come into it.'

'You're bloody right,' she said. 'Now, ring for her and she'll let you out, and I'll go upstairs and see if I can bear the sight of my face.'

I said, 'Oh, Bianca, if I had your looks, I'd never move away from the glass; I'd keep looking at myself all day long.'

She said, 'You are not so bad yourself; you're exquisite; don't be so bloody silly.'

Riding in the bus along Park Lane, on my way back to Peel Street, my thoughts returned to John H. and his carping. I thought about why I would have liked to have been married to him in spite of it, and why James's nagging was becoming unbearable to me, and I sorted it out, at last.

John H. was calm and he was sarcastic and he was superior and he made one convinced that he was always in control. He was in a position of strength.

Whereas James's carping was due to weakness; whining or angry, he was always clutching at me with demands. He was insatiable, wanting proofs of my love and care and devotion, and when I'd threaten to leave him he would fall into abject humility, and say that he could not live without me, and he even pretended to be suddenly taken ill, with an attack of vertigo or nausea, trying to arouse my pity. And whenever, on such occasions, I wanted to call a doctor, he got angry, saying that it was heartless of me to want to call a doctor, that it was I who should be looking after him and trying to get him well. He was always trying to force me into the role of being motherly, which was not my nature.

John H., on the other hand, was fatherly and protective, and this was probably what I wanted. Bianca, if I'd told her, which I would not, because I was ashamed of it, would have said that this was owing to having lost my father at two years old. But I did not think it was needful to bend over backward and indulge in such fancies. It was, surely, simpler than that. It was just my nature and I was hopelessly weak.

James was about Bianca's age, in his late forties; brown-haired and brown-eyed, tall, well-made, he moved in a loose-limbed way. He had the haughty grasshopper profile of the intellectual and, though his shirtmakers were in St James and his tailor in Savile Row, he gave his appearance donnish accents with knitted ties, cardigans instead of waistcoats and, at home, tweed coats with lozenge-shaped leather patches at the elbows.

At the time I first got to know him he had just opened a gallery of modern art in Old Bond Street with two other partners, the money provided by him entirely. And his decision, two years later, to leave England and to settle down abroad, was due to his embitterment at being bought out by the two others in the meantime, to which they were entitled according to their initial contract. By this time the gallery had begun to flourish and they had taken the first opportunity of getting rid of him.

His resentment over this, what to him was an act of betrayal, never left him; in fact it deepened as he watched the budding gallery unfold, within the next ten years, into the biggest gallery of its kind in the world, based in London, and with branches in New York and in Tokyo.

I had first met him at one of Bianca's brandy-and-champagne parties in the late afternoon. I had been standing on the landing, pretending to look at a print of a Canaletto *veduta* of Venice while wondering whom to approach among the few people I knew in the drawing-room.

He said, 'Do you admire it?' and I said, 'Yes, I do, but not wholeheartedly. There is something about Canaletto – something sober, chilling, too meticulous, that puts me off.'

He said, 'What you mean is, it's pedestrian.' Then he said something that he had probably said a hundred times before, but which I found tremendously impressive. 'In my opinion, people can be divided into those who like Canaletto and those who like Guardi. And you, I believe, like Guardi.' I exclaimed, 'You are so right!'

I had continued to be impressed when he asked me to dinner in his house in Peel Street, which he had restored and made over from what had been an early Victorian butcher's shop. When, for instance, I had hesitated to use a flat terracotta bowl as an ashtray, he had said, 'Go ahead, it's Attica; it's more than two thousand years old. If it's lasted that long, it will last a bit longer.'

He liked to say that there are many kinds of bad taste but only one good taste. About Bianca, to whom he referred as a society tart with the paint chipped off, he was disdainful. The furnishings of her Queen Anne house in Curzon Street he dismissed as banker's bastard baroque, and, when she came to Peel Street and was shown some of his treasures, he said that she was one of those people who admire the right things for the wrong reasons.

He went with me to the dressmaker's and spent hours

there, harrowing them with commands as to how to fit and drape the cloth on my body, and Bianca did admit, with reluctant admiration, that the dresses James had had made for me were on the level of those of the Paris *haute couture*.

He gave me chains to wear which had been taken from Egyptian mummies and a turquoise necklace from sixteenth century Persia. Which made Bianca remark that he did not dress me so much as decorate me, and that, in doing so, he turned me into a piece of his decor, an addition to the Hellenistic terracotta figurines, the bronze mannerist Bologna statuettes, the Hispano-Moorish bowls, the Isnik plates, the seventeenth-century Delft china, the Bohemian ruby-glass goblets.

Bianca said, 'And this antique jewellery he gives you, it's a scream; it's good for a laugh. What is it, lapis lazuli and turquoise and stuff? I'd throw it in his face if I were you; it's a load of rubbish. Has he never heard of diamonds, in that village he comes from? If he believes he can fob you off with that, he still believes in Father Christmas.'

James was obsessed with stains. He not only created them on his clothing and on the cloth by spilling food and drink at table; he also spotted his desk and the carpet around the desk with sealing wax, candle grease and ink blots. And, as though driven by a malicious demon, when buying the house in Peel Street, he had had the panelling in the two downstairs rooms painted a dull white, as well as the skirting and the doors, and had furnished the drawing-room with white-painted Regency chairs. Thus, every time one opened a door or shifted a chair or touched a wall to take a book from the open shelves, a constellation of fingerprints arose on the surface, like dark stars on a pale sky.

And, linked to this constant soiling and staining of his surroundings, was his unceasing urge to remove the traces of the soiling and staining, which went so far as to make him walk with me round the rooms, pointing to each stain that had to be removed, and demanding that the deep-pile carpets, which showed every footprint, be swept over with a brush so as to restore their uniform smoothness. When he came home and saw an ornament turned at an angle slightly different from how he had placed it himself, or a cushion askew, or a duster dropped beneath a table and forgotten and left there, he flushed with rage, saying that it was like receiving a slap in the face and that it showed that I did not care for him.

Bianca said that he was trying to make me feel guilty all the time because he was feeling guilty himself, and that the constant re-enactment of removing the marks of his slovenliness was due to the desire to obliterate the perversion of his amorous peculiarities.

When James decided to leave England I saw this as the obvious, the easiest way to break with him. It was Bianca who stopped me. She said, 'He's gone from London now, so you've got a breathing space. The house is up for sale. You carry that through, and you see to the packing and clearing up and storing of the bloody stuff; that's no work; the removal men are paid to do it and you don't have to lift a finger. Then you go to Estoril and look around for a house; it'll be a paid holiday for you and you still won't have to have James around. Once he gets down to Estoril, you clear out and come and stay with me. Living in Curzon Street isn't as bad as the salt mines in Siberia – not that I've been there. Then we'll see. No use crossing your bridges.'

Like all Bianca's advice this was eminently reasonable and acceptable, and, as to my thus playing an underhand game, Bianca said, 'It is our duty in life to make people happy. And this way, you'll make him happy, I bet,' and, seeing her malicious conspiratorial smile, I said, 'Oh, Bianca, you are wonderful. I wish I had your sense of humour.'

Peel Street branches off Kensington Church Street and leads up the rise to Campden Hill, and there is a Barclays Bank in Kensington Church Street. Yet, while living with James I had kept my account in their Westbourne Grove branch, which had been the most convenient for me in those days when I had been living in a tiny bedsitting-room on the fourth floor of a house in Clanricarde Gardens, of which the bedroom part had consisted of a narrow divan and the sitting-room part of a low button-quilted stuffed chair.

It was a week before my departure.

The teller greeted me with, 'Good morning, madam. Lovely morning, this morning,' and when I kept silent, he added, 'Sunny Portugal, is it? I can't say I envy you.'

I was struck by the calm malice of his words. It was the same tone of voice that Bianca had used, only the day before, when she had said, 'One thing I do know, if another man comes along, James won't see you for dust.'

I kept looking at him; I knew I could afford to look at him without meeting his eyes. His head was bent; he was writing on a pale green form – not really writing but dashing his pen across and above and under the printed lines, without stopping or hesitating, a virtuoso performance of an inky ballet on a pale green stage.

He had a narrow, well-shaped head with thick, smooth, black hair – jet black, not like mine or Bianca's, which seemed black but was really black-brown – and long fleshy lips in a smoothly white face. There were no lines on his face; there could not be; he was not a man who would show his emotions. He looked calm, clever, and brutal.

He said, 'In fives, tens, and twenties? And hundreds? A mixture? Or any particular preference?'

I said, 'No, no, I leave it all to you. Whatever you think fit.'

'Whatever you think fit,' he repeated after me, speaking low and with almost closed lips. 'Whatever I think fit. And what do I think fit? You'd be surprised.'

He raised his eyes briefly, and said, 'Lisbon, will it be?'

I said, 'No, Estoril.'

He said, 'Ah, yes, royalties in exile, once so beloved by their people, I don't think; and a freezing wind all the year round which is all to the good; it keeps away the flies and the mosquitoes. That's something,' and, without glancing up, he reached out and seized yet another form from the stack of papers by his side.

I said, 'Oh, good. Flies are a nuisance but mosquitoes are dreadful. One, just one, is enough to give you a sleepless night.'

He said, 'You may find other ways of getting a sleepless night. Apart from that, I advise you to go to Lisbon when you want to change money. You get a better choice of banks there; shop around and see their rates of exchange. Sign this please. If you call tomorrow at the same time it will be ready for you.'

In the afternoon I went to see Bianca. She came down the stairs herself, to let me in. She was in a dressing-gown of thin dark green wool, sprigged with tiny roses, the green of her eyes deepened by the tint reflected from her gown.

She said, 'I put this on for you specially; roses, roses all the way, for that provincial bad taste which you have – yes, you do, despite James and his coarse-spun austerity.'

This was an allusion to James's dislike of glossy figured damask tablecloths and his preference for rough linen, with every thread showing.

I said, 'How come you've answered the door?'

She said, 'Because it's the maid's day off, that's why.'

I said, 'You don't say. When isn't it her day off?'

And, when she did not speak and kept looking at me with the mischievous conspiratorial smile that always delighted me so much, I said, 'Yes, still, I suppose you are right.'

She said, 'Of course I am right. Better let her out than keep her in; once they start bringing their men inside it's the end. And, as you know, I've hardly any stuff in the safe in the bank. Look at this, for instance; it'd be worth murdering me in my bed for this alone.' She raised her hand and we both contemplated her ring, I respectfully and she with a solemn gravity which she only accorded to jewels and to models of *haute couture*. The diamond was as large as her thumbnail, square, with stepped-up edges, in what was called an emerald-cut, and I had never liked it. To me it was a sorry stone; it had none of the burst of myriad lights one expects to break forth from a diamond; it was confined, imprisoned, deprived of its birthright.

She said, 'You go and do likewise. Yes, I know, you'd want a rosette brilliant, with your provincial bad taste, but the main thing is that you get it.'

In the drawing-room I kicked off my shoes and lay back on the love-seat. I said, 'Talking of maids, I went to Screes the other day. Farewell visit. Violet was there too. And she said such a – '

'What's she like now?' asked Bianca. 'I haven't set eyes on her for ages. Still the buxom dairymaid, and hair like the stuffing spilled out of a mattress and on top of it that sunny nature which she really oughtn't to have?'

I said, 'Bianca, really – '

'Bianca, really. When you have that kind of mouth, showing your gums above your teeth every time you smile, you can't afford to have a sunny nature.'

'But she's fresh-looking, isn't she,' I said, 'and she's got a sweet nature, don't you think?'

Bianca said, 'Oh, quite, and I don't like her much, either. But what was it about her you wanted to say?'

I said, 'She came out with such a remark, you'd never guess; it shook me. And you, with your maid, and giving her the day off, it made me remember. We were at lunch and Claire was belly-aching about getting and keeping servants out there in the country, what with Screes being in the sticks and no transport for the slaves, and how the maid of people nearby got raped only the other night, coming home, walking from the bus stop down a lane. And Violet suddenly utters, "Some women don't know their luck." Can you beat it?'

'She might have kept her bloody trap shut,' she said, 'but I'm not surprised. So many women want to get raped. When I was in that spa place in Bellinzona, some years ago, the doctor in charge liked to tell the women patients, "You are the Brünnhilde type; you want to be conquered." Women love to be told that kind of stuff, and that was a polite way of putting it, don't you see. I'll tell you what the trouble is, Eve, though. The trouble is, one is always wishing for something, but not thinking the thing through to the end. Like saying you want to live forever. You don't realize that if you live forever, you have to get very old; you think that you can go on living as though you were twenty-five. And it's the same with this rape wish. You'd like to be raped, and I mean, you, Eve; yes, you too, be honest. But what you want is to be raped by the right man.'

'Oh, Bianca,' I said.

For a while we were silent.

Then I said, 'You know how the other day I said no man attracts me, nowadays. I went to Barclays today to see about my travellers' cheques – and the teller.'

'What about the teller?' asked Bianca. 'And, by the way, has it never occurred to you that James has just paid thousands into your account for your travel expenses and for your expenses with the removal men. Why don't you draw out the lot and stay here? You could live for years on that money. He can whistle for you; there's not a bloody thing he could do about it; it's in your account and in your name, and he wouldn't even be here, in England. He can't be, can he? He's got the wind up with that fiddle he did, and the Bank of England watching him.'

I said, 'Oh, Bianca. I couldn't. I'd despise myself. Not because of James and what he'd think of me. It's because of me. I've got to live with myself and if I don't like myself, how can I stand it?'

She said, 'Eve, you are hopeless; you botch every chance you get, with your divorce to start with – ' and she would have continued on this well-beaten track if it had not been for the ring of the bell from downstairs, followed by two sharp raps with the knocker on the front door.

'How now brown cow,' said Bianca. 'It's got to be a person – but that bitch of a dressmaker said she couldn't deliver before next week, and that means not next week either. It can't be anybody, though. Not at this time of day. Do go down, Eve; be an angel.'

I said, 'But what if it is somebody and not a person? Are you in?'

'No, I'm not,' she said.

The fanlight above the door was too high for me to see through. When I opened it there was a man facing me, about forty years old, barely of middle height, of dandified elegance, in a pale fawn ulster and with yellow gloves, and as he took off his hat, I saw the familiar broad, domed forehead.

He said, 'I needn't ask who you are – not that I've ever met you before, but I'd have known you anywhere. Is Bianca in? She must be, if you are here,' and he followed me as I preceded him up the stairs.

'Bianca, it's your brother,' I said, and she rose, coming forward to meet him, smiling, though not with her malicious conspiratorial smile. That smile she reserved for me.

She said, 'Ships that pass in the night. I didn't know you were in town. When did you get here, and where are you staying?'

'Usual. Rooms in Half Moon Street.'

She rarely spoke of her 'little brother'. I knew he was living in Zurich, where he had permanent quarters in the Elite Hotel and that he was in the stockbroking business.

I barely listened to their talk, still dwelling on my scene with the teller. I thought, if he'd only said a word, one word, I'd have cancelled the flight and the travellers' cheques. Something like, 'I'll be off duty at three this afternoon; would there be any chance of seeing you?' Oh, God. And I know tomorrow'll be no good; he probably won't be on tomorrow, and even if he were, it'd be hopeless, because if he'd wanted to, he'd have come out with it straightaway; he is that type of man; it's everything at once or nothing and never. He's like Reggie Burns, in the taxi that time, after the party; the same type. Not English, Sicilian-looking I'd say; and I said, 'But you are married,' and repulsed him, and I could have kicked myself afterwards. And he did give me the right answer; he said, 'What's that got to do with it?' but it's Bianca's training, never touch a married man, *c'était plus fort que moi*, and he let go of me at once too, worse luck, as Violet would have said. But then, he couldn't, not in the taxi; no, of course not; that was just a try-out for afterwards; and I wouldn't have gone with him, not of my own free will.

I was recalled from my shameful reverie by Bianca's brother turning to me. 'Of course, as I was saying, you do take after your mother. But you are not a patch on her. Pity.'

I said, 'You are not the only one to say that,' while he kept looking at me, shaking his head.

Bianca said, 'Let's get off the bloody subject, shall we? And, if Eve doesn't take after her mother too much, it's all to the good, in more ways than one, isn't it? Or do I have to beat it into your head with a hammer?'

There was some more talk to which I paid scant attention, thinking it was just as well the brother had turned up and had stopped me going on about the teller and that Bianca would have been derisive about it instead of consoling.

I decided to leave, saying, 'I'd better go; you'll have heaps to talk about,' but he rose too, saying he had an engagement and that he would walk me to the bus stop in Park Lane.

When I went to see Bianca on the following day, I kicked my shoes off and huddled on the love-seat, on which the pink brocade looked dull, like faded rose petals, owing to the gloomy light, while the madonna and Atlas were rising from the blue-green satin like figures rising from the sea, against a summer sky, at dusk.

Bianca said, 'We were talking yesterday about how women want to be raped and men want to live forever, and never think it through. It's like men when they think of getting married. They want the perfect wife. She must be a lady in the drawing-room and a cook in the kitchen and a whore in bed. And, once they are married, they find they've got a whore in the drawing-room and a lady in the kitchen and a cook in bed.'

I said, 'Oh, Bianca, you are so wickedly clever, if you'd

lived in the middle-ages they'd have burnt you as a witch.' And seeing that smile of hers, which always delighted me, I said, 'You know, we are not really like friends. We are a club. With you chairman and me the only member and anyone else who wants to get in being blackballed.'

She said, 'Yes, and my little brother did rather burst in on our committee meeting yesterday, didn't he.'

'Is he going to stay long?' I asked.

'A week or two, then he's going back to Zurich.'

'Zurich is welcome to him,' I said, 'and I hope the weather stays nice for him.'

'Any particular reason? Because he didn't fall for you?'

I said, 'Oh, Bianca, that's just it, only you've got it the wrong way round. Because, you know, when we left here and by the time we got into Curzon Street he started telling me about how sculpture was his hobby. *Il ne manquait plus que ça.* I've always loathed lawyers who write poems and bankers who paint flowers, but then, just in front of Gunthers, he stops and asks me, wouldn't I like to come to his place, just round the corner in Half Moon Street, and see his sculptures. And that really annoyed me.'

Bianca said, 'I didn't think my little brother was as randy as that.'

I said, 'Who cares about that? I just thought it was such revolting cheek.'

'But Eve,' she said, 'don't take on so; be your age. This isn't the first time a man has asked you to his place to look at his etchings. Or whatever.'

'But Bianca,' I said, 'how dim can you be? Don't you understand? First he runs me down, tells me I'm not half as attractive as my mother was, and the next thing, this. What does he expect? What goes on in that brain of his? So typical of men. Like the husband of my cousin Vera. After fifteen years of marriage, Vera is still the most exciting woman in the world to me. Fine. Not that I asked him. Next thing, he wants to, with me, in the same breath. I could have howled. Not that I'd ever touch him with a barge-pole but that's beside the point. The point is that men are so dumb when it comes to sales talk. How can a woman – how can any woman – say yes, when she's been given to understand that she's only second-best.'

Bianca nodded, looking at me quizzically.

I said, 'Another thing I can't stand is when they say, you are so warm and soft. Of course, I'm warm and soft. What woman isn't? It's just that they can't be bothered to think up something particular, something that will fit me, and me only. Oh, Bianca, I'm sick and tired of men. At least, I am of the men I meet.'

I kept looking at her but she was avoiding my eyes, pleating a fold of her dressing-gown above her knee. Then she raised her head and I could see her giving me the special smile again.

She said, 'Anyway, at least my little brother, clumsy though he was, did it in the proper way, not the wrong way round. The wrong way is when a man entices a girl to his flat by promising her a night of love-making. And once he gets her there, he keeps her up all night, showing her his etchings.'

I went into shrieks of laughter, while she said, 'Really, Eve, you are the most grateful public. What'll I do without you, when you are in Estoril, with no one to palm off my oldest jokes on?'

I said, 'But Bianca, isn't it odd that even my going to Estoril is really owing to you entirely, and if James hadn't come here that time, and pondered the wall hanging, I might be going to Beaulieu or Malaga or Salerno.'

She said, 'That's just one of your ideas, you know; it's make-believe, but if it makes you feel better about Estoril, that's all that matters. And once you are back from Estoril, bereft of James, I'll see what I can do for you.'

I said, 'But next time, it must be a man who works, because James is at home all day, he says only donkeys work, and that's what makes it so bad; because if he were diluted, the way other men are – who come home at night from the City –

just think – and even late at night, perhaps because first they go to their club and then, weekends they play golf and go shooting – even Claire having John H. at home now that he's left the City, she hardly ever sees him except at mealtimes; he sticks to his study and never shows his snout. Oh, Bianca, they had a row over that last time I was at Screes. Claire said she wanted to have a gong in the hall to call John H. for meals, and he put his foot down. Mind you, I think he's right; he said he was not living in a blinking castle, but in a blinking cottage, and being a simple cottager it was good enough for him if the maid came to fetch him for lunch and dinner. That is, assuming always she had the use of her feet.'

It had been the only time, ever since I had gone to live in Peel Street, that Bianca had asked us to dinner, and even then she had not made an occasion of it and there had only been one other man to make up the fourth.

As soon as we entered the drawing-room, James had started talking about the wall hanging, saying that on previous occasions, with the brandy-and-champagne routine, he had not been able to do so.

And when Bianca had begun, 'It's seventeenth century, that's for certain, but it may be Spanish or Portuguese – ' he had interrupted her, irritably, putting a hand over his eyes for an instant, and saying, 'Mrs Brainylow, I beg of you – spare me, please,' and had walked round the wall hanging in half-circles, peppering it with short, suspicious glances. Then he had come to a halt in front of one of the windows, leaned against the sill, put his hands in his pockets, thrown his head back, and said, without looking at anyone in particular, 'It's very late baroque, of course, but that doesn't mean it's seventeenth century; it could be early eighteenth, for that matter. But one thing I do know. It cannot be Spanish; it must be Portuguese. I can't think who put it into your head that it might be Spanish. Why, a child of five could see it. You've got the Flemish influence; not so much in the man, but it's very clear in the madonna – the two are not by the same hand, needless to say – and the Flemish influence was very strong in Portugal, from the fifteenth century onward; the angularity suited them, what with their being so down-to-earth themselves and against all show and pretence – quite unlike the Spanish. But apart from this, look at the colour scheme. It tells you the whole story; sober, discreet, no flamboyance, and every time where the Spanish would use gold and silver, the Portuguese use yellow and grey instead.'

I had been genuinely interested, while Bianca had pretended to be so.

She had also pretended to be amused by his 'I beg of you – spare me,' which was so brusque as to be a naked insult, and she had continued playing the benevolent hostess by turning to the other guest, a straw-blond young man with slightly protruding calves' eyes, and saying, 'Aren't we lucky, getting a real expert's opinion, just for once?' to which he had responded with, 'Jolly good show, I'll say,' a remark of such perfunctoriness as to increase the ill-humour I knew to be smouldering within her.

The young man had then crossed over to me and, proffering his gold case with its row of king-size cigarettes, said, 'Do have one of these; it's your last chance, because they don't make them any longer,' and had started to laugh loudly, overjoyed by my not, at first, grasping the double-meaning of these words. This move too, although productive of hilarity, was wrong, because it made Bianca feel left out.

It was therefore not surprising that the mood at dinner was uneasy and restrained, with Bianca forsaking her usual mischievous frivolity, turning solemn and speaking of me as 'this dear little girl', and of how our families had always been linked in friendship and how, now that I was without a family and alone in the world, she felt responsible for my well-being. These remarks, aimed at James, were received in silence and they made me feel embarrassed, because they were tinged with the meretricious. Bianca achieved real solemnity only when speaking of diamonds and *haute couture*.

It was at this point that the calf-eyed young man, who had, clearly, not been following the discourse, broke in with, 'That curtain, in the room yonder. Ever tried to sell it? Bit of a white elephant, what?'

James said, 'This is like the finger of fate pointing. Why haven't I thought of Portugal before?' He went on to say that the house in Ascona was not suitable for living in all the year round; there was snow in the winter, in the Tessin; the summers were close and airless; and if he had to live abroad, Portugal was just what he wanted, with no snow in the winter and the Atlantic climate, with its cool summers, so much to be preferred to the other countries in the south of Europe, with their Mediterranean aspects.

Bianca had given us what she called 'the best small treatment', a lace cloth laid over pink damask, the lace and the damask both being too short to cover the table when it was extended to its utmost size, seating twelve, and there were pink candles in the double-branched holders, sparkling in wreaths of crystal prisms of the same kind as those on the chandeliers that were such a neck-twisting labour to clean. The soup was served in bowls of flowered china with spoons of the same china to go with them. These, too, belonged to the 'small treatment'. Originally there had been six of these bowls, but two had been broken by the maid.

This splendour, though, was lost on James, who loathed lace, cut glass and flowered china.

And, as though feeling that by setting a festive table she had done enough, Bianca had not bothered to provide a decent meal. The mushroom soup was out of a tin and thinned with milk instead of with cream, and with the main course she had skimped on the garnishings by serving a single dish of rice, left-overs of roast chicken, chicken-livers and green peas. For pudding there were halves of peaches reposing on chunks of the most common ready-made vanilla ice, swimming in raspberry syrup, and which Bianca blithely called Pêche Melba, daring anyone to contradict her by sweeping each of us with her delightfully malicious smile.

Once we were out in Curzon Street, James, still spinning the Portuguese thread, remarked how extraordinary it was that Bianca's house should have been, first, the place where he had met me, and, second, the place in which he had been given the pointer to go to Portugal, and how he felt that we both, he and I, were starting a new life, walking together hand in hand, and he might have continued thus had it not been for the sight of an approaching taxi-cab.

While we were getting in, I felt convinced that he would transcribe those last sentences into the diary he kept. I had only glanced at it once, briefly, when he had left it lying open on his desk, having been called downstairs to the telephone, and this short perusal had been sufficient for me to know that he intended it for publication.

I had, on that page, recognized the rendering of an ugly scene of the day before when he had shouted at me that he had never come across anyone as ignorant and inefficient in housekeeping as I was. My reply that I had not thought it worthwhile to see to the mending of the broken sash in the window of the small room at the rear, as it was not in use, and as we were going to leave the house, anyway, was the reply of a bad servant, and he implied that, altogether, I was like a slovenly maid.

In the diary he had written, 'Eve, strange, eerie, graceful creature, with her foreboding of leave-taking and divination of the misty shapes of things to come.'

To James I owed my understanding of modern painting; my appreciation of some of the darker byways of applied art of former centuries; the skill of letting a few flowers slide into a chalice by holding them above it, instead of bunching them in a vase; a predilection for washing grapes in wine instead of in water; and a conviction that tea or coffee had to be served in different porcelain, depending on whether one was taking it in the library or in the drawing-room.

He said, 'My dearest child, I have to go back to Lisbon now, and I shan't be able to see you for a day or two.'

I said, 'But, will he take me back in the car to the Coimbra?'

He said, 'My sweet child, surely you do not think I'd let you go back there. I do not like the idea of your staying in the Coimbra, for reasons which need not concern you.'

I did not query this, nor did I protest. This was partly due to my feeling drained and light-headed and partly to his 'I do not like the idea of'. He had used the same phrase the night before when explaining why he had removed the key from the bathroom door and, recalling this, I realized that this was his way of confronting me with a decision against which there was no recourse.

He said, 'I've asked the McGregor woman to call here; she'll be here in about an hour's time. There is a house in the Rua Viveiro I want you to have a look at. It's a bit run down, from what she tells me, but it's all she had at such short notice, and I want you to understand that it's only for the time being, till we find something better for you.'

I said, 'You want me to move into a house, just like that, at a moment's notice? How am I to manage? This is sheer madness,' and, seeing his amusement, I added, 'I can't even begin to think about it, what with having had breakfast at teatime. The bacon and eggs were devastatingly good, though, I'll say that for them. I presume the criminals that perpetrated the plaited fish have been put back in prison where they belong?'

He said, 'My dearest child, I know I've exhausted you. Why don't you lie down for an hour till she gets here and if there is any thinking and worrying to do I'll do it myself.'

'Thank you, yes,' I said, 'I will lie down. And at least now I've got the blouse and skirt to put on, that they've sent over from the Coimbra. I couldn't have faced Katie, at this hour of the day, in my dinner dress, even if it hadn't been ruined.'

'You still feel badly about it, don't you? It makes you feel guilty.'

'Yes,' I said. 'Not because of the dress itself, but because of

Bianca; she took such pains over it, getting it just right, and those flat black daisies, that was all her own idea.'

He said, 'And then a beast of a man comes and rips it all to shreds, is that it? My sweet child.'

The Rua Viveiro was a street leading from the rear of the Casino uphill to the Monte Estoril Hotel, where, hardly more than a week before, I had stepped out of Stafford's Bar and, after listening to the arrogantly loud voices of Ginny darling and the forget-me-not, had taken a cab and driven back to the Coimbra.

Katie McGregor, when she came to fetch me, said in her most determined manner and with a lavish use of Scottish rolled 'r's, that she had found the very thing for me – that is, for the time being; that is, anything would be better than staying on in the hotel; which, though being a nice hotel, was not really very nice in the long run. And when she had driven me to the house, she had not even made a pretence of asking me whether it was to my liking or not, remarking only, in order to forestall any objections I might make, that despite the central heating it would be damp in the winter, but that, as we were getting into April now, there was no point worrying about this, and although the poor dear Pinto Bastos, whose house this was, still had old-fashioned fires instead of oil-fired central heating, this was not going to be my worry as she could guarantee to get me something really decent before the summer was out.

She refrained from mentioning any of the obvious questions, such as those regarding the lease and the price, and I had not inquired.

Pleading another appointment, she walked, with me following, from the drawing-room into the hall, where she stopped, facing me, and said, 'You take a thorough look around now, on your own, and let me know if there's anything further you might want, cutlery or stuff,' and she gripped the edge of her beige knitted suit and pulled it down vigorously over her flat hips in a gesture intended, no doubt, to convey her businesslike keenness.

I was about to thank her when, at this instant, a door at the rear opened and there emerged, probably from the kitchen quarters, the tall, gaunt Maria do Carmo dressed in the white and blue striped smock.

Katie said, 'That's fine. She's found the way, all right. I see you're settled now.' Not noticing my speechlessness, she allowed the maid to show her out of the door, addressing some graciously benevolent words to her in Portuguese.

The house had been built by the two Misses Pinto Basto at the beginning of the century and was so irregularly planned that it seemed to be composed of wings only, with the main central part missing, and with each of its six rooms contained in a wing of its own. This wilful untidiness, this rebellious asymmetry, was underscored by its aspect of genteel, self-respecting indigence, with the red-brick walls and the red-tiled roof showing square and oblong patches of duller and deeper red, where repairs had been done, and this, together with the streaked and unevenly faded green of shutters and paintwork, would have made it conspicuous in a street formed of larger, higher and evenly-fronted white stucco villas. However, it was tucked out of sight and faraway from the pavement, behind a sloping lawn, which, in its turn, was partly hidden by thickets of flowering shrubs.

I knew none of this vegetation. They were all subtropical plants, and if some of those blooms looked vaguely familiar to me, it must have been because I had seen them displayed in a Mayfair florist's window. And yet I found them consoling. Because when I beheld them from a distance, all massed together, they recalled to me the small-petalled medley on Bianca's *mille-fleurs* silk peignoir.

The furnishings of the house would have been called out-of-date, cheap gim-crack by Bianca and Claire and John H., and while this was true, they would have been unable to perceive the charm that still pervaded the place like the imprint of a blunt seal, and where a cultured good taste, once high-brow and avant-garde, had been trying to assert itself against straitened means.

The cheap basket-chairs had been painted lemon yellow and peacock blue in an attempt to raise them above the ordinary; the rickety bamboo tables had been chosen for the grace of their outlines; rough deal tables were hidden under Paisley wraps or squares of embroidered counterpanes of Balkan origin; and the bowls of beaten copper and rustic ceramic were obviously meant to be filled, not with conventionally pretty roses and carnations but with berried branches and coloured shells and pebbles.

I was convinced that the Pinto Basto sisters, whose home this had once been, had been spinsters, excessively clean in their persons, the surrounds of their bathtub heaped with loofahs, sponges, and body-scrubbing brushes, always untidy in dress, and with their hair coiled in twisted strands on the crown of the head and curling in a fringe over the brow, always wispy and dishevelled.

They had danced poems according to the teaching of eurhythmics, had been attracted by Rudolph Steiner's anthroposophy, had been slim to the point of emaciation owing to their vegetarian diet, and had, with their fringed shawls and floating wide sleeves, kept catching their clothing on the rims of the fretwork shelves affixed to the walls, which were now bereft of the multitude of curios and photographs and miniatures, they had no doubt once harboured.

Dazed as I still was from my night at the Montemar, wandering idly through the front rooms, and indulging in my fancies about the Misses Pinto Basto, I caught sight, through the drawing-room window, of the chauffeur leaving the garden with his eagerly tripping step; and when, some time afterwards, I went to the bedroom, I found that the wardrobe was filled with my clothes and that all my other belongings had been ranged with careful neatness in the drawers of the chest.

I never set foot in the Coimbra again.

He said, 'But my dearest child, what is so extraordinary

about my asking you whether you've had any news from Bianca, and, if so, what she's got to tell you?'

We were in the drawing-room. He was sitting on a Victorian couch with rolled-over ends, the only heavily sturdy piece in the room, the mahogany frame of which had been painted a peacock blue in an attempt to harmonize it with some of the basket-chairs painted likewise.

I had kicked off my shoes and sat leaning against him, with my legs stretched out in front of me.

I said, 'You are like John H. He always says, "What is it with you and Bianca?" He doesn't much like her, and I think you don't like her, either.'

He said, 'When John H. used to say this, did he have his hand where mine is now?'

I did not reply.

He said, 'You are a bad liar.'

I said, 'I haven't lied to you.'

'There is lying by omission. Don't play hide and seek with me. I'm grown-up, even if you aren't.'

'Yes,' I said, 'I did have a letter from her.'

'And you've thrown it away and can't remember what's in it.'

'No, I've kept it,' I said.

'Will you show it to me?'

'There's a lot about a dressing-gown she's had made, in tiers, with three shades of blue; not the sort of thing that'd interest you.'

He said, 'Hardly,' and when I did not speak, he said, in that low voice he had used on two occasions before, 'I'm still waiting.'

I had often pondered about it. It was the voice of authority, and authority is the power to enforce obedience, and no one had ever spoken to me like this before, I had not known it, and yet, with him, I had recognized it, with overwhelming certainty. I had never been afraid of a man before and, even with the American, I had felt easy and on equal terms, and while I kept saying to myself, what are you afraid of? what can he do to you? I found no answer and I only knew I had to obey.

I said, 'You'll be frightfully cross. She writes, "Who is this slimy, greasy, oily Portuguese lawyer you've gone off with? And what kind of a hole-in-the-corner lawyer is he? And how do you know he is a lawyer at all, if it comes to that? Have you been to his office? In Lisbon? It probably doesn't exist. And his English. It doesn't mean a thing. Every superior waiter speaks English, nowadays. For heaven's sake, come to your senses; you are twenty-seven not seventeen. And might one know his name? If he's been in the Anglo-Portuguese bank in London – if, I say – then I can ask John H. and he could find out about him. And probably be told that he took in the mail and made the tea.'

He tightened his arm around my waist and I gave a sigh and leaned closer to him.

He said, 'My sweet child, at last. I thought I'd have to go and fetch a tin-opener.'

'That's not funny.'

'You've got an excellent memory. I don't think you left out one word,' he said.

'I can always see it in my mind, the way it's written, on the right side of the page or on the left or on the top or on the bottom. But how do you know I haven't left out a word?'

He said, 'Because I have an excellent memory too, being a hole-in-the-corner lawyer.'

'How do you mean?'

'I never say what I mean and I never mean what I say. Work it out yourself.'

Wrenching myself from his hold and turning to face him I said, 'You've read it? You knew all along?'

'My dearest child, of course I've read it and of course I knew all along.'

'You've gone into my chest of drawers,' I said. 'Oh, God.'

He smiled in his lovely soothing way. 'My dearest child. The top drawer, right-hand side, under the handkerchiefs and scarves, that's where every woman keeps her secret treasures; every burglar knows it. But I am not a burglar and not a maid-servant. I do not rummage in drawers, I promise you.'

I said, 'In that case you've just tricked me; you never saw it; you've been playing cat and mouse with me.'

He said, still with his soothing reassuring smile, 'My sweet child, I didn't trick you; I did see it; I read all the letters you get before you get them, and I decide which ones you should have. I don't like the idea of your being upset. But this letter of Bianca's I gave the *laisser passer*. I had my own reasons which need not concern you just now.'

'You are too much for me,' I said. 'You make me shiver, sometimes.'

'Just as well. *Odint dum metuant*. And you needn't come to my defence with Bianca, either. You shall write to her that, indeed, you have never been to my office in Lisbon, that my name is such and such, that you first met me in the Montemar, and that, for all you know, I might be a waiter. With a command of English.'

Looking up at him, I saw that he was laughing silently. I said, 'You are not a bit cross. No, of course not. You told me the first night. That you are like Talleyrand and never get offended at what people say to you,' and I felt again the icy chill invading me, as I had felt it on that first night with him, when he had told me he would never let me go.

He said, still laughing, and sliding a hand under my blouse and up my back, 'Keep still now. I'm getting very good at it; I can undo this fastening with only one hand.'

'I thought we were going to have tea,' I said.

'Of course we shall. Eventually. My sweet child.'

It was nearly six o'clock when Maria do Carmo entered, pushing the tea trolley, and placed it alongside the bed.

The high, strongly marked cheekbones in her narrow face and the thick, straight, protruding brows seemed to imprison the small, dark eyes between them and gave her an air of sullen obstinate dignity. It was this dignity that made her jealous regarding the household. Thus, for instance, she had forbidden me to touch the trolley, ever, on the pretext that it was too heavy for me and unwieldy, owing to one of the castors being stiff.

I said, 'I hope to God she made the tea right, she always wants to save on the boiling water for rinsing the pot. I couldn't understand it, till Katie explained it to me. They never have enough water; they get more murders for water-rights, among the peasants, than for love or money or anything else. The tea does look a bit on the strong side. But don't get depressed about it, will you?'

'I won't get depressed.'

I said, 'John H. does though, when it gets brought in and looks too strong. Then, to take it out on Claire, he says, "If this is tea, bring me coffee, and if this is coffee, bring me tea," and Claire hits the roof.'

'I shan't hit the roof.'

'In some ways you are wonderfully considerate,' I said.

He said, 'I can afford to be. Because every time I touch you, you make me feel very welcome.' And when I did not speak, he added, 'And yet, you'd run away, if you could. There's an elusiveness about you, and if a man can't cope with it then heaven help him.'

'Now that she's gone,' I said, 'I want to ask you – because they know when one is talking about them, even when they don't understand the language. Like dogs; a dog always knows when you are talking about it. Why doesn't she ever wear an apron? Only blue and white in the morning and black in the afternoon?'

He said, 'My dearest child, yes, anything to change the subject, I knew it. Well. Yes. Maria do Carmo. She's been with the family for so long now, almost forty years, she does not want to be considered as a maid; she would rather be thought of as a housekeeper. Not that it makes any difference, because she doesn't get a salary, anyway. At Christmas I give her a chain or a bracelet, heavy gold; she likes that. And every year I put something into her savings book; I never tell her how much; it's never discussed.'

And when I looked at him incredulously, he said, 'She is from the same village where I come from, in the north, near Viana de Castello. When one needs servants, one always takes them from the place where one comes from. She was one of five sisters; she came with us to Lisbon when she was eleven years old, and we sent her to school, from our house, in the mornings and for the rest of the day she had to get along with the other servants and get trained.'

I said, 'Now I remember. The hall porter in the Coimbra who spoke English so well. He was the valet of the owner too, to start with. He took him along with him, from his village. I got this from the elegant young policeman; he told me, in between trying to pick my brains about Shepherd.'

'Did he try to get off with you?'

'Not really,' I said. 'Only pretended to. Anything to make me talk. He knew perfectly well that I was – already spoken for.'

'Were you?' he said. 'I had no idea. Should I have? Have I said anything wrong?'

'Please, stop it.'

And when I saw his silent amusement, I said, 'But, talking of good English, this elegant young policeman, he was absolutely perfect. I never asked him about it, though.'

He said, 'I don't know who he was. He must have been a Reynolds or a Cobb or a Stillwell, Anglo-Portuguese; port wine, mostly; two hundred years in Portugal and the sons get sent to school in England, and then to Oxford and Cambridge. And they don't marry Portuguese girls either; it's all English brides or Americans, and when they speak Portuguese they pride themselves on speaking it with an English accent. They'll always tell you they had to learn Portuguese when they were grown-up, and back from Oxford.'

I said, 'Maria Teresinha tried to get me off with him. She kept at me, saying and not saying, in that way she has – wash me but don't make me wet – all hints and feints – I don't know why.'

He said, 'Can't you guess? Don't you know what game she was playing?'

And when I said, 'What on earth – ?' he said, 'She hated the American. Because he was unblackmailable. One look at him and you knew. And he was quite capable of getting himself a girl. Without the help of Maria Teresinha, thank you very much. But even if he'd been different, he'd have soon been gone, so there would be no chance of squeezing anything out of him – not like this young Reynolds or Cobb – she could have always turned round and – at least, tried it on.'

'But what is there – I can't see it.'

'But, my dearest child,' he said, 'you were there, she had you. She knew you had come to Estoril to look for a house to live in, not on your own, but with this Mr James Hepburn, whom you had been betraying in his absence, in your wicked, flighty way.'

'How are you, madame? And you are well? And you have good news from you husband? That's how it always went. Husband.'

'She knew quite well he wasn't; that was her *façon de parler*. And she couldn't have cared less either; it would have made no difference when it came to making you pay her for shutting up about it.'

'How very odd,' I said. 'Because I've been in this kind of awkward situation before, in a hotel, and with James. One day I'll tell you about it.

'One day, when you know me better, is that it?'

'You see, I never even told Bianca about that episode in Paris. She'd have thought it screamingly funny, but on the other hand it made me think that there was a noble side to James and she wouldn't have understood it. And it's one of the reasons I stuck it out so long, with James. And when he was always on at me about how inefficient and stupid I was about the house, and Bianca saying, "It's the old game, putting you down to build himself up" – she wouldn't have understood that in some ways he was a better human being than I was.'

And, as he was looking at me with that tight-lipped amusement which made me feel uneasy, I said, 'It's all very well for you, you can afford to be superior. Bianca and I, before I left London, we'd worked it all out that I'd clear out from Estoril as soon as James got here; but now I'm here and I can't clear out.'

He said, 'Can't you? Who's stopping you?' and when I did not speak, he added, 'Now, come, come; we are not going to have tears, are we? Don't upset yourself about James; I'll settle him. And, in the meantime, you write to Bianca, as I told you to.'

'Yes, I will,' I said, 'I'll tell her you are not a young man with long eyelashes. That's a joke between Bianca and me. Once, at Screes, when we were both staying there, there was an old girl invited too, a do-gooder, all church and mother's meetings, and there was talk about a certain young man who was a very pretty boy with such lovely long eyelashes, and how he did the flowers so beautifully in the church – and Bianca said to her, very loud, into a sudden silence, "You must beware of young men with long eyelashes. Because, usually, you'll find that they are impotent." Claire was ready to hit the roof.'

He said, 'My sweet child, you're making me feel quite at home at Screes, far away as it is. But I'll get up now. I've brought some work to do. You stay in bed, till dinner.'

I first met James in front of that Canaletto *veduta* at Bianca's, and after that I only met him a few more times. He had to go to New York, he told me, and, knowing that I was living in a tiny bedsitting-room in Clanricarde Gardens, he asked me to move into his house in Peel Street during his absence. He said I'd be doing him a favour living there, his man-servant would only be looking in twice a week and he did not like to have the house empty; all the more so, because, not wishing to bother about minor stuff like Sickert and Zadkin, he had recently bought a Utrillo and, successfully crowning a longing of many years, a blue period Picasso. He proposed that, on his return to Europe, we should meet in Paris and that, after spending a few weeks there, we should return to Peel Street together. He took it for granted that I was going to live with him in Peel Street.

When I got to Paris James was supposed to arrive within the next few days. He had not made a booking for me at an hotel, nor had he sent me any money, and I was annoyed at what I felt was cavalier treatment on his part, typical of the rich man who is unaware that other people are poor.

I drew out a few hundred pounds, which was all I allowed myself for fear of depleting my bank account, and when I got to Paris I went to an address my cousin Vera had given me, a small hotel in the Rue Monsieur le Prince in the Latin Quarter, one of those places not patronized by tourists and almost entirely inhabited by students. I had never before stayed in an hotel of such grim dilapidation. The cracked wash-basin had only a cold-water tap, and it occasionally filled with dirty soapy water, which slowly drained away, and which was the discharge of another basin, in a room above.

The owner's wife brought me hot water in a small metal jug every morning and the owner served me with my breakfast coffee.

James had written that I should keep in touch with him through an art gallery in the Place Vendôme. They would convey his messages to me. Every day when I went there, I was told that he had sent yet another telegram from New York, saying that he was being delayed.

On the fifth day, in the morning, when I was about to go out, the hotel owner, who had come to retrieve the coffee tray, stopped in the doorway, and asked whether he could make love to me.

Taken aback, I turned to him, to this man who, until now, I had regarded as a walking coffee tray. I looked at him, properly, for the first time. He was a short man in his thirties, square-headed, with bristly brown hair and widely spaced, yellowish teeth.

I said, forcing a smile, trying to be gentle, 'I'm sorry. It is not possible.'

He said, '*Quelle pitié. Madame est très belle*,' and left the room, while I thought, pityingly, 'You should see Bianca. You ain't seen nothing yet.'

But this 'madame is very beautiful' kept resounding in my head. Another telegram which I was shown and which I could not make sense of, while being assured by the man in the gallery that he too could not make sense of it and that altogether he found Monsieur Hepburn rather *emmerdeur*, increased my resentment toward James. This truculence now became infused with thoughts of, 'Who does he think he is, leaving me hanging about here, with my money getting less every day, and thinking I'm going to be faithful to him, on top of it?'

It was on that same morning that, in a coffee house on the Boulevard St Michel, I got into conversation with a young man, a student of medicine, vigorous, bullet-headed, with round blue eyes, who neither interested me nor attracted me, took him to my hotel, and went to bed with him. He spent several nights with me there, not realizing that his presence, including his eager, short activity, gave me a twofold satisfaction, enabling me to spite both James and the owner of the hotel.

A few days later, the man from the art gallery sent word to me that James was due to arrive.

He turned up at the hotel early in the afternoon, annoyed and disgusted upon seeing the place, and yelling downstairs, where the owner's wife was sitting behind her desk, to ask the taxi to wait, and the bill to be brought.

Without taking off his hat and coat, he took the bill presented by the owner on the familiar little metal tray, while the man stepped back and remained standing in the doorway.

James laid the paper chit on the table in the middle of the

room, took out a pencil and began to note down some figures. Then he said, in his excellent French, 'But this is all wrong. I see here so and so many days, at such and such a price, but it doesn't add up correctly; it's almost double what it should be.'

The owner said, raising his eyes with calm modesty, 'Monsieur will find it correct, if he considers that madame has had a man in her room, at night, and, that a double quantity of hot water had to be provided. If Monsieur will go through the account again, I shall retire in the meantime, and leave Monsieur and Madame to their explanations.'

Barely glancing up from the bill, James said, 'Oh, that. Oh I see,' and he bent once more his arrogant grasshopper's profile over the table. The hotel-keeper walked out of the room backwards, without taking his eyes off James, and, moving near to me, said in a low voice, 'What did you expect, madame? You did not want me.'

I looked at the door, now closed. I was filled with a spiteful delight. I thought that the owner had behaved superbly, getting his own back, in a most unexceptionable manner, and I was filled with the determination neither to explain nor to offer excuses, quoting under my breath my beloved stand-by, 'If it be farewell for ever, 'tis for ever, fare thee well.'

Turning to me and stepping away from the table, James said, haughtily, calmly, 'Have you packed your cases? If you have, we'll go downstairs. I'll pay, and I hope they've kept the taxi. I want to go to the Hotel du Bac in the Rue du Bac; it's quite small and *tout ce qu'il y a de plus chic*. They've got footmen there, in silk breeches and buckled shoes. Rather sickening rococo, but it's got character.'

He never once referred to this scene, in which he had, I thought, behaved in an amazing fashion and which had made me feel guilty toward him for ever after, although I kept telling myself that, after all, I was not married to him, not even engaged; I had made no promise of any kind to him, before his going to New York, and I was ignorant as to whether he had had any dealings with women during his absence. It did not occur to me that James's magnanimity had not been a question of choice. He must have sensed from my attitude, my defiant silence, that I was ready to break with him completely. And, at that time, he was already too taken with me to risk it.

He said, 'My sweet child, Maria do Carmo tells me that now she's got this niece of hers here with her, she'll find it difficult to manage, because there is not another maid's bedroom in the house.'

It was about four o'clock in the afternoon. We were in the drawing-room, I, as usual with my shoes kicked off – as I had used to do in Curzon Street while huddling on Bianca's love-seat – and leaning against his chest.

I said, 'I don't really know what she needs her for, except that they go in for orgies of cooking all their ghastly regional dishes.'

Just as James had said, at our first meeting, that one can divide people into those who like Canaletto and those who like Guardi – meaning the tidy, sober, down-to-earth ones and the slap-dash romantic ones, fired by the glow of imagination – I had always thought that one could divide women into those who were, basically, chamber-maids, with similar traits of neatness, tidiness, preciseness, and a liking for rituals, and those who were cooks, who liked to indulge their fancies in composing dishes whose taste, fragrance, and texture they would change, according to their mood, and who did not care for measuring and weighing, but relied on eye and hand. Maria do Carmo belonged to the former type, while the niece, a young woman, fair and round-faced, short, thick-legged and sturdy like a pony, belonged to the latter, as I did.

I said, 'As it is, Maria do Carmo is a bit sniffy because there's no chauffeur's bedroom and bathroom here, and when I say, I haven't got a car, anyway, she say's that's not the point.'

He said, 'My dearest child, the Pinto Bastos are agreeable

to your staying here as long as you want. But I do not like the idea of your living in a rented place and I've seen a house which I think even Maria do Carmo would approve of. There'd be room in it for two nieces as well as the non-existent driver's bed-and-bathroom, boiler room, laundry room, ironing room, everything she is used to. And I want you to go and have a look at it. It's empty, which is all to the good; you can furnish it however you want; and if you say the word I'll buy it tomorrow.'

I said, 'God, I never dreamt – '

He said, 'As we are on the subject, I don't like the idea of your feeling lost and vulnerable, with Bianca and those at Screes wringing their hands and waiting to find you, sooner or later, in the proverbial gutter. I want you to be completely dependent on me but at the same time I want you to know that you are provided for. I'll put down a trust fund for you in Liechtenstein. I'll tie it up, of course, so that you won't be able to touch it during my lifetime. The details need not concern you; I'll only want a few signatures from you, the rest is up to them and their notaries. And you needn't think it's charity on my part; you'll be doing me a favour. I'll be only too glad to be rid of some of my money; the less I have, the better. But, again, this need not concern you.'

I said, 'I don't really understand a word of what you're saying, and about wanting to have less money – how daft can you get? Do you think John H. would think it sensible?'

He said, 'He would, my sweet child, I promise you.'

I said, 'I made a devastating pudding for tonight. It's got mocha cream, and a sponge cake made with hazelnuts instead of flour, and the cream is in three layers, in between. It's all ready, and I'm glad it is, because otherwise you'd have thought I was being mercenary, what with the house and the trust fund. And you could have it for tea but I'd rather you didn't, because I've made a soup with rice and green peas and a ham bone, to go first, and then a veal stew in a white lemon sauce with nutmeg and carrots and turnips, the first new ones this year, and potato croquettes, and I'd rather like to have a dignified ending with the mocha cream.'

He said, 'My dearest child, in that case, I quite understand; I'll make allowances for it. But I want something else and I want it at once. And I'll tell her we'll have the tea in the bedroom but in our own time.'

The house he had told me about was one of several belonging to the Vasconcelos family, whose footman, Angela's brother, had been among the early suspects in the Shepherd murder case; as I had left the Coimbra without even packing my things, I had not seen Angela again, and thus I did not know what had become of him.

When I called at their house, there was no man-servant in sight. Instead, there was a young maid, black-frocked, whose bonnet repeated on a minor scale the three-tiered embroidered frills on her tiny apron, and whose appearance was a gratifying example of Veblen's 'vicarious consumption', when seen side by side with her mistress. The latter was a pasty-faced, dishevelled, fat old woman, in a baggy tweed skirt, a creased pink silk blouse and a red cardigan frayed on the right-hand sleeve, a combination that revealed her to be ignorant of one of James's dogmas that 'one should never put pink together with red, because then pink tries to look green, and can't.'

I had been told that my formal visit was to last no more and no less than the prescribed twenty minutes. While we were seated facing each other in front of the hearth, conversing in French, the maid had come in, at short intervals, to replenish the fire of the lazily burning logs by the addition of fir cones, placing these beneath the logs with her white-gloved hands, and retreating each time by stepping backward until she reached the door, which she then closed, still facing us.

I described this white-gloved fire-tending scene in one of my letters to Bianca, hoping it would amuse her, and I also wrote that the house he had bought for me was in the same street as the large shabby villa where the ex-king Carol of

Roumania had lived and died and which was still inhabited by Madame Lupescu, while the former minister of protocol and his wife, remnants of the king's entourage, had to live in a small house in a side street round the corner, but were expected to be on call and duty all day long. I even added the limerick I had learnt from young McGregor, 'Have you heard of Madame Lupescu, who came to Roumania's rescue? It's a wonderful thing to be under a king, is democracy better, I ask you?'

I filled my letters to Bianca with these trifles, careful to avoid all but the briefest mention of Mascarenhas.

Thus, while I kept silent about my gratitude to him, knowing it would increase her hostility, I also kept silent about the heavy-handed ruling with which he oppressed me and fenced me in, always with his soothing, reassuring smile, never admitting of any discussion.

To begin with, there was his control of my incoming mail. Moreover, I had found out that I could neither make nor receive any telephone calls outside Portugal in the house in the Rua Viveiro, where I was still living and would be living for some time longer, till the newly bought house was ready.

He had told me that he had ordered this limitation of the telephone so as to prevent Maria do Carmo or her niece from making calls to Canada or Brazil, where several members of their family had emigrated to. I had not believed this. But I had not dared to say so.

Also, I had no money. He had taken my passport away, saying that, as there was no safe in the house in the Rua Viveiro, it was desirable to entrust it to him, and, bereft as I was of my passport I was not able to cash any of the traveller's cheques provided by Barclays Bank in London and issued to me by that teller, who, I now realized, had been like a *fata Morgana* in the desert of my emotions, and whose remark about 'finding other ways of having sleepless nights' had come true.

And while I got some pocket money I was in no position to ask for more. The grocer's boy called at the service door of the house every morning, even on Sundays, to receive his orders, and returned a few hours later with the groceries. The grocer's bill was paid once a month, not by me but by Maria do Carmo, and when, from time to time, I went to the grocer's myself, to get something out of the ordinary, like German rollmops or English marmalade, I was received with smiles, bows, and hands rubbed against each other in a show of deference, and never expected to pay in cash.

Equally, I had been told that I could go into any shop in Estoril, and, no matter how costly the dress or scent I might be wanting, ask for the bill to be sent to the Rua Viveiro.

Further, he had told me that 'he did not like the idea' of my going to Lisbon on my own. If I did so, I was to be accompanied by Maria do Carmo. And when I pointed out that it was awkward to take her along to such places as the British Institute or the American Library, where I went about once every three weeks, to get books, he said he would engage for me a suitably cultured lady, an erstwhile governess or school teacher, who would not only be helpful in showing me the town, but would, by conversing, help me to acquire a more suitable Portuguese vocabulary. I was picking up, from Maria do Carmo and the niece, various vulgar expressions which were the equivalents of, say, 'ever so nice', or 'something cruel', one of the most distasteful of which, to the educated, was the habit of saying, '*pois, pois*' instead of the '*sim*' which meant 'yes'.

It was with painful wistfulness that I now recalled Bianca, standing on the stairs in Curzon Street, after having opened the front door to me on that afternoon, holding out her hand with the large though not sparkling diamond on her finger, saying, 'Go and do likewise.'

Because in my present situation, the only way I would have been able to get hold of any money, would have been by owning jewellery, and I had none, having sold all that had been left to me after my mother's death.

I was certain that in my place, Bianca would have at least tried to be given some. I would rather have bitten my tongue off, as the saying goes, than do so. And I had kept silent in agreement, when he had once said to me, 'I don't like the idea of buying you any jewels; you never wear them, not even costume jewellery; it is not your style; it isn't you, and besides, jewels are a bad investment,' while I fancied I heard Bianca's voice, saying, 'Eve, what a bloody fool you are.'

In the Coimbra, the American had not taken me by force; I had melted as soon as he had lifted me up in his arms. Whereas Mascarenhas, on the settee in the Montemar, in a few moves had trapped me, and in a few words had brought to bear on me an authority that could not be questioned. In the same manner, he had now imprisoned me and fenced me in.

He had told me that with Portuguese servants in general, and with Maria do Carmo in particular, I was to say simply what I wanted done and never to explain why I wanted it. And, in the same vein, when they had done something of which I did not approve, I was never to reprove them or ask them why they had done it. I was merely to tell them not to do it again.

Thus I never found out whether Maria do Carmo liked the house he had bought. I was aware that, behind his smiling, insistent virility and her sullen, obstinate dignity, they were both united in the power of exacting my submission, whereas the niece, impressed by my cooking, and eager to learn, followed me with loyalty and sturdiness, half spaniel, half pony.

Again, when I wrote to Bianca about the house he had bought, I did not dwell on details, for the same reason as when I referred to him, and I did not even express my delight.

It was the most modest-sized house in that street of imposingly large villas in vast gardens, though its grounds were as large as theirs. But apart from its size, it was altogether singular in aspect when compared to most of the other houses in Estoril.

It was early nineteenth-century Gothic, with two round

towers flanking the front. The roof was half hidden by crenellations. The windows, tall and narrow, with pointed arches and panes divided to repeat the ogival pattern, were spaced alternately singly or in pairs, and the stark symmetry of the design was underscored by the rose trees and laurels, planted to form quincunxes, with their crowns cut so as to be precisely rounded.

The black-tiled roof, the yellow woodwork and the white walls, with their glossy black, yellow and white, enhanced the naïvely rigid charm of the house.

He said, 'My dearest child, Madame Vasconcelos is very pleased to have met you. She tells me that if you'll have tea with her one of these days, she'll arrange for you to meet one of the former governesses they had, when the daughters were still at home; if you take to her, she can teach you Portuguese and go with you to Lisbon. Will you ring her up, tomorrow morning?'

I said, 'That's very kind of her. And she'll really have me to tea? Katie McGregor told me you can live in this country for thirty years, and do business with them, and they'll never ask you to their homes.'

He said, 'Certainly.'

I said, 'Then it isn't just because she sold the house to you and I'm going to live there?'

He said, 'No, that's nothing to do with it. If a foreigner had bought the house ten times over, she'd never have asked him to tea. She will probably ask you to lunch too, but not to dinner. They don't entertain. As far as I know they only have a family dinner once a week. Thursday is the day. They only invite the closest family – forty people or so. They find this sufficient.'

I said, 'Oh, God, you can say that again.'

It was the late afternoon, and Maria do Carmo had just taken the tea-trolley away.

I was sitting up in bed, watching him as he paced about with his hands in the pockets of his dressing-gown. Owing to the milder weather he now wore one of burgundy-red silk patterned with white pin-point dots, of the most conventional kind, and I was certain that John H. wore one exactly like this, in the summer.

I had not seen him for several days. He never telephoned, and I never knew when he would be coming, and while he often came in the afternoon, I sometimes found him in my bed, in the middle of the night. If I asked him, on the following day, at what time he had come to Estoril, I would nearly always be told, 'Oh, about three in the morning, my sweet child. I like to work late at night.'

This never letting me know when to expect him was another way of making me feel how helplessly I was in his hands.

He said, stopping by the dressing-table, and leaning against it, 'Tell me, my dearest child, have you ever stolen an electric radiator?'

I pushed away the pillows behind my back and sat up straight. I said, 'Not just one. I steal two every week,' and, seeing his smile I added, 'Did this come over you all of a sudden, or have you been feeling peculiar for some time?'

He said, 'Indeed, I have been feeling peculiar for some time past. I was not aware of it until now.'

I said, 'What on earth – ?'

He said, 'For some time I have been reading James's letters. I never let you have them; I decided against it.'

He was not smiling now. And, looking at those long, straight lips, now closed tightly, at the firmly rounded chin, at the low, wide forehead framed by the handsome arc of white hair, I thought that when he did not smile and was not wearing the gold-rimmed glasses there was only the glossy white hair left to carry the benevolence which his countenance usually conveyed, and it suddenly occurred to me how harmless James had been, and then I heard a faint tinkle of glass. He must, by leaning more heavily against the dressing-table, have set the jars and bottles shivering.

He said, 'I got a lot of entertainment out of them. Besides, they are easy to read. He's got good handwriting.'

'Where is he now?' I asked.

'In Zurich.'

'Where does he write his letters to? I didn't give him this address in my farewell effort. You told me not to.'

He said, 'He writes them to the Coimbra, of course.' When I remained silent, he went on, 'He gave that last letter of yours to a friend of his, a graphologist, German, called Else Kronheimer. Useful to know her name; I might ask her myself one day to explain your inmost nature to me, my dearest child.'

I said, 'You are not being funny.'

He said, 'I didn't intend to be. I only wanted to keep you on tenterhooks a bit longer. Where were we, are we getting nearer to the radiator? Ah, yes. Else Kronheimer. Now, it appears that you do not make thick and thin strokes, up and down, when you write; you keep your strokes evenly thin all the time. This means that you have a fear of life.'

I said, 'Yes, that is true.'

He said, 'It is. Or you wouldn't have stayed with him for that length of time. She also said that you are exceptionally decent in money affairs, great integrity, scrupulously honest. She also said you were utterly passive; you did not want to do, you only wanted to be.'

I said, 'Yes, that's true, too. But why doesn't he get himself a big, active, large-bosomed motherly woman, because that's what he wanted all the time. For instance, once, someone called on him in Peel Street, and afterwards James made a scene. At first I hadn't a clue why. It was because the man had stayed too long. I should have seen that James was getting tired; I should have found a way of getting rid of the man. It is always the woman's duty to take care of the man. Sickening.'

He said, 'Now, Else – will you allow me to call her Else? – she says, what with your being so passive, if he wants to keep you, he must fight for you. He'll come here and fight for you. That is, he intends to. Now don't look at me with those wounded-deer eyes, my sweet child. You see how right I was not to have given you his letters.'

I did not speak.

Leaning back against the edge of the dressing-table, and setting the glass tinkling, he went on, 'What I can't make out is that, on the one hand, here you are, brimful with integrity. On the other hand, there is the missing radiator.'

'Have you come over all queer again?'

'The matter being, that your James, on whom I now look almost as my James too, as well I might. Considering he never had you.'

'Please stop that.'

'Forgive me for being so crude, my sweet child. James. As I was saying, he has now received the inventory from the removal people who are storing the stuff for him, the contents of number 47 Peel Street, and they have listed therein three electric radiators. Whereas he knows that there were four. Where is the fourth? Where is it, I ask you? How is it possible that it was not handed over and packed and taken away? Can you account for it? Did you, perhaps, take it to Bianca's, or to Screes, seeing as, at that time, you were still living in Peel Street?'

And when I kept silent, he went on, 'Do you realize, my dearest child, that he is accusing you of having pinched the radiator? Furthermore, on the one hand – you must forgive me talking like this, but I am trying to be fair, weighing one fact against the other, as though I were in court – on the one hand, then, he is going to fight to get you back. On the other hand, he wants you to return all your dresses to him, because he bought them for you, with his own money, intending them to be worn by you while you were with him. I do admire him, don't you? I have never come across such a thing before, not even in the nastiest divorce cases. Not that I do divorces; I'm strictly a financial lawyer. Greasy, oily, and slimy I may be, but I am financial, and I hope you specified this to Bianca in your last letter.'

I said, 'Yes, I did, in my last-but-one.'

And, seeing his heartening, soothing smile, I added, 'Oh, Bianca. She is like a stone on my chest. I don't know why she is so livid with me.'

He said, 'We shall deal with her in due course, my sweet child. Let it be now; I won't have you upset.'

He went to a side table and brought a box containing cigarettes and matches to the bedside. It was not the luxurious green malachite of my first meeting with him, in the Montemar. It was a copper box with a domed lid and a broken hinge, in keeping with the cultured good taste and indigence peculiar to the house. It was, despite its battered appearance, a valuable piece. I had once turned it upside down and found on its base the engraved W. & W. of the famous *Wiener Werkstätte*.

He said, while giving me a light, 'You are smoking less now. That's in my favour; I can't be such a beast, after all.'

I said, 'You are a beast. It's just that I've got more used to you.'

He said, 'I haven't quite finished yet, with James. I wanted to keep the best bit to the end. Sit tight. Put the cigarette in the ashtray. I don't want you to singe the bedclothes, or Maria do Carmo will never forgive me,' and he took the gold-rimmed glasses from the bedside table, put them on, and pulled a tidily folded sheet of letter paper from behind the handkerchief in his breast pocket. He was smiling again, and, once more, I thought how odd it was that I had never felt a touch of fear with James, despite all his red-faced anger, or his maudlin nagging, nor had I felt submissive. And yet this man who seemed so agreeable, who never showed rage or irritation, who did not complain or criticize, could always force me into surrender and overcome my every reluctance without even a hint of a threat.

He said, unfolding the sheet, 'You may notice he's writing on the thinnest onion-skin letter-paper; no use wasting money on stamps, when one can avoid it. No, I'm not giving it all to you, I'll just read out a para or so.'

I watched him as he slowly slid a thumb down the edge of the sheet. Then he came to a halt, murmuring, 'Close harmony, walking hand in hand,' and then, raising his voice, 'Now, here. I cannot live without you. I am desperate. I cannot control my turmoil. I am liable to commit any folly at any moment and you will have me on your conscience for the rest of your life. I do hope you did not forget to put mothballs into the blankets.'

I was shrieking with laughter. He gave me his handkerchief, and, while I was dabbing the tears from my face, he said, 'I must say, I wouldn't have missed James for the world. There are things one cannot make up because they are beyond one's imagination. It's the best suicide letter I have ever seen.' And as I reached for my cigarette, he said, 'It reminds me of the little boy who says, "Lady, what's in this paper bag? Can I have a look?" and she says, "Never you mind; don't touch it; it's moth balls," and he says, "Some moths!"'

I said, 'You were in London too long; you learned English too well.'

He said, 'There is one joke which is the absolute touchstone for a foreigner. It's about the auxiliary policemen they used to have in London during the war. There is this man driving in his car, and he stops at a crossroads where he sees a policeman on the kerbstone. He lets down his window, and yells, "I say, constable, how far is it to Camden Town?" and the policeman puts his head inside the window and says, "My dear, it's simply miles away."'

I said, 'That's devastating. Do you know who'd have loved it?'

He said, 'Yes, I know, my sweet child. And he's dead and buried. Love is the sphinx with the riddle never solved. It's not only moth balls, it's also murder. And, talking of the sphinx, Oedipus solved her riddle – that's to say, he thought he did – and he went into Thebes, feeling very proud of himself, and look what a mess he made of his love-life. They've been talking about it for ever after; they call it a tragedy; but, as Talleyrand would have said, it was worse than a tragedy, it was a mistake. And, on the other hand, there was the sphinx. She committed suicide because he had solved the riddle. But I've never believed it. She took it with her, when she threw herself down the rampart at the entrance to Thebes.'

For a while we were silent.

Then he said, starting to smile, 'Talking of riddles, in another, earlier letter, of despair – he wants to know whether you took with you those recipes you had, for almond croissants and vanilla slices and – '

I said, 'Yes, I know. What about them?'

He said, 'Because, don't you see, if he doesn't commit suicide, he'll want you to bake them, every day fresh, for his tea. He still hasn't grasped the fact that you've left him. He's convinced he'll get here, take one of those residences you got ready for him with the McGregor woman, and while he sits upstairs in the library, perusing one of his rare books, you'll be downstairs, at the stove, baking, and every so often he'll call out to you not to forget to put the moth balls into the blankets.'

I slid out of the bed and he lifted me on to his knees, and I hid my face on his silk-clad chest, grateful for the coolness on my hot cheeks.

The end of April brought a return of what the inhabitants of Estoril called 'winter', with a thread-like, dense, chilly rain, though, as Katie McGregor liked to assure me, this was 'not a very nice way to talk', because winter might, as likely as not, mean sunshine and sunbathing on the seafront. But the tangled flowering shrubs in the garden now looked as though they had been freshly varnished, more like chintz than Bianca's *mille-fleurs* peignoir.

In the drawing-room a fire of olive logs had been lit and a pile of logs and a wicker basket with fir cones flanked the hearth.

Adhering to the taste with which the rest of the house had

been furnished, the fireplace was backed and surrounded by tiles, that were, in defiance of the commonly seen Portuguese patterns, of an art-nouveau design, deep blue-green with black-stemmed white tulips; while many of these were cracked or chipped, others had been replaced by plain green ones.

I had been sitting in front of the fire in one of the basket-weave chairs, shifting irritably from time to time.

I had put on a pleated woollen skirt of Royal Stewart tartan and my amber-coloured lambswool jumper which went so well with it, and my sleeves kept getting caught on the sharp spikes protruding from the defective caning.

The central heating had been lit in the morning and then been turned off again because the chimney was not drawing, and there was no telling how soon the chimney sweep, who lived in Monte Estoril, might come. As a reminder of this failure, the smell of soot and coaldust still permeated all the rooms.

As soon as he arrived, I joined him on the settee, kicking off my shoes, and letting myself be enfolded in his arms.

He said, 'It won't be long now. And the central heating in the new place has been converted to oil-fired. Only a year ago, they told me.'

I said, 'I'd have thought it would be early nineteenth-century Gothic, to go with the house.'

He said, 'I'd rather have had antique Roman central heating, with airducts beneath the floor. For efficiency, give me the Romans every time.'

I said, 'That's just it, the Roman efficiency. Do you remember how you told me about Portuguese servants and how they can't stand being taken to task when they've messed up something? I got Tacitus out, the other day, from the British Institute. The Annals – in English, of course. I loved him at school though he was devastatingly hard to translate, and now it's lovely to sit back with somebody else having done the hard work. I got to a passage about Portugal

– part of Rome in those days – and it was amazing really, just exactly the way you described them to me.

'It was somewhere in the north of Portugal – all the names were different, of course – and there was a Portuguese town clerk who got his accounts wrong. In Rome, at the ministry of finance, they knew he had been cheating and embezzling in a stupid way, because, if he hadn't been stupid, he'd have cooked the books better, and they sent a high-ranking civil servant to look into it.

'When this Roman got there and started to ask probing questions, wanting a precise answer each time, the town clerk could not bear it. Tacitus says exactly that: he could not stand being faced with these exacting questions.

'One night, when the Roman was riding home to his lodgings, the town clerk was waiting for him behind a rock on the narrow road, and killed him. But he did not run away. He went to the police station and gave himself up. Tacitus doesn't comment; he never does, he always keeps a poker face; but he drives home his point. That the Portuguese are not dishonest, but they are inefficient and they can't bear being found fault with. And in this, Rome couldn't understand them.'

He said, 'My dearest child. That's marvellous.'

I said, 'If you were John H., you'd say, "What is it with Tacitus? You can't eat him or drink him." But no. Perhaps not. If it was to do with accounting, he'd take an interest.'

For a while we were silent, looking at each other, he with his soothing, reassuring smile, which might have been mistaken for a benevolent one, the practised smile of the professional consoler, which I had recognized that first time I had met him at the Montemar.

Then my mind went back to our second meeting, when he had asked me to dinner. I recalled him as I had seen him then, in the dark red velvet jacket, the glossy waves of white hair, the calculating intelligence of the blue-grey eyes belying the heartening smile – it was the red velvet that now completed the picture for me.

In the castle in Salzburg, the erstwhile residence of the ruling Prince Bishops, there are corridors lined with portraits of those reigning cardinals, mostly of the baroque and rococo periods, and it was there that I had seen him, over and over again, white-haired, clad in red velvet, ambiguous with paternal kindness and cynical calculation. He was the typical *éminence grise*, the schemer behind the scenes.

And I thought, now it is easy; when I meet Bianca again, and she asks me, 'What's he like?' I'll say, 'Think of a cardinal of the eighteenth century, and you've got him.'

He said, 'Maria do Carmo tells me that there was a phone call for you today; a woman, English speaking. I hope you told the McGregor woman to refer to me, whatever it was.'

I said, 'It wasn't Katie.'

'Who was it then?' he asked.

'It was Ginny Sutcliff; Ginny darling I call her, because she isn't a darling, if you see what I mean. I know her and she knows me, though we've never spoken.'

'What did she want?'

'She was trying a *rapprochement*. She'd heard I was going to live in the Vasconcelos house, and was trying to find out how I had brought it off. The Vasconcelos had been holding on to it for years, keeping it empty and not wanting to sell; and then she went on about Shepherd, how we'd both known him and wasn't it dreadful, and how she had always wanted to get to know me, and couldn't we meet now that I was going to settle down in Estoril.'

'Ah, yes,' he said. 'She is one of the Stafford crowd, isn't she?'

I said, 'She is; she is with Baron Vierwald and company, and she's not like me; she's tall and big and silver-blonde and she hasn't got a fear of life.'

He said, 'Ginny darling taking you under her wing in the Stafford. And if you were lucky, another American barman behind the counter. Did you say you'd meet her?'

'I left it open.'

He said, 'I absolutely forbid you to see her or anyone else

of that lot. Is that understood?' And when I did not speak, he added, 'And while we are on the subject, I forbid you to see anyone, unless I approve of them. Is that clear?'

And he took me round the waist and held me tight against his chest, and I thought that I could never tell Bianca how he oppressed me, because, what with her being so down on him, she'd want me to come back to London and she'd say, 'You bloody fool; you couldn't stand James, and now you've gone from the frying pan into the fire. With James at least you were free to move about and he was proud to show you off. You must be crazy.'

I said, 'Has there been any more from James?'

He said, 'Oh, yes, reams; eight pages the last time. He's got his visa now from the Consul and a room reserved in the Coimbra – not that it was needed because they're half empty anyway, this time of the year, so he might have saved himself the cost of the wire. If only he had consulted me.' After a pause he added, 'I'm not going to tell you the date of his arrival. I'll tell you when it's over though, I promise you.'

He released me from his arms and when I sat up straight he caught me round the waist again and slid a hand beneath my skirt and up between my thighs and I gasped and tried to twist away from his insistent fingers.

He said, 'My sweet child, you are so delicious in your pleated skirt; you are like a schoolgirl of fifteen, and you behave like one too, always trying to resist me and to get away from me. The only time you are good and don't put up a fight is when you are asleep. Then I feel like a satyr with a sleeping nymph, because I'm really taking advantage of you.'

I tried to sit up but he tightened his hold on me. I said, 'When I'm asleep. Oh, God. You couldn't.'

He said, 'I could and I do. What am I to do when I get here, at three in the morning, and I haven't seen you for days? Take on Ginny darling, big, blonde and not afraid of life? We are not going to have tears, now, are we?'

I sank back into his arms.

He said, 'I know you are upset because I've put my foot down about Ginny darling in particular and the rest in general. Keep still, now, my lovely child. I've got you pinned down like a butterfly under glass.'

The thin rain continued, steady and chill. The chimney sweep had come, with an assistant. After having finished his task, he had changed into an excellently laundered white shirt, bundled the soiled one under his arm, and walked away, followed by the youth, who had remained in his blackened clothes.

There was little improvement. The radiators were warm now, all day long, but barely warmer than blood-heat, and though the chill was taken off, the rooms became frowsty.

Maria do Carmo was convinced that, as the boiler had been originally intended for anthracite, and as this was unobtainable, at least in Estoril, the fault lay with the inferior South African coal which had been supplied. However, she also suspected that the unsatisfactory performance might be due to the defective lining of the boiler.

I realized that, had I been married to John H., the central heating question could well have taken the place of the tough silverside at meals and there could have been reproaches about my not being firm enough with the coal merchant, and I wondered why I had not had any letters from Screes, and how much Bianca had told them.

And then, as though begging John H.'s pardon, I recalled that there was a lyrical streak in him, though buried, and remembered how, at Screes one spring, he had been looking out of the window at a flowering plum tree, and remarked, 'Once every year the tree is a bridegroom and in love.'

I was sitting up in bed, leaning against the pillows, and watching him as he paced about in the wine-red silk dressing-gown, and thinking what a pity it was I couldn't ask them at Screes whether John H. had one exactly like it.

He said, 'My dearest child, when she comes in to clear away the tea, tell her to bring you a bed jacket.'

I said, 'I haven't got one.'

He said, 'Then she must bring you a cardigan. And, in the meantime, cover yourself up better,' and he stopped, looking at me with a smile, as I obediently pulled up the blanket to my throat.

He said, 'Did you read Bianca's letter? I have a good mind to make this the last letter I am going to let you have.'

'Why?' I cried, sitting up.

'Cover yourself up,' he said. 'This is more important than Bianca's letter. This is more important than Bianca. It's about time this whole Bianca business stopped.'

'But why?' I cried again, clutching at the blanket which had slipped down.

He crossed over to the window and leant against the sill. 'For various reasons.'

I said, 'Are you going to treat me like a Portuguese servant, giving me an order and not explaining why?'

'Calm yourself down, first, my sweet child. I must admit I have been tempted for a long time to treat you, yes, like a Portuguese servant. In this matter.'

I said, 'It's true, of course, that Bianca's got her knife into you. And I can't really see why, what with John H. being all over you. Really, if you knew him, you'd know he's been simply raving about you.'

In her last letter Bianca had written, 'This Dr Barros Torres de Mascarenhas of yours. You will be interested to know that I have asked John H. about him. He never met him but he knows exactly who he is. He was in the Anglo-Portuguese, as you said – though that's neither here nor there, nobody knew him at the time – but when he went back to Lisbon he was the right-hand man of Fasao, the lawyer who cheated Gulbenkian out of the foundation money and made it over to the Portuguese treasury, while Gulbenkian looked on, helpless. There was even a book written about it. It was a unique scandal of financial piracy, and it's never been forgotten in the banking world. You say 'Mascarenhas' to a banker, and he'll say, 'Fasao and Gulbenkian', and whistle. John H. says he'd love to meet the man, though I can't see why; he's a notorious crook, a criminal; he's down in the annals of finance like Crippen or the Yorkshire Ripper. I'd rather you'd taken up with an English-speaking waiter, as I wrote in my letter before. You say that James is due to come over and I only hope to God he'll get you out of this. What do you want, after all? If you play your cards right and if you really can't stick him in the long run, you can always give him a kick and come back here, as long as you get out of this.'

I said, 'Yes, Bianca is simply livid; she's never been like this before, over a man I've been with. No matter how miserable I was, she always stood by me, and she never carried on in this way. It's odd.'

And when he did not speak, I said, 'Perhaps it's because, in the past, I always met men through her. Claire says Bianca gave me her cast-offs, not only dresses but men too; but that's not true. Claire can never say one good word about Bianca, and what's she got to be so stuck-up about? She isn't all that pure. Look at Violet; she isn't John H's. Bianca did get to know them first, that's true, but only in a drawing-room way; like James, for instance, whom I met at Bianca's, but who was never keen on her. And now she feels devastated. She even writes in the post-script that she isn't like an umbrella which can be put away in a corner when it isn't needed any more. I suppose she feels out of it because I got you on my own.'

He said, 'My sweet child, you did not get me. I got you.'

And I thought, yes, you've got me and I haven't got you; I'll never have you; I'm inside the cage and you are out of it. But even if Maria do Carmo had not come in just then, I would not have dared to say it aloud.

When we were alone once more, he came over to the bed and buttoned the cardigan over my throat and breasts and then he sat down on the edge of the bed.

He said, 'You really are like a child; one has to think of everything for you. When I call you my sweet child it is not only because you are twenty-seven and I am more than twenty years older than you are, which makes me old enough to be your father. And you, my little girl.'

I said, 'You are being ridiculous. Because if I were your daughter – you couldn't.'

He said, 'You mean, if you were my daughter I couldn't penetrate you. But of course I would; you don't think it would stop me?'

'I wish you wouldn't make that sort of horrid joke.'

He said, 'There was another occasion when you said the same thing to me – do you remember? And I was not joking then, either. And when I say that you make me feel almost incestuous, it is not a *façon de parler*. Because I knew your father. And you were born by then. If I were a bad journalist, I'd write, "When the two men met, little did they know that one day in the future one of them would – ."'

For a while we remained silent.

Then I said, 'If you did know my father, then it's more than I did. I was too young. I was two years old when he was killed, and Bianca says it really was a scream, his death; it's one of those sad stories that while you're telling it, you can't keep your face straight for laughing. And Bianca says it was all due to drink at the time and no harm done, because he and my mother were just on the point of divorcing.'

And, growing embarrassed when he did not speak, but continued to look at me in a calculating way, as though lying-in-wait, expecting me to tell him a lie and ready to trap me, I felt like the Portuguese town clerk when faced with the Roman civil servant. Casting about, playing for time, I said, 'It's devastating. As Maria Teresinha said to me, that time you rang up and asked me to dinner, about it being like a bolt from the blue that you knew me and yet she wasn't surprised, because the world is so small.'

He said, 'The world is not small, it is the circles we move in which are small. I was in London, in banking, and he was in the City in banking. With Lazard Frères, wasn't he? In arbitrage.'

'Yes, and the Brothers put up with him for a while because

he was a Thurlow – that is, he was a Tugendhardt from Kassel, though you wouldn't know it, they changed their name to Thurlow in the 1914 war, like the Battenbergs did, to Mountbatten. And he was an offshoot really; the main Tugendhardts are in America now, and going frightfully strong, like the Reinholds from Dresden, who are now part in Brazil and part in New York, but the Sao Paulo branch have folded up and gone into edible oils, whereas the New York branch, you've no idea – '

He said, 'My dearest child, let us not get lost in the mazes of the Reinholds and the Tugendhardts. Let us get back to your father, in arbitrage, with the Brothers. How do you go on from there?'

I said, 'Don't you know? He went down the drain, left banking and took up motor racing; ghastly crowd, Bianca says; rough diamonds, though there was a prince in it too, Prince Mirza from Siam; that's why his death is such a scream, Bianca says, and should be written up as reading-matter for six-year-olds in prep schools, because it's really a moral tale, and it just shows you.'

He said, 'My dearest child, Bianca is either a fool or a liar, and I'd opt for the liar. She must be. I don't know what her story is, but your father's suicide is not a fit story for six-year-olds.'

'Suicide?'

'Yes, suicide. Didn't you know?'

I did not speak.

He said, 'People couldn't understand it at the time; there seemed to be no reason for it. But if they'd asked me, I could have told them exactly what had happened. I'll tell you about it later. Let's hear Bianca's story now, scream and all.'

I said, 'Oh, God, John H. always says that Bianca is such a liar and that I always fall for her lies. But, perhaps she didn't lie to me; perhaps it was hushed up and she herself – '

He said, 'My dearest child, shall we steer clear of conjectures, now?'

I said, 'The Brothers had put him into arbitrage – you've

said so yourself, that's no conjecture – and he left. Because he couldn't stand the strain. But Bianca says it was more a case of, we don't know how we'll be able to get on without you, but from next Monday on we're going to find out.

'He'd been hanging round with this motor-racing crowd before, but once he was sacked, he went wild on it, on the big international courses, so he had plenty of opportunity to get himself smashed up, and if he didn't, it wasn't for the lack of trying. You see, that's the screaming part of it, because when he went to stay with the Milne-Uppings in Newmarket for the weekend he fell down the cellar stairs and broke his neck. That's the beauty of it, Bianca says. It shows you, you can't get drowned if you're born to be hanged, sort of thing, and that's why it's almost a moral tale.'

'Very ingenious.'

'And he wasn't even drunk at the time. That's to say, Bianca says of course he was tight, but the Milne-Uppings gave out that he wasn't, what with it being before dinner; he'd just changed for dinner, and he wanted to show the butler something down below. He gets on top of the cellar stairs, he calls out, and the butler says, "Coming, sir," and by that time my father is at the bottom with his neck broken.'

He said, 'Yes, I see; accidental death in the ruling class. But the real accidental death was ruling class too, because your father shot himself with a revolver, gentleman that he was. It's only poor devils who hang themselves.'

'Like the cook in the Montemar? The elegant young policeman told me about him.'

'My sweet child,' he said, 'I know full well that this is painful for you and that you are trying to shield Bianca. Please stop dragging in the cook from the Montemar and everything else but the kitchen sink.'

I said, 'Does Bianca know? That he shot himself?'

He said, 'My dearest innocent child, knowing isn't the word for it.'

I said, 'But she wasn't there at the time; she didn't know the Milne-Uppings, only by hear-say.'

He said, 'Probably. And now I'll tell you how it happened and you won't like it. Not the least little bit of it. I have to go back in time, to when he was with the Brothers – and about that, too, by the way, you were deceived by Bianca. He didn't leave because of the strain involved in arbitrage. And he wasn't sacked, either. He did well there. He left for quite another reason.

'The reason was that one of the junior partners at Lazard Frères took a great liking to young Thurlow and kept asking him to his home. At that home there was a young wife, and she too took a great liking to young Thurlow, though in a different way, owing to the difference between men and women, which I'm still trying to work out. In my vile way. Even if you don't like it.

'The wife was about twelve years younger than the husband. She was chased by all the men and hated by all the women, but even those women who hated her had to admit that she was faithful. The men said she was a block of ice from the waist down.

'But with your father she melted. He was quite beside himself at the conquest, and in that state, he was reckless; it was a wonder they were not caught *in flagranti*. Which I always think is such a poetical way of putting it; awesome too, because it means in the act of burning.

'They were not caught, I said. But she burnt out sooner than he did.

'In the final row she says, "You bloody ignorant fool; you conceited clown. I never loved you, but my husband loved it; he was looking on. He was watching all the time, and every time, in our own house, in my bedroom, with that large mirror facing the bed. Didn't you ever wonder why we never met away from the house? Have you never heard of a *garconnière* or a *pied-à-terre*, or such like, in the village you come from? And do you still believe in Father Christmas?"

'This, you must understand, was shattering to your father. Think it through. Put yourself in his place. The story got round and he became the laughing stock of the City, Salomon Brothers, Coutts, all of them, up and down the menu.

'He took to motor racing as a way of bolstering up his pride; his manly valour, they said. But I believe he saw it as a way to destroy himself. Or perhaps both.

'At the same time he became prey to the obsession of chasing after women. Not just any kind of woman; only those who played hard-to-get. And every time he succeeded it made him feel better, but soon he was driven on again, because an obsession can never be appeased, no matter how hard you try.

'Now, we are in Newmarket. Houseparty. The hostess a dried-up old hag. The only worthwhile woman staying on her own is a major's wife; husband stationed abroad with his regiment. In the morning, Thurlow shot dead at the foot of the cellar stairs. Found by the butler. Mystery. I wasn't there, but I do happen to know what went on. Never mind that now; I'll come to it later. He says, "When can I come to your room tonight?" Then, "If you won't, I'll shoot myself." Then, "Is that your final word?"

'And this was where his fatal obsession took hold of him; his sick pride. He had to be true to his word. You might say, he died a heroic death.'

He looked at me for a long time.

He said, 'My sweet child. That junior partner of Lazard Frères is still about; less junior of course; I'd rather lost sight of him, so to speak. Naturally, I've been out of the City for years now, but I believe you told me that he lives in an apartment in the Ritz all the year round, is senior partner at Selwyn Reeds, and that his name is Albert Brainylow. A rare name; and there can be no mistake about it; and his wife of former years is called Bianca. Which I never knew. Until you told me.'

'It isn't true,' I said. 'You've made it up, every word of it, about Bianca and Albert Brainylow, and Bianca isn't a liar. Why should I believe you? How could you possibly know what went on at Newmarket at the Milne-Uppings, you never went near the place; and if you've made that up, you could have made up the other part too, about Bianca when she was still living in Hampstead and married.'

He started to laugh silently.

I blushed with indignation. 'It's logical, what I've been saying, isn't it?'

He said, smiling, 'There are things one cannot make up; like, for instance, James's suicide letter about the moth balls. The major's wife was Swedish, by the way, and she looked very much the part: icy blonde, with a broad face and wide cheekbones. Bit broad in the beam too. But quite a dish.'

'You knew her?'

'I knew both of them, her and her major husband.' He paused. Then he added, 'But I knew her better.'

I said, 'Then it's really true? I still can't believe it.'

'It's true,' he said. 'And even before I knew you and that Thurlow was your father, I knew that Bianca was responsible for Thurlow's death – without having had the privilege of knowing her name was Bianca, that is.'

I said, 'It isn't true. Bianca was my mother's best friend, they were at school together. And ever after – Bianca saved my mother's life – in Cheyne Walk – you know what I mean. And think, all she's done for me. I can't even begin to tell you. But you've always hated her. From the first, when I talked about her. You've even had my dress thrown away, the dress which was hers and which she gave me; the dress you spoilt on the first night. And I believed you, I was such a fool. I didn't understand what Maria do Carmo was saying; I believed you, and I didn't even bother to have a look at the dress. Now you make me feel as though – as though I've betrayed her.'

'My dearest child.'

'You had Bianca thrown into the dustbin on our first night. That's how you put it, yourself. It isn't possible, your story. You are a beastly liar. Think of it, only think of it – she and my mother.

He said, 'Exactly. She and your mother. Don't you know

that Bianca hates men? Imagine how she and your mother must have laughed together, after your mother had married Thurlow; what a bond it was between them. And it was a bond. Cast-iron and water-tight.'

He moved to the head of the bed and slid his shoulders behind me and enfolded me in his arms. 'My dearest child, don't you know that Bianca has been in love with you, ever since you came back from school in Menton, ever since you were eighteen?'

'Nineteen,' I said. 'I took the *baccalaureat* at nineteen. That's the usual age at a Lycée, though you wouldn't know that, because you are ignorant as well as a beastly liar.'

He said, with his soothing, heartening smile, 'My dearest child, so be it, nineteen. But don't you understand that she looked on calmly, on your marriage to Badham, on your affairs, on James; she could afford to, because you were never happy, and that's why she was so marvellously loyal to you, just as she had been to your mother. And don't dare tell me that she was being kind and decent. She wasn't. She was in love.'

I went limp and he held me closer. 'My sweet child, I have been hesitating a long time over whether I should tell you or not. But after Bianca's last letter I decided it was about time to put a stop to it. When she lashed out against me.'

I said, 'Oh, God, only now do I begin to understand. Bianca always saying about Albert being a senior partner at Selwyn Reeds and in bed a zero. And then, how she had to get a divorce, because she had to get free; I didn't understand that, either. Because I kept wondering, why did she want to get free, when he gave her *carte blanche* with men; she could have affairs, and she didn't even have to go to bed with him, ever. It all fits in, now. Poor Bianca. And it's all your fault, really; it's you who are disgusting; it comes from reading my letters. You shouldn't read other people's letters.'

He said, 'My dearest child, you really are priceless. After all Bianca's filth and lies and betrayals you get morally indignant with me because I have been reading your letters. And thank God I did. I had a feeling all along there was something unsavoury and unhealthy about this so-called friendship of yours.'

I said, 'Now you're talking like John H. He's always told me that Bianca was a liar and that I shouldn't believe her. He's all there, really, though you wouldn't think so, what with him always going on about the meat and the cheese scones; and he knew who you were and what you were, even at a distance, while I, being here with you, didn't have the faintest. Odd, really, isn't it?'

'Nothing odd about it; it was only to be expected that he should know who I was. What was odd, what was – well, I suppose it was to be expected, too – was that Bianca used it against me and made me out a notorious crook. Which I am. It just depends on which side of the fence you are.'

The rain continued steadily and the flowering shrubs in the garden, though now bedraggled, dim and soggy, still kept reminding me of Bianca's *mille-fleurs* patterned dressing-gown.

It was in the early afternoon. He had just arrived and we were in the drawing-room, sitting in front of the fire.

I said, 'I still think you're being unfair to Bianca. You should be grateful to her. Because, if James hadn't seen the wall hanging in her room and set out to prove it was not Spanish but Portuguese, he'd never have got the idea of settling down in Portugal and he wouldn't have sent me to Estoril and you'd never have met me.'

He said, 'And I must be grateful to the American professional killer; if it hadn't been for him I'd never have met you. And I must be grateful to Shepherd having gone to the dogs and been a wash-out as a spy, or the American would never have come here. And so on. Where am I to start being grateful and where am I to stop? What a child you are.'

I got up and put two short logs on the fire.

He said, 'I don't want you to do that. Next time ring for her and let her do it. I don't want you to get a splinter in your hand.'

I said, 'Yes, you are right. But it'll be a problem. Because Maria do Carmo, being a housekeeper, will find it beneath her dignity, and she won't let her niece come here, into the drawing-room, ever; she keeps her tethered in the kitchen quarters like a goat. Though goats aren't tethered in kitchens, but you know what I mean.'

And, seeing his smile, I went on, 'That reminds me of the time I went to see Madame Vasconcelos, when the house was bought. She had a white-gloved maid to replenish the fire. It was devastating. I wrote to Bianca about it; I knew she'd be thrilled.'

He said, 'But I have no intention of providing Bianca with thrills. And you must stop writing to Bianca, now.'

I did not speak.

He said, 'My dearest child, you still have not understood the Bianca situation. But, before we go any further. What was there between you?'

I said, 'Nothing. I know very well what you are driving at, and you're barking up the wrong tree. I've never even – seen her.' I got up and, with one foot, pushed the basket with the fir cones farther away from the hearth.

He said, 'That's not true; don't lie to me. I've told you before that you are a bad liar.'

Turning round, I said, 'Bianca is very discreet and modest. She'd never dash out of the bathroom with nothing on, the way I do. And when I went upstairs with her, to talk to her when she was getting ready to go out to dinner, she was always in her peignoir and with her underclothes on.' I remained standing, leaning against the mantelpiece.

He said, 'My dearest child, where is your reasoning? May I remind you that on our first night, the first time, on the settee, you were fully dressed. And I got there just the same.'

'Stop it,' I said, and, turning to the hearth, I put my crossed arms on the shelf of the mantel and burst into tears.

He said, 'I'll stop if you tell me. Come here.'

He took me on his knees. 'I only saw her naked once. She asked me what lotion I put on, after my bath, and then she said she used pure olive oil, all over her body, every day, though she didn't really know whether it did any good. And would I like to see. And I said, "Yes, please, very much." So we go upstairs and she takes off her things and stands herself in front of the tall, tilting looking-glass by the window, and turns round and round, slowly, like a figure on a revolving stand in a shop window.

'And I say, "Bianca, thank you very much, it was lovely." And she inclines her head. Like an actress on the stage. Then I went out of the room. I didn't want to see her getting dressed again. It would have spoilt it. It would have been like – a profanation. Of a secret.'

'I see. It was a sacred act between you, was it?'

'Yes, that's the word.'

'My sweet child, it is even worse than I thought. Adoring and being adored. A mystical union. Eternal love. Beyond the grave.'

'Stop it,' I said. 'I've told you the truth and now you make fun of it; it isn't decent.'

He said, 'My dearest child, I'm not making fun of it. I just wanted to get my bearings. Now, you must write to her and tell her it's over.'

I said, 'But why? I'm here and she's there; I can't go round to Curzon Street any more, the way I used to. Why can't I at least – why should I hurt her? She's never hurt me.'

He said, 'You don't understand. That kind of woman – she'll make endless trouble. I want you to keep in with them at Screes, but with her, it's got to stop, once and for all.'

'I can't do that. Never.'

He said, 'Never say never,' and, when I did not speak, he added, 'Besides, once you say you will never do something, you are getting near to doing it.'

'But what am I going to tell her?' I asked.

He said, 'You needn't go into details. No whys and wherefores. Put the blame on to me; say that I am a beast and that I have forbidden you any further contact. Which is the truth. And the only truth she'll understand. Because, once you come with reasons and arguments there'll never be an end to it. Now will you do this?'

I dabbed my eyes. 'You mean, treat her like a Portuguese servant?'

'Exactly, my sweet child.'

For a while we were silent.

Then he said, 'Well, at last we've settled that. First you can't and then you can. You never can give in at once, can you? All according to rule. *Mulier semper variat.*'

I said, 'It's much prettier in French. François I, the king, translated it as, *Femme toujours varie, fol est qui s'y fie.* Our Latin teacher, Monsieur Ruelle, taught us the two together. He was a defrocked priest, and grim and strict, but whatever he taught, he knew how to make it stick forever. For life.'

He said, 'As long as Monsieur Ruelle kept strictly to teaching you Latin, in his strict way. Did he or didn't he?'

'Whatever makes you think not?'

'Because, my sweet child, even when you can control your voice, you cannot control the expression in your eyes. Now, tell me.'

'There is really nothing to tell.'

'Tell me the nothing first, and then the really.'

'I was his favourite,' I said, 'and I never knew it. At the time. I only found out later, a year after the *baccalaureat*, when I came to Menton for a short time – my mother had just died – it was in the summer, the Lycée was closed and I thought, I felt so – I wanted to ring him up. First a woman came to the phone and was very sympathetic, saying, "An old pupil, yes, of course, he'll be so pleased." And then he came on. He said, "Eve, so frail and pale and graceful, always my favourite. I always thought of you as a ballerina; you have the ballerina face and the ballerina figure. What's become of you? You haven't gone into dancing, by any chance?" And when I laughed, he said, "For four years I've watched you, the graceful Eve. Now, as you know, in the classical epos there are two kinds of adjectives: the *constans* and the *ornans*. When I say, graceful Eve, which is it?'' I said, ''The *constans*.'' He said, ''Excellent. I'm satisfied.'' And click, down went the receiver. Didn't even say goodbye. That was the way he was. Grim.'

He said, 'My sweet child, I'm going to do now what Monsieur Ruelle had been wanting to do for four years.'

As April drew to its close I felt touched by the opposite of persecution mania; that is, it seemed that people were being nicer to me.

It had started in the post office, when, standing beside me at the counter, she had said, speaking in French, 'I see that you have a crocodile bag; I've seen you with it nearly every day. When the time comes to freshen it up, I've got just the man, in Lisbon. He doesn't touch anything but crocodile. He's from Timor. He's very clever.'

She was one of the ladies of the circle. She might have been the elegant young policeman's cousin, whom he had greeted by kissing her on both cheeks.

I could not have picked her out had I seen her among the others, all with their hair dyed, not an extreme black or blonde, but a discreet brown, and dressed in the same smoothly domed shape, all trim and flattened, all looking at the world with the sullen eyes of victims.

She had bidden me goodbye, saying, 'Do come and join us, next time you are under the arcades, and I'll have the address ready for you.'

I had asked his permission. There had not been the stark, 'I absolutely forbid you,' or the equally adamant but more tempered, 'I don't like the idea of'. He had said, without hesitating, 'I'm perfectly agreeable, my dearest child. I know the lot of them, and if I don't know them, I know about them, and, if I had to, I could probably tell you to a penny the solvency of each of their husbands.'

I had thus achieved without trying, what Katie McGregor had not been able to do in thirty years, and now, the rain having ceased, I could take my place in the circle of seats, beneath the hugely spreading tropical oak, and be received, not with smiles, because these were exceedingly scant, but with looks of benevolent resignation, the looks of sufferers ready to welcome one of their own kind.

It was rather like the case of Bianca's butler who had said, 'Sorry sir,' upon seeing Bianca in the bath. Up to the present time they had seen me, without looking at me. But now their knowledge of Mascarenhas behind me had carried me out of a shadowy distance into a lit-up proximity.

I had even gone so far as to probe their permanent lack of gaiety. 'You are always so sad,' I said to one of them, and received a clear-cut prompt reply, 'One never laughs; laughing is vulgar. Though with men it's different.' And when I asked him about it, he had agreed, adding, 'You are expected to look – not discontented – but wistfully melancholic, and you'll have to adapt yourself to this.'

They none of them spoke English, and they all spoke French, and their talk was exactly as I had known it would be, when I had watched them enacting it, while sitting at my table under the arcades.

To my surprise it never bored me. I put this down partly to the glow of satisfaction I felt at belonging to the circle, partly to relief at the return of serene sunshine. I knew that I did not really fit in and this was not because I was twenty-seven to their late forties, or because I was non-Portuguese. Bianca would not have fitted in, either. But if Claire had come and sat down under the tree, she would have so entirely belonged that no one would have even noticed that a newcomer had joined them. I never found out by what runnel the gossip about me and my situation had trickled down to them. Yet, obviously, they now accepted me. Though I was a 'woman of fate', as the elegant young policeman had put it, when telling me about Maria Teresinha. Yet I knew that Maria Teresinha, more elegant and better groomed than I was, and with perhaps, more winning ways, could never have been admitted to the ladies' circle.

Although the rain had ceased and the weather was fine, and April was at its end, one could not have said that spring had come. There was no spring in Estoril. Some flowers had vanished, others had taken their place, and others again would take their place in winter. The only sign of spring which I could recognize was the scant appearance of cherry or pear in bloom, and these to me were shockingly wrong, humiliated as they were when seen outlined against a sky of such deep blue that it seemed to crush the modest delicacy of their blossoms.

We had not quite finished dinner.

The dining-room, which was small and square, made it obvious that the Misses Pinto Basto had never intended to give dinners for the forty closest members of their family. The round table resting on a handsome pedestal carved in the shape of outward-curving foliage, could seat four people comfortably and, at a pinch, six.

Maria do Carmo had told me that it was made to be drawn out into an oval, large enough for twelve, by inserting two leaves. Which were missing. She found them a few days later, in two of the spare bedrooms, each board in a bed under the mattress, from which I drew the, perhaps erroneous, conclusion that the Misses Pinto Basto, avoiding the main bedroom and the lascivious implications of its large double-bed, had preferred the chaste discomfort of single narrow beds, and had both suffered from back-ache.

In the dining-room too, one could perceive the struggle of straitened means against cultured good taste. The lamp above the table was a wreath of handwrought iron, but the four small lights crowning it were shaded by cheap pleated paper, and the chairs on which we were sitting, like those ranged against the walls, were kitchen chairs.

An attempt had been made to disguise their humble rush-seats by providing them with peacock-blue linen cushions on which the plentiful stains might have been due to spilt grease and wine.

Young McGregor, though, on a short visit with Katie, had ascribed them to the menstrual bleedings of the Misses Pinto Basto. His mother, furiously tugging at the string of pearls at her throat, had said that that was not a very nice way to talk, while agreeing with him afterwards when he said that the whole place was a bloody disgrace and in need of being done up and refurnished. Neither mother nor son could feel the charm of the house.

I said, 'I'm awfully sorry, there's only the fruit now. I'd counted on the cheese.'

He was peeling an orange with knife and fork, without touching it with his fingers, in that beautifully elegant way he had, which, I knew, I could never achieve.

I had ordered a Camembert from the grocer's boy that morning, but it had turned out to be both immature and rancid, and Maria do Carmo had thrown it away.

I said, 'It's heartbreaking. They sell the best French cheeses and yet they are inedible. They get them but they don't know how to look after them.'

He said, 'You remember. At our first dinner. I told you to leave the cheese alone. There's only goat and sheep, regional stuff, and I hate all regional dishes.' He began to cut the orange into quarters in an elegantly ruthless way, ignoring its natural divisions. 'And it's not only that they don't know how to take care of the French cheeses. They are left lying for weeks in the customs before they get cleared.'

I said, 'Is it true that there is a dish from the Alentejo, very garlicky, of course, where they put pork with mussels?'

He smiled. 'I'm afraid that's true.'

I said, 'She and the niece, they cook like mad for themselves, all the time; *bacalhao* and chick peas and that oil which has to be rancid, otherwise they don't like it, and other things about which I'd rather not enquire.'

He said, 'When you get to the new place, you must teach the niece how you want something prepared and then let her get on with it. I don't like the idea of your spending so much time in the kitchen.'

'You're spoiling me.'

'I'm not spoiling you, my dearest child, and I don't want to spoil the servants.'

'Anyway,' I said, 'I'm not suffering, the kitchen here is pretty decent, with all this marble on the floor and on the walls and even the kitchen sink carved out of a block of marble. I know marble is as common as dirt here, but for me it's devastatingly rich. The kitchen in Peel Street was grim; that was one of James's rising to heights and sinking to depths ways; the rooms were bristling with antiques and the kitchen, where he never set foot, was a slum. There were even slugs. When I came down in the mornings, there were the silvery slimy traces, in meanders all over the floor. They came in from the back-yard.'

He said, 'James. Silver slime. I quite forgot to tell you.'

'Oh, God.'

'Don't look at me like a wounded deer.' And, putting down knife and fork, shifting his plate to one side, and throwing his napkin on the table, he contemplated me for a long time, smiling soothingly, all the while.

He said, 'My dearest child, shall I leave you on tenterhooks or shall I start with the end, first?' When I did not speak, he went on, 'It's all over now. Finished. He's been and gone. Now, I'll begin at the beginning.

'You see, my sweet child, James got his visa from the Consul, as I told you, putting down an honest twenty Swiss francs on the counter – I even know this; he doesn't spare you anything in his letters – and in the train going back from Bern to Zurich, he sweated copiously, as he put it, the train being overheated. Tugging at you, all the time, to make you feel sorry for him. So far so good.

'I should explain that once a foreigner is here in this country, if he's well behaved it isn't easy to get rid of him. It's only naughty journalists who get booted out at the proverbial twenty-four hours' notice. On the other hand, when you arrive, you have to pass through the usual controls, immigration, police, and they don't have to let you in. No recourse and no explanation given, visa or no visa; the Consul is one thing, the police another.

'When James touched down at Lisbon airport, they made him turn round. I have no idea why; I was not there, and it had nothing to do with me.

'And so as to ensure that he would not turn rancid by being kept hanging about, like a Camembert cheese, they put him on the first plane out. He wanted Zurich, but, as it happened, it was going to Paris.

'And now you can go to the McGregor woman and tell her to forget about the gentlemen's residences she has been getting ready in Estoril.'

I said, 'You are wonderful. In your beastly way.'

He said, 'My dearest child, this has nothing to do with me. Surely you do not think I could influence the decisions of the police. These things are out of my hands.'

I said, 'God, and the booking at the Coimbra.'

He said, 'My dearest child, that was never made. I told them not to, at the time.'

'Sometimes you give me the creeps,' I said.

'Just as well.'

'How do you mean?' I asked. 'Do you mean, just as well it's only sometimes and not all the time?'

He said, 'No, my dearest child. You are afraid of me all the time, but it is only sometimes that you are aware of it.'

He had not come in the afternoon but at eight at night. Now, as we were eating the pudding, it was nearly nine o'clock. I was finishing the red wine I still had in my glass, but he had made Maria do Carmo bring back the white wine which she had removed after the first course.

There had been no soup. I did not have any ready, as I had not thought he would come, and I would have despised myself had I served anything out of a tin, the way Bianca had done when she had asked me and James for dinner.

The red wine had gone with the meat-loaf.

I said, 'Now, if John H. were here, he'd say, "What's this,

chopped dog? And, by the look of it, I'd say it's been an Airedale," and then Claire would hit the roof.'

'Ah, yes.'

'Do you think Bianca told them at Screes about my letter?'

'I doubt it.'

'So do I. She'd be too proud to tell them.'

'Ah, yes.'

'There is no cream with the apple crumble,' I said. 'I want you to understand that it's on purpose; I don't want you to think I've forgotten it; it's because there's already a devastating lot of butter in the topping. You can't be expected to know this, so I'm telling you. I don't want you to feel neglected.'

'I don't feel neglected.'

I said, 'Will you have more pudding? Because there is no cheese; the cheese you'll have to imagine, as John H. would say, though here he couldn't blame me for it; we're not at Screes.'

'My dearest child, help yourself first and I'll have the rest; or, better still, you can finish the lot.'

'Can I really? And you won't hold it against me, afterwards?'

'I promise, my sweet child. And I shan't have any coffee either. I have to go back to town tomorrow, and if I take coffee now, I shan't be able to sleep in the office tomorrow morning. But I'll have a whisky in front of the fire.'

I said, 'It's odd how one still wants a fire at night, despite the fine weather. Katie was right; the house is damp. But, you know, the weather being so fine again, it's all wrong; it makes me feel offended; it's sort of proof of how inefficient I am, because it should be raining now that we are moving into the new place. It always rains when one moves house, just as it does when one goes to the hairdresser and at funerals.'

He said, 'My sweet child, there is no need to upset yourself. Let them all get on with it in their various ways, and keep out of the way yourself. Madame Vasconcelos is going to send her own housekeeper along too; she's such a battle-axe no plumber or electrician could stand up to her. They say she'll live for ever because the Devil himself will be afraid to carry her off.'

'How devastating,' I said.

When we got into the drawing-room he put his glass on the mantelshelf and lit my cigarette and his, and Maria do Carmo brought a small bamboo table to my side and, as an ashtray, a pewter bowl which might have been an antique porringer.

I said, 'Good job you put down your drink over there, because this spidery table isn't safe. And it's no use Katie saying the place is dilapidated; if you ask me, it's always been like this, from the beginning, and there was never a table which didn't limp or wobble. I have a feeling the Misses Pinto Basto just liked lame-duck furniture, and I'm sure they went in for lame-duck people too; frightfully charitable and understanding. The whole place is symbolic of them.'

He said, 'My dearest child, you may well be right. But you haven't a sixth sense, have you, by any chance?'

'No, I haven't. Why?'

He went up to the hearth and took a sip of whisky. 'I was hoping, in a way, you had. What with your talking about the dead Misses Pinto Basto and those at Screes and Bianca and funerals.'

I said, 'I wish you wouldn't make that sort of horrid joke.'

I could not see his face because he was now taking another gulp of whisky.

Then he turned round and remained leaning against the mantelpiece. He kept looking at me for a long time, unsmiling, and with a calculating air. 'I do read your mail, as you know, but there are things I can't keep from you. Not in the long run. Besides, you'll have to write them a letter at Screes.'

I got up so fast from my chair that I knocked into the bamboo table at my side. It tilted over and went down with a splintering crash, followed by the dull rumble of the pewter bowl as it rolled over and over on the boards before coming to a halt.

He said, 'She was twenty years older than you are, wasn't she? Forty-seven; forty-eight? Typical case I should say, of the frustrated beauty with five-minutes-to-midnight panic; can't face getting old.' He reached behind him and took another swallow of whisky.

I gripped the arms of my chair and pushed it away from me. 'She committed suicide, did she?'

He said, speaking from the other side of the river bank and so far away that I could barely see him, 'Yes, of course, my dearest child,' and then, as the dark rushing waters came roaring over me, he said, still getting farther away, 'Steady now, we are not going to faint, are we?'

I said, 'No, of course not.'

'Of course not what, my sweet child?'

I looked at him. He was standing in front of me, bending down, holding both my hands. I was lying on the settee.

I said, 'I don't know.'

He was smiling in that lovely soothing way.

He said, 'Here is Maria do Carmo with some iced water; would you like that? I'd rather you didn't have the brandy one usually gives on such occasions. Do you want to sit up? Take it slowly.' And he sat down on the edge of the settee and put his hands under my arms and raised me up.

Looking beyond Maria do Carmo's shoulder I could see the niece, standing in the open doorway. It was only when I saw the bamboo table, lying on the floor, to one side of the hearth, that I fully regained my wits.

I drank some of the iced water and then I wanted to sit up straight, but he would not let me, holding me close to him, with his fingers gripping the soft insides of my elbows.

Maria do Carmo left, the niece having retreated already.

I said, 'I'm perfectly all right now. Really.'

He said, 'That's because you had a decent dinner. I took care not to spoil your dinner. And now you've got your colour back again; your usual pale colour; frail, pale, graceful

Eve. What wouldn't Monsieur Ruelle give to be here now, in my place.'

'Must you always rub it in?' I said, and I moved my shoulders and tried to get out of his grasp.

He said, 'I knew that would get you. I can see you are quite yourself again.'

'How did she do it?' I asked.

'Usual stuff, sleeping pills. You don't think she'd disfigure herself, like your father did.'

'In Curzon Street?'

'Yes, in the bath and fully dressed. She'd given the maid the day off.'

'She always gave the maid the day off,' I said. 'We had an argument about it, only a week before I left London; it was because of her thumbnail-size diamond, mainly, but you wouldn't understand; it's too complicated to explain.'

'Like the lobster. We still haven't got round to that, have we?'

'Stop it, please.'

'For the time being. Anyway, I hope the maid didn't swipe the diamond, when she found her. Pity you can't ask them about it at Screes. When you write. Your letter of condolence. Because that's always the only interesting thing about a death; who gets what and if not, why.'

'Must you be so dreadful and hard-boiled, the way you talk?' I said.

'Yes, I must, my dearest child. I'm not going to break my heart over a hysterical bitch. And I must say, they've taken it with great composure at Screes, too. Claire writes, "We must not grieve because this was what Bianca wanted." And John H. has surpassed himself; he writes, "You can imagine what we all feel like." Well, I know what they all feel like. There's nothing to rake in, is there? She had this allowance from Brainylow, didn't she? But that's expired now, and there can't have been much else.'

I said, 'I suppose not; I've no idea; she never talked to me about her money affairs.'

'And there is a Tindy staying with them now, at Screes. Who's he?

'That's Anthony, the younger brother. Claire's and Bianca's. He lives in Zurich.'

'You know him?' he asked.

'I only met him once, at Bianca's, just before I left. He recognized me too, just like Alvaro did.'

'He sends his regards,' he said. 'His fondest regards. And he tried to make you, didn't he?'

'Must you always – ?'

'Yes, I must. Answer me. Yes or no.'

'Yes, he did try it on.'

'And you told Bianca about it?'

'Of course I did.'

'And what did she say?' he asked.

'That men are ghastly.'

He said, 'Just what I thought. And here you are, far out of reach, and with a ghastly man holding you down. She can't have much liked the idea, can she?'

'Do you think she did it because of my it's-all-over letter?'

'My dearest child.'

'And when she asked John H. about you and he told her who you were. And then she got so frightfully nasty about you. And said how she'd rather I'd taken up with a waiter. Did she imagine – was she afraid, do you think – that you'd tell me about what she did to my father?'

'My dearest child,' he said, 'that's all conjecture, isn't it?'

'But, what if she did the same thing as my father. With the Swedish Major's wife. What if she wrote me a letter which I never got? Something like, if I broke it off with her for ever, she'd – '

He said, 'My dearest child, haven't we had enough of that with James and the mothballs?'

He was wearing a dark blue pin-striped suit, and with it, as he always did when dressed formally, a butterfly bow of the most conventional kind, dark blue with white dots, and his hand went up now to his collar and he straightened the bow in a gesture of fastidious disgust.

I said, 'But how can I know? How do I know, with you being as beastly as you are? Even with James, you never showed me a single one of his letters.'

He said, 'There is a golden rule: when a husband asks you whether you have seduced his wife, never admit and never deny. What am I to say, my sweet child? If I haven't done it, I cannot admit to it. And if I did, I have to deny it. In which case you'll never believe me. Will you?'

'You are too much for me,' I said.

'I know I am. Go to bed now. I'll call Maria do Carmo. I'll come a bit later.'

Maria do Carmo always took my clothes away after I had undressed for bed, to wash or brush or press what I had been wearing, and he never came into the bedroom with me.

He always expected me to be in bed when he came in.

But this time, after I had put on my nightgown and she had left, I did not go to bed; I was sitting on the edge of the bed when he came in.

In the weak, circumscribed light cast by the pair of wrought-iron sconces flanking the head of the bed, the dark red silk of his dressing-gown and the wave of white hair framing his forehead recalled to me once more the ambiguous countenance of the *éminence grise*.

He said, untying the belt of his gown, 'My dearest child, why haven't you gone to bed yet?' And when I did not reply, he said, placing his gold-rimmed glasses on the bedside table, 'If you won't tell me, I shall tell you, shall I? I can always make you weep, but you haven't wept at all for Bianca, and now you think you'll take it out on me, for her sake, in her memory; men are ghastly, and she wouldn't have wanted you to lie down for me. Am I right?'

I did not speak.

He said, 'My dearest child, you think I should respect your sacred grief, and you shouldn't let me.'

He took off his dressing-gown and threw it over the foot of the bed.

He said, 'Men are ghastly. With them it's, when you want to you are not allowed to, and when you are allowed to, you don't want to. When you can, you shouldn't, and when you should, you can't. But do stay as you are, my sweet child, by all means.'

And he came over to me, bent me back from the waist and, standing, took possession of me.

Robert Morley's second Book of BRICKS

JOHN MINNION.

Robert Morley's second Book of BRICKS

Cartoons by John Minnion

CORONET BOOKS
Hodder and Stoughton

First published in Great Britain 1981
by Weidenfeld and Nicolson Ltd

Coronet edition 1982

British Library C.I.P.

Morley, Robert
Robert Morley's second book of bricks.
I. Title
828'.91407

ISBN 0-340-28443-9

Printed and bound in Great Britain for Hodder and Stoughton Paperbacks, a division of Hodder and Stoughton Ltd., Mill Road, Dunton Green, Sevenoaks, Kent (Editorial Office: 47 Bedford Square, London, WC1 3DP) by Richard Clay (The Chaucer Press) Ltd., Bungay, Suffolk.
Photoset by Rowland Phototypesetting Ltd., Bury St Edmunds, Suffolk.

Contents

Introduction

ROBERT MORLEY

In preparing a sequel to the first *Book of Bricks* I was, at first, somewhat hesitant. The fact that we'd sold nearly a hundred thousand copies in hardback and it is e'en now selling successfully in paperback, tempted me to believe that it might be wiser not to try to repeat our triumph. However, both George Weidenfeld and the National Society for Autistic Children convinced me we should try our luck again.

I would like to start by expressing my deep gratitude to all the contributors and especially those who, like myself, have not left the fairground and are insisting on another ride on the roller-coaster. Some, including Dame Edna Everage, Ronald Harwood and Professor James Sutherland, have very kindly researched various aspects of brick-dropping and, whatever my earlier qualms, as soon as I got round to editing this book my spirits were immeasurably lightened by the sheer fun of reading the misadventures and entering again the mad world of those who, like Theo Cowan, hailing a taxi, almost squashed to death the incumbent passenger and then dissolved into helpless laughter.

We must assume that by the time this book is published the heir apparent will have successfully wed and, while hoping the whole adventure did not prove too hazardous to the various branches of the family, it might be perhaps permissable to start with a delightful collection of Royal Bricks generously contributed by Hugo Vickers.

Mr Vickers instances a number of bricks dropped by the late Duke of Windsor. In Tasmania in his early youth and on board the Royal Train, he espied in his drawing-room an indicator revealing the speed at which he was travelling. The dial registered eleven miles an hour.

'Bloody nonsense,' he is reported to have observed. 'They might at least have seen that this was working properly.' And, adjusting what he believed to be the regulator, he inadvertently applied the vacuum-brake. The train came to an unscheduled stop and the timetable for the day was considerably disorganized, especially as His Royal Highness was loathe to take responsibility for what had occurred.

In New Zealand H.R.H. was credited with having knighted the wrong man, while in Fiji at a ball at Government House, he opened the proceedings by claiming as a partner the lady typist of the chief Indian agitator on the island. In Melbourne, when the Prime Minister pointed out his son in a far corner of the room, the Prince went happily to where two men stood and shook hands with the one in evening dress only to discover that he was a waiter. At another dinner party in Australia the guests were invited to close their eyes and draw pigs on the menu. The Prince of Wales turned to his hostess and heard himself saying, 'I shall look at you and get my inspiration.'

I have my own personal reminiscence of a brick once dropped on him by my late father-in-law. The Prince at that time was President of Buck's Club, but for some time relations between he and the

President had become strained. My father-in-law was not a great reader of the gossip columns and one evening set forth blithely with the beautiful socialite Audrey Simpson for an evening on the town. At the Embassy Club, the equivalent in those days of Annabelle's, the great Luigi conducted them to a table next to one already reserved for the heir to the throne. My father-in-law was slightly nervous of his reception but when His Royal Highness arrived, all was apparently to be honey and flowers.

'My dear Buck,' said the Prince, 'how very nice to see you. I would like to introduce Mrs Simpson.'

'And may I in turn introduce *Miss* Simpson,' Buck said.

Something about the way he pronounced 'Simpson', as if it were in inverted commas, gave the unfortunate impression that they were both out with ladies of the town. My father-in-law was never spoken to again, although he narrowly escaped injury some years later on Sunningdale golf course where, as the expression has it, King Edward VIII drove through him.

Prince Edward's brother, the Duke of Gloucester, Mr Vickers reminds us, was not exactly a dab at light conversation. On one occasion, after witnessing a display of belly-dancing in Cairo, he was subsequently introduced to the performer. They sat in silence for several minutes before the Duke enquired, 'Do you know Tidworth?'

There are few instances of the present Queen ever being disconcerted or put out by the inane remarks made to her by her subjects although, when Robert Graves went to Buckingham Palace to receive a gold medal for poetry, the Queen told him it was the first time she had presented such a medal. 'Congratulations, Ma'am,' replied Graves, after which the audience terminated rather abruptly. But I prefer to think that Her Majesty had a busy day in front of her – possibly a Royal Garden Party.

It was on one of these occasions that I – flushed at the success of my riposte to Prince Charles who had enquired what on earth I was doing there, replied, 'The same reason as yourself, sir. It's good for business,' – then found myself conducting the late Prince Chula of Siam to a chair explaining that this was an admirable vantage point to observe Her Majesty actually sipping the Earl Grey. The Prince shook me warmly by the hand, stepped over the ropes and made

his way to the Royal Tea Tent where he stood for some time munching an éclair and making conversation with the Monarch.

Finally, as we step off the Royal Carpet, I am indebted to Mr Vickers for his delightful account of a dinner party presided over by Sylvia Brooke, the daughter of Lord Esher, then newly married to the last white Rajah of Sarawak. A lull in the conversation occurred, but, to her relief, she was able to announce to her guests, 'Listen, it's started to rain at last.' The guests remained dumb in silent horror as the young Ranee turned to see the old Rajah blithely relieving himself over the veranda.

Which reminds me of a tale still told at the Melbourne Club of an elderly grazier, unwilling to trust his bladder another second, seizing the sugar bowl, emptying out its contents and hastily transferring it to his lap. Alas, the sugar bowl was inadequate and for some minutes his guests were treated to the sound of rushing water. It became a favourite joke at the club for irreverent strangers to test the sugar for moisture and, on one occasion at least, demanding 'one of your dual-purpose tankards'.

I leave it to Andrew Sinclair to provide, in this volume, yet another gem of this genre. If we were giving prizes again this time, I would award it to the lady who prefers to remain anonymous but told me how, as a young girl, she was introduced to a blind man successfully manoeuvring his tea-cup at a party to which she had been bidden by her mother to keep him amused. Another guest had brought her dog and our heroine, temporarily at a loss for conversation, made an extravagant play for the creature, petting him enthusiastically until the blind man enquired, 'Is that a dog you're talking to?'

'Yes,' she told him.

'Do you like dogs?' was the next question.

'Very much, she said.

'Have you got a dog?'

'We did have a dog but he went blind and we thought it kinder to put him down.'

For me the charm of many of the stories in this book – such as Prudence Leith's account of the cat collar in the salad, or the wonderful slapstick moment when the bus conductress sat down abruptly on the pavement having been yanked off her bus with her own ticket punch machine – lies in the visual images they conjure up and we have thought it best to leave most of these to your imagination.

I have sought to include in this volume not only bricks but examples of absent-mindedness, though there is not a word of truth in the remark by Billie Whitelaw that I once left my own mother-in-law on the doorstep. With Gladys Cooper, such a folly would be quite unthinkable, though in my presence I heard her retrieve a brick with brilliant fielding. Talking of a friend with whom she had had an unexpectedly boring luncheon, she told myself and Robert Hardy, who was of course also her son-in-law, that she was 'sick to death of hearing complaints about sons-in-law'. 'I told Mildred,' she explained, 'that it was simply not the slightest use hiding herself in the garden when they came round. Make the best of it, stop belly-aching, don't hope for miracles. Even if the marriage should break up, your daughter might make the same mistake or even worse next time round. I told her she must learn to live with them [here there was the slightest change of expression] and she will get as fond as I am of both of you from the very first day we met.' She was, of course, guiltless of further brick-dropping. A brick was dropped in her absence for her, though, by my father-in-law who read aloud a letter from Gladys while my wife and I sat over coffee with him: 'I am so glad Robert seems to be turning out all right after all your fore . . .'

'After all your "four" whats, Buck?' I pressed home my advantage.

He turned to my wife. 'I can never read your mother's writing,' he told her.

It was my turn again: 'I thought you were doing rather well. Might I try and decipher it?'

'I think the word is encouragement.' He stuffed the letter into his pocket and bought me another brandy. 'I don't know when I've encouraged you exactly,' he remarked a little later on regaining his composure over the Remy Martin.

'You came to the wedding,' I reminded him, 'and when the registrar took us into his holy of holies and asked if you were still alive, I was the one who volunteered to pop out and see.'

'I never thought that was very funny,' he rejoined, and we were back, mercifully, on our old footing.

Returning to the absent-minded, I recall the tale told me the other day by a lady who, regaining her car in the car park, looked with dismay at the havoc wrought by vandals: 'I realised they had neatly removed the radio cassette player. One expects that sort of thing these days, but I was amazed at the skill with which they had not only pinched the instrument panel without damaging the upholstery but also completely removed the steering wheel. It was only when I searched for the handbrake that I realized I was sitting in the back seat.'

By some curious chance I seem to have thrown away a letter from a lady who wrote me about her husband who must, therefore, remain anonymous. 'Eustace', she wrote, 'is becoming increasingly absent-minded and has lately embarked on a course of "memory-mending" by post. Anxious to test his progress the other morning, he picked up from the kitchen table my shopping list which he briefly perused then, replacing the list, he departed for the supermarket, assuring me that he would return with all the items listed within the hour. When he did return, three hours later, it was to explain that although he'd undoubtedly remembered every single article on the list, when he emerged from the supermarket he was unable to remember where he'd parked the car.

'"All's well that ends well," I told him. "Let's check the groceries."

'He shook his head sadly. 'I think I must have left them in the Police Station when I reported the car as stolen."'

Finally, my deep gratitude is due to you, gentle purchaser, for helping an autistic child and we hope that you will enjoy our effort on their behalf.

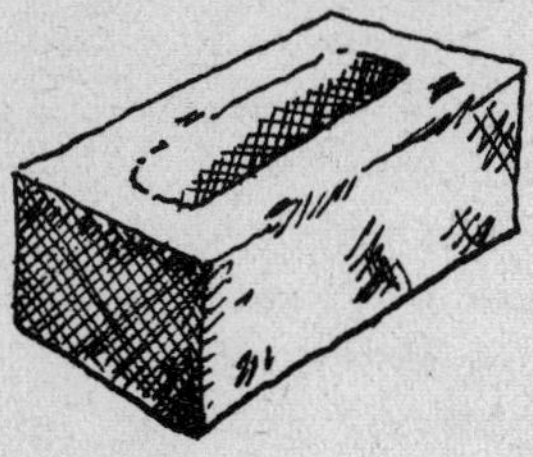

Katie Boyle

TELEVISION PERSONALITY AND WRITER

As a much-publicized and very genuine dog-lover, I have not one, but two stickers on my car voicing the opinion that 'Dogs Deserve Better People' and I always feel that if my own don't live well into their teens, I have failed them miserably. I have always gone in for portable dogs, and found that the old-fashioned Italian egg baskets complete with a small cushion are the best way to keep them both with me and out of everyone else's way. I'm so conscious of my dogs' comforts that I also carry a thermos-flask of water and assorted toys for them.

One day, I got into my car and had driven about a hundred yards when I saw a woman, then a man, then a child all making the most agitated gestures. (Oh well, fame is fame.) Then a woman virtually hurled herself under my wheels and, by a miracle, I managed to stop in time. When I, in turn, hurled myself out of the car to abuse her for doing something so stupid, I realized to my horror that there on the top of the car roof was Tessa (my Yorkshire terrier) sitting bolt upright in her egg basket and wondering what all the fuss was about!

Harold Evans

EDITOR OF 'THE TIMES'

I was with a party of fellow journalists and their wives at an eatery in the King's Road where they had a fiddler who came to the table to play love songs and his attentions greatly embarrassed the wife of my friend. He thought he knew the best way to cope with the unspoken entreaties. He took a £10 note from his pocket, showed it to her and then attempted to tip the man so that he would go away. To do this, without disrupting the host's conversation and upsetting him by appearing not to like the entertainment, he folded the £10 note and then leaned over the back of his chair to put it into the pocket of the violinist.

He found it difficult to get the tenner into the flap of the pocket and pushed and pushed. What he could not see, but everybody else watched with astonishment, was that he was trying to push the tenner into an opening at the top of the violinist's fly. The harder he pushed, the more the violinist bent his body to escape what he thought were amorous hands. But the violinist played gallantly on.

Brian Aldiss

SCIENCE FICTION AUTHOR

In the 1970s I was a guest at a large conference at Poznan in Poland. To give you an idea of how important it was, we were blessed by the presence of a live Russian cosmonaut – the Eastern bloc's equivalent of having the Pope to open the Birmingham Motor Show. I was the only English guest, but there were large delegations from all the eastern European states.

The official proceedings were deadly dull, but the 'après ski', as so often happens, was fun. In particular, I found myself the recipient of much hospitality from the Bulgarian group. This was before Bulgarian Technology had invented the Death Umbrella, and all was comradeship. Of course, Bulgarian national habits differ from ours: they drink fomented mares' milk, put their surname before their given names, and smoke a lot of cigarettes without incurring any Government Health Warnings. I also observed on that occasion that they have a wide variety of drinks – *kvass* apart – unknown in the West. I investigated that phenomenon whilst they plied me with questions about science fiction. In particular, they wanted to know a great deal about *Brave New World*. It so happened that I had boned up on that novel recently and was, therefore, able to respond rather fully, squeezing my replies through the language barrier, and waiting patiently, glass in hand, whilst the interpreter of the group translated what I said to the others. This took place in their suite. Rarely have I had a more attentive audience.

I told them what I saw as the sterling virtues of the novel, also pointing out a few seeming flaws. When we got to the flaws, some of them protested rather politely, somewhat in the matter of Canute, who bidst the mighty oceans deep their own appointed limits keep, without expecting much by way of response.

Finally, they had had enough and said, 'Mister Aldous, you have been very frank about your wonderful novel, and we thank you so much. You have been marvellously modest about it.'

Bill Tidy

CARTOONIST

Punch magazine, ever eager to submit their contributors to new dangers, had agreed to my idea that the life of a modern submariner warranted investigation. It wasn't my idea really but followed drinks on HMS ——— in Liverpool, where someone suggested I accompany a boat to sea and under.

Within days I was hanging, hands clasped at my side, beneath a helicopter somewhere off Gibraltar, while below me a very narrow submarine wallowed in a surprisingly brisk Mediterranean. Submarines have an aura of mystery and danger about them (What, go down in one of those things?) so I was determined to be cool and casual once I was on the thing.

Touch down. I was professionally undone, and hands pointed towards the tower or fin on which officers and ratings looked down with the detachment that the professionals delight in. The helicopter and wind noise made speech impossible, but I was a bit peeved at the sailors' wild gesticulations towards the fin. Christ, did they think I was going to walk towards the bow and jump in the sea? Smiling reassuringly I 'thumbs-upped' them and walked carefully, but knowledgeably, towards the fin. I knew from research that this type of submarine had a door in the fin. Ha, right in front of me was a nice hole for some unsuspecting idiot who had never been to sea before to

plummet down. I skirted it carefully, miming 'Yes, all right, all right I can see it' to the wildly waving fool in the frogman suit who was to save stupid me from falling into it, or over the side. Do they think I am ga-ga? Confidently I gripped the rail around the fin and inched my way along the narrow casing to the door which was closed. No handle! Hell, what should I do? Don't let the side down, Tidy. I pushed the door hard. Nothing, oops, nearly slipped – bloody hell, they are all watching from the top of the tower and waving. What was that? A tap on the shoulder, and a glaring frogman pointed back to the hole in the casing. Crimson with embarrassment I retraced my path to the manhole and descended the ladder.

Below, the greeting was sincere and cheerful enough, but to a man who'd studied *Jane's Fighting Ships 1978* (£34), 'This your first time on a submarine?' was the putdown of all time.

Mrs R. Wheller

My daughter Nicola works at the Technical College in Taunton, and has been deeply involved with the organization of a comparatively new department. Recently she had occasion to show an inspection committee over the new unit.

'How do you feel, Miss Wheller,' asked one member, 'now that you've got this project off the ground?'

'Actually,' said my daughter, 'I'm exhausted after only two days into the course.'

A shocked look spread over the face of her questioner. 'I beg your pardon?' he said. 'I'm exhausted', repeated my daughter, 'and we're only two days into the course.'

'Oh, I see.' He looked relieved. 'I thought you said after two days' intercourse.'

EXIT
HIS
HERS
JM

Michael Bentine

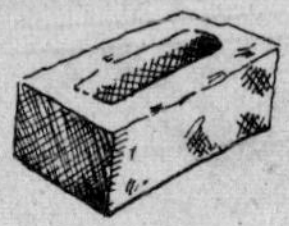

COMEDIAN AND WRITER

I was at an audition. There was a woman singing on the stage; her voice was so awful, that I turned to the man sitting beside me and remarked upon it. He replied very frostily, 'That is my wife.' Pink with confusion, I hastily stammered, 'I didn't mean her voice was awful, only the song she was singing.' To which he replied, 'I wrote it.' I slunk away.

Diane Cilento

ACTRESS

I was returning from Australia to Italy, just after I had produced my first child. At the time, my daughter was about five weeks old and I was carrying her in the usual wicker basket and was armed with mounds of nappies, gripe water, booties and bonnets. We had already been travelling for many hours from Sydney to Darwin, to Singapore, and then to an unscheduled stop, Bangkok.

I was anxious to take advantage of this unexpected stroke of luck, as I had heard that the Thai carvings, jewellery and paintings were beautiful, cheap and unobtainable anywhere else.

Having left my basket-load of baby in the hands of two enchanting ladies in the Mother's Room at the airport, I hurried off to examine all the tempting goods displayed in the stores. After an energetic and invigorating bout of bargaining, I became the proud possessor of a set of Siamese knives and forks carved with dancing figures, a large roll of Thai silk of varying purple hues, and a poster of some Thai boxers hurling themselves into the air at each other.

I rushed back to the airport clutching my booty in my arms and was hurried aboard the plane as the last flight call had been made some time earlier. The engines roared, sweets were passed around and I settled comfortably into my seat, contemplating with pleasure the surprise with which my delightful presents would be greeted. The great plane moved out on to the run-way.

As the roar of the engines gained momentum, I noticed that the chief steward and an air-hostess were whispering to each other, peering down the cabin past me, frowning and gesticulating as another hostess joined them and whispered urgently into the ear of the worried steward. It was quite clear that something was up. I wondered vaguely if we had a terrorist on board.

The sound of the great engines decreased. I glanced out of the window and in one blinding, heart-in-mouth moment the whole mystery was revealed: rushing down the runway were two lovely old Thai ladies carrying a basket between them which they lifted up momentarily for inspection. They were shouting but I couldn't hear a word.

The body-blush stayed with me for a good twenty-four hours; the disbelief and condemnation in the eyes of my horrified fellow passengers made the remainder of my

journey quite memorable. But there is no use denying anything: I just totally and utterly forgot that I was no longer a foot-loose and fancy-free woman whose oyster was the world. Listen, it can happen to anyone. . . .

Rudolf Nureyev

BALLET DANCER

It was the last day of my holiday and I was standing on the deck of a yacht in the harbour of Piraeus outside Athens. We had just had our last bathe. There was some delay about going ashore and I suddenly decided to have one more farewell swim. I flung off my dressing gown and jumped over the side. As I hit the water I realized that I had already taken off my wet bathing trunks. It was okay while I was in the water, but a bit more difficult when I had to climb back aboard the boat. But nobody seemed to mind.

I'm sure they weren't disappointed.

Roger McGough

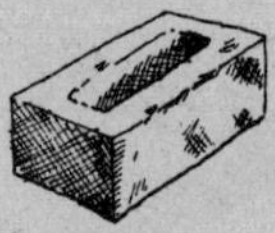

POET

Last November I was invited to give a poetry reading at Walton Jail. I was pretty nervous about facing a 'captive' audience of young long-term prisoners, some of whom were in for life.

It was a filthy morning, cold, grey and rainy, and I was led into the room after much unlocking and relocking of iron doors. I took off my mac, shook it, and said cheerfully, 'Cor, it's terrible out – you're lucky to be inside.'

Tom Conti

ACTOR

This was a situation in which I didn't know how many bricks I might have dropped.

Some years ago I went to meet the producer of a series called *The Explorers*. I was then taken to meet the director. In true British fashion, I didn't listen to the name, but his face was so familiar that I knew he was an actor turned director. We chatted amicably for half an hour or so. He knew my wife's name and that I had a daughter; I complimented him on having done his homework. The film was to be made in the Australian outback and we talked of the inadvisability of taking families on the 'shoot'. I asked whether he was taking his wife with him and the ages of his children, etc., all the while struggling to think who was the owner of this so familiar face.

As I left the office the name came – along with a cold flush and a mild buzzing in the ears – Lord Snowdon. I showed nothing of course, but made my customary exit, trying to open the door the wrong way, catching my belt on the handle and trying to say a controlled 'goodbye' before calmly walking into the tea trolley in the corridor.

I tried to 'play back' the conversation. How many bricks must I have thrown at him? What ghastly questions might I have asked? What was the last thing I saw you in? Is your wife an actress?

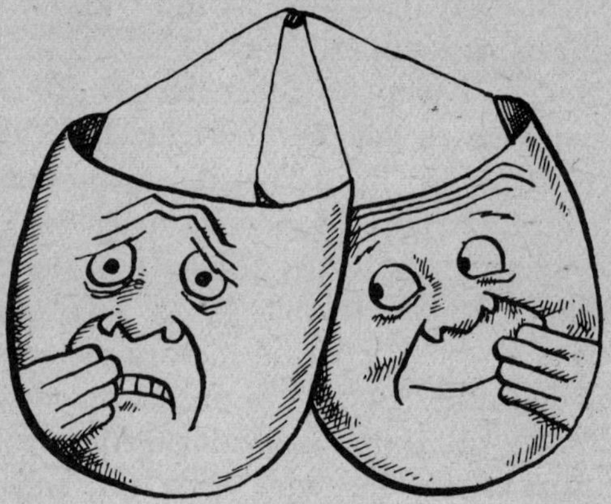

Theatrical Bricks

RONALD HARWOOD

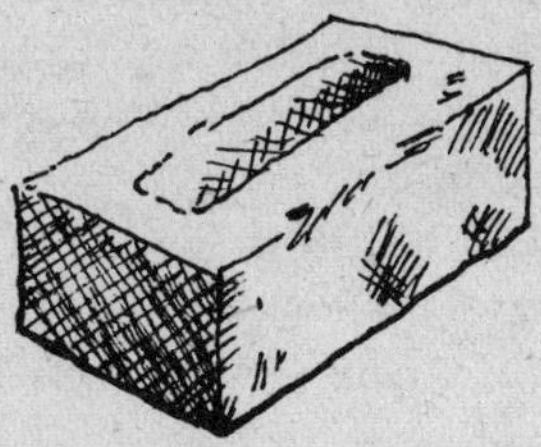

Theatrical bricks: the very words conjure up a flamboyant image as though to qualify for the category they have to be dropped with certain glittering panache. The truth, however, is, that theatrical bricks differ very little from any other sort of brick except in two important respects: the sound they make on the way down, and the damage they do on landing. Because more often than not they are loosed by the famous or in the presence of the famous, every nuance of tone and timbre is recorded and reproduced by the wags and wits with malice and mischief. And because actors, for all their outward show of bravura, are for the most part inwardly timid, easily hurt and childlike in their need for encouragement, the theatrical brick can be a lethal missile which will dent an already insecure ego, shatter a fragile self-confidence and cause irreparable cracks in elegant and celebrated façades.

Audiences can be devastatingly, if unintentionally, savage. Perhaps because we live in the Age of Television audiences are slow to realize that stage actors can actually hear what is being said in the stalls. During a performance of *Waiting for Godot*, the well-built Peter Bull heard an elderly dowager utter in a clear voice, 'I do wish the Fat One would go!' And in Edinburgh, while watching a distinguished actress as Cleopatra, a genteel Scots landlady said to her neighbour, 'Does she not put you in the mind of Mrs Wishart?' Bricks destined to haunt.

The late Henry Kendal once told me that an elderly woman seated opposite him on a train leaned forward, tapped him on the knee and asked, 'Excuse me, but didn't you used to be Henry Kendal?' I myself was once introduced to a genial old man at a party who didn't at first catch my name and asked me to repeat it. I did so in good clear tones. Clutching my hand tightly he said, with some relief, 'Oh, thank God, I thought you said Ronald Harwood,' a moment not easily forgotten.

The printers of theatre bills also have the habit of hitting the bull's eye. In Libya I saw a poster announcing 'Edward Jackall in *The Day of the Fox*', and Athene Seyler was once billed as 'Ateeny Sailor'.

Actors are at their most vulnerable after a performance. Tired but hopeful they wait in their dressing-rooms for friends and fans to coo and congratulate. Inevitably then, the dressing-room is the most common setting for a pile-up of bricks. For example, to Robert Helpmann who had just played Hamlet, Esmé Percy is reported to have said, 'My dear, you're the best Hamlet I've seen since Sarah Bernhardt.'

Sir Seymour Hicks, famed as a light comedian, once played a loutish cruel villain who was beastly to animals and ended up by killing his father. The great Henry Irving came round to see him after the performance. 'You held the audience in the palm of your hand, my boy,' he said. Hicks was understandably flattered. 'Did I, Sir? I'm proud you think so.' 'Yes, I do,' Irving said, 'but light comedy is your game. I shouldn't annoy them with this other stuff if I were you.' There is, incidentally, an infallible method of avoiding the dressing-room brick. If you are unlucky enough to have to be back stage to see an actor after a bad performance, take a leaf out of W. S. Gilbert's book: 'My dear chap,' he used to say, '*good* isn't the word.'

The actor's natural habitat is, of course, the stage and here the damage is often self-inflicted and always public. I am told that one young man still has nightmares about the following disaster. The play was *Anthony and Cleopatra*; the place Stratford-on-Avon; a full house; the long season nearing its end. Enter Antony and his servant towards the finale of the tragedy. Antony, defeated in battle, is disrobing in preparation for his suicide. 'Pluck off,' he says, wearily, in the hope that the man will remove his cloak. On that night the servant had lost all concentration, his thoughts were a million miles away. 'Pluck off,' Antony said again, a little more tersely. Still no response. '*Pluck off!*' he hissed. The servant came to and, misunderstanding, left the stage. Some say he has now left the profession.

In an amateur production of *Dracula*, the ball scene was held up by the non-appearance of the actor playing Count Alucard. The Grande Dame of the company, intending I suppose to save the situation by sheer force of wit, said in a booming Birmingham accent, 'Isn't it terrible about that man going about sucking all them people?' And Peter Wilson reports that an actress friend playing the co-conspirator in a murder mystery was startled to hear her fellow conspirator say very slowly and distinctly, 'I'll wear fingerprints so I won't leave any gloves.'

A story that nicely embraces the on-stage disaster and the insecure ego concerns a performance of *Hamlet* at the Old Vic in the late 1920s. Robert Speaight, as the Prince, lunged in the fight scene, ripped his tights and exposed himself in all his male glory to the entire house. He was a sensitive man and deeply embarrassed. The company tacitly agreed never to refer to the incident. During the course of the season Speaight also played King John and scored a great success. Ralph Michael, a member of the company, found himself beside Speaight in the gentlemen's lavatory. The two had not been particularly friendly but Michael thought he ought to pay Speaight a compliment. Standing there side by side, doing what they had to do, Ralph Michael smiled at Speaight and said, 'By the way, Bobby, may I say how much I admired your John?' Speaight glowered at him fiercely, buttoned up and fled.

One does not instantly think of directors as sensitive souls, yet one cannot help but have sympathy for Sir Peter Hall, the director of the National Theatre, when he revisited one of his productions of an opera which had been rather extravagantly re-rehearsed with a new cast by a young staff producer. Sir Peter fumed at the changes the man had made. After the performance, the two met.

Sir Peter (furious but controlled): 'Good evening.'

Staff Producer (blithely): 'Wotcher, Peter. How's tricks?'

Sir Peter (with great control): 'You've altered my production.'

Staff Producer (merrily and with a hint of suicide): 'I know. Better, isn't it?'

Another young man, fresh from university, had the nerve-racking task of directing a great actor of the old school. It could have been Sir Donald Wolfit. At the end of the first week of rehearsal the young man wanted to say something encouraging to the star who was obviously holding himself back until there was an audience out front. 'Well, Sir Donald,' the director said uncertainly, 'it's . . . er . . . coming along . . . very nicely.' 'Coming along? My dear boy, that's *it*!'

In the theatre, one man's brick can easily become another man's witticism. What usually happens is that a brick dropped by some poor unfortunate unknown is nimbly caught by the famous and hurled back with terrible venom. Take for example the young actor who was appearing in a comedy by William Douglas-Home. After a performance one evening the young man sidled up to the playwright and said rather grandly, 'I say, Willie, I wonder if you could give me another laugh in Act Three?' Douglas-Home's reply was masterly. 'Funny you should say that. I was about to ask you the same thing.' The inspiration of this book, Mr Robert Morley, is not unknown for his bricks but his numerous admirers, of which I am one, like to pretend that Morley-bricks are in fact Morley-witticisms. His old friend Llewellyn Rees once met Robert in Jermyn Street. The two had been firm friends in youth but had not seen each other for many years. Rees, known as Lulu, has a circlet of saintly white hair and is ideal casting for an archbishop. 'Lulu, my dear,' Robert said, 'where have you been? I haven't seen you for ages.' 'No,' replied Lulu, 'most of my friends think I'm dead.' Said Robert, 'Not if they look closely, surely?'

No discourse on theatrical bricks would be complete without reference to that Gold Medallist among brick-droppers, Sir John Gielgud. I have two favourite Gielgud-clangers. Once, when lunching at the Ivy Restaurant with the impresario Hugh 'Binkie' Beaumont and the actress Athene Seyler, Sir John discussed the casting of his next play. 'I don't know who to get for the old

1
2
3

woman. All the best actresses are busy. There's only poor old Athene left.' Beaumont closed his eyes; Miss Seyler smiled sweetly; Sir John must have sensed his clumsiness. 'Not you Athene,' he said quickly, 'the other Athene.'

In 1953, Sir John took a company to Salisbury, then in Rhodesia, now in Zimbabwe, to play *Richard II.* At the final curtain-call, he stepped forward to make his speech. As is the custom on such occasions, Sir John thanked all those who had made the event possible. 'In conclusion,' he said, 'I want to thank the wonderful stage hands. They've all worked like blacks.' They all were.

Geoffrey Bryson

A very dear friend, now alas deceased, was not noted for thinking deeply before she spoke. She was present at an entertainment in (would you believe) the Floral Hall at the Valley Gardens in Harrogate and one of the items in the show was a fairly impromptu fashion parade in which audience participation was invited. As the audience largely consisted of matronly Harrogate ladies, you can imagine what it was like. When the parade had finished, the compère – who as a professional entertainer should have known better – asked if anyone had spotted the Deliberate Mistake. My friend leapt to her feet and declared, 'Number four is a man.' Needless to say number four was a Harrogate matron in full sail.

Sally Bell

In the summer of 1966, when we were travelling on the ferry from Brindisi to Patras, I was standing patiently in a queue (very British) for coffee when Robert Morley's voice boomed over our heads – in Greek – asking for two coffees. In a flash he was served. I had to wait another ten frustrating minutes. If I'd had a brick I would have dropped it in his coffee!

ΔΕΝ ΦΤΕΩ ΕΓΩ ΑΝ ΔΕΝ ΜΙΛΑΣ ΤΗΝ ΓΛΩΣ-
ΣΑΝ ΚΥΡΙΑ. ΕΣ ΑΛΛΟΥ ΕΚΕΙΝΕΣ ΤΙΣ ΜΕΡΕΣ
ΣΥΧΝΑ ΜΕ ΣΥΝΧΗΖΑΝ ΜΕ ΤΟΝ ΜΑΚΑΡ-
ΙΤΗΝ ΚΥΡΙΟΝ ΟΝΑΣΗ.

JOHN MINNION

Carol Channing

COMEDIENNE

I was living in a rather smart apartment block in New York some years ago when, one morning, I discovered that my telephone was out of order. I had a very busy day ahead and a lot of calls to make, so I rushed downstairs to speak to our switchboard operator who handled all the calls for the building. Whilst I waited impatiently to speak to her, I distinctly heard her say, 'Oh yes, ma'am, I'll gladly book that call for you if you'll just confirm your full name – is it *Mrs* or *Miss* Duchess of Windsor?'

Tony Benn

MEMBER OF PARLIAMENT

This true story concerns the late Percy Wells, who was the MP for Faversham in Kent. His last train from Victoria Station ran at about 10.30 p.m. and therefore he was always anxious that he might miss it when we had a division at the end of the Commons debate at 10.00 p.m.

As a result, he used to push himself to the front of Members queueing up in the Division Lobby and, as soon as the doors opened, he would rush through and, having been counted in the Division, would dash downstairs and get a bus to Victoria Station to catch his train.

One night Percy brought his wife to dinner at the House and after dinner they were sitting having a cup of coffee when the Division Bell rang for the ten o'clock vote. Percy went upstairs into the Division Lobby, where colleagues pushed him to the front as usual, and then he rushed off to Victoria Station, where he caught the last train. But, when he got home, the lights were out and the house was locked, and he realized that he had left his wife sitting in the House of Commons. She presumably discovered what had happened after an hour or two and was obliged to spend the night in a hotel in London.

This story went round the House of Commons very quickly and ever after that, whenever there was a late vote, people used to make way for Percy and push him to the front, but they would always tap him on the shoulder and say, 'Have you got your wife with you, Percy?'

Percy was a charming, modest man, and this story used to amuse and embarrass him at one and the same time.

George Moor

For years I had taken the old pony through the woods to the stable. The path was very crumbly and dangerous at one point and I was using my accustomed soothing phrases when I noticed that I was addressing my bicycle.

Lord Clark

ART HISTORIAN AND AUTHOR

Although I have been elected to nine clubs and have paid the entrance fees, I have resigned from all but one simply because I have been too embarrassed to speak to any of the members. This is a ridiculous shortcoming, the more so as I am very fond of talking; but I am still unable to conquer it. My only recent effort to be clubable confirmed my fears. A dinner was given in the St James's Club for Oliver Chandos, who had been its chairman for many years and had just been made a Knight of the Garter. As he was an old friend of mine, I thought I ought to attend. I found myself among a group of members, none of whom I remembered having seen, who naturally did not address a word to me. After about ten minutes a man who looked like a Naval Officer, wearing a claret-coloured bow-tie, advanced towards me and said, 'You're Sir Kenneth Clark.'

I agreed.

'The Bart, of course,' he said.

'No,' I said, 'I am not a baronet.'

'But you must be,' he said, 'the other Sir Kenneth Clark is a fearful shit; everybody says so.'

'Well, I'm afraid I'm the only one.'

Simon Curtis

STUDENT

Early last year, soon after starting at a college in North Carolina, I was introduced to two attractive girls in the campus bar. One was coloured and the other white. I invited them to have a drink and they both asked for wine.

'Well, what's it to be,' I eagerly enquired, 'white or black?'

Leonard P. Belson

OPTICIAN

Every optician spends a considerable amount of his professional life adjusting spectacles which, through normal wear, have become loose and uncomfortable. We become quite used to hearing tales of woe from our patients who have sat on their spectacles, lost their screws or are suffering from broken 'arms' and 'legs'. But the demure, little old lady who confronted me this time was completely original.

'Can you tighten me specs, luv?' she asked. 'They drops orf every time I goes to the toilet'.

My waiting-room, crowded with patients, suddenly came alive. Magazines with the latest news of the *Titanic* and eye-witness reports of the crash of the R. 101 were put down and all heads swivelled round at this unheard-of phenomenon. I knew instinctively that I should not ask the inevitable question, but curiosity got the better of me.

'How can your spectacles fall off when you go to the toilet?' I asked.

I was treated to the type of withering look reserved for the imbecile, as she bent down to illustrate her reply: 'Simple, luv. When I bends dahn to pick up me knickers, they falls orf!'

Good enough for *Punch*, in which periodical circa 1900 I feel it must have been illustrated by the late George Belcher.

Lady Diana Cooper

AUTHOR

Not recognizing people has always been the cause of dropping bricks. I'm always telling people grotesque stories – which turn out to be about themselves.

The other day, when thousands of us were celebrating Sir Robert Mayer's hundredth birthday at the Royal Festival Hall, five hundred of us repaired to a special room during the *entr'acte*. There I was mooching around without an escort, when a nice little woman equally unescorted came to my side to ask me if I did not think it wonderful.

'Wonderful,' I replied, 'and isn't he marvellous?'

'Marvellous,' she replied, and so we rippled on in praise off-handedly for several minutes – during which time I noticed the size, sparkle and splendour of the diamonds round her throat.

The penny dropped. I bungled an arthritic 'bob' saying, 'Oh, Ma'am. Please, Ma'am. I'm so sorry, Ma'am – I didn't recognize you without your crown.'

Neither surprised nor coldly, she said, 'I thought it was Sir Robert's night, not mine.'

Of course I've dropped much more hurtful bricks all my life – through my eyes, not my heart.

Terry-Thomas

ACTOR AND COMEDIAN

I was fifteen and on summer holidays in Coombe Martin, and very ambitiously invited two girls and their very severe mother to tea in a grotto café in Lynmouth.

Having rehearsed the ordering of the tea, I was able to converse with the waitress in a lordly manner. I then relaxed for a few seconds, beaming with satisfaction at my impressed guests. Suddenly something clicked and I realized I had forgotten a vital ingredient. 'Waitress,' I called, 'I nearly forgot to order my very favourites – please add some Lemon Turd Carts.'

John Cleese

ACTOR AND WRITER

My favourite absent-minded story concerns (I believe) Soren Kierkegaard, the Danish philosopher. He wandered off one morning deep in thought and entered his local park. Utterly distracted by the demands of the problem that was absorbing him at that moment, he wandered across the lawns and right into the middle of a huge flower bed.

He was brought back to consciousness by an irate head gardener rushing towards him shouting, 'What are you *doing* there?'

'What are *any* of us doing here?' cried Kierkegaard.

Cynthia Isserlis

My mother to my husband: 'Oh, George, you *must* come and live in Suffolk. It's such a wonderful place for widows!'

Paul Dew

I once visited the home of a friend to leave a message concerning a jumble sale which we were jointly organizing. When I looked in the front door along his passage I saw a number of boxes containing clothes.

'Collecting plenty of stuff for the jumble sale I see,' I remarked to him, 'but I'm afraid you'll have a bit of a job with some of this by the look of it.'

'I happen,' he told me, 'to be rebuilding my wardrobe upstairs.'

Norman P. Coxall

In the 1960s, when London was swinging, the Beatles were at their peak and Carnaby Street was the Mecca of all the young trendies, it was very smart amongst the young set to go to 'in' places such as bistros or bistrotheques (which is a bistro and discotheque combined). The society photographer Tom Hustler ran such a place in Maddox Street called Fanny's; it's probably still in existence today.

My friend and I booked a table and took along two girls we hoped to impress. We told the girls that we were involved in Music and Fashion and anything else we considered to be remotely trendy, and they were very impressed.

On reaching the bistro, we were shown to our table and the waiter busied himself with the menus and napkins.

'Is young Hustler in tonight?' my friend enquired.

'You mean Tom Hustler, the guy that owns this place?' said the waiter.

'Yes, of course I do,' replied my friend. 'We're great chums.' This really impressed the girls.

'That's odd,' said the waiter, 'I'm Tom Hustler and I've never seen you before in my life.'

Lady Antonia Fraser

BIOGRAPHER AND MYSTERY WRITER

I have a particular fondness for literary bricks, having started very promisingly in my teens by insisting on conducting a whole conversation on the assumption that a man called Tristram Shandy wrote a book called *Laurence Sterne*. In vain my interlocutor tried, tactfully, to put me right. I gamely battled on: 'Ah, but Shandy's understanding of Sterne . . .' It might sound rather brilliant these days.

Two other literary bricks concern my great-uncle and aunt, Eddie and Beatrice Dunsany. Aunt Beatrice charmed me as a child with the story of the rich and romantic American Lady touring Europe – before the First World War, I imagine. She was enchanted with the Europeans – especially the titled ones. Overhearing a conversation about Machiavelli's *The Prince*, she contributed enthusiastically: 'Oh, the dear Prince! We met last fall and I just fell in love with him. . . .'

Uncle Eddie Dunsany – a man of wonderful and terrifying aspect – casually referred to a book called *Peace and War* during a conversation about Tolstoy with Maurice Bowra (then a young don). For a while Maurice Bowra managed to keep the conversation going without mentioning the title at all, thus avoiding the twin perils of contradicting his host and compromising himself. Finally,

trapped by the turn the talk had taken and deciding to go for politeness, he too alluded to *Peace and War*.

'*Peace and War! Peace and War!*' roared Uncle Eddie. 'You mean *War and Peace*.' And he retired absolutely delighted with the low level of culture among young Oxford dons.

Irene Handl

ACTRESS

Shambolic night began like any other night of my season at Watford. We were doing *Blithe Spirit*, a play which I adore, and I was playing a part which I adore, Madame Arcati. The company was in great nick, the laughs had been coming a treat right through the show. Only the last act to go: I arrive at Charles Constandine's house at the witching hour, fetchingly clad in Chinese pyjamas, bowed down by assorted herbs and strings of garlic, plus a deep sense of shame at my failure to definitively dematerialize that teasing, obdurate sprite Elvira.

I put my herbs down somewhere handy, in case they are needed for last-ditch tactics, and am starting on preliminary incantations when I become aware of a sensation that cannot be but recognized throughout the civilized world: the unmistakeable slither of trousers falling down. Suavely, inexorably my black satin trousers slid down towards my ankles, where they were firmly taken into custody by Madame Arcati's cycle clips. I was left standing in my Chinese jacket, my suspendered hose and my private underwear – a single garment of silk and lace known to the lingerie trade as 'cami-knickers'. Mine were red – a beautiful cerise, which lights more brilliantly than anything I know except tinned cherries.

The actor playing Charles's part exploded. Gripped by the terrible clips, I shambled into what I hoped would be the dimmest corner of the stage and tried to effect repairs. No use: the divorced ends of the waistbelt refused to be re-united and I would have to play the rest of the scene holding everything up. Ostrich-like I had my back to the house, so I didn't know that a malign moonbeam was lighting my tinned cherries.

After that nothing seemed to matter, as the whole place went up in an explosion of laughter which could be heard out in the street and wasn't extinguished on either side of the curtain till long after it had finally come down.

Olwyn Holden

One Easter Sunday morning my husband sneaked a caramel chocolate from our daughter's Easter egg. The next moment he was writhing in agony, the chocolate having impacted or trapped a nerve in a tooth. I rang the dentist, who offered to come down to his surgery in about one hour's time. I then rang the doctor who said to come over to his house and collect two very powerful pain-killers. I jumped in my car and drove the twenty minutes to his house, twenty minutes back, to find my husband practically passing out with pain. I rushed into the kitchen, poured a glass of water, and swallowed the tablets myself.

Hunter Davies

AUTHOR AND JOURNALIST

When my wife, Margaret Forster, went up to Oxford in 1969, fresh from her council estate in Carlisle, all the other girls in her college, Sommerville, seemed to be the daughters of famous people. There was Teresa Waugh who turned out to be the daughter of Evelyn, Julia Gaitskell, the daughter of Hugh, Judith Pakenham, a genuine Pakenham, and Annabel Asquith – a real Asquith.

In an effort to keep up her end, she started agreeing that the novelist E. M. Forster was her father. In those days, Mr Forster's private life had not been extravagantly explored and no one, apparently, expressed disbelief. Years later, however, an academic from an American University somehow heard the legend and wrote to my wife for confirmation. Had E. M. Forster been secretly married and would she supply some information about her mother?

By this time Mr Forster was, of course, dead and his version of the love that dare not speak its name had been published posthumously.

Anecdotes for the Interval

Lord Delfont

IMPRESARIO

Joe, feeling unwell, went to his doctor for a check-up. After a thorough examination the doctor pronounced that Joe only had a short time to live.

Shocked, the doomed man said, 'Will the end come in months or years?'

'No,' said the doctor, 'in a matter of hours, and, if I were you, I'd go home to bed and make myself comfortable.'

Joe did this but, becoming nervous, he called his friend Mo and said, 'I'm dying. Won't you come over and talk with me in my last hours?'

Mo did as he was asked and, after some hours of reminiscing, he fell asleep. Joe immediately roused him and said, 'Please, Mo, don't go to sleep now.'

Mo rubbed his eyes and grumbled, 'It's all right for you, but I've got to go to work in the morning.'

Serena Fass

TRAVEL AGENT

A friend of mine was driving along happily minding his own business, when all of a sudden a woman driver came tearing round the corner in the opposite direction on the wrong side of the road. Passing him, she rolled down the window and shouted 'Pig'. My friend, quite astonished by this insult, went on his way, muttering 'Silly old cow'. On turning the corner he drove straight into a herd of pigs.

Sir Fitzroy Maclean

AUTHOR

Some thirty odd years ago, as a very young and rather nervous Member of Parliament, I stayed a week-end with a prominent and influential constituent. His wife, also a pillar of the local establishment, had a fine head of red hair.

I have always been fascinated by the contents of other people's medicine cupboards. Combined with a strong urge to experiment, I have also always held the possibly rather dangerous view that, whatever it does to other people, no medicament is likely to have any effect on me. That night in the medicine cupboard I found a large bottle labelled 'peroxide'. I had heard of 'peroxide blondes', then much in vogue. My hair in those days was dark brown. 'I bet,' I said to myself, 'this stuff doesn't make *me* go blond,' and, rubbing several lavish handfuls into my hair, I went to bed.

When I woke up next morning and looked in the looking-glass, I found to my amazement that my hair had in fact turned bright red, exactly the same colour as that of my hostess, who, as she presided over the breakfast table, quite clearly viewed me with the wildest surmise. Since then I have been rather more careful – at any rate with peroxide.

Cleo Laine

SINGER

Like lots of mothers with first-borns and first walks to the shops, I left my baby outside the butcher's and walked back home alone. While preparing the tea, I experienced a strong feeling of loss, of something misplaced. When my mother came in to ask where young Stuart was, I didn't wait to reply but sprinted back to find him quite happy, still outside the family butcher's shop.

Our third child also suffered, but not in the same way. Moving to a new house necessitated a change of school for young Jacqueline, my daughter. I enrolled her at the village school and proudly took her on the first day. Arriving home after school, we questioned her about what she'd done. She wasn't very forthcoming, but pressed further said, 'Well, it's a bit babyish for me.' A little worried, we went to see the Headmistress.

Talking through the problem, she took our Jackie's enrolment papers and said, 'Let's see, she was born in 1964, so she *should* be in the infants, but as she seems so advanced we will . . .'

'What year did you say?' asked her father.

'1964,' repeated the Headmistress.

John looked at me knowingly and accusingly: 'You made Jackie a year too young, she was born in 1963.'

The Headmistress quietly closed the folder: 'I think someone should come back and have arithmetic lessons, don't you?'

Sir Nicholas Henderson

AMBASSADOR

Before paying an official visit to a town in France, I was given the usual briefing about leading personalities so as to help make the *entente* as *cordiale* as possible. I was told that the Préfet's wife was pregnant and that the Mayor's wife was very ill. At my first meeting I expressed pleasure and congratulations over the happy family news I had heard; at my second I commiserated, saying that I hoped Madame's condition would soon be *rétablie*, a phrase I had mastered with pride.

It was only after both interlocutors had remarked upon the eccentricities of the British and the pleasure that they had had in experiencing it at first hand that I made enquiries and discovered that I had got them the wrong way round.

John Gardner

JOURNALIST

After the war, I was – like most hopeless sons – destined for the Church, as my father was a High Anglican priest. I took my degree at Cambridge and then went on to complete things at a theological college in Oxford (saw the light there, also, and became a journalist instead).

The theological college was, naturally, very high church and strict. During one Holy Week, I found myself in a whirl of services and much ritual. Easter came and, having given up the cinema during Lent, I took myself off to the pictures at the earliest, and most seemly, opportunity.

The rigours of religious ritual must have really got to me. As the performance ended, I left my seat, gravely genuflected to the screen, and only realized what I had done when I saw people looking at me. I left with red cheeks. The film was, in fact, one of the early *Carry On* movies.

Margaret Drabble

NOVELIST AND BIOGRAPHER

How I welcome this opportunity to relive one of the nastiest moments of my life! It occurred when I was watching for the first time what I think is called a rough cut of the only film I ever wrote that ever got made. Naturally I found my own story deeply moving, and was weeping copiously by the end. However I was not so far carried away as to forget that I was sitting next to the composer of the music, to whom I had just been introduced. Politely I blew my nose, turned to him, and said, 'I thought the music was wonderful.' He looked surprised (or was it offended, I dare not recall) and said, 'But I haven't written it yet.' I think I went on to explain that I wasn't really very musical, that I was in fact tone deaf, but I don't suppose it did much good.

Norman Plastow

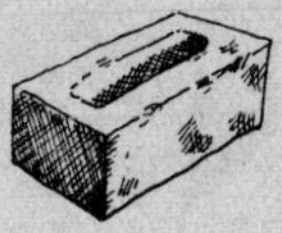

ARCHITECT

I worked for several years with a Hungarian woman architect whose command of the English language made one realize how versatile and subtle it can be. One of her best efforts occurred at a meeting where a scheme for an old people's home was being discussed. The discussion was brought to an abrupt halt by her profound observation: 'A woman is as old as a man feels her, but a man is as old as he feels himself.'

Lord Longford

AUTHOR AND CAMPAIGNER

I recently attended a film show given by my old friend Aidan Crawley, the famous cricketer, etc., following his travels in the Himalayas. On the way in I saw a rather lonely figure sitting in the corridor. It was the great explorer Sir John (now Lord) Hunt. I said to him cordially, if a trifle condescendingly: 'You look a bit lonely, John. Why don't you come in with our party?' Lord Hunt is the most modest man in the world. It is said that when he received an invitation to become a Knight of the Garter he thought it must have been intended for the other Lord Hunt. After considerable hesitation, he explained to me: 'They've made me the President here [that is of the Royal Geographical Society]. I'm afraid they want me to take the Chair.'

James Herriot

VET AND AUTHOR

My absentmindedness, though constant and long-standing, has usually manifested itself in trivial ways. Brushing my teeth with shaving cream and wondering why the new toothpaste tasted so foul and made me foam at the mouth. Stopping in the middle of a veterinary round and trying to think where the devil I was going. Forgetting to put my dog back into the car after a country walk and having to dash back to the spot where, showing more sense than his master, he would be patiently waiting. Enclosing letters in the wrong envelopes with wildly embarrassing results.

However, there are two incidents which, though not world-shaking, may have caused certain people to doubt my sanity.

The first was when my wife asked me to take the sitting-room clock to be repaired. With my two young children in the car I drove into the market place of our little town and, clock under arm, entered the shop. Only it wasn't the right shop, it was the butcher's. My children, who always delighted in their father's affliction, watched, giggling, as, with my thoughts far away, I stood staring into the butcher's eyes.

I had been a customer for a long time and the good man smiled in anticipation as he twirled his cleaver in his hand and I clutched my clock. This went on for several very long seconds before I realized where I was. There is no doubt I should have calmly purchased a pound of sausages, but my return to the world was too sudden, the prospect of explanation too unthinkable. I merely nodded briefly and left.

The other man in our town who probably thinks I am unhinged is a Mr Craythorne. Some years ago he was manager of Mead's grocer's shop, his children went to the same school as mine and he and I knew each other quite intimately.

He was standing in the doorway of his shop one day when I passed, my brain, as usual, wrestling with some distant problem, my eyes staring into space.

I heard his voice: 'Now then, Mr Herriot,' and turned a blank gaze on him.

Only fellow sufferers will understand that at that moment I had not the remotest idea who he was. To whom, I desperately cogitated, belonged this very familiar face? Then, as I floundered, I noticed the word 'MEAD' in foot-high letters above the shop window.

'Good morning, Mead,' I cried heartily, giving him a smile compounded of friendliness and relief.

I had gone only a few steps before I realised that my greeting had been not only impolite but somewhat arrogant. I turned back and addressed him again.

'Good morning, *Mister* Mead,' I said.

It was only when I had turned the corner of the street and come to the surface that it dawned on me, too late, that his name was Craythorne and the time was late afternoon.

Andrew Sinclair

NOVELIST AND BIOGRAPHER

A friend of mine from Australia was asked to an elegant party in Eaton Square. Caviar was to be served after the champagne. Having drunk too much of that, my friend found his way to the bathroom. He groped around for a light switch, but did not discover it. He then groped around for a lavatory, but did not discover one. Finally, he found the edge of the bath and settled for that. He relieved himself slowly and fully, then turned on the taps to swill away the evidence.

Going back to the party, he asked his hostess where the caviar might be. 'Packed on ice,' she said, 'in the bath. I am just going to get it.' He went instead, walking quickly back to Australia.

MANAGER

Dame Edna's Bricks

Many moons ago, long before I became a bi-hemispheric megastar, my manager Barry Humphries was at a function in Oxford. Who should he bump into there but Sir Osbert Lancaster, the clever cartoonist, who was then just plain Mister Lancaster. Barry introduced himself as an Australian comedian, but he must have mumbled his name with uncharacteristic modesty because Sir Osbert said: 'The only other Australian comedian I know is that awful chap who dresses up as a housewife and waves daffodils.' I bet Barry went a bit quiet after that.

Mind you, possums, it's funny the number of people who used to think Barry was one of those twisted types who went in for female impersonation. Just because he and I are never photographed together is no reason to believe that Mr Humphries sometimes dresses up as me! What a sick suggestion that is.

However, a few years ago, when I went to Royal Ascot, an incident occurred which reminded me how many intelligent people still believe this libellous rumour.

At the race meeting in question I wore a gorgeous hat based on the Sydney Opera House, Casino and multi-purpose conference and convention complex. It was so spectacular that it attracted the world media and, I'm afraid, rather 'up-staged' a very famous lady whose Ascot hats usually make headlines year after year. As luck would have it, she and I bumped into each other outside the gates, and as the cameras jostled to snap us for posterity, her son (who also designs her clever hats) said to me rather sharpish: 'At least my mother is a *real* woman!'

Would you call that a brick possums?

Talking of incredible mothers, it was my own wonderful mother who once said to me: 'Edna, every time you open your mouth it's just to change feet.'

The day came when I had to bundle her off to the St Peter's Close Twilight Home in Melbourne, and she naturally – bless her! – wanted to pack her entire lifetime's collection of memorabilia.

'You'll only need a nightie and a toothbrush, darling,' I said gently as the attendants escorted her caringly into their spotless unmarked van. 'If you happen to need any of your favourite old frocks or bygones, tell matron and we can always fetch them out of the incinerator.'

What a ghastly slip of the tongue that was because I'd meant to say wardrobe. Luckily, my precious old parent had her mind elsewhere at the time – as she so often had in those days – so my 'brick' fell on deaf ears, but Mummy certainly wouldn't have thanked me if she'd known what a big spring-cleaning we had planned just as soon as she had been comfortably re-allocated. I know Oxfam wouldn't have been overjoyed to receive my precious darling's mammoth collection of nostalgia and moth-fodder.

I'm glad super old showbiz chum Robert Morley has asked me to rack my brains to recall any little bricks I've dropped, because quite frankly there have been times in my career when something untoward has popped out that shouldn't have. Most married women have had the same experience!

There was the time when a famous female member of the Royal Family (no names, no pack-drill) once visited me in some distress at the Dorchester Hotel in Park Lane Street and flung herself sobbing into my arms. The first thing I said was, 'How did you get past my security, darling?' Again I was saved from embarrassment because the poor little mite was, for once, too upset to have noticed my big macho bodyguard discreetly stationed outside the door.

On another occasion I was at a Royal Garden Party in the gardens of the Queen's gorgeous period home at the end of Mall Street and to my embarrassment an enormous queue of distinguished guests and upper-echelon high-fliers thought they recognized me and besieged me for autographs. Normally I would have obliged with pleasure, but that day I felt I owed my sovereign a word of apology for slightly up-staging her (to use a show business term). 'Oh, Ma'am,' I blurted out, 'if I'd known that this was going to happen, I'd never have worn my tiara.' My hostess smiled charmingly but not without a funny little hint that I'd put my Gucci peep-toe sling-back in it well and truly.

JM.

Christina Foyle

BOOKSELLER

In the 1930s, I spent a holiday in America and watched Duke Ellington perform to an enraptured audience.

Coming home on the ship, we met some rich Americans, who were very conscious of their wealth and importance. One of them said to me, 'My, I am looking forward to seeing your country. Do you know, I am related to Duke Ellington?'

'Really?' I said. 'We saw him perform with his band in New York and he was wonderful.'

'I said the Duke of Wellington,' was the frosty reply.

Yehudi Menuhin

MUSICIAN

My wife agonizes between my infinite capacity for forgetting names and my equal skill in triumphantly misappropriating them. Of the two habits, she would appear to prefer the former, for at least, she says desperately, she can be called upon like some dematerialized telephone directory to furnish me with the missing name. Whereas with the latter she has, as it were, hastily to erase the misnomer with as much speed and tact as possible, redressing the balance with a sweet smile for the victim and a venomous glance at myself.

The illustrations I could offer of this kind are so numerous that it is difficult to choose from among them. However, one particular instance I remember taking place in the foyer of the little Opera House in Monte Carlo. It must have been, I suppose, after one of my concerts, which in that sociable spot are never left unadorned by some party to send the musician happily off to bed however poorly he may have played.

There was a milling crowd of overdressed people of both sexes – by which I don't mean over-covered but rather under-draped – the women with large expanses of flesh leaving a splendid field of jewellery and men in dinner-jackets made of every imaginable material from plum-coloured plush to Turkey carpet (circa 1910).

Diana, with our youngest son Jeremy in tow, had become separated from me – a most dangerous situation socially – and I suddenly espied a smallish man with a shock of white hair, a brown face and alert black eyes. Darting forwards, for fear he would be engulfed before I could nab him, I seized him by the shoulders, embraced him on either cheek, exclaiming delightedly: 'Chagall! *Cher Marc, comment ca va?*'

The expression of blank surprise on the face of the assaulted man totally failed to deflect my joy and I continued in much the same vein, asking him what new work he was doing (oils or water-colour?) and it wasn't until my hands – possibly more perceptive than my eyes or mind – registering the thick furry white flannel of his jacket (the poor fellow was still imprisoned in my grip) that I sensed dimly that something was awry.

Releasing my captive uneasily, I turned to find Diana at my elbow and muttered to her 'Chagall, darling,' in a kind of dying fall. She, of course, had taken in the utter stranger at one glance – ghastly 'who's for tennis' jacket, black satin propellor of a black tie, velvet shoes and all – and placed him somewhere half-way down the list of Greek ship-owners without whose drachmas the tower-blocks and gambling temples of that once exquisite little town would have tumbled into the sea. Offering an apology with her second-best smile, she extricated me from my predicament, adding that, especially after a concert, my faculties were dimmer than usual and that, in order to protect herself, she usually greeted me back-stage with a kiss and the reminder that she was my second wife – a position that she had by then stoutly maintained for some thirty years or so.

With true Greek courtesy, the utter stranger told me that he considered I had bestowed upon him a great compliment and that he was indeed often mistaken for

Chagall. I turned triumphantly towards Diana and was discomfited by a veiled glare tinged with desperation. 'Well,' she said, 'at least you didn't mistake him for Indira Gandhi.'

Jeremy Thorpe

FORMER LEADER OF THE LIBERAL PARTY

Princess Beatrice, who was one of Queen Victoria's daughters, was sitting next to a rather pompous, ill-informed politician, who in order to make conversation said, 'Ma'am, I've just come back from Spain. Is it a country you know?' To which the Princess replied, 'Oh, yes indeed. My daughter is Queen there you know.'

Frankie Howerd

COMEDIAN

Just before the last General Election, I was attending a Sunday luncheon party. I entered the room looking for a friendly face, when a man came forward and held out his hand. I thought to myself, 'Good, somebody I recognize – Peter Saunders, the impresario who presented *The Mousetrap*.' So I said cheerily, 'Hello, are you still running? Is business good?' And he replied, 'I'll let you know soon.' 'Funny,' I thought, 'what a strange reply.' It took me thirty seconds to realize that it was in fact Lord Carrington, who the following week became Foreign Secretary.

Hilary Fletcher

I was travelling to a friend's home and wasn't sure where to get off the bus; when I did decide, I left it until a large queue was half-way through getting on. I darted through them in a panic and in my hurry I got my handbag strap caught around the bus conductress's ticket machine and yanked her off with me. As she sat on the kerb, the entire bus collapsed with laughter, including me, and I had to make a quick exit because for some strange reason she didn't seem to find it funny.

Billie Whitelaw

ACTRESS

Life for those who know me can be perilous, because I'm sometimes very absent-minded. I've never left my mother-in-law behind on the doorstep (as Robert Morley has apparently done), but I did once lock my mother into the lavatory for a couple of hours before I noticed she was missing. But the most excrutiatingly absent-minded thing I've ever done occurred at a lunch given by the Variety Club of Great Britain. At the lunch was a very well-known actor who had been married to a very well-known actress. He and I talked for a while, and he told me how ill and unhappy he had been since their divorce. I decided he needed cheering up, so I said in my brightest voice, 'Oh, good. There's a very dear friend of mine across the room. I know you'll like her – you must come and meet her.'

It wasn't until my two friends stood staring in horror at each other that I realized I'd introduced the actor to his ex-wife. I wanted to die and I still have nightmares about it.

Frank Muir

WRITER AND BROADCASTER

I once dropped an awesome brick in circumstances so weird that the whole thing, like so many true happenings, comes out like a lie so implausible as to be an insult to the reader's intelligence.

I once ran over a man when my car was standing stock still at traffic lights. It was many years ago and the traffic lights were at the top of that little hill in Camden Town. It was a Sunday morning and I was driving to a lunch party with friends who lived in Ongar. I had no idea how to get to Ongar but, as I was setting off, somebody told me to follow the red Singer sports car of a friend who was also going to the party. The trouble was that the friend did not know that I was following him, so I had to keep his car in sight. All went well until the beastly lights in Camden Town went red just after he had crossed, trapping me. I sat fuming at the wheel, watching the red car getting smaller and smaller in the distance. Just as the lights changed to green and I was reaching for the handbrake I saw out of the corner of my eye a man backing out of the paper shop across the pavement. He was making amiable remarks to somebody inside the shop. Waving happily to his invisible friend he backed towards me, stumbled, fell over the kerb, rolled over and wedged himself firmly under my front nearside wheel.

The little red car had disappeared from view round some corner which I would never find, and my chances of getting a free hot meal went with it. In a sudden rage I wound the window down and shouted at the flustered face two feet away: 'You . . . You . . . You c . . . !'

It was then that I noticed his clerical collar.

Gaia Servadio

AUTHOR AND JOURNALIST

I had been promised one of those things which make journalists happy and which could rightfully be regarded as a sign of acute masochism by those outside the trade: to be granted a special visa for a visit to the car factory at Togliattigrad on the Volga. In fact, I must say right away that the visa never materialized since the Soviet factory, which had been provided by FIAT, was running into disastrous delays and was not ready. However, as I was in Turin, I asked to see the Mirafiori factory and, at the end of my visit, I was given a superb little model of a FIAT 128 (I think, I am never sure about models).

Back home my son coveted this perfect little car and so I gave it to him: it became his favourite toy. But on one of my visits to his room, which was in a state of chaos, I promised him that if he did not put it in order, I would throw everything out of the window. On the following day the room was chaotic and I kept my promise. How could I do otherwise? Mothers must keep their word. But Owen was miserable: the one toy he really cared for had fallen four floors and was in pieces. So I suggested that he should write to Gianni Agnelli since he had stayed at his house and, after all, he was FIAT's chairman. Owen wrote. I didn't see the letter and some time went by.

A few weeks later a telephone call came from British FIAT and the manager was on the line. 'The car is ready,' he said, 'but won't some spare parts do instead? At Bradford we can make it as good as new.'

'No,' I said, 'it is really smashed up.'

'Which colour do you require?'

'Mine was blue, but it doesn't actually matter – any colour will do,' said I.

Slightly embarrassed but very kindly he enquired how it had fallen and from what height.

'Well, it was from the fourth floor, from my son's bedroom window.'

There was another pause. 'But can you tell me how it came to fall from there?'

Embarassed, too, I had to confess that I myself had thrown it out.

Visualizing the person with whom he was talking as a mighty strong woman with the muscles of a Hercules, he remained silent until, unfortunately, I added that it had been my son's favourite toy.

A model of the car arrived on the following day.

David Niven

ACTOR

When I was a very impecunious young officer in the Regular Army aged nineteen (long before I became an actor and perhaps could have carried it off) I was invited to a Fancy Dress Ball at a *very* smart house in Leicestershire.

I took a lot of trouble and went as a clown complete with pompoms, a bladder, a string of evil-smelling sausages, and a very long false nose.

I arrived early, eager to meet the immensely smart and important people I knew would be there. Few cars were about when I showed up and the butler looked a little surprised, but anyway he opened the drawing-room door and announced me. Lots of smart and important people were indeed there and they were all in full evening dress.

I had got the right date but the wrong month.

The host and hostess insisted that I stay for dinner and I spent a miserable night in my greasepaint seated between two dowagers who never spoke to me and beneath the pitying eyes of butler and footman.

Sir Ralph Richardson

ACTOR

During the war I was given special leave from the Navy to make a film about submarines. We were shooting in a submarine lying in Liverpool Docks. On the way back to our hotel after the day's activity, the late Charles Victor and I shared a taxi to the Adelphi Hotel. Charles was heavily made-up with full beard and dressed as a naval officer. I was more or less playing myself and in civilian clothes. We were just about to get into the lift at the hotel when the manager approached me and expressed his pleasure and gratification that I was patronizing his august establishment.

'You will let me know,' he urged, 'if there's anything at all we can do to make your stay comfortable.'

'A bottle of wine?' I suggested.

'We'll have it sent up to your room immediately.'

By this time Victor was growing a little impatient. He was manifestly not to be included in the celebrations. The manager accompanied us into the lift and pressed the button for the sixth floor.

'If it's not too much trouble,' said Victor, 'I would like to get out at the floor below.'

The manager reluctantly halted the lift and Charles got out.

'Do you know, sir, who that was?' the manager said to

me, and before I could reply, he continued, 'That was the actor Ralph Richardson.'

Who he imagined I was remains one of the great unsolved mysteries of the Second World War.

Glenda Jackson

ACTRESS

At about the age of fourteen I was sent to do the weekend shopping, taking my youngest sister aged three in her pram. I finished the shopping, returned home and only then discovered that pram plus baby had been left behind. I was not actually beaten until pram and baby had been safely returned.

Bricks in Literature

PROFESSOR JAMES SUTHERLAND

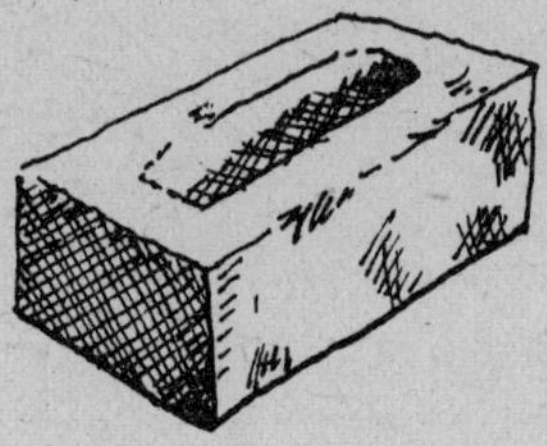

So far as the lexicographers are concerned, the first brick appears to have been dropped as recently as 1923, when someone wrote in *Punch*, 'I had dropped a brick, as you say.' The following year the phrase acquired unimpeachable respectability when John Galsworthy used it in *The White Monkey*. About twenty years later the irresistible modern desire for the emphatic ('My dear, it was absolutely *devastating*!') induced us to start dropping peculiarly heavy bricks, which were called 'clangers'. I take these facts from the recent *Supplement to the Oxford English Dictionary*, where 'to drop a brick' is defined as 'to commit a verbal indiscretion, make a "bloomer"'. The word 'bloomer', apparently a shortened form of 'a blooming error', has been traced back to Australian prison slang of about 1889, and has nothing to do with 'knickerbockers worn by women for bicycling'. But 'bloomer' was not (and so far as it remains current, is not) confined to verbal indiscretions. The same is true of 'making a gaffe', which we started saying in the first decade of the present century. We began 'putting a foot in it' a good deal earlier. In a slang dictionary of 1823 the phrase was glossed as 'to get into a scrape by speaking'; but it is older than that, going back to the last years of the eighteenth century, when a contributor wrote in the *Gentleman's Magazine* of 1798: 'The General has put his foot into it again.' We were already talking of a *faux pas* in the seventeenth century; but for some time the words usually meant 'an act which compromises one's reputation; a woman's lapse from virtue'.

That little burst of erudition is not meant to provoke astonishment that 'one small head could carry all he knew', but rather to suggest that our ancestors were just as likely to drop bricks as we are, though they didn't call them that. One of the most successful plays in the reign of Charles II was Dryden's *Sir Martin Mar-all*. Samuel Pepys thought it 'the best comedy ever was wrote', and went to see it ten times. 'I never laughed so in all my life,' he wrote in his diary after seeing it for the first time; 'I laughed till my head ached all the evening and night with the laughing.' What Pepys found so funny was Sir Martin's unfailing tendency to put his foot in it, to drop bricks both in speech and action, to goof every brilliant scheme he had thought up. Restoration comedy rested on a number of assumptions that are not always easy to define precisely, but one of them is awareness. The Restoration gentleman was socially alert, in entire control of himself and of the situation, and quick to respond and adapt himself to changing circumstances. Poor Sir Martin was at once 'dumb' and endlessly talkative, unaware but supremely confident, moving about, like Wordsworth's child, 'in worlds not realized'. (Sheridan's Mrs Malaprop, that inveterate dropper of verbal bricks, may be said to have moved among words not realized.)

Forty years after *Sir Martin Mar-all* and in the reign of Queen Anne, the dramatist whom her contemporaries called 'the celebrated Mrs Susanna Centlivre', had a resounding success with a similar play called *The Busy Body*. The luckless hero Marplot, 'a sort of silly fellow' who 'generally spoils all he undertakes, yet without design', goes from one blunder to another. On his first appearance his friend Charles, son of Sir Francis Gripe, introduces him to Sir George Airy, and Marplot promptly drops his first brick. The conversation gets round to Sir Francis, and Marplot cannot contain himself:

Marplot: 'Ah! he is a covetous, cheating, sanctified curmudgeon. That Sir Francis Gripe is a damn'd old—'
Charles: 'I suppose, friend, you forget that he is my father—'

Marplot: I ask your pardon, Charles; but it is for your sake I hate him.'

This is only the beginning; Marplot has still to boob and goof his way through five acts.

One doesn't have to be a fool to drop a brick, though it always helps. At all events, we sometimes come to grief because we are ignorant of some vital fact that we couldn't possibly have been expected to know. In his *Memoirs of Count de Grammont* Anthony Hamilton recounted one such blunder made by Richard Talbot, a gentleman of the bedchamber to the Duke of York, Charles II's brother. Writing long after the event, Hamilton got his dates wrong, and perhaps a good deal else; but the story he told could easily have happened. The Duke of York, who was every bit as promiscuous as his brother, had commenced an affair with Lady Carnegie, the wife of a Scottish peer. The lady was amenable, and everything was proceeding most satisfactorily, the more so as Lord Carnegie happened to be in Scotland paying his respects to his father, the Earl of Southesk. During this filial visit the old earl died, and his son duly returned to London, no longer Lord Carnegie, but Earl of Southesk. Rumours of what had been going on in his absence soon reached the new earl, but for the present he decided to do nothing more than keep a watch on his wife. The Duke for his part, realizing that he would now have to be rather more circumspect, made a point of never visiting the lady unless he was accompanied by a friend, who would give the occasion the necessary appearance of formality. I leave the rest to Anthony Hamilton:

> About this time Talbot returned from Portugal: this connection had taken place during his absence; and without knowing who Lady Southesk was, he had been informed that his master was in love with her.
>
> A few days after his arrival, he was carried, merely to keep up appearances, to her house by the Duke; and after being introduced, and some compliments having been paid on both sides, he thought it his duty to give his Royal Highness an opportunity to pay his compliments, and accordingly retired into the antechamber, which looked into the street, and placed himself at

the window to view the people as they passed.

He stood sentry, very attentive to his instructions, when he saw a coach stop at the door, without being in the least concerned at it, and still less a man whom he saw get out of it, and who he immediately heard coming upstairs.

The devil, who ought to be very civil upon such occasions, forgot himself in the present instance, and brought up Lord Southesk *in propria persona.* His Royal Highness's equipage had been sent home, because my lady had assured him that her husband was gone to see a bear and bull baiting, an entertainment in which he took great delight, and from whence he seldom returned until it was very late; so that Southesk, not seeing any equipage at the door, little imagined that he had such good company in his house.

But if he was surprised to see Talbot carelessly lolling in his wife's ante-chamber, his surprise was soon over. Talbot, who had not seen him since they were in Flanders, and never supposing that he had changed his name: 'Welcome, Carnegie, welcome, my good fellow,' said he, giving him his hand, 'where the devil have you been, that I have never been able to set eyes on you since we were at Brussels? What business brought you here? Do you likewise wish to see Lady Southesk? If that is your intention, my poor friend, you may go away again; for I must inform you the Duke of York is in love with her, and I will tell you in confidence that at this very time he is in her chamber.'

Southesk, confounded as one may suppose, had no time to answer all these fine questions. Talbot therefore attended him downstairs as his friend; and, as his humble servant, advised him to seek for a mistress elsewhere. Southesk, not knowing what else to do at that time, returned to his coach; and Talbot, overjoyed at the adventure, impatiently waited for the Duke's return, that he might acquaint him with it. But he was very much surprised to find that the story afforded no pleasure to those who had the principal share in it; and his greatest concern was that Carnegie had changed his name as if only to draw him into such a confidence.

It is not given to everyone to drop two such bricks in close succession. The Duke, however, must have forgiven Talbot, for on succeeding to the throne as James II he rewarded him (for rather more important services) with the title of Earl of Tyrconnel.

Dame Rebecca West

AUTHOR

Years ago in Washington a lift stopped and then shot up with only a nice looking lady and myself. We were both guests at a big dinner. I looked at her and said pathetically, 'Do tell me who you are.' And she said, 'Well, I am Mrs Truman, but I often wonder.'

I am bound to say that her smile was so sweet that I might have been giving her a bouquet rather than dropping a brick.

JM
BURKE'S PEERAGE

Bernard Levin

WRITER AND JOURNALIST

I claim (and there will be few challengers) to be the only man who has ever introduced Lord Longford to his own wife and, moreover, presented her under the name of Lady Pamela Berry.

What an extraordinarily short sentence for Bernard Levin!

Prudence Leith

COOKERY AUTHOR AND RESTAURATEUR

I once had the marquee tent for someone's wedding party put up in the wrong garden – next door, in fact.

When I first started cooking for my living I had an Abyssinian cat who used to watch me filleting salmon and making gateaux from the window-sill. One day the telephone rang: 'Is that 229-0684?'

'Yes.'

'Is your name Benny?'

'No, but my cat's is.'

'Well what the hell is his name-tag doing in my salad?'

But my favourite catering disaster is the true story of the couple who went to the Far East on holiday. They wanted, besides their own supper, something to give their poodle. Pointing to the dog, they make international eating signs. The waiter understood, picked up the poodle and set off for the kitchen – only to return half-an-hour later with the roasted poodle on a platter.

Behram Kapadia

ART DIRECTOR

I was asked to take a photograph of Jimmy Greaves to appear on the jacket of his autobiography *This One's on Me* which tells the story of how pressures at the top drove him to alcoholism, wrecking his career and marriage. He was now painfully on the way to recovery with help from Alcoholics Anonymous.

I telephoned him with details of the photographic session and added, somewhat absently, 'If we finish early, Jimmy, how about a quick drink?'

Wendy Toye

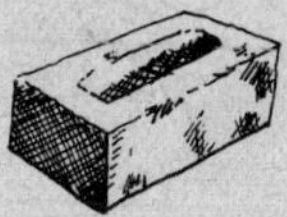

DIRECTOR AND CHOREOGRAPHER

Deep in thought about a new production, I went to the ticket office in Leicester Square underground, asked for a ticket to Sloane Square, took from my handbag my powder compact, opened it and handed the man the powder-puff and – what's more – confidently waited for the change.

One night some years ago, suffering from the universal complaint, I was at Boots the chemist standing in a queue behind quite a number of people, with a lot more behind me, all waiting to get their drugs. When it came to my turn, I asked in my embarrassment for a large packet of Hemeroids. The chemist, thinking I was taking the mickey, kept saying wearily, 'Packet of what?' and I kept repeating louder each time, 'Hemeroids'. It wasn't until I heard the giggling queue behind me that I realized something was wrong – 'Germoloids' I should have been saying.

Lady Longford

BIOGRAPHER

I was married in November 1931 and was told by my kind and helpful mother-in-law that it was the correct thing to be presented at Court on marriage. So my name was put down for one of the early Courts the next year. Meanwhilc I realized that I was going to have a baby in the following August. Should I cancel the Presentation? 'Oh, no, no one will notice. The first baby never shows.' Re-

assured, I practised my curtsey, but cautiously, not descending too low.

However, when the great day arrived, two things happened. The baby had evidently made a sudden spurt and, loaded with feathers and frills, I was unwieldy to say the least; and the graceful creature who was presented to their Majesties just before me, swept a magnificent curtsey right down to the ground. In the Spirit of emulation, and forgetting what I had learnt at rehearsals, down I sank to the floor and – there remained for some of the worst seconds in my life. Could I rise again? I made several attempts to no effect. I could see the concerned courtiers on either side preparing to dash in and frog-march me away. At last, with a frantic heave I staggered to my feet and disappeared into the crowd, conscious that I had not only dropped a brick but might also have dropped a baby at the foot of the throne.

Barbara Kelly

TELEVISION PERSONALITY

I do rather tend to put my foot in it. Recently at an ambassadorial cocktail party, I became like a beleaguered 'dodgem' car, completely immobilized in the crush. Struggling to regain momentum and at least seçure a canapé, I volunteered to no one in particular, 'This is just like the Black Hole of Calcutta'.

'Were you there?' enquired Mrs Indira Ghandi delightedly.

Michael Bartman

MARKETING DIRECTOR

It was a cold, rainy night and I was passing a friendly fish and chip shop when my wife and two children decided they would like to grab a bite to take home. The shop was in a busy road and I parked on the opposite side of the street and suggested they might like to stroll across in the rain and pick it up for themselves. However, as they all refused, I reluctantly negotiated the traffic and joined the queue and, some fifteen minutes later, found myself at the head of it, to receive four soggy bags of fish and chips. I dashed across the road, threw myself into the driving seat, flinging the greasy parcels at my wife beside me in the passenger seat and, muttering words of abuse, insisted that, in future, if the family wanted fish and chips they should bloody well go and fetch it themselves. My wife unaccountably started to scream, only it wasn't her but a total stranger! I looked up and through the windscreen to see my family in the identical car in front making strong come-hither movements.

'Where's the fish?' was their only comment when I rejoined them.

Norman St John-Stevas

MEMBER OF PARLIAMENT

I was going to Cambridge for the day and my car was being repaired. I said to my housekeeper, 'May I take your Mini?' She agreed and told me it was parked outside the door, but warned that it would not go very fast. I had some difficulty opening the door, but eventually got in and then had some difficulty getting the ignition key in, but it started up and off we went. Far from being slow, it positively flashed along.

I stopped on the motorway for petrol and found to my horror that there was a padlock on the petrol tank, but no key. So I asked the garage attendant for a jemmy and passed it off saying jokingly, 'If anyone saw this they might think I had stolen the car.'

'You'd be arrested,' he chuckled.

So off to Cambridge and back, and I had the car washed and filled with petrol as a thanks offering, and parked it outside the door.

Next day, when my housekeeper brought me my breakfast, she said, 'Why didn't you take my car yesterday?'

'I did,' said I.

'No,' she said, 'it's been outside the house all the time.'

'Nonsense,' I replied and jumping out of bed I went over to the window and, pointing, said, 'That is the one I took.'

'That's not mine. Mine's the one behind it.'

As the ghastly truth began to dawn I heard merry laughter outside and a voice say, 'Darling, your car's back.' I heard another voice say, 'Goodness, so it is, and look it's washed and full of petrol.'

I didn't wait to hear any more, but crawled back into bed and ate my boiled egg.

Years later I mentioned the story to my new secretary. 'Good heavens,' she screamed, 'that was my car.'

Dame Peggy Ashcroft

ACTRESS

I think my best piece of absent-mindness was during the war when we were playing *The Importance of Being Earnest* at the Phoenix, where it was excessively cold. After the matinée I put on my husband's largest pair of woollen socks. In the evening when the curtain went up on my first appearance as Cicely watering the roses in a pink muslin dress I looked down and saw that the socks were still on my feet. There was no chance of removing them – I could only bend at the knees and cover them up.

Daddy, what did YOU do in the War?

Nigel Nicolson

AUTHOR AND PUBLISHER

Early in 1940 I was a 2nd Lieutenant in the Grenadier Guards, stationed at Wellington Barracks, and was ordered to take forty men as reinforcements to the battalions in France. It was a simple job. I was to march them to Waterloo Station, entrain them for Dover, cross the Channel, deliver them to somewhere like Arras, and then return.

The war had scarcely started. There was no fighting in France, no bombing of London. But it was my first independent command, and I marched off my little detachment with inflated juvenile pride. We were accompanied by a small section of the regimental band, and one or two people cheered.

We crossed Westminster Bridge. On the far side I marked the entrance to Waterloo Station. 'Left wheel!' I cried. The columns responded. We passed under the great portal into the courtyard beyond which I expected to find the waiting train. There was no sign of it, nor of any locomotive activity whatever. Instead, tall office buildings enclosed us on all sides. A typist looked out of a window, then a dozen or more, tittering, and a few guardsmen risked a wave or two in response. The band faltered.

It was not Waterloo. It was the courtyard of the London County Council. The exit on the far side was barricaded, and there was no room for a U-turn. 'About turn!' I commanded. While this manoeuvre was possible, and indeed smartly executed, it left me and the band at the wrong end. We scurried round.

Then the second disaster occurred. I tripped on the kerb, fell into a puddle and rose drenched, filthy and diminished. Cries of derisive encouragement volleyed from the now crowded windows. My men were kinder. I signalled to the band that any musical accompaniment to a retreat would be inappropriate. We marched to Waterloo in total silence.

Magnus Magnusson

JOURNALIST AND BROADCASTER

When I was at Oxford, a fellow-undergraduate got himself engaged to a delightful undergraduette, a jewel of the county set in Wiltshire. She was the daughter of an Admiral; he was a totally unsuitable suitor (as he proved later by becoming a very successful journalist).

The betrothal was fiercely resisted by the girl's parents. But eventually they relented sufficiently to allow the young man to be invited for a country-house weekend. Everyone found it a difficult occasion, socially.

On the Saturday evening, Daddy had invited a lot of his seafaring cronies to dinner. Our hero found himself seated well below the salt, and not even next to his affianced.

The talk was all of seas and ships and sealing-wax, and our hero found himself out of his depth (he was reading P.P.E., which only qualified him to have opinions about cabbages and kings). So, for solace, he applied himself all too diligently to the claret.

Then, from the far end of the table where Daddy was holding court, there wafted down a word he felt he could recognize. The old sea-dogs were discussing 'buttocks', which, for the benefit of the uninitiated, means in nautical jargon 'the breadth of the ship astern from its tuck upwards'.

Here at last was a chance for our hero to make his mark on the conversation. Leaning forward, he bellowed up the

table: '*Buttocks!* Did you say *buttocks*? My future wife has a splendid pair!'

The marriage did not take place.

It's obviously Magnus's own experience, so we've taken the liberty of including him in the illustration.

Graham Payn

ACTOR

I was only seventeen. I was playing a very small part in *The Tempest* on television at Alexandra Palace before the Second World War, while Peggy Ashcroft had the enormous responsibility of playing Miranda. We met in the corridor at the awful moment just before the performance (performances went out 'live' in those days) and Miss Ashcroft very sweetly wished me good luck.

'Thank you,' I replied, 'I am so nervous.'

'Don't worry, so am I.'

'Well,' I said, 'you have every reason to be.'

Dannie Abse

DOCTOR AND POET

That particular Friday, because I was going to spend the weekend in South Wales, I hoped to leave work early but the relief radiographer proved to be incompetent and slow. All the x-rays sent to me were either under developed or overdeveloped, under-penetrated or over-penetrated, or partially fogged. Patient after patient had to be returned to the x-ray department for a repeat x-ray.

At last it seemed that there were no more x-rays for me to read and it was time to leave. I would catch a later train from Paddington than I had intended. I was at the door when the telephone on my desk again rang insistently; it was the inept radiographer.

'Could you hang on, sir?' he said. 'There's one more patient. Dr Wicks would like you to report on it now. When it's ready, I'll bring the x-ray to you.'

I can't remember exactly how I responded; I suppose I gracelessly said something like, 'All right, but don't bugger up the film this time.' I returned to my desk and to pass the time read the current *British Medical Journal*. Then I looked at my watch. I had missed another train and now half an hour had passed since the radiographer called me.

I was half-way through a paper on '*Pseudomyxoma Peritonei*: An Unusual Case' when I decided that enough was enough and I stamped out of the room towards the x-ray department, where I at once encountered the radiographer emerging from the dark room. 'It's just developed, doctor,' he said before I could say a word. 'Will you read it wet?'

In the dark room there is a screen on which wet x-ray films can be hung. The radiographer placed the film on it and turned on a switch so that the screen lit up brilliantly behind the x-ray. I looked at it astonished. The posterior-anterior view of the patient's chest – the usual view – was at an extraordinary tilted angle of forty-five degrees: the left shoulder was way up, the right shoulder way down. I had never seen anything like it.

Sarcastically I tilted my head at an angle of forty-five degrees as I scrutinized it and said tightly, 'How the hell did you manage that?'

'Well . . .' he said.

'For God's sake,' I roared, 'all day you've messed things up and now this is utterly skew-whiff.'

'The patient's behind you, sir,' the radiographer urgently interrupted me.

I turned from him towards the open dark room door, put on a suitable smile and approached the patient in order to reassure him.

'Your x-ray is normal,' I said. 'It's fine, though it's tilted somewhat. The radiographer has somehow cleverly contrived to make you look like a cripple. That's what I was complaining to him about. Don't *you* worry.'

'Can I go now?' asked the patient.

'Of course,' I said smiling benignly.

And the patient, unsmiling, rose, one-legged, to limp pronouncedly over the brown linoleum of the x-ray department and through the door to disappear from my sight but never entirely from my mind. I turned to the radiographer who lounged, rather than stood, against the wall, his face a study of sweet magnificent triumph.

Heather Sherratt

BOOK DESIGNER

I was sitting on a crowded bus about a year after I got married when a young man leapt on, came and stood opposite me, and said, 'Hello,' looking obviously delighted to see me.

I gazed blankly at the beaming face, puzzled, until I finally asked, 'Who are you?'

'I'm your husband,' came the injured reply.

André Previn

COMPOSER AND CONDUCTOR

The process of adopting a Vietnamese orphan is, quite correctly, fraught with difficulties. My family has now been graced by these children three times, but I still remember one slightly insane moment during the first adoption attempt. Visiting my house, prior to the final sanction, was a remarkable lady named Rosemary Taylor, who had led a selfless existence in Saigon, running an orphanage. I doubt whether I will ever meet anyone more suited to eventual sainthood than this extraordinary woman. She was a weekend guest in my house in Surrey and, needless to say, we underestimated her sense of humour and her sense of occasion, and bent over backwards to make everything with which she came into contact seem to spring from the pages of an ideal home magazine.

Now, at the time, my small sons were addicted to an admixture of health-food cereals, which they consumed with gusto each morning. I personally thought it vile, but they loved it, and I presume it was good for them. The stuff was kept in one of several large glass containers in the kitchen. On her first morning in my house, Miss Taylor appeared for breakfast. She asked for cereal, and I gave her a large bowlful, lauding the energy-giving qualities of this blameless concoction. She poured milk over it, disdained the use of sugar, and fell to. She ate in silent contemplation, and if there was any dissatisfaction on her face, I missed it. Finally, the bowl empty, she pushed it away. 'I have to be honest with you,' she said, 'I'm not really crazy about it.' My eyes happened to glance at the various glass jars around the cupboard. A realization hit me. I blanched. Finally I managed to answer: 'Actually I'm not surprised,' I said as gently as possible, 'I've just made you eat a large dish of hamster food.'

Michael Noakes

ARTIST

I had been commissioned to paint a portrait of the newly-appointed Chief of Defence Staff. Since there was to be a domestic background in the picture, the first two sittings were to be held in his home rather than in my studio.

I arrived and laid out my equipment happily, and we tried out his chair in various positions in different lights. My first error was when, trying to be helpful, I attempted to pass his Field Marshal's baton to him (delicate gold filigree top, velvet-covered, presented to him by the Queen just two weeks before). Somehow I missed – and it dropped with an echoing thwang into a tin waste-paper bin. That, not surprisingly, did not go down very well.

Determined to prove that painters are not really clumsy idiots, I set to work – deliberately painting with deft, rhythmic arm movements. But I knew, as that fully-loaded brush sprang out of my hand and hurtled like a rocket across his drawing-room, that it was going to touch down on the one bit of the Aubusson carpet, in the far corner, that I had not protected with dust-sheets . . . and Alazarin Crimson, just right for painting the ribbon of the Order of the Bath, is unfortunately so powerful a colour that it is virtually impossible to remove the stain completely.

We had to stop for twenty minutes whilst I did what I could to put right the damage with my turpentine and his

LINSEED

detergent. Before starting again, I asked if I might wash my hands. The Field Marshal was obviously only too glad to be rid of me for a bit, and directed me to the little cloakroom by the front door.

While there, I thought I would take the opportunity first to spend a penny; as I washed my hands, though, I became aware that the loo was making the strangest noises. I went across to have a look at it and, incapable of action, I watched as the water-level gurgled over the brim and several gallons were deposited all over the floor.

The next time I had a sitting at the Field Marshal's home, I was filled with good resolutions as I drove up to the front door. He, looking slightly strained I thought, greeted me there. He was, though, still surprisingly courteous: holding the door wide open for me as I carried my portable easel through, he gave me a weak smile. 'Good morning, Field Marshal!' I beamed, as I eased past him with a caricature of extreme care. Then the collapsible leg on the easel fell open, and removed a large chunk of the door.

Michael Aspel

BROADCASTER

I was once, and only once, invited to a reception at the Iranian Embassy. A well-meaning colleague at the BBC provided me with what he described as an all-purpose greeting in Farsi, which I learned by heart. When I was introduced to the Ambassador, a large hairy man, I recited the phrase perfectly. He gave me a wintry smile and moved away. An interpreter explained that I had just told the Ambassador that I would not exchange the moles on his cheeks for all the riches in Samarkand and Bokhara. No wonder the poor fellow looked puzzled: His Excellency was wondering, no doubt, who had told me about them.

Magnus Pyke

SCIENTIST AND TELEVISION PERSONALITY

It is well-known – or by now it should be, since Gaspard Coriolis wrote a paper about it in 1835 – that in the Northern Hemisphere bath water corkscrews its way down the plug-hole in an anti-clockwise direction. You need to understand this if you are concerned with the exact placement of communications satellites up in the sky. There I was, with a full-scale transparent bath, explaining the reason for this to the multitudinous television audience, telephoning Sydney to allow a scientific colleague there to describe how differently bath water behaves in Australia, sending a man to Nanuki in Kenya where bath water runs away left-handed or right-handed with equal facility, plug-holes being exactly on the Equator there. And then, when I pulled the plug out in Leeds, the water started twisting round (or so the little floating flag seemed to show) the wrong way.

And yet . . . and yet . . . Goaded from my humiliation by a gesticulating cameraman, I turned back to look at the bath water again. I found that it *was* twisting anti-clockwise after all. If you imagine the long limp sausage of water extending up from the plug to the surface, when the bottom starts twisting left-handed, the top drifts round for a while right-handed – which is what had caused my heart to sink – before the whole thing gradually gets itself together and (in the Northern Hemiphere) spins round its anti-clockwise way. My brick did indeed start to drop, but Gaspard, dead though he may have been for nearly a hundred and fifty years, caught it nicely for me.

Unbelievable, isn't it?

William Douglas-Home

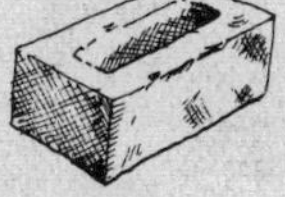

PLAYWRIGHT

In early youth, while sitting with the grown-ups at lunch, I remember hearing my elderly Aunt Margaret assuring a retired schoolmaster, who had asked her if the county she lived in in Wales were over-populated, that it was, in fact, 'very sparsely copulated indeed'.

Warren Mitchell

ACTOR

Scene: Sir Peter Hall's office at the National Theatre, Thames flowing outside, the hock inside, just finished the smoked salmon, my reward for being terribly talented in *Death of a Salesman*.
Sir Peter: You know I'd like to see you tackle *The Tempest*.
Me: Caliban?

Sir Peter: No, Prospero.
Me: You're joking.
Sir Peter: No, you see the part is often misunderstood. Prospero is concerned with power – it's a great play.
Me: I'm not mad about it. Saw it once at the Old Vic with Sir John. Mind you, it was an awful production, I couldn't believe it. Do you know what the director did?

Slow freeze. Cut to M.C.U. Sir Peter – tiny smile playing round his lips, he nods.

Sir Peter: Yes, it was my production.
Me: Can I have another glass of hock, please?

Of course everyone knows that M.C.U. is maximum close up.

Diana Rigg

ACTRESS

I was in my dressing-room at the Old Vic changing after a performance of *Jumpers* and chatting to my mother when there was a knock at the door. The visitor turned out to be Albert Finney, who was rehearsing *Hamlet*, the next production in the theatre. My mother, anxious to prove herself in the theatrical swim, turned to Albert Finney, enquiring brightly, 'And when are you going to give us your Hammy?'

Theo Cowan

PUBLICIST

One day, as I rushed out of my office late for lunch, I found a taxi waiting at the kerb, opened the door and jumped in, shouting my destination to the driver. A moment later I realized I was sitting on the lap of another passenger. As I am of rather unusually heavy build, my first thought was that I might have done him an injury. I manoeuvred myself into the space beside him and enquired, 'Are you all right, sir?' Obviously temporarily winded, he seemed unable to speak. At this moment the cabbie turned round and said, 'I already have a fare,' whereupon I burst into uncontrollable laughter. I scrambled out crab-like and, regaining the pavement, watched a little man in a blue suit sitting bolt upright and staring fixedly ahead, being driven slowly away. The last thing he expected, presumably, when he hailed the cab was that he would be engaged so soon in a game of musical chairs.

William Whitelaw

MEMBER OF PARLIAMENT

I was attending a reception at the American Embassy several years ago and was introduced to an American whom I did not know. After I had spoken to him for some time, I went to a friend and said, 'Do tell me, who is that American I was talking to about golf? He doesn't appear to have much sense of humour.' My friend replied: 'Bob Hope.'

Life with Danny, Emma, Christopher and Jane

As this book has been compiled to aid the National Society for Autistic Children, it might be helpful to describe briefly what autism is and to give some idea of what life is like for some children and their families.

Autism is a syndrome present from birth or beginning almost invariably in the first thirty months of life. Responses to auditory and visual stimuli are abnormal and there are usually severe difficulties in the understanding of spoken language. Speech is delayed in developing; if it does develop, it is characterized by echolalia, the reversal of pronouns, immature grammatical structure, and inability to use abstract terms. There is generally an impairment in the social use of both verbal and gestural language. Problems in social relationships are most severe before the age of five and include an impairment in the development of eye-to-eye gaze, social attachments, and co-operative play. Ritualistic behaviour is usual and may include abnormal routines, resistance to change, attachment to odd objects, and stereotyped patterns of play. The capacity for abstract or symbolic thought and for imaginative play is diminished. Intelligence ranges from severely subnormal to normal or above. Performance is usually better on tasks involving rote memory of visuospatial skills than on those requiring symbolic or linguistic skills.

The following anecdotes, which first appeared in 'Communication', the magazine of the National Society for Autistic Children, were collected by the children's parents over several years.

To know autistic children is to love them; but to love them it is necessary to develop a very thick skin. They are outspoken and direct to the point of insult by normal standards. They can be agile and hyperactive to the point of damage and danger, and then siblings can suffer physically and mentally from their obsessions and rituals. In spite of all this, the awkward situations that occur are often quite funny when you remember them later.

Danny was at his first concert. To keep him from fidgeting, we handed him a pair of opera glasses. At first this was a blessed diversion, but for some reason, every time the horns sounded, he would turn round in his seat and carefully adjust the focus on to a woman sitting just behind us.

At first the woman ignored this scrutiny, but as the horn-playing became more frequent I noted her face changing – from a one-time pink, it appeared to take on an ominous shade of puce.

In the end I turned round and whispered an apology. 'He's handicapped,' I added.

Puce-face glared. 'You might have told me before,' she spat.

Incensed, I retorted, 'What do you expect me to do? Stick a notice on his back saying "I am handicapped"?'

'It would help,' she answered.

The incident could well have closed at this juncture, had it not been for Deborah – always a champion of her brother – who rounded on Puce-face. 'In that case,' she said, 'you ought to have a notice on your front saying "I am cross".'

Danny was belatedly going through a phase of imaginative play – goblins, fairies, giants, little people. The house was full of them. Elaine's cello teacher – a charming and shy man – arrived at our home for his first visit. Danny, a normal-looking eleven-year-old, approached him. 'Hey,' he said in a confidential tone, 'I think you're really a fairy.'

Emma had a particularly nasty habit of sinking her teeth into her brothers and sister when frustrated. There were days when a ring at the front door conjured up visions of some benevolent N.S.P.C.C. inspector shaking his head in utter disbelief that a two-year-olds arm, bruised from wrist to shoulder could be caused by autistic teeth. We watched her, of course, as best we could and pounced to remove the two-year-old when sister bared her teeth. It was the seven-year-old who suffered the final indignity. Having been warned not to put her hands through the bars of the cot where her autistic sister was warming up for her all-night trampoline session, there was a wail of anguish. No sympathy from a weary mother: 'I told you not to put your hand near her.' The response was heart-rending: 'I didn't, it was my nose – I only wanted to kiss her goodnight.'

At the age of eight, Christopher decided that a friendly approach might be 'a good thing'. On entering the Primary School where he attended a special class, he bounced up to the Headmaster and said, 'Morning Usherwood, d'you want a kiss?'

At the age of ten, Christopher greeted guests with the invaluable information, 'You mustn't pee down the drain!'

Most people reading this book may feel they have never actually met an autistic child, but think carefully – maybe you are fortunate enough to be able to say you remember one. Perhaps you are one of the people our family used to meet when we took our autistic daughter out.

Maybe you can remember lying peacefully on the beach when, for some unknown reason, a very attractive toddler suddenly jumped to her feet and ran down the beach; nothing unusual so far – but – perhaps did feel something was different about her, for instead of running on the sand (as normal, boring people do) Jane thudded over you. Now, it may be that you are fond of children, but one foot in your face and one in the middle of your stomach cannot, I am sure, be the best way to further relationships between children and adults. I am sorry we did not stop to apologize, but look at it from our point of view: wasn't it better to catch her? And anyway, as you were doubled up gasping for breath, it hardly seemed fair to disturb you again.

If you still don't remember us, maybe it was your sausage Jane stole as we were sitting down in the restaurant. One minute you had egg, sausage and chips; the next you just had egg and chips. But you must be honest – you never really saw it go. You just felt the little girl two tables away munching a sausage had something to do with it, but you couldn't be *sure*, could you?

Perhaps you met Jane and me out shopping. When Jane wanted some sweets and I very firmly said no, a favourite trick of hers was to take off her pants and hurl them in the air.

So please think back – maybe we have met before. Thank you for buying this book and you never know, you could be the next lucky person to meet us.